BREATH
AND
SHADOWS

By the same author
————

The Knight, Death and the Devil

Last Courtesies

Rumors of Peace

Love out of Season

Mrs. Munck

BREATH
AND
SHADOWS

ELLA
LEFFLAND

WILLIAM MORROW AND COMPANY, INC.

NEW YORK

Description of cavern on pages 310–311 based on *A Guide to Maximiliansgrotte*,
used courtesy of Naturhistorische Gesellschaft Nürnberg E.V.

Poem by Ludvig Bødtcher on pages 6, 7, and 8 originally published in English
by The American-Scandinavian Foundation. Reprinted courtesy of
The American-Scandinavian Foundation.

Library of Congress Cataloging-in-Publication Data

Leffland, Ella.
Breath and shadows / Ella Leffland.
p.   cm.
ISBN 0-688-14271-0
1. Danish Americans—History—Fiction.   I. Title.
PS3562.E375B74   1999
813'.54—dc21   98-8830
                                                      CIP

Printed in the United States of America

First Edition

1   2   3   4   5   6   7   8   9   10

BOOK DESIGN BY VICTORIA HARTMAN

www.williammorrow.com

Man is but breath and shadow, nothing more.
—SOPHOCLES, fragment

FAMILY TREE OF THE ROSTEDS

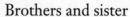

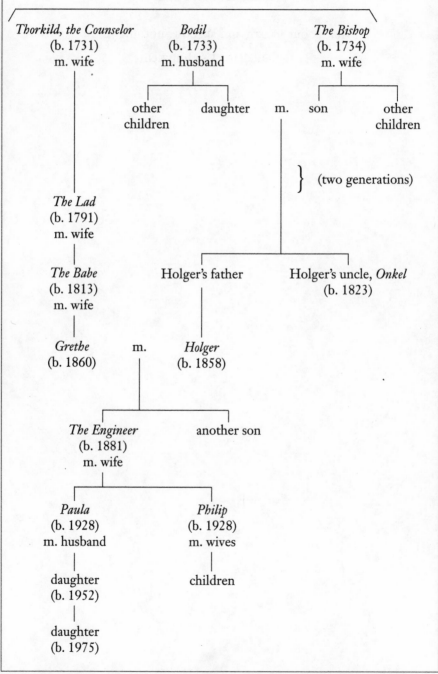

Brothers and sister

Thorkild, the Counselor
(b. 1731)
m. wife

Bodil
(b. 1733)
m. husband

The Bishop
(b. 1734)
m. wife

other
children

daughter   m.   son

other
children

} (two generations)

The Lad
(b. 1791)
m. wife

The Babe
(b. 1813)
m. wife

Holger's father

Holger's uncle, *Onkel*
(b. 1823)

Grethe
(b. 1860)

m.

Holger
(b. 1858)

The Engineer
(b. 1881)
m. wife

another son

Paula
(b. 1928)
m. husband

Philip
(b. 1928)
m. wives

daughter
(b. 1952)

children

daughter
(b. 1975)

BREATH
AND
SHADOWS

The absolute darkness is familiar to the great creatures making their slowly shuffling way down through it. They shelter here from time to time, as those before them have done for hundreds of thousands of years, bones now lying in strata beneath the cavern floor. The bears as they descend give off a shaggy, living stench that scarcely touches the vast sovereignty of damp stone. Their slapping feet, the scratching clicks of their long claws, are swallowed by silence. In time, deep beyond the reach of saber-toothed tigers and other foe, they settle themselves in the blackness. They sleep.

· 1 ·

"Take care!"

The cry is heard simultaneously with the banging open of the double doors; and still hooting imprecations, the nursemaid follows hard on the heels of two blue-smocked small boys who come pounding into the room with a cat madly struggling in the arms of one.

"Oh, poor Olaf," their mother calls imploringly from over her needlework, "oh, do put him down."

But Olaf is already leaping wildly free with ears laid back, and now he shoots across the Turkish rug to crouch, striped fur on end, beside a potted palm: a small, ratty-looking stray whose scarred body and notched, unsymmetrical ears—one is permanently twisted—bear witness to his early wanderings. He is still given to wandering, and disappears for days into the woods that spread away from the house; but he always comes back to the creature over there, she who coaxed him in from the snow one freezing dusk long before.

His alert, pale green eyes followed the boys, whom he saw as two frantic beasts, as they ran first to their mother's chair for their good-night embrace and then to their father's and then dashed back out, almost colliding with the maid and her tray. "Take care!" cried the nurse again, pursuing them on down the hallway as the maid in her white lace apron and beribboned cap came into the room.

3

It was a spacious, richly upholstered drawing room with tall windows overlooking the Øresund, the sound that lies between Denmark and Sweden. A great floor-to-ceiling ceramic stove, with flowers and winged animals painted on its sea-green tiles, radiated a broad and cozy warmth. The walls were covered with paintings in carved gilt and ebony frames—seascapes, landscapes, ancestral portraits of bishops and army officers. Fresh flowers stood everywhere.

The maid, very young though heavy-featured and square of shape, took in her surroundings with a pleased and cavalier air. She carried a Florentine tray on which stood a carafe and two small glasses, for the master and mistress liked their sip of apricot liqueur of a quiet evening, and they liked it served on this tray from their Italian wedding trip. That was before her time, she'd been with them only a few weeks, but she knew everything about the trip because she'd asked. Why not?

First by carriage down the coast to Copenhagen, then by steamer down to Germany, then by train down the rest of the fantastic long way, and she herself had never even been to Sweden—not that there was much there but poor people emigrating to America—but so near that as she passed the windows she could see the glow of coastal lights across the water.

She glanced from the tall windows to the tall potted palms. She had never imagined, coming from a cramped little row cottage, that there could be such a thing as trees inside a dwelling. They had made her nervous at first, but now she felt entirely at ease with them, as with everything else in the house. She even made improvements in her mind. For instance, she'd sweep out the cat. Peasants kept cats, not people of standing. And not even a peasant would keep a wretched eyesore like Olaf.

But she didn't hold this against her employers, for you couldn't find a more generous, easygoing young couple, especially the mistress. And both of them a great pleasure to look at, for the maid very much liked comely, glossy-haired, well-dressed people. These two had more than their fair share of good looks—as they had more than their fair share of everything—and even resembled each other a bit, being cousins, if only distant, having in common a great-great-great-grandsomething-or-other back in the mists of time. She knew this because she'd asked. She'd asked about the bishops and soldiers on the wall. Why shouldn't she? Why should she hang back?

Having set the tray down by Hr. Rosted, she turned to Fru Rosted with enlarged and tragic eyes.

"I know it's fearful late to ask—but could Fruen *please* give me tomorrow off 'stead of Thursday? I'd never ask—not on my mother's grave I wouldn't—only tomorrow's the last day of the Hørsholm fair, the very last day! Oh, if Fruen only knew how much I been wanting and wanting—"

"But go then," Fru Rosted's mild voice broke in. "Go to your fair by all means. Peace be on your agitated soul."

At which the girl bobbed brightly and left the room.

"I know," she said to her husband as she drew a wool thread through the material on her lap. She was making a small needlepoint rug; a design of pale and dark yellow roses was woven against an almost finished background of russet.

"Too soft, Grethe," he said, lowering his book with a good-natured headshake. Hr. Rosted was a very tall, strapping young man not quite thirty, clean-shaven, with a mass of bronze hair, and dark strong brows over eyes of deep warmth. "Every maid in the universe is given a half-day off. But not ours. No, they must all have a full day. Well, that's fine, that's as it should be. But this one—this one has already grown so bold as to choose whichever day suits her. Too soft, my love. And here comes another petitioner."

Finally seeing his way clear, Olaf was swiftly loping to his creature's side. It was a standing joke between Hr. Rosted and his wife that she was more concerned with the cat's welfare than the children's.

"But a cat isn't like a person," she said, leaning from her chair and stroking the animal by its twisted ear. "A cat is all alone, Holger. A cat cannot express itself in words. Olaf cannot say what he feels inside him."

"My dear Grethe, the only feeling inside Olaf is the wish for a big juicy herring."

And he gave a mock duck of his shoulders as she, with smiling aim, threw a tangle of thread at him, their eyes meeting in a look of shared and familiar humor, and of deepest, most intimate love.

His eyes lingered on her as she took up her needle and thread again, the unsightly animal nestling in the folds of the gown around her feet. The lamplight fell on her honey-colored hair, parted in the center with small locks along the brow, above them a smooth broad plait like a crown. On her lowered cheek he knew just where the captivating dimple appeared when she laughed. He knew the exact shade of her so much more than pretty, so much more than captivating gray eyes, candid, witty, tender. If he were a poet, like Bødtcher, whose open book he held in his lap, he would write one of the world's great love songs.

Olaf slept in the warm folds. Suddenly he woke as the huger of the two creatures came looming over him in what he experienced as a towering confusion of movement and noise, and which sent him speeding back to the potted palm.

Hr. Rosted, carrying the two small glasses, seated himself on the brocade arm of his wife's chair. They sipped, they talked, and from time to time their faces came together in a protracted kiss. They were a couple who on their walks always held hands, no common sight in the 1880s, who at the dinner table would each move a foot to seek and caress the other's, whose bed in the morning was a wildly tumbled map of ardor. Thus it was a good while Olaf waited before Hr. Rosted returned to his chair and Fru Rosted to her sewing. Then the cat ventured back and settled in once more.

Presently Hr. Rosted began to read aloud from his book.

> . . . *waters that languished in winter's chain*
> *break glittering loose again.*

From sheltered shade, in darkening glade,
my ears may capture
the nightingale's rapture . . .

Grethe listened with savoring pleasure. It was a poem they both loved, "In the Spring."

. . . and deeply my heart those tones inspire
with sighs, with longing,
with sweet desire.
Love dips his dart in the rose's glow
and smiling waves his bow . . .

From one of the woven roses Grethe brushed aside a long honey-blond hair, and was suddenly swept by the question of how many hairs are lost in a lifetime, falling to shoulder or lap and brushed to the floor—perhaps thousands, yet they are nowhere . . .

. . . with fragrance of myrtle
his dart will hurtle . . .

And one's skin sheds particles endlessly—like a fine colorless dust they must be, all those bits of oneself, numberless, where are they? In a lifetime would they not create a pile quite high? Then where are they? And those bits of earwax one ekes out with a twist of cotton wool—if all those bits were put together at the end of a life, would they not compose something the size of a cobblestone?

Yet they are nowhere . . .

. . . it strikes like lightning,
thy heart's on fire . . .

Blood. Where is that? Each month when I wrap my soaked red cloths in newspaper she takes them, the washerwoman, and stirs them with a broom handle in a bucket of cold salted water, and then she pours the reddened water down the drain, yes, that is where the blood goes, down into the earth—dear God, month after month, year after year. So much blood—what if it should come gushing up through the soil, what if it should surround us in a dark red marshland . . . ?

. . . with sighs, with longing,
with sweet desire.

Holger softly closed his book. His wife sat rapt, the fingers of one slim hand spread across her brow. After a time, the fingers came away, revealing eyes that were grave.

"It is so beautiful, that poem," she said quietly. "I have always loved it."

"But it has made you sad?" he asked.

Grethe gave a small shake of her head. "I am not sad." And her eyes kindled, smiled. "I am not sad at all. I am but sighs, longing, and sweet desire."

Olaf was again obliged to jump away as Hr. Rosted came over to his wife, and the two of them, with many nuzzling pauses, putting aside the little rug and skeins of russet, agreed that they should retire early.

But Fru Rosted does not forget Olaf. "Come now," she says, stooping with a rustle of her gown, and lifting him gently in her arms as her husband begins extinguishing the gas lamps. In the hallway she sets the cat down, and kneels to its upturned gaze. Olaf feels his face cupped in the creature's hands, his forehead pressed by her lips.

"Dearest Olaf, do not be lonely," she whispers. "Do not be lonely."

· 2 ·

"Every family has its tragedy," the old Counselor's old sister tells him, standing with her back to the crackling warmth of her white marble fireplace. "Your son chose to join Napoleon and died through his bad judgment. That is now several months in the past. A greater tragedy, a national tragedy, is that we have lost Norway."

"Norway—! What do I care about Norway!"

"You had better care," she replied sharply. "We have been dealt the last blow. Denmark's sun has set for good. This year of 1814 will ever be remembered as having tolled our funeral."

"I do not care!" he shouted from the settee. "Bodil, I cannot care!" And he sat back in a violence of tears.

The drawing room, gilt and white, with precisely appointed Louis XV furnishings, was spacious and high-ceilinged. The house stood on a broad Copenhagen street down which the wind keened, striking and shuddering the windows. The old woman turned around, presenting her silk-shawled back to her brother, and extended her faded long hands over the flames.

All at once the old Counselor lunged to his feet. He wheezed hard from the abrupt exertion, for he carried an extraordinary paunch, and indeed was of extraordinary dimensions in every direction except upward, a dwarf, a squashed mushroom of a man, a grotesque, as broad as he was high.

"You ice-block!" he yelled up at her. "Why should I expect concern from you! It is not *your* son who has been killed!"

"That is now some months in the past," she reminded him as she turned around. But he was raging on.

"It is not *your* wife who is long in her grave, or *your* daughter-in-law who has died the same in childbed! No, and it is not *your* beloved son who is gone! He is gone!"

"People die continually," she said. "It is the nature of existence."

"I hope you will be next," he spat out bitterly, pacing the floor with his heavy, waddling gait, and frantic with grief, striking his old fist against his breeches.

"But what is it?" she asked. "What have you come about?"

"Nothing!"

Bodil watched the short, thudding steps. He was so total a miscreation, so meager in height, so broad of girth that he rocked from one side to the other. His legs were small pegs, but his head and hands were large and coarse. She watched the crude, meaty fist that rubbed his wet eyes.

"You really must curtail your self-pity, Thorkild. Think of it this way: you have his child, at any rate."

"I do not want the child. I want *him*!"

"You will not have him again."

He shot her a look of hatred. Grabbing his walking stick, he stomped out of the room, down the stairs to the entrance hall, where he reached up and tore his cloak, gloves and hat from the footman, and plowed through the hastily opened door into the street, where he was at once knocked halfway around by the wind.

"She has never been aught but a block of ice! A rationalist. Bloodless. Bloodless!"

He struggled with his cloak, its multiple shoulder capes flapping wildly in the wind. He dropped his hat, heaved after it with laborious wheezes, and clamped its height down on his lashing, coarse gray hair. He pulled on his gloves. The wind sounded like an ocean in his ears.

"It were no loss if *she* went from this world. For her coldness and hardness, I wish it upon her—I wish it upon her!"

And dragging out his handkerchief, he wiped his small, deep-set wet eyes, and blew his great potatolike nose. Then he set off along the snow-crusted cobblestones, heaving from side to side in his massive waddle and muttering fiercely to himself.

Bodil watched her brother from a window, hoping she had seen the last of him for a very long time. Both she and her younger brother, the Bishop, though they could agree on nothing else, had always shared the opinion that to be in Thorkild's company was a sore trial. It had nothing to do with how he looked, monstrosity though he was. No, it was his character—excessively emotional, always furious, always barking, snapping, shouting, boiling with rage because his head came no higher than people's thighs. Evil-tempered, yet also ludicrous, with his waddling and wheezing and spluttering. Small wonder that he had not managed to scrape up a wife until he was nearly sixty, in spite of having endeavored for decades to get himself mated. Indeed, he was a plum catch in respect to family fortune, but as Bodil had put it to the Bishop long ago: "Imagine a girl's finer feelings, picturing herself in his bed."

The Bishop had frowned. "Our Lord enjoins us not to entertain such thoughts."

"Any thoughts at all."

"My dear sister!"

Which was why they seldom visited.

Hunched over his stick, the old Counselor pushed against the wind that came roaring in from the Sound down the broad street, which was lined with tall, splendid baroque buildings of pale yellow and pale gray. He himself lived in one, not far from his sister's, but he seldom traversed the short distance.

"Nor should I have today," he muttered, "but I have no grip on myself. It is the letter—the letter. Not that I would have told her of it. Nor would I tell the Bishop, did he live here in Copenhagen, for he is even worse than Bodil. They are useless creatures on this earth! They have no right to exist—she with her empty logic, and he with his empty God!"

It was a little past two o'clock, the cold light of day was waning. As dusk gathered, the old dwarf toiled along narrower streets. The wind roared in his ears. Hanging shop signs were lifted straight out like wash on a line. Straining passersby, rumbling carts, clattering carriages all grew dim in the roaring, deepening darkness around him.

Then there was nothing. No buildings, no traffic. He realized that he had come to a part of the city destroyed in the British bombardment of seven years ago. Fires had raged for days, vast areas had been laid waste. Much rebuilding had taken place since then, but there still remained black desolate stretches like this.

He stood looking.

"What madness these wars have been!" he cried.

And his grief for his son broke forth again, so that again he dragged out his handkerchief, more as a companion than anything of practical use in this ferocious wind, which in fact tore it from his hand and sent it flying into the darkness.

He turned back. He could not indefinitely postpone his return home.

He let himself in with his latchkey. His housekeeper came slapping into the entrance hall with her mouth already going.

"*Gudbevares,* Hr. Counselor, take a look at your face. It's practically blue"—reaching down and dragging him out of his cloak, yanking off his hat. "They say the Sound's frozen solid as a rock straight to the bottom."

"That is impossible," he grunted, twisting aside to work off his gloves himself.

"Solid as a rock straight to the bottom"—tossing his things in the direction of the clothes rack, and giving a hard thump to the top of his head to flatten the wind-raked hair. "They say folk are taking walks to Sweden. Don't tell me that's what you got into your head to do— tramping across the ice at your tremendous age."

"Of course not, you imbecile."

"Wind's finally left off"—throwing his gloves over with his other things. "The windows got a fierce shaking, I can tell you. But not a peep out of the babe, he doesn't make no fuss, he's good. But how would you know? Never even have had a look at him. Unnatural, if you ask me."

"I do not ask you! Go see to your tasks, you big slovenly good-for-nothing!"

But she was already slapping off, unperturbed.

In the library, in the darkness, he maneuvered his bulk into a chair, his fingers too cold to light the candles on his desk. After the noise of the wind, the room's silence was profound. The wind, its ocean roar, had been a comfort. Now in its place was the stillness he had so dreaded. He sat with the icy folds of his face pressed into his hands. Then he got himself scowlingly down from the chair and went into the hall, where he labored up the stairs to the nursery.

When the wet nurse answered his sharp knock, he ordered her out. Inside he took up the candle from where she had sat darning, and clumped over with it to the cradle, whose hangings he lifted aside with his free hand. He studied the infant for some moments, squinting at the tiny fingers that fidgeted aimlessly on the coverlet, at the shining little eyes that darted about, following movements that were not there.

"Idiot!" he muttered. "How could you be anything but an idiot, having existed for so short a time?" And he seated himself heavily on the stool by the cradle. He set the candlestick down hard on a small table beside him. His eyes were furious. "Century after century you were nothing. Absolutely nothing. Then a spasm in the womb, nine months of darkness, now a few of light—for all the use you make of light. Here stands a candle, but you might as well be blind. Recognizing nothing, understanding nothing. Idiot!"

He broke off and sat silent, smoldering. Only his wheezes could be heard. His thick, coarse gray hair, still disorderly in spite of his efforts, was gilded in the candlelight. He always wore it powdered, indifferent to the fact that powdered hair had not been in fashion for more than a decade, but hardly a flake remained after the wind's scouring. His pendulous lips were blue-tinged, but his great nose had been reddened like a winter apple. He sat rubbing one cold, thick hand with the other.

"All right, I apologize! But you must try to understand how difficult it is for me to see you lying there full of mindless contentment, blowing bubbles on your lips, while your father . . . while he, while my lad . . . while for him, it is all finished."

His shaggy brows knotting, he fumbled inside his coat and withdrew a folded sheet of paper. It was sealed with red wax that had not yet been broken.

"It is from him. It is addressed in his hand. Here, as you see."

He held the missive to the cradle for a moment, then brought it back, and for a long while sat looking at it in his hands.

"When it came this morning, I began to laugh like someone demented. I could not stop. It was from him—from him, he was alive! Everything his fellow officer had written me about his death was swept from my mind. I thought—I thought—I do not know what I thought, my mind was soaring in all directions, the joy, the joy! I could not stop laughing . . . and then I realized, from the date of the franking, that it had not been sent recently. No, I saw that it had been posted months ago, in October, a few days before the battle at Leipzig where he perished. It had been detained in the mails, gone astray, I do not know . . . I only know I have carried it with me all day without opening it. For I cannot. I cannot bear to read it . . . you can understand that, can't you? Even if he has only written about the weather, or how his horse is keeping? I cannot bear to think of his dear hand moving across the page. I cannot bear the pain."

Without his handkerchief, the old Counselor presses first one eye with the heel of his palm, then the other. Then from inside his coat he withdraws his square, metal-rimmed spectacles and gets the stems clamped around his ears. He sits on for a while. Finally he wipes his nose with his cuff, and slowly works his broad thumb under the sealing wax.

· 3 ·

"I'll be finished in a minute," she says, snapping a pea pod. Her fingers are calloused, her nails chipped. Her gray-streaked, dark brown hair is pulled back in a knot. "Do you want more coffee?"

"No, thanks."

Philip, sitting across from his sister Paula at her kitchen table, presses a stamp to a postcard. When he is abroad, he always sends a picture postcard to his office staff in Chicago. Everyone sends postcards, staff and customers alike: the bulletin board bristles with Kodachrome views from every corner of the globe. Turning the card over, he looks at the Swiss village his sister lives in: a few weathered buildings clutching the green slope of a mountain too high to be contained by the card, which he turns over again. His fingers drum a little on the oilcloth.

The oilcloth was frayed. On the windowsill next to him were red wildflowers in a jar. The sill was ulcerated with dark sores where the paint had chipped away.

"We'll have time for a walk before dinner," Paula said.

"Good," he replied cheerfully, although in the two days they had been together, they had hiked up and down so many steep paths and roads, not to mention the climb to her top-floor apartment, that his feet throbbed. Nothing around here was level, not even indoors. The big stone sink in the corner sloped frankly to one side with the weight of the ages. The refrigerator and stove were newer, probably thirty years old. They too stood at a slant, if only slightly. If you put a marble on the linoleum, it would roll. Paula finished the shelling of the peas and set the bowl aside.

They went down the three inner flights of stone stairs out into a volley of sunlight that revealed Paula's dress to be in need of ironing. He could not fathom the way she looked and lived. For years she had made her home in Neuchâtel with her second husband, a Swiss attorney she had met back in Chicago, but after the separation—and it struck him that he and his sister now had five ex-mates between them—she had chosen to move up here to this meager village, into those three shabby little rooms. What she had begun to look like, undeniably, was something between a peasant woman and a bag lady. He remembered when she was stunning, with a gardenia behind her ear.

At the closetlike post office, he mailed his card and made a phone call. Paula did not have a phone. He talked with his assistant, whom he had left at a Zurich hotel, and with whom he would fly on to Cologne tomorrow. He came back outside with a laugh.

"My assistant wants to know how I'm enjoying my hikes up here in the Alps. I can't get it through her head that it's the Jura, not the Alps. To her, Switzerland's the Alps and that's it. Case closed. This woman's been to every last spot on the globe without absorbing the faintest idea of its geography."

And he laughed again, shaking his head.

"She sounds like a fool," his sister said with the directness he admired but which sometimes set his teeth on edge. He knew his assistant was a fool, but she was a fool with a good grasp of business; and in addition, their nights were comradely and athletic, with nothing beyond.

Crossing the small square with its folded, contemplative cats, they

descended the road that curved down the green slope. The valley
spread out below them. Philip's ruddy baldness shone in the sun, the
remaining hair thick, grizzled, vigorous. An extremely tall man, heavy-
set, he wore well-pressed chinos and a white polo shirt that would be
damp with sweat by the time they climbed back. His feet already hurt.
Nor did he care for this part of the road, where something ghastly
had once happened. Paula had told him yesterday, when they had
walked by. He could envision the young farmer driving his harrow,
its blades chopping and flashing in the sun. Foolishly, he has allowed
his two small children to ride with him. The thing tips over, the children tumble into the blades, the young father climbs like a madman
to his house and cuts his throat from ear to ear.

The farmhouse disappeared behind them. Wildflowers of every
color rippled in the mild breeze. They talked of one thing and another
as they walked: friends from their youth, former spouses, their grown
children scattered across the States.

Philip's feet burned in his shoes. He gave an inner sigh. They walk
in the morning, they walk in the afternoon. Between walks, they sit
at the kitchen table and talk. At night, like the rest of the villagers,
they retire early. Every light is out, the night is black. He undresses
in a smell of stone dust, for she has set up a cot for him in the room
she uses for her labors: a worktable, chisels, mallets, rocks. She used
to sculpt in clay, now it's stone. And she has no talent, never did have.
It is incredible to him, and embarrassing, that she does not realize
this. He tries to sleep, but the cot is hard, the room unheated. Lying
in the cold silence, he sometimes hears what sounds like a distant,
confused orchestra: the clunking bells of cows moving across steep-
nesses. And he thinks of things tipping, tumbling. He thinks of the
room's faintly slanting floorboards, of the sharp chill they give off,
hardly diminished by the small threadbare rug next to the cot. He lies
listening to the distant, swaying disharmony of the cowbells, and only
toward morning does he drop off. When he wakes to sunlight and
puts his sore feet on the worn little rug, gray and gritty with stone

dust, he yawns tiredly and wishes he were elsewhere, even though he is very fond of his sister, who was saying now, as they walked across the road, that it was a shame he couldn't stay longer.

"Do you really have to fly to Cologne tomorrow?"

"Afraid so. In a year or so, say 'eighty-nine, all the morons running around clicking their Nikons will be running around triggering their video cameras. There'll be an extensive display of video models at the exhibition, so naturally I'm eager to see it. Panting."

"It's always amazed me how much you dislike photography," Paula said. "Anything to do with it."

He shrugged. "I don't dislike it. I'm indifferent to it."

"Come on. I've heard you often enough. A mushrooming frenzy of duplication, a fucking fraudulence of bits and pieces. That's a verbatim quote, Philip. You repeat yourself, in case you don't know it."

He gave a laugh. He had a rich, voluble laugh.

"I don't know why you laugh. Maybe I agree, but I don't own the biggest camera and photographic supply company in the Midwest."

"Why not laugh?" he said, and followed her onto a dirt path that led back up the slope. He plodded behind the run-down heels of her briskly moving shoes, glad to have stopped talking, for he was out of breath. The muscles of his thighs ached with every step. He was not an unactive man, a jogger and tennis player, but he was unused to climbing, and unused to the great highness, the great silence all around. When they paused, turning around on the path to catch their breath, he felt for a moment that he would topple into the distances below, and stepped back. And it wasn't even the Alps, only the Jura, which brought his assistant fleetingly to mind. He could imagine her down there at that farmhouse, darting around with her Nikon F3, snapping rapid-fire shots of the crazed wife and stunned neighbors before dashing on to the red mass in the overturned harrow.

They climbed on up through a sprawling flower garden to the back of Paula's apartment building, and sat down on a wooden bench. Damp with sweat, he stretched his burning feet before him. Clothes hung on lines out here. The level strip of ground had been paved with cement, but was cracked everywhere by grass in rampant growth. Chickens walked around pecking. The sun was well over in the sky, but the air was still warm. It was only the nights that were cold, but after dinner he would be driving his rented car back to Zurich.

Their conversation resumed. Paula, pushing back strands of hair with those calloused fingers whose sight he could not accustom himself to, got onto their childhood in Evanston a hundred lifetimes ago. She remembered more than he; maybe because she was older, if only by ten months. They talked about their mother, they talked about their stepfather. Maybe, Philip agreed, they had socialized and traveled too much, but they'd been great whenever they were around, especially their stepfather. Their father they never talked about, because there was nothing to talk about. They had never known him, had heard only a few scraps from their mother, whom he had bored unconscionably. A brief shipboard romance—she on holiday, he a Scandinavian structural engineer on his way to South America—followed by a marriage of less than a year. Stuck in the Uruguayan interior, the back of the back of beyond, as she called it, with a man both boring and too old for her, she had just up and left one day; took herself back to Chicago with a weeks-old infant in arms and another freshly conceived. Then a burst appendix had solved all problems: lethal peritonitis down there in the back of the back of beyond, and the man was no more. He was an eyeblink in their mother's life, to Philip and Paula even less. But their mother was a vivid memory. She could be great fun, even more so their stepfather, who had sometimes played charades with them. They talked about their childhood games.

"Remember when we squeezed toothpaste into all the keyholes, and the maid chased us outside with a broom?" Paula asked.

"Wasn't it a vacuum cleaner?"

"How could she chase us outside with a vacuum cleaner?"

"I don't know."

"Do you remember the ants?"

"Ants?"

"In the back garden. How they fascinated us."

"Kind of."

"They fascinated us."

And she thought how long ago all that was. More than fifty years had passed, an immensity of confused and rushing time.

The sun was going down. They climbed on up to the front of the house, still talking. They had talked about everything, Paula thought, except her reasons for coming here. She knew what was behind her brother's affectionate but somewhat bored and restless eyes: what does she want up here? What does she do? Takes walks. Hammers on those pathetic stones. Sits around that squalid apartment. Why is she up here in this godforsaken place? Well, you could ask, Philip. Why don't you ask? Because I could tell you. It has to do with that immensity of confused and rushing time. Why don't you ask?

They continued their climb up the three inner flights of stairs. The kitchen was brilliant in the last of the light. The flowers on the windowsill blazed.

That evening after dinner, Philip makes the long drive back to Zurich. The next morning he is on the flight to Cologne, his assistant, her shoulder draped with camera straps, in the seat beside him. His palms are damp. It's curious, he reflects, looking down the aisle, how casual people seem during takeoff. Yet they can't conceal an odd look of politeness, as if by appearing obedient and courteous and good, they might escape God's wrath. God's wrath didn't express itself often. Only once had he known its fury, years back on a flight in bad weather. Wrenched in every direction from behind the clutch of his seat belt, he and the window beside him careering high and low, he had felt a racing horror in which one single, comprehensible thought stood out: that he should have one single, comprehensible thought in this final confusion.

The categorical silence is broken by a roar. Stalagmites are crushed by boulders torn from ceiling and walls. The sheltering cave bears disappear in the fall of stone. When the earthquake ends, there is silence again.

· 4 ·

The pressure of lips still fresh on his forehead, Olaf remains sitting on the polished parquet floor of the hallway. The two creatures have gone up the stairs. The hallway is dark. Olaf sits on.

He would soon go out into the night woods by way of the kitchen window, which was always left open on its hasp. He would go hurriedly, even though the house was dark now and the kitchen empty and safe. It was not a place he liked. He felt no gratitude to the kitchen beast who gave him his scraps. He could smell the enmity on this creature, could hear its mute snarl when it set the bowl down with a clatter. The plowing feet of this beast would flatten his tail if he did not keep it nervously curled around him while he ate. He always got out fast. He got out of most places fast, but did not always escape the two small chasing beasts who yelled and swept him into their arms. When he burst free, they bouncing back with arms outspread, it was with fury. The other, much bigger creature, the one with the glint at its center—this being Hr. Rosted's gold watch chain, looped across his waistcoat—this one was not as threatening. But often it came like a blot between Olaf and the other, the one that was Olaf's. He knew this other creature as well as he knew anything: its scent, its sound, its touch. It was the only one of these creatures he ever desired to be near.

Now it was no longer present. His reasons for staying were few: a rasping of leaves against a pane, some glassy pings from above as a moth involved itself with the chandelier. Olaf followed these sounds with flicks of his good ear until they paled on him. But still he did not leave; he was being pulled by habit down the hallway to his night post at the far window. With a crouch, he hopped up and settled himself on the sill. Only at night did he do this; on the single occasion he had sat here in the daytime, one of the several beasts of busyness in its beribboned cap had smacked its hands together and shaken the curtain, so that he had fled in terror. But at night he possessed full, serene command of what lay below.

This was the Øresund, the Sound. Great, black, still. It was Olaf's custom to observe this great black stillness with close patience unless he suddenly felt the need to wash himself, as he did now, licking a paw and with it stroking his face. It might have been a glorious face, a prize, for the delicate care he put into its cleaning. Its abradedness, its starkly twisted ear, were unknown to him; he licked and smoothed with equanimity.

Then, as often happened, his eyes flared at the sight of other eyes: very small, bright yellow eyes, which stared back at him as they moved slowly through the dark—these being the rigging lights of one of the great seagoing schooners, perhaps on its way to Africa or Asia—his riveted gaze holding the riveted gaze of these yellow eyes until they disappeared from view. Then, suddenly, an owl's hoot sounded from the woods. He jumped down and ran swiftly into the kitchen, pausing to savor with a sniff the traces of mingled scents—meat, juices, blood—and to sharpen his claws on a leg of the table. Then he sprang to the window and squeezed out into the pulse of the night.

C<&<

The dark mass from which Olaf leaped was in daylight a large and pleasing structure with ivy-covered half-timbered brick walls, and high gables bordered with openwork carving in the Viking style. With a fine view of the water, the house was set among gardens around which stood the majestic beech woods that were a feature, along with meadows, moors and streams, of one of the loveliest regions in all of Northern Europe. A faint crescent moon had risen.

In the Rosteds' bedchamber the eiderdown had been pushed aside. The couple still breathed heavily, lying naked and gleaming with sweat, the propriety of trammeling nightclothes as alien to them as the inclination to seek slumber when the building frenzy and enraptured release were over. It was as if they could never have enough of each other, whether of each other's flesh or thoughts; and having drawn the eiderdown back over them, they lay talking, limbs entwined, until gradually, reluctantly, they suffered sleep to part them.

Later Grethe woke drowzily to the thought that one of the boys had called out. Gently disengaging herself from her husband's arms, she got into her slippers and white cashmere peignoir, and pushing back her disheveled hair, went along the corridor to the nursery. Both children were peacefully asleep. She touched her lips to their brows, very lightly, not to waken them.

Perhaps, she thought as she returned along the corridor, it was the Pierced One who had called out. And she paused at the oddness of the thought. The Pierced One hung among the ancestral portraits in the drawing room, the only likeness there which was not painted, a profile only, a silhouette cut from black paper. He had died too young to have sat for a portrait. Perhaps it was a black paper cry she had heard?

"You are absurd," she whispered to herself, coming back into the bedchamber and removing her robe and slippers. But she was no longer sleepy. Often it happened that she was unable to sleep; then she would wander around the room for a little until she felt ready for bed again. She never minded the interval of wakefulness; it was pleasant to walk about quiet and naked in the dark. She drew her hand along the furnishings as she moved—smooth velvet, rougher brocade, carved wood—and lowered her face to a bowl of flowers. It was always strange to smell flowers when you could not see their colors; there was something untold about them in the darkness, as there was about oneself, wandering slow and soundless on naked soles.

At the window she drew aside the curtain. A thin slice of moon hung high over the garden and woods. From the woods the night wind brought a sound of massed rustling, like the sound of the surf. Everything was as black as the black sky, where a few scattered stars hung with the curved crystal thread of moon. In the gardens the flowerbeds were still covered with straw, but in another month or two they would be in bloom. And in the woods the nightingales, with their rapturous, sobbing song, would have returned from their southern migration. Snow still lay throughout the grounds, in hard frozen traces, though she could not see them. Nor could she see the greenhouse or the stable or the carriage house.

She wondered if Olaf was curled up on the carriage house roof. She knew that he sometimes slept there, for she had seen him from the window on summer nights, when every inch of the grounds was as distinguishable as if it were not night at all, but soft gray dusk. Foreign guests were always surprised by the pale beautiful nights of the northern summers. It had to do with the earth's tilt, the angle of the sun's rays; a principle, in any event, a law of nature, like gravity, like the moon's control of the tides. But if the moon crumbled, she thought, the Sound would swoosh like a geyser into space, and all beings everywhere would vanish like shot arrows from the face of the earth.

Her heart suddenly pounding, she looked up to be certain that the crescent moon hung intact, and appalled at herself, put her hand to her face. Such odd, terrible, invasive thoughts. And earlier this evening, when she had sat sewing on the little rug and Holger had read aloud, had she not then also been gripped by unwanted thoughts? She could not clearly remember, but it seemed so. Nor had it been the first time. She did not think so. Nor was tonight the first time she had heard the black paper cry of the Pierced One. She did not think so. She did not think so.

"But let it be the last," she whispered. "Let it be the last, for it is dreadful."

After a time, she begins to feel calmer. She cannot remember exactly what it was that had so troubled her. Everything, after all, is as always—familiar and good: the regular tock-tock of the clock as she walks back across the room, and the lovely, nearing sound of Holger's breathing, that slow, indrawn lightness followed by the deep, rich sigh as she climbs quietly back into bed.

· 5 ·

The wet nurse never before having glimpsed the old Counselor, for he has never before come to the babe's room, feels her mouth drop when at the sound of a rap she opens the door. She looks down on something ancient, wheezing and low to the floor, a horribly bulbous miscreation from which blazes a command to get out.

"At—at your bidding, Herre," she stammers, and betakes herself downstairs to the kitchen.

"Didn't I tell you he's a vision?" asks the housekeeper, busy slapping dishes down on the table. "So he finally went up there, did he? Only because I gave him a severe talking-to. You have to beat a thing into his head, he's that thick. I tell you, it's not easy living with that foolish, furious old freak, and not another soul about. 'I don't need a house staff and I don't want them!' he declares of a sudden, some dozen years back, and out the door he pushes them—maids, cooks, footmen, coachmen. 'Take the carriage, take whatever you want, out, out, away with you all!' he cries, and that's that. Why? I haven't a notion. Nor probably had he."

The wet nurse, who had heard all this before, sat down at the table and waited for an end to the clattering of chipped bowls, all of which contained leftovers. The great kitchen, with its unswept red tile floor and its walls hung with every kind of pot, pan and ladle, all of them tarnished with disuse, was lit by the moving amber reflections from the blazing, soot-blackened hearth. It was the warmest room in the house. The wet nurse enjoyed her meals not for the uninspired fare, but for the blessed heat, and for the break in her solitude with the babe upstairs. The housekeeper's flapping tongue was something that came with it.

Hair poking out from under her soiled cap, greasy ends of a knitted shawl dangling down her apron front, the housekeeper flopped into a chair, stuck her elbow on the table, and speared a cold dumpling.

"Does a gentleman walk?" she asked through her chewing. "Do you ever see a gentleman on foot? But many's the time I been buying fish on Gammel Strand or coming from the market square and seen him stomping and glowering past. It's all he's got on his mind, such as it is: barging up and down the streets. And never think it's an oddness come of his great age, for as I hear it, he's been blundering through alleys and avenues all his life—why, all Copenhagen must know him by sight, a big humiliation for his family you can be sure. But he cares about nothing. That's how they are, grotesques—witless. True, he was a financial counselor once—and to Christian VII be it known—but how long do you suppose that lasted? A week, then out on his ear. What on earth could *he* counsel? Why, he's so daft he'd have come quick to grief in this life if it wasn't for all those generals and landowners and high churchmen of his going back to God knows when, money pouring down from one generation to the next and plopping into his lap at birth so he never need do a thing but stamp about the streets heaving from side to side like a ship in high seas. And never a kind word for the concern I show him, only shouts and insults and nastiness even when you're bone-tired from all the work around here—"

To the wet nurse, adding a heel of bread to the cold sausage and eel on her plate, it seemed that the housekeeper seldom cooked and never cleaned, but spent the greater part of her days snoring by the hearth with a handful of sugartop candies in her lap.

"But sure he must appreciate your tremendous work," she said with a smile, to which the housekeeper shook her head, wiping her mouth with the back of her hand.

"Never. No appreciation. But he remembers what I done for the lad. If it wasn't for that, I'd of been out on my ear with the rest of the house staff he kicked out the door that day. But me he kept on and made housekeeper. Well, I'd saved the lad, hadn't I? Saved him outright?"

"Aye, pulled him off that thing he was stuck on," sighed the nurse, who had many times heard the tale.

"Aye, the iron-spike fence out there in the courtyard. There I am. I'm standing by the fence getting some sun on me, being a scullery maid and always damp. And I see the child right above me, he's standing between the spikes and reaching up to a tree branch. Now he pulls himself up on it, and now he slips! He falls! Like lightning I'm stretching my whole self up and catching him round the legs as he comes down so the spike can't go in no further. Pierced him just by the heart the doctor said, and would of gone deep and mortal but for me. Not that it did him much good in the end," she added. "Gone now anyway, and scarce two and twenty."

The wet nurse—who had been raised hungry in back alleys, who made a living only because she was endlessly impregnated by an ale-sodden spouse, endlessly brought to bed of puny babes who mostly died but left her full of milk, who knew the irreversible truths of life but welcomed whatever light moments came her way—was not disposed to snuffle at the demise of an officer. No one forced those peacocks into battle. The Army was their choice. Not everyone had choices.

She remarked dryly, "I trust he didn't look like his papa."

"Not on your life he didn't. The opposite. Bonny. Oh, he was bonny, make no mistake. Not in *no* way like that repulsive beetle. You'd think he'd try to make up for how he looks by acting decent, but no, there's nothing in that big ugly head of his but—"

The head appeared as the kitchen door was pushed open. Something about the old gnome's face as he entered, the eyes, their extreme redness, caused the wet nurse to rise from the table and take her leave, as if by remaining she would infringe on his privacy.

The housekeeper wiped her mouth with her wrist.

"So, what think you of your grandson?"

"Passable," he grunted.

"Passable indeed. Well, that's more than can be said for you." She drummed her fingers among the crumbs on the table. "What is it you want? Will you eat?"

"A cutlet and seltzer water only. And don't look so put-upon. Surely you can bestir yourself to make a cutlet. Move!" he snapped, waddling over to the hearth.

The housekeeper remained where she was. She forked up a piece of jellied eel and sat chewing.

"You've been crying again. I can always tell by your eyes. Look at them."

"I cannot look at them, can I, they being in my head? I want none of your twaddle. I want silence."

"Always weeping. Weeping and weeping over him. But do you ever weep for your little daughter-in-law?"

"That is for her parents to do," he muttered.

"What are you talking about? She hadn't any, that's why the babe is with you."

"Don't tell me what I know!" he barked, and turned back to the fire. "So let God weep for her, I cannot weep for everyone. Make me a cutlet."

The housekeeper sighed and got to her feet.

"Go then," she said. "I'll bring it into the dining room."

"Here is good enough," he muttered. "I want the warmth."

"For being out in the fierce cold, stomping about like a fool as usual."

"Not as usual!" It burst from him.

"Oh, so we're an unusual fool today. What accounts for that?"

"Hold your tongue!" he yelled.

"You're not to be endured," she threw over her shoulder, and slapped across the dirty floor to the larder. "Passable indeed. And let God cry for her. Fie! Fie! And running about the streets like a half-wit on the coldest day in all history—for that's how it will go down in the books, you mark me, what with the Sound frozen solid as rock straight to the bottom—"

Thorkild stood at the hearth thinking of his daughter-in-law. A sapling of a girl, a little green sapling laid away. The parents gone too, both taken by influenza last year, in their prime. It was true what Bodil the ice-block had said: people die continually. Sudden disappearances everywhere. There. And there. And there. That people vanished was almost less surprising than that people remained. One should be comforted by the prodigality of death, by its broad, familial gathering in of its arms, and should not grieve as if one's gathered-in lad were the only one, solitary and forlorn. All that remained of the boy's beloved face was his framed silhouette hanging on the library wall, a bit of cut-out paper, nothing. He knew his sorrow seemed excessive to others. Reddened eyes always, sudden overflowing tears, handkerchief to the nose. Had not some months passed, after all? As if time meant anything. It only drove the truth in harder. Harder. Harder.

"I shall eat in the dining room after all," he says in the midst of the housekeeper's shuffling and clattering. It will be colder there than in the kitchen, but he will be alone, and if further weeping comes upon him, of the great shuddering, unstoppable kind, as happened in the babe's room when he read aloud the letter, he need not hold back. He had not held back with the babe. The babe had understood.

· 6 ·

Locked behind his safety belt, Philip reflects that landings are the same as takeoffs: just beneath the casual expressions, the idle talk, there exists that same hopefully appeasing quality of obedience, politeness, goodness. God's small children sitting row on row, all trying to be worthy of the wheels' meltingly sweet first bump.

Or maybe it's all my own projection, he thinks. Certainly there's no sign of covert beseeching in the figure making its way down the aisle from the rest rooms, swaying against the plane's vibrating slant with not a damn that the aisles are supposed to be cleared. The arms look like sausages, encased in the sleeves of a padded, fluorescent-orange Mao jacket. Below are black rubbery skintight biker's pants with neon slashes. Enormous pink and white running shoes, like two baroque fortresses, are on the feet. The face is round and young, overseen by a blond-tinted cascade of tiny kinks and corkscrews. The species is so ubiquitous that he always has to look twice to be sure this one is his assistant.

She climbed over his long, cramped legs, lifted her cameras by their straps from the adjoining seat, and sat down talking. He was grateful for this, it obliterated his thoughts.

Something about Howard Hughes. Howard Hughes's fingernails.

She'd caught it on TV in Zurich yesterday. "Gross," she said, snapping on her seat belt. "They were so long they curled under his fingers. So what I want to know, how did he unhook bras? Just a minute, darling, I've got these weird fingernails."

The plane lurched, Philip's heart with it. Now she was talking about Martin Luther. "Did Martin Luther have fingernails? No way." Her flights of fancy were informed by the rules of stand-up comics: leap from one reference to another, effect the startling, but keep that theme building. "No way did Martin Luther have fingernails. He was a peasant. Peasant fingers are totally worn down by toil, like right to the knuckles? Like I'm trying, my strudel, have patience, just a couple more hours. What I want to know, how did he have time for the Restoration?" Another lurch, the voice sailing on with something about Rome, "all the Restoration shit hitting the fan." Had she lost the fingernails? Wasn't that the theme? Maybe there was no theme. They were zooming in now, tops of wet buildings, the voice still sailing on. "Probably warm in Rome right now, not like sodden Cologne here. They're probably screwing al fresco in the Pincio—"

He felt the wheels' first skipping bump, then another, and now they were shooting along the runway. It wasn't done yet. But finally there came a mammoth holding back of power, a sense of giant heels digging into the ground in lengthening ruts, and at last a shuddering deadlock which flowered into the smooth, silent taxiing that marked arrival.

He released a long breath. Outside it was drizzling. It had been drizzling in Zurich. It was probably drizzling in the Jura, yesterday's big clear distances all mist. They came to a full, conclusive stop. He unbuckled his safety belt, and stretched his arms as the aisle began to fill.

"It's really grabbed me," she said. "What d'you think? Photos and text."

"Photos and text of what?" He had stopped listening, no longer in need of distraction.

"Ber*lin*. The Wall. I photograph the Wall. I photograph the Berliners. I interview them about their feelings."

"You speak German?" he asked, getting to his feet. "News to me."

"So?" She stood up, hoisting her camera straps over her shoulder. "I get an interpreter." The comedian's tone was gone. She had her serious side. "The Wall's just sitting there waiting for an in-depth exploration. All I've ever done before is snap the graffiti. But this time I'd do photos and text both. Interviews. Get firsthand personal stories on both sides."

"What do you know about the Wall?" he asked as they wedged themselves into the snailing column. "Or Berlin? Or Germany?" And he added: "Reformation. Not Restoration."

"So? I don't count those pompous hairsplitting terms as any kind of relevant truth."

"I forgot," he laughed. For she always made him laugh, finally, with a kind of hopeless, contemptuous disbelief.

෦෪

It was three days of swarming bodies and endless display booths: film, tripods, developing paper, chemical mixtures, plastic filters, filter umbrellas, and cameras, cameras, cameras *ad nauseam.* The video models, he knew, would be obsolete in six months, overtaken by newer designs; but his customers, like customers everywhere, clamped hands on the first thing out; they relied on him for merchandise excitation, and he was reliable, always willing to cram their hands, eyes, brains with the most recently hatched Stella Nova.

Damp interiors of cabs that splashed between exhibition hall and hotel. Jammed lounges and suites where contacts were made with manufacturers' reps, where you had to yell over yakking photographers and technology buffs. Late hours and elbow-jogged drinks, then a few hours' sleep before he and his assistant were again sloshing boothward in a dank cab. When it was over he had negotiated a substantial number of orders, in the video field a whopping one.

"So, do we go to Berlin or not?"

He shrugged. "Why not?"

❧

From their hotel off Kurfürstendamm they took a cab to the Brandenburg Gate. She was off clicking her Nikon as soon as they got out. In the Berlin dress code of disaffiliated youth—black boots, black jeans, black leather jacket, yards of hanging sullen scarf—she made a disdainful detour around gaudily clad tourists, most of them fellow Americans as busy as she with their cameras. Philip wandered around to blarings of transistor rock, schlock. It wasn't raining but had been. Glistening tour buses, streaked wooden souvenir booths, shining ropes of litter snagged in weeds, and the dank Wall with its multicolored graffiti inscribed mainly by tourists over the years. Small chunks of Wall, more likely small chunks of pavement, were being bought at the booths. Flowers were also being bought, to place at its foot. Why not? Why not a good pull of the heartstrings, whether the pulling was done by some TV trauma-unit docudrama, or by a publicized slab of scrawled-over concrete? He watched the purchasers lay their wreaths with bowed heads. His assistant was one of them, except that she had chosen a more distant spot. She laid her spray as someone separate, unique. It began to rain.

They stayed a day and a half. They shopped along the Kurfürstendamm, ate at Kempinsky's, dropped in late at a rock-pounding all-night dive off Savignyplatz. Then he was fed up with Berlin. He had never liked Berlin. Too big, too ugly, too noisy. And the rain. When he suggested Rome, there was no argument from his assistant. Her photo-and-text enterprise, with its dreary, long-range prospect of locating a translator and finding interviewees, had gone the way of indefinite postponement, as he had known it would. But on the ride back to the airport she had things to say about the Wall as a tragic symbol of the modern world's schizoid nature—a fresh-caught cliché apparently tossed from the same source as Howard Hughes's finger-

Glaciers have begun moving down again from the polar regions. Over thousands upon thousands of years, by infinitesimal degrees, grinding the earth beneath them, they cover vast areas of the earth's land masses. For thousands upon thousands of years the air is frigid. Then the glaciers begin retreating. With the same stupendous languor that marked their arrival, they grind their way back out of Europe, leaving behind scored soil and crumbled rocks, lakes annihilated by alluvial deposits and coastlines altered. Warm weather again prevails for thousands upon thousands of years, until the glaciers return. And again retreat. And return, and retreat.

In the limestone caves common to parts of the Continent, the glaciers' ponderous journeys pass unknown. Whether permafrost lies above, or trees circled by noisy birds, it is all the same to a chamber of rock millions of years old. Water trickles, stalagmites build up unseen. The great cave bears still come, down and down, slapping their slow steep way, but they come less often, and there are fewer of them. Like the mammoths and bison and saber-toothed tigers, they are dying out.

· 7 ·

The windows of the house stand open in the heat of summer. The curtains of reticella lace are drawn aside to views of the Sound and of the gardens and beech woods, all imbued with a quality of basking stillness. Occasionally a breeze from the water stirs the long edges of the curtains, which then fall motionless again.

Down in the garden a social comedy is being enjoyed by Hr. and Fru Rosted and Hr. Rosted's uncle. They are having tea with a foreign, a Philadelphia, couple, guests whom Onkel has brought from Copenhagen, saddled with them for the day—a pair so phenomenally stodgy that they had stiffened, as if shot, when their carriage drew up before the house just as the two small boys, hastily followed by their nurse with towels and sand bucket, came running down the steps stark naked. Onkel, a scholarly, flinty-faced man who behind his pince-nez and severe gray goatee harbors a strapping sense of humor, had turned to his two stricken companions and said in his accented English:

"Going for a bathe in the Sound. Filthy custom in our land, allowing children to cavort nude on the beach. Revolting."

Not a glimmer of perception had met his irony. Unbelievable, he thought with high amusement as they emerged from the carriage to the greetings of Holger and Grethe, who had come out to welcome

4 3

them, and who received two coldly affronted handshakes. And as if the children had not been enough, a servant girl came skittering around the corner of the house, flinging up the backs of her skirts for the benefit of some unseen pursuer.

Onkel was delighted.

"Really, this is all quite unendurable," he said. "What must our guests think?"

Grethe smiled.

"I think perhaps our guests would enjoy a stroll. May we have the pleasure of showing you our gardens?" she asked them.

Holger's wife had many excellent qualities, among them a mildness, a kindness, and a shimmering beauty that warmed and gladdened. In this case, however, these qualities did not even minimally appease. The guests retained an absence of cordiality amounting to rudeness.

Nor did the massed and radiant flowers undo the distasteful scenes the couple had suffered, nor the peach and pear trees ripe with clustered fruit, nor the Viking dolmen nor the goldfish pond. As they came to the sandstone griffin, mythical beast symbolic of the sun's wealth, Holger gave his uncle a wink and drew the couple's attention to the ferocious eagle head and wings and talons, to the extended tongue like a scimitar, and to the rampant lion body with its barbed genitals.

"What?" he asked in his pleasant, courteous voice. "It does not please you? Is it the savagery? But in order to draw the flaming sun through the sky, it must possess a certain savage strength, mustn't it? Ah, but that may be too archaic a concept. Well, one is flexible. Our friend here may also be seen as the embodiment of Christ—"

"Really," Onkel interrupted. "This is sacrilege."

"Not at all. Our guests will recognize it as an accepted Christian interpretation. Perfectly proper. The winged part represents our Savior's godly, judgmental nature; the lower His shall we say more human aspects. Perfectly proper. Yes?" he asked the pair with his pleasant smile.

Managing to keep a straight face, Grethe suggested they walk on.

But in spite of her amusement, she was sorry for the couple. So sour. And so hot. Such heavy, inappropriate attire, as if they refused to accept the fact of summer in so northern a country. The lady's hat alone—an enormous, weighty, sweltering affair of veils and plumes— must be contributing as much to her grimness as the intolerable sights she was undergoing.

As they walked, Grethe felt the sleeve of her dress with her fingers. It was an eyeletted white muslin gown, not charred, not disintegrated. Once, it seemed to her, the griffin had dragged her up between its stone wings and borne her to the incineration of the sun. She gave a shake of her head to dislodge the peculiar thought, and gestured toward the small white tea pavilion.

"I hope you will take some refreshments after your drive?" she said to the couple, who responded by telling Onkel that they wished to leave in sufficient time for their visit to Helsingør.

Grethe ignored the insult. They could not conduct themselves otherwise, they were too displeased and unhappy. Nevertheless, she tried again as they sat down in the pavilion.

"You will be more comfortable here, I think. We are very nicely shaded by the trees, as you see."

But the couple in their stifling clothes looked no less condemnatory than before. As the maids came with trays, Grethe tried once again, indicating the lovely views from where they sat. She looked out at the bluegreen Sound, with its dotting of sailboats, and at the massed, vivid hues of her beloved flowers, and suddenly she heard the Pierced One's cry—abrupt, fleeting—and saw his framed black silhouette before her. She looked down and concentrated on the passing of dishes. There was coffee, iced tea, freshly baked white bread with butter, fresh shrimp in chipped ice, glistening strawberries. When she raised her eyes, the Pierced One was gone.

"And you will continue from here to Helsingør?" she enquired of the couple, who ate with no discernible appreciation, but as if to fulfill an obligation to their escort.

"Our friends naturally wish to visit Hamlet's castle," Onkel replied, and held a hand up warningly. "And please, Holger, do not belabor us with the fact that Hamlet never existed."

"Never did," Holger told the guests with a charming smile. "Never trod the halls of Kronborg. The real prince, he on whom the good Shakespeare based his tale, was from a more primitive era. Amleth was his name, lived on a miserable windswept island over in the Jylland fjord. And like his namesake feigned madness: but his took a cruder form, such as rolling about in the mud. And his gibberish wasn't as wonderfully quotable as Hamlet's—still, it had flair. For instance, he once complained that the beer tasted of iron, the bread of blood, and the lard of dead men's flesh—"

Onkel clicked his tongue. "Really, Holger."

"—and it was found that rusty swords lay at the bottom of the brewer's well, and that the wheat came from a battlefield where men had been slain, and that hogs had eaten human carrion." Holger nodded reflectively at the couple. "Gives one pause, doesn't it, as to the nature of truth? Indeed, I see it does, for you have stopped eating. But pray continue; I will speak no more of philosophy, which may not be digestible fare."

And Grethe thought: to feign madness merely. To roll in mud and then to wash it off. To be restored so easily.

Aloud she offered the couple more tea, adding with quiet humor, "No, truly it has not been brewed with rusty swords."

But their offendedness was great. They declined with hard eyes.

"Shall we speak of something more agreeable?" asked Onkel, who was enjoying himself very much, and turning to his two guests, he began to describe the flora and fauna along the coastline.

Grethe exchanged a look, a smile, with Holger. Had they sat nearer, one foot of each would have sought the other, shoe caressing shoe. Grethe's toes curled and stretched. She remembered herself aglow in the morning's early freshness; the encircling heat of his arms, her cheek pressed in languor against one strong, beautifully made hand; his crisp bush of hair and his sex, softened now from its ecstatic thrusts, lying against her wet thigh. She never felt a wish to wipe his exudation from between her legs; it was natural and good, his inner fluid which had mixed with hers and trickled back out to bathe her thighs. Sometimes he used a sheath, in which his fluid was caught; and sometimes she inserted a sponge into the unseen regions within her; they alternated in these precautions, believing in fairness, but the very idea of precaution, of artifice, was uncongenial to them both, clumsily inhibiting. Usually they used nothing, and if conception took place, then that was what was meant to be, and was good.

"My nephew has painted many scenes from our coast here, both landscapes and seascapes. And very fine they are. I hasten to add that Hr. Rosted is a gentleman painter. Amateur."

"I'm glad you added that, Onkel. I shouldn't care to be taken for a professional."

"Apaches. Riffraff."

"And most of them are so preoccupied with the nude. Have you noticed," Holger asked the visitors, "that there is an excess of nudes in contemporary paintings? And no evidence whatever of drapery. Why, not only exposed bosoms but—"

"Oh, please," entreated Onkel.

Grethe's eyes shone wet with suppressed mirth. Unable to speak for the laughter inside her, she shook her head at the cigarette case Holger was passing around. Customarily she took a cigarette after a meal, but her guests would be caused further unhappiness by the sight of a woman smoking. Surreptitiously, she wiped the corners of her eyes. She sipped her coffee and gazed out at the garden. There was Olaf, walking along the path. He looked hot in the pouring sun. But he knew a cool place in the woods, where he was very likely going. He and she had been there together. More than once they had been there together. It was by a small spring, the ground was moss-covered, soft to lie on. She wanted to go with him now. She wanted at least to turn in her chair and keep him in sight as long as possible. But she sensed this would not do in front of others.

"And you, Grethe, what are you working on at the moment?" asked Onkel, and he explained to the guests: "Fru Rosted is an accomplished translator who specializes in modern French literature. Modern but not frivolous, I assure you. Is that not so, Grethe?"

She smiled.

"Indeed, it is. At present I am working on a novel by Emile Zola."

"What, Zola? I had no idea!" exclaimed Onkel, who had arranged the contract.

The couple's lips tightened, and tightened further as Grethe took a cigarette after all, and lit it. She was tired of their unhappiness. If they could not tolerate other ways of life, why had they not stayed home? She was also growing tired of Onkel and Holger's game, entertaining though it was.

"Unfortunately," Holger was saying to the couple, "nothing is as it appears. You might think as you come up the drive that you're approaching a decent bourgeois establishment, but—"

"No, don't say it," Onkel protested. "Don't say it is actually a sink of nonconformity, a den of bohemianism—"

"And worse."

"Worse? Pray don't unburden yourself to our guests if you mean such things as—"

"I do. You've arrived in a barbarous land," he told the pair. "Yes, we who live in the northern outskirts of civilization, lashed by gales of ice for eleven and a half months of the year, we worship the sun in ways you can never understand. The griffin you saw, and the Viking dolmen—these relics of a savage past are our idols. We set our sacrifices before them. We are Amleths, primitives—all the rest you see around you is veneer."

"It's true!" Onkel brought his face close and intent to the guests. "One tries to deny it but cannot. Savagery boils in the blood—throbs in the eyeballs!" And he gave a sudden sharp fingertap to his pince-nez.

If the couple was shocked or by now merely enraged by these

goings-on, Onkel could not tell, nor did he care. Rude and pompous rectitude called for humorous pinpricks, but, like Holger, he was an essentially serious man for whom the comedy had run its course. He put his serviette aside, and on behalf of his guests thanked his host and hostess for a delicious repast.

The guests looked at him with utter, glittering dislike. Grethe felt sorry for them, deprived of their trip to Helsingør; for they would not now want to spend the rest of the day in Onkel's company, but would ask to be returned directly to Copenhagen. But as the party walked back through the garden, the couple made it clear that Kronborg was their destination and to Kronborg they would go. She then felt sorry for Onkel, who was not one to renege on a promise and thus faced hours more of the wretched pair. Whereas she and Holger would be released.

There would still be time to join the children for a bathe; to be immersed, liquid diamonds all around. She had never known water so intimately until she had married and moved here. She was city-bred, a Copenhagener. And she thought of her father, whom she remembered quite clearly. Not so her mother, who had died in childbirth. That was a fate that seemed to run in her family, though she herself had escaped it: her births had been easy, small hips but also small babies. Who grew at once like sturdy, rosy blooms, their two lovely boys whose shouts at play were carried to her ears from the shore.

Birth, she thought. Perpetual reproduction. The flowers all around. Roses, tulips, lupin, laburnum, bluebells, convolvuluses, forsythia, golden chains and bursts of fiery reds and lakes of blue, of violet, of sparkling white. They were a horror to her when she dwelled on their fecundity. Blooms bursting up everywhere only to flake and shred and in their seeding decay gave rise to more of the same. Everywhere you looked: petals, leaves, shapes, colors, a massed tangle, confusing, suffocating. She longed for her needlework in her hands. Her own clearly drawn floral pattern. Her own steady route. The thread follows the needle. There was no pattern here, no route in this terrible overgrowth of death and birth. If she had gone with Olaf, she would not have been assailed by the garden's horror.

She concentrates on the blue clarity of the sky, and by degrees, she feels herself return to equanimity.

And now they have arrived at the carriage, Onkel throwing them a look of mock despair. The grim, sour, perspiring couple are being helped in by the coachman. On to Helsingør, on to Hamlet's castle, where no Hamlet ever dwelled.

· 8 ·

In Helsingør the wind blows hard off the Sound. It strikes the passengers broadside as they climb down from the mail coach to wait, with stamping feet, for their frosted baggage to be unstrapped from the roof. The monstrous little beetle of a man and the garrulous woman having no baggage to wait for, they can be seen already setting off down the street in a flapping of garments.

It is the first time they have ever traveled together. The house-keeper's errand is to look over a property left to her by a deceased aunt. The Counselor, despite his hatred of coaches, has come along to advise her. This ridiculous notion vexes the housekeeper; and far more than vexed is she to be seen in his company—the other passengers sitting there the whole time staring, or trying not to. In dissociation, she had sat almost with her back to him. She had conversed a great deal in the coach, but now she is mute. She has nothing to say to her companion. He, for his part, rocking alongside her with clacking stick, hopes to persuade her to move into the property. Then he will be rid of her.

The door opened straight from the cobblestones into a single room with a beamed, low-pitched ceiling. There was a hearth, a crude table, some rush chairs. Toweling hung at the windows instead of curtains.

Thorkild scowled with disappointment. She would rent it out or sell it, but she herself would not move into this one-room hovel. Yet never having been inside a hovel, he could not suppress his curiosity. Where, for instance, did one sleep? Seeing an alcove bed, he waddled over and peered into it. Deep, shadowed, it held a pillow of coarse cloth and some blankets. From above hung a rope, evidently to aid the old aunt in rising. On the floor below stood her slippers. He picked one up. It was made of folded rags carefully sewn together, with sewn-on soles of layered thick string. He set it down, his breath visible in the room's chill, and went over to an open wooden box filled with white sand. Possibly the sand was used to sweep the floor with. The floorboards were very clean. The toweling at the windows was clean and white. Rising on his toes, he peered up at the rack where she kept her dishes. In pride of place stood a yolk-yellow glass bowl, cracked and glued, with faint, timeworn bands of cheap gilt. A family heirloom perhaps, or a wedding gift. The bowl gave color to the surroundings. It was a snug little room, or would have been if the hearth were going. But the room was bitterly cold, with a cold sheen of absence everywhere.

The housekeeper tied the strings of her bonnet more tightly for the wind that blew outside.

"If you're through fiddling about, we can leave," she said. "A cow stall, but looks to hold up another hundred years. Solid enough to fetch something if not much. And a few kroner from the rag-and-bone man for the trash what's inside."

Thorkild followed her furiously out the door.

"What's got your back up now?" she demanded. Then her face softened. "Of course, you're out of sorts from so much walking. But you needn't accompany me to the assessor's office. Spare yourself, Hr. Counselor. Let us meet when the coach leaves."

"Good! I have things to attend to here in Helsingør! Go then, you stinking codfish!"

Pleased, the housekeeper proceeded on her way alone, while

Thorkild, who had nothing to attend to in Helsingør, or anywhere else for that matter, stuck off in the opposite direction. Along the gray whistling streets he stomped, lurching from side to side in his enveloping black cloak, with no thought of entering a *Kro* for warmth and a bite to eat, for he would not sit down in public places where he felt eyes swarming all over him. The coach ride had been torment. And for nothing. He was stuck with her until he died, for he would never turn her out. What she had done for the lad—to that memory he was loyal.

He was brought up short by the harbor. Turning, he pressed on toward Kronborg, outlined against the gray sky. He would have liked to go back to the small room and sit there. But the room was very cold, and he must keep his body moving, keep the blood circulating until he returned to that odious wretch of a woman—out with it all to the rag-and-bone man, bowl, slippers, everything. And in the coach, pretending she was not with him, her back practically in his face. And off to the assessor's office alone, released from the mortifying lump at her side: spare yourself, Hr. Counselor. "Counselor!" he spat out aloud. He did not claim the appellation, it was not he who used it, but others, a tossed crumb. He stared up, enraged, at a passerby.

Why do I glare? Why do I add viciousness to the burden of my appearance? Why have I not instead cultivated a winning personality? A delightful wit, a charming smile?—and earn indulgence. No thank you! No thank you!

He stomped along the Kronborg approach, remembering that he had first walked here some eighty years ago, in the midst of an unbearable childhood. His parents were kindly but could not rescue him. Here he had walked with them, and with Bodil and the Bishop. His brother was called the Bishop even as a child, for his nature was that of a bishop and one knew he would become a bishop. Just as one knew that Bodil would become the highly effective wife of a highly placed government official. And he? So terribly much shorter than they, though older, in clothes sewn to contain an abnormal squatness—he did not look ahead. He had spent his few years on earth endeavoring to deal with each moment as it came. He watched. He concentrated.

Then watch! Concentrate! It is demeaning to sink into these squalid thoughts. Here before you is the sea, the wind, here soar Kronborg's green copper spires! And he stamped along the Flag Battery, only to come to a wheezing stop, for beyond this point the Battery was limited to the military. Beyond this point one saw cannon and pyramids of cannonballs.

"Damnation to you!" he spat at the weapons.

Damnation to that which had taken his son's life! His jaw trembled. A year had passed, but the pain had not passed. He turned sharply and strode to the parapet. He planted his big kid-gloved hands on the silver knob of his short stick, and stood battered by the wind. He looked at the gray churned water, at the dark ships rolling. Every foreign ship that passed to or from the Baltic was forced to pay the fortress of Kronborg a toll fee, and had fumingly done so for centuries. Vessels of all nations were obliged to dip their flags, strike their top-sails, and fork over. An impressive sight. And a profitable tradition. Perhaps this income was all that now kept Denmark going, left bank-rupt by Napoleon's wars—filthy, unspeakable Napoleon, who had brought his lad extinction!

Cloak whipping, he turned and made his way back along the Bat-tery. He had loathed war for as long as he could remember. As a child he had listened to his grandfather reminisce over the Scania War of 1676, when as a young officer he had participated in the savage battle of Lund, smashing Swedish skulls all around. And there was the earlier ancestor who had fought on the city ramparts when the Swedes at-tacked Copenhagen, and who had passed down gratified descriptions of the clambering foe as lye and boiling water came pitching into their faces. A yet earlier officer ancestor had been present at the Stockholm Massacre in 1520, and from him there had passed down through the family a still vivid account of the daylong, hectic chopping until the square was nothing but heads and blood . . .

It was difficult to think of the mighty northern empire Denmark had once been: ruler of Sweden, Finland, Norway, Greenland, Iceland, and large parts of northern Germany. Over the last two hundred years they had lost it all, bit by bit. All but Iceland and Greenland and Norway. And now they had lost Norway too. He did not care. He lacked communal spirit. Naturally he was sorry that his country was bankrupt, wrecked. But it had known dire straits before and had always recovered. It just grew smaller and smaller.

In the driving wind, his face cold as marble, he took out his pocket watch and held it close to his eyes. An hour and a half remained before the coach departed. Hunched over his stick, he pressed on with his outing. Here was the moat. Shards of ice floated on its choppy black surface. Here was the drawbridge, its ornate stone portal set in the dark massive brick of the fortress wall. The massiveness was streaked with frozen snow. White jagged tongues hung from frozen rainspouts. The only sound in the wind was the single, long cry of a gull.

It was dusk when the coach began to load. The housekeeper, chilled to the bone but not discontented as she stood talking voluminously to her fellow passengers, espied a cloaked form, like a broad, low tent, heaving from side to side into view. She had hoped he would miss the departure. Her hands in their cloth muff twitched with the desire to pick him up and fling him across the street.

Sitting in the jounce and rattle of the coach, his feet not reaching the floor, Thorkild glowered at the eyes that examined him, his heart pounding with fury. Then darkness fell and his confinement was more bearable. Except that the wretched housekeeper, sitting with her back to him, never relented: her opinions of the weather splattered out over everyone, and the scandalous price of firewood, of turnips, of fish, and the many merits of the house she was putting up for sale. And he thought of the little room growing smaller with every kilometer, colder, and he reached out and drew it to him, and sat with the yellow bowl between his hands and was warm.

But the truth was that he had dozed off; he was jolted awake when the postilion blew his horn. Minutes later the horses clattered to a stop in Copenhagen's Raadhuspladsen, and they climbed out in sleet-wet wind, he and his housekeeper who more than ever seemed to him a low form of vegetable life, or some species of blind overlarge worm. Unbearable was her continued proximity in the hired chaise home. Once through the door he pushed roughly past her down the hall, while she, untying her bonnet, blew out a relieved breath to feel the thing no longer at her side.

ॐ৪৯

The household resumed its daily ways. In the babe's room the wet nurse had been replaced by a nanny in towering white headdress who, but for exceedingly generous pay, would have packed her bags, so uncongenial was the disorder of the great house and its hanging silence and its monstrous old party, although, fortunately, he was usually sequestered in his library or gone from the premises.

Spring came. In sunshine the Counselor stomped beneath green copper spires and the shining domes of great churches, across canals and down flowering lanes, and through raucous alleys astink with vom-ited ale; through the bustle and cries of market squares he stomped, and past the rearing bronze of equestrian statues. He stomped by hurdy-gurdies and chimney sweeps, and drunken lurching sailors, by peddlers and beggars and servants with baskets, and through the swarming rumble of wagons and carts, and past gentlefolk in lightly bouncing landaus, and he never slowed, he never stopped. On the rare occasions that he thought about his health, he supposed that any doc-tor would deem him a phenomenon: at eighty-four a bull of strength and endurance. It was true that his legs were little pegs, but little pegs like iron. And it was true that he huffed, he wheezed, for he carried an immense load. But he never gave out. Seldom did he even grow markedly tired. Indeed, the more he stomped along, the greater was the churning vitality within him. He was a projectile. You will see my back before you can gawk. I leave you. I am forever leaving you behind me, like so much debris, like the trash you are.

He took himself through the city's east gate, past the plumed guard with his musket, and set off for the East Commons. Sometimes he went to Sun Hill, but today he would not, for tomorrow was Pentecost and hordes of people would already be gathering on the hill to greet the sun in the early hours of the morning when, presumably like the spirit of the Holy Ghost revealing itself to the Disciples, it appeared in all its glowing splendor. From that spot, for thousands of years before Christianity, hordes had gathered to worship the sun's release from winter. What had Christian conversion meant? Very little. In fact, nothing. What meant much, always and forever, was to gather in hordes.

He was still thinking about this as he walked through the meadows of the East Commons. Hordes had once gathered here to the tune of fifty thousand people—more than half the city's population—and camped till dawn. From the upper windows of his house, he had looked out at the distant glow of bonfires. And as he had stood there, the old Counselor—who had not been so old then, if not so young either, getting on for forty—had wished he had a wife to converse with, to tell of his connection with what was happening. For very briefly, a few years earlier, he had experienced court life. This had been due to some wire-pulling by his sister Bodil, about which he knew nothing at the time. He, with no credentials beyond a couple of law courses during his few and wretched university years, had suddenly been summoned to Hirscholm Castle and appointed a financial advisor to the king.

You understand, my dearest, that I did not desire the post. I?—to be surrounded by bulging eyes? The thought was excruciating, you know how I am about eyes. But I went because summoned, and I discovered that the confusion was so enormous that I need not have worried—they were all far too preoccupied with themselves to send the smallest blink in my direction. Indeed, I even returned a time or two. What was it like, you ask? Feverish intrigues in every corner, dandified cutthroats, fabulously wigged opportunists, and popinjay advisors like myself created overnight. Everything hectic, lawless, dis-

solute, and the king of course entirely mad. I glimpsed the king but
once. His face is pale, like tallow, and emptily active. I saw the queen
in her riding habit. I saw Bishop Münter, my brother's idol, and be
assured that the Bishop's every step rang with political acuity. The
Church always knows how to get along. But did I see *him*? Struensee?
That is what you want to know, and that is what I want to tell you.
Yes, I saw him close enough to distinguish his pale reddish eyebrows.

I am not political. What's more, I knew that Struensee was not only
a German, but that he had grave faults of character. But when he
seized power last year, when he threw out undeserving nobles from
high office, established freedom of the press, and distributed corn and
foodstuffs to the people, I was in favor of it, for it was just. And I felt
a perfect delight—though my sister Bodil was greatly displeased, her
mother-in-law gasping her last—when he decreed that funerals of the
wealthy must take place at night to discourage ostentatious display.
And I said good! when he flung open theaters on the Sabbath. And I
said good! when he abolished the morning star, that iron-spiked club
used so freely on lowlife along our night streets. And I said good!
when he got the queen with child, for surely she could not abide her
mad husband. But of course it all had to end. For everyone was against
him: royalty, aristocracy, bourgeoisie, common people. Yes, the common people too, who stood to gain so much! What they cannot forgive
is his bedding the queen. For them, Struensee's single but inexpiable
crime is this insult to the holy person of their king. Just think of it!
It makes one throw one's hands up in despair. Yes, it makes one sigh,
it makes one sad, it makes one hopeless. Do you not agree, my love,
that we should turn our backs on such a world and repair to bed?

And alone, he had gone from the window with its distant glow of
bonfires.

A week after that, he had walked out to the Commons. The grass
had been trampled flat by fifty thousand pairs of feet. Refuse lay scattered among the charred vestiges of bonfires. Where the execution
block had stood was a dark spread of dried blood. Nearby, tied to two
cartwheels on the ground, were the decapitated bodies of Struensee

and his deputy, broken into shapelessness by the blows of an iron bar. The arm of one exhibited a stump, for Struensee's right hand had been chopped off before his neck was severed. The heads were impaled on two sharpened poles. In a buzzing of flies, his hand over his nostrils, he had stood for some moments looking at the pale reddish eyebrows.

The meadow that the old dwarf clomped across today had long since been a meadow only. And though it held an old and dreadful memory, it had also, in later years, been the site of some of his happiest moments, for he and his lad had used to walk here together, and to sit on the grass. But in the year and a half since his son's death, he never paused on his meadow walks, never sat down among the wildflowers, for then the sorrow, the longing, came battering in like tidal waves.

☙ ❧

Late in the afternoon the Counselor could be seen back on the city streets, eyes glaring from his potent onrush. With bitterness he thought what an irony it was to give a man such great strength with which to accomplish so little. Apart from pounding the streets of Copenhagen, he had never applied himself to anything. Unless it could be said that being buried in his library with his quill, covering sheet after sheet with thoughts on the nature of truth, was something. It was not. His cabinets were stuffed with the scrawled pages of decades, but they were worthless scrawls. He knew that. He was merely driven, as he was driven to pound along the streets.

He winced to think that he had once actually written a letter to Johann Wolfgang von Goethe expressing his thoughts. Goethe had not replied, as why should he have? What could he, Thorkild, say about the nature of truth? His perspective was that of a grotesque. He would not be out of place among those other miscreations who, one heard, were displayed in the tents of traveling circus troupes, to the shaking of a tambourine.

He understood himself in this matter, and thus had no understanding of himself. Was his hatred of war, cherished since childhood, based less on the gruesome slaughter of those old family tales than it was on the knowledge that he was excluded, would never sit astride a rearing mount, sword held high? He did not know. Were his radical political leanings merely the perverseness of someone rebuffed by his own class? Was that what his sense of justice amounted to? For he liked the common people no better than his own people. When he had gazed at Struensee's impaled head, grieving the loss of that great reformer, was he not thinking less of those shattered reforms than: here is one like me, rebuffed, scorned, who has been subjected to the ultimate exclusion? Did not Struensee's terrible end actually please him for bearing out his ferociously low opinion of mankind? He did not know.

His route home was roundabout, prolonged. For he was never eager for the sight of his noxious housekeeper, and he no longer visited his grandchild. After his first visit to the nursery he had gone often. But no more. It was too painful for both of them. The babe was terrified of him. He would burst into wild tears and scrabble away if the Counselor tried to touch him. And now that he was almost two years old, and could run, he fled to his nurse with heartrending wails. The babe's father had not been like that when he was small. No, the bond between himself and his lad had been extraordinary from the first. The babe was very different. The babe belonged already to the outside world, with the world's judging, repulsing eyes.

As he stomped along, he felt the air turning cold. It was almost evening. On Sun Hill the devout hordes would be flattening the grass in their vigil.

He went through Gammel Torv. He passed Sankt Marie Kirke, slowly being rebuilt since the British bombardment eight years ago. And now, he thought, since Napoleon's recent escape from Elba, a new war was brewing. The very thought of Napoleon stabbed his heart with grief, with rage. He stomped yet harder, down one street and up the other, until he came to Lystbadhavn, the Sound before him. The air is now very cold, but the water lies golden in the last of the light, as if the sun had dropped down into it and were illuminating it from beneath, in a smooth, warm sheen. He thinks of the yellow bowl in the little room in Helsingør, and he can imagine that it is the bowl which is spreading its glow up through the waves, and he can imagine reaching out and lifting it as it dripped with light, as with dew or honey.

· 9 ·

⟡ The early morning sky is pale, pure, vast. In a heavy sweater pulled over pajamas and bathrobe, Paula stands looking out from her workroom window with a mug of coffee held forgotten in her hand. The immense sky, the mountainside rising into it, the distances below, even the floorboards' slight incline under her feet, all give a sense of brink, risk, imminence. Setting the mug down, she rubs her hands and blows on them for warmth, and turns to her work.

The villagers often see the rumpled foreigner out with gunnysack in hand. Up in a field. Along the roadside. A woman with run-over heels, gray-streaked hair half-undone, who, with or without the sack, did a lot of wandering around. At the beginning they had stared, but now she was just someone marginal whom they had grown used to.

The villagers might unknowingly have laid eyes on her in times past. When they took a drive to Neuchâtel and went window-shopping along one of the more fashionable old streets, they might have crossed the path of someone who belonged there as clearly as they did not. Stylish Italian pumps, skirt and jacket of soft burgundy suede, silken scarf in delicate hues, dark hair smoothly coiled, a face to which lipstick, blush and eyeshadow had been applied with the finesse of many years' practice.

With her calloused fingers, covered with small black cuts, she grinds a heavy file back and forth across a fieldstone. At the heart of the stone is the true thing. At its very center, within its tiniest, innermost grain, there truth is. But you can't isolate something that minuscule; you have to make do with what's around it, with what takes shape as you chip and file and sand, with the form, the indication. Indication of what?

The question did not discourage her. Nor did the stone's unsteadiness. It seesawed under the motions of her filing and sometimes tipped over, heavy though it was. She had used a bench vise when she had first begun working with rocks, but their rigid immobility had bothered her. She had put the vise away. The rocks should have their freedom, even if this made her chipping and filing more awkward. And too, the rocks in their freedom were inspiring, for when one tipped as she worked on it, she could see that it was presenting itself from a new angle alive with fresh possibilities.

With her mallet she struck the point of the file against the stone. Small chips flew. A dime-sized shallow crater had been created, an awesome valley for some wandering micro-organism, a stony plain without end.

She felt sunlight on her shoulders. It was already midmorning. She went into the kitchen and opened a can of mushroom soup. While it heated on the stove, she washed at the bathroom basin, ran a brush through her hair, twisted it in a knot, stuck some hairpins in and went into her bedroom, where she put on the wrinkled cotton trousers and sleeveless shirt that hung over the chair from the day before. In the kitchen she poured her soup and took it to the table. When her brother Philip had visited her last fall, she had cooked extensively. Alone, she ate whatever was on hand whenever she was hungry.

The old refrigerator and stove glinted in the brightness. Each tiny room was flooded with sunlight. They were laid in a row: kitchen, bedroom, workroom, one leading to the next, simplicity itself. In summer heat she opened a couple of windows for the breeze. In winter she turned on and opened the oven for warmth. When things got too messy, she briefly swept and straightened. Occasionally she did a washing and hung it out back.

She enjoyed her soup, but she was eager to return to the stone she was working on. Fieldstones, the commonest treasure. Yet she had not really been aware of them until one morning in Neuchâtel, in her garden, when she had picked one up to prop against a leaning heliotrope. With a strange welling of excitement, she had carried the stone upstairs to her studio where she sculpted in clay.

Eventually the gardener had come to her with a complaint. She was decimating the border of stones along the path. She had gone to her husband, had asked him to sit down. She was a frank person. She told him that she was now working with fieldstones, and that she wanted to live where there would be more of them; therefore she was leaving him. Naturally, he thought she was making a joke. He had never taken her sculpting seriously. And with good reason. She had no talent. The figures she wrought from her clay were relentlessly prosaic, amateurish, unrealized. But she had kept on with them. From her youth she had kept on with them. Then came the stone from the garden. Fieldstones were not the usual reason for breaking up a marriage, but in her case they were.

The only thing she regretted leaving was Lake Neuchâtel. Always she had felt strongly about water, its depths as mysterious, as soul-stirring as mountain heights. She felt moved even when she watched the bathtub filling. Her favorite childhood book was *The Water-Babies*, infants cavorting in river spouts, bubbles, whorls. And the book about the Rhine Maidens. Their water was deeper, darker, glassier. She remembered that their hair spread out behind them in fans. Water is to go down into. You think you will discover something. It draws you, it comforts and excites you that there is something to be discovered. Even in the bathtub, there is something to be discovered. You know this the moment you sink into its miniature rocking waves. You know.

But if you confided this to someone who said yes, yes, that's exactly how I feel, you and they could go no farther. You would both be dumb. Your two submersions in discovery are something that can never be discovered.

Still hungry when she finished her soup, Paula brought a roll back with her. From time to time as she worked she gnawed on it, crumbs mingling with the stone dust on the tabletop. She blew. A Gobi windstorm, perilous, blinding, steppe ponies too small to see racing in all directions. Then the storm settled. With mallet and chisel she struck the rock, part of it breaking off, a landmass plunging to great distances below. You never knew what would happen. It was all uncharted territory.

Leaving Neuchâtel had also been a striking off into the unknown. Her first night in the little bedroom, which was furnished with alien things—sallow mirror worn through in black stipples, old bed with wire twisted around one of its legs that had cracked vertically, old disheartening things somehow damp-seeming, like garbage, and the inhuman dense darkness outside, the ear-pounding silence—her first night here had been spent in misery and regret. What did she care about rocks? For rocks she had left a lovely home, a husband she liked, a richness of shared activities; and she thought of their skiing and sailing and convivial dinner parties, and of Paris, Munich, Vienna, no more than an hour away by plane whenever they wanted: theaters, galleries, concerts. But it had to be done—and so here you were, self-shipwrecked in a remoteness of heights, in three squalid little rooms whose floors had a slight but awful tilt, and time and silence all around and only yourself in it.

"You must have left him for a good reason or you wouldn't have," her daughter had written from Malibu in a surprised but supportive letter that had ended, ". . . meanwhile, the scenery sounds great and you've got your hobby to keep you busy. In fact it sounds like an ideal spot to regroup in. What's the place like that you're renting, chalet-sort of thing? Are you near some decent-size towns you can drive to?"

Her daughter had not been quite as sanguine when it was her dad whom Paula had left; natural, of course, even if her daughter was grown and married by then. Paula herself had been surprised to end a union of twenty-six years. Each year its comfortableness has sucked her in deeper. It was a marriage of similar tastes and shared interests and occasional discreet affairs on either side, of mutual tolerance and understanding, a pleasant marriage really, no little quarrels, no big blowups. Then she had blown up the whole thing and run off with a Swiss attorney, ironically to a life in Neuchâtel very much like the one she had left behind in Chicago, right down to the clay sculptures that never came out as they should.

She had put down her daughter's letter with a sigh. Hobby. Chalet. Her daughter hadn't the faintest idea what she was doing here. Not that Paula herself, waking from that first miserable night, could understand why she had come. She had had to set her jaw. But the place wasn't so bad after she had unpacked her own things: her tools, linen and towels, a few scatter rugs and throw pillows, some books. Then she had brought up flowers from the back garden and set them around in jars from the peeling kitchen cabinet. This was the place she had chosen. Here by God she would stay.

Her husband had come from Neuchâtel to talk with her. He looked around as if she were demented. "Well, that's the thing," she had said. "For your purposes I'm demented, so you must do as you want. Permanent separation? Fine. Divorce? Fine. Whichever is simpler. You can put everything that's mine into storage. My car too." Already she was bored thinking about these things, while he, who had not even sat down yet, must have found her succinctness startling; he had the look of someone in a weird dream full of odd angles that bang the nose and bark the shin. Nothing worse, however, and she was glad, for he was a pleasant man whom she liked. "I want you to be happy," she said, "so the thing to do is to find someone else." And he had. She was obliged to take the bus into Neuchâtel to sign the divorce papers, a simple procedure; she had independent means. But it was boring, irksome, all she wanted was to get back.

It was true, the only thing she missed was the lake, and for that she had her bathtub.

In the afternoon she stopped working and got up to take her hike. Stones were ranged around the little room, some not yet touched, others finished. These finished works might euphemistically have been called abstract forms, with a few that vaguely resembled some human or animal shape. But what they truly looked like, she said to herself, were rocks with dents. And that was as it should be. It was not art that she was pursuing, art was beyond her. This was accident, experiment, a continual quest to unlock something for herself alone, of no merit or meaning to anyone else.

Before leaving for her walk, she dumped a pile of wash into the big stone kitchen sink. She turned on the water and poured in powdered soap. After a couple of scrubbings and rinsings, she wrung out the tangled mass of clothes and linen, heaved it into a red plastic basket, and went into the workroom for the small rug in there. The rug had been dingy for many years, even before turning gray with stone dust. When she refilled the sink and submerged it, the water grew dark with dirt, as dark as black coffee. She pulled the sink plug and the dark water drained away, leaving behind a field of grit.

In the cluttered basement of the family home in Evanston there had stood an old-fashioned steamer trunk with cracked leather straps which she had once unbuckled, with some difficulty, for her child fingers were small and weak. Inside, the trunk was lined with what looked like wallpaper in thin brown stripes. There were folded jackets and trousers, books, bundles of letters and brownish photographs, possibly more things underneath, but her eye was caught by a patch of color, and she drew out a small folded rug and spread it on the floor. It was old and worn, but it was very pretty. And it was child-sized. She spanned its breadth with her two small sandaled feet. And she had closed the trunk, which later vanished during a Salvation Army drive, and brought the little rug to her room. It had gone with her to college, to her studio apartment afterward, had grown increasingly dull and threadbare with use, had been relegated to her walk-in closet during her first marriage and to her dressing room during her second, where, haphazardly packing to leave, she had scooped it up into a suitcase. Then it had graced the workroom.

Having kneaded it in soapy water, she rinsed it again, wrung it out, and dropped it on top of the other wash. Then she struggled downstairs with the sodden load. The breeze outside was hot and smelled of grass. She untwisted and hung up a sheet, sunlight billowing through it in a bright milkiness. When she hung up the rug, which smelled of clean damp wool, she saw with surprise how its colors leaped out: the pale and dark yellow roses, greengold leaves, background of rich russet. She had almost forgotten what the colors were. Though frayed in several places, the aged little rug looked almost as fresh as it must have when it was first woven. She knew nothing about needlework, but it was evident that whoever had done it had been very skillful. Hundreds and hundreds of tiny upraised squares, each one a carefully executed stitch in perfect alignment with the next, each one a part of the complex and delicately nuanced pattern. She smiled at the rug's refreshed beauty as water fell from its hem in big sparkling drops. Then she hung up the rest of the things and went down past the garden for her hike.

Paula was a woman on the tall side, like her brother, and like him had shown a tendency toward fleshiness in middle age. She had kept this tendency in check by eating balanced, nutritious meals and working out on her NordicTrack in the spare room. Now with no desire to keep anything in check, she found herself slimmer than before, maybe the word was gaunt. It was due to the long tramps, and to the preoccupied bites in lieu of real meals, and possibly even to her intense concentration over her work. To be gaunt, she thought drily, was appropriate for the village idiot, or whatever she was considered to be, although her status was not something she pondered.

She had pondered it, somewhat, in the beginning. Of course she was an oddity: the villagers lived well, sometimes in her building she glimpsed the interior of an apartment if its door stood open—solid, roomy, well kept, a television in the corner. It wasn't just that she went around with a gunnysack collecting rocks, but that she lived in those run-down little rooms up there under the rafters. The landlady hadn't wanted to rent them until they'd been refurbished; they had stood like this for years, much work was needed. But so great was Paula's impatience to begin her new life that she had insisted. The landlady had shrugged and relented, but had looked at her as if she weren't all there. That was the look she subsequently received from all the villagers, and she had thought about it at first.

She did so no longer. She spoke French well and greeted them politely, and was greeted politely in return. That was sufficient; her face as she climbed down the path bore an expression far removed from questions of a social nature. It was a face with fine-boned features, and with light blue eyes which in youth, combined with pale coloring and dark hair, make a striking impression. The face was thinner now, hollow-cheeked. The dark brown hair, no longer touched up by the hairdresser, was streaked with gray. The skin was browned by the sun and lined.

From time to time she stood still, taking in the distant valley below: heat-hazed meadows, darker woods, a road along which cars like dots moved slowly, although sitting at the wheel you'd be in rushing wind with trees flashing by. Possibly the ants—she stood before a battalion that marched across the path—experienced that same huge rush and noise as they scaled dirt boulders and descended in slides of rubble to press on in all directions. They seemed not to know where they were going; they backtracked, bumped into each other, yet gave the collective appearance of being possessed by some specific goal. Crouching, she put her forefinger down and felt a tickling tread. She raised the finger, watched the ant run along it hither and yon, then gently blew it back to its brethren, where it hurried on among them, no doubt in a roar of pounding feet and collisions.

She stood up from the ants, an abrupt giantess, dwarfed when she looked up the mountainside, and went on through the grass, through sweeps of wild narcissi and bluebells.

That day there had been bluebells in the jar standing on the kitchen windowsill. She was sitting at the table with a sandwich. And across the slope, off in the distance, she saw a madly climbing figure. It vanished behind the leaves and flowers in the jar. A moment later it burst back into sight from behind a blue petal. And unknowingly she had watched the young farmer wildly climbing with maybe two minutes left of his life. What must his mind have held? A blizzard. A blizzard consisting of two things only: the red mass in the harrow blades and the razor that would deliver him.

A blizzard of such surpassing agony is beyond human imagining. His young widow—I've overheard talk of it at the *épicerie*—still clings to the belief that he was numbed by shock. There was no suffering in him as he ran. He thought nothing, knew nothing, his feet carried him as a robot is carried, his hand snapped up the razor as a robot's would. His actions were disconnected from his heart, his soul, which remained as cloudless as the moment before the accident happened. The woman clutches the same passionate belief about her children. Shock rendered them unconscious even before they struck the blades. They tumbled lightly, lightly into sleep, as into an afternoon nap in their beds. It is essential for her to believe this. But I don't believe it, I can't. And I wonder if it is the blizzard that is in the tiniest, innermost atom of the stone.

The sound of the cowbells was unusual today: extremely loud, concentrated, a clanking density that grew nearer with her every step. Then she remembered that today the cows were being taken higher up the mountain for summer grazing. And there they came, up the dusty, sun-flooded road as she stepped onto it. They were garlanded with flowers of every color. Their bells, which looked as if they were made of pale polished gold and were beautifully engraved, were very large. Paula was reminded of one of the few conversations she had had with her landlady. The landlady had remarked that the farmers were very proud of the bells, and when Paula asked if the cows might not find them cumbersome, the landlady repied: "Of course not. The cows are just as proud of them."

And so they are: fine handsome creatures who know their worth, who, all brightly garlanded, walk at their own chosen pace while two or three cars submissively line up behind them. The bells ring out high and low, and through the ceremonious rumble of hooves a feeling of some ancient, festive joy spreads through the air.

The only inhabitants of the cave are bats hanging in hibernation. Occasionally a rodent advances a few feet through the entrance, then turns back from the unpromising terrain.

Deep below the entrance the cave spreads out in chambers. In the largest, a stitch of light shows faintly in the ceiling high above, where a fissure has eroded into existence over the ages. The darkness below is unaffected. Stony pools lie in the undifferentiated black. The unseen walls are thick with calcite deposits in labyrinthian formations. Bats hang from these, and from the stalactites that descend in every jagged length from the ceiling.

· 10 ·

In the summer warmth as she rides down Købermagade in her landau, Bodil suddenly raises her lorgnette. Framed in the glasses, her brother pounds along the street, his pygmy bulk heaving pistonlike from side to side as people turn to stare after him. Sharply she lowers the lorgnette, two points of angry color burning in her old cheeks.

Once, many years before, she had tried to reduce the onus of being related to Thorkild by persuading her husband to finagle a court appointment for him, simply to obtain for him a dignified title. A freak with a title, she had explained to her husband, was slightly less a family blot than a freak without one. She had used the harsh word because it was accurate. She did not stand on euphemisms or half-truths.

The landau turned the corner. She was relieved to put distance between the two of them. Yet her dislike of Thorkild was not a matter of his physiognomy. Indeed, she had felt kindly toward him in the beginning.

As a child, on long light summer nights, she and her younger brother, the Bishop, would slip from their beds and patter over to Thorkild's. They did not tiptoe, for Thorkild's slumber was so profound that nothing, not even the nursemaid's first shake in the morning, could disturb it. His shape under the eiderdown was a lump. He lay on his back, breathing regularly, with his characteristic wheeze. And his small eyes were open. They were not widely open, but they were not slits either. One could clearly see his blue irises and the white of his eyeballs. His lashes were short and scant. They fluttered faintly, with a continual small twitching of the lids, giving him an appearance of worry and concentration. She would lean over and shut the lids with a forefinger, first one, then the other. Immediately they would reopen. The meager lashes fluttered on.

This was a fascinating thing to watch, yet she was sorry that he should wear a look of such anxious vigilance even in sleep.

"He is afraid of death," murmured the little Bishop, and added with some anticipation, "I shall pray for his soul when he is taken."

"No, he is afraid of everything," she corrected him. "But of course he may well die." If so, she would cut a lock of his bristly hair in remembrance.

It was possible, Bodil told herself as they passed through Kongens Nytorv, that her kindly feelings toward Thorkild had in fact rested on the prospect of his imminent demise. He was a sickly child; he tired easily, coughed, wheezed, and had digestive problems. Surely he could not last much longer. Her sympathy for the stunted, dreadfully malformed creature could afford to be bounteous.

And in her landau she gave herself a severe nod, for her spirit of objective inquiry was brought to bear as keenly on herself as on others. Yes, the child Bodil would have been quite content with that lock of hair.

Still, one should not be too hard on oneself. Thorkild had not been a likable child: solitary, watchful, obstinate. He would not come forward to visitors, and was rigid in the presence of her and the Bishop's little friends. Neither grownups nor children could find their way past that intense look of distrust, as if he foresaw either a commiserate pat on his big head, or an extended tongue followed by screams of laughter. It was true that he had experienced both; but must he make dire suspicion his very core, so that he was like a squinting little toad all shrunk into himself, whom only their parents could tolerate?

He was given the same fine quality of clothing, if sewn to a different measure, as she and the Bishop. Like them, he had his toys and his books. He did extremely well in his lessons with the governess, and later with the tutor, and showed a pretty voice when the singing master played "Niels Ebbesen" and "Roselille og Hendes Moder" on the clavichord. He was praised in all that he did. He lacked for nothing, not even health, for he grew sturdier all the time, his rocking gait firmer. Yet if anything, he became more dislikable: irate, scowling, snappish, though still sunken into himself, watchful like a toad.

It was this involvement with himself that she could not accept. Not as a girl, not now as an old woman. Truly, it was not his terrible dwarfism and misshapenness that sat foremost in her mind. It was his character. If he were a man who could be conversed with quietly, in a civilized fashion, who could smile at a witticism, and perhaps offer a few himself, who observed life clearly and reasonably, she did not think she would be unduly aware of his appearance. It was his self-consciousness, his intensity, his querulousness, like that of a snarling, barking, nasty little dog, that made one despise him for his lack of manhood. He had not the least sliver of inner resourcefulness. Not the smallest spark of courage. He had been blessed with an iron constitution, an excellent mind, wealth, yet had allowed his appearance to determine his entire life, to crush him into anger and oddness and futility.

The horses drew to a stop before her house on Bredgade. Straightening her shawl, she gathered together her lorgnette and brocade reticule as the coachman opened the door of the landau. Never once had her brother told himself: the concept of equality holds true only in mathematics. I shall not waste thought on my difference from others. I shall make the best of what I am.

That would have been an enlightened, an admirable attitude, and she would have admired him.

⊂⊗ℬ⊃

Later that day, in her drawing room, the old woman received one of her several grandsons and his wife and small children. As a matriarch, Bodil required her family members to present themselves regularly but not to stay overlong. It was a brief, dutiful call: a bit of a chat, some bonbons for the little ones, then she proferred her face to be kissed on both cheeks in farewell. It was always amusing, she thought afterward, to realize that her grandchildren and great-grandchildren were also those of the Bishop; for her daughter and one of the Bishop's sons had married. It was humorous that she and the Bishop were conjoined in their progeny when they were so radically opposed otherwise, unable to visit without quarreling. They did better on paper. That evening she sat down in her elegant little writing room and wrote him her biannual letter.

> *11 August 1815*
> *Copenhagen*
>
> *My Dear Brother,*
> *I write you not with a quill but with something new and rare, this being a metal nib which one inserts into a holder. My stationer imports them from England where they are crafted in very small and thus costly quantities, and they are well worth their cost in that they achieve far cleaner and finer strokes, as you see before you. However, though I write with something new and rare, I bring you no tidings of the same nature, all things here remaining much the same as when we last corresponded.*
>
> *I trust you are in strong health and that you continue to fulfill your office with the vigor for which you have always been known. I too find my vigor scarcely diminished by the years, and give thanks to the vital stock from which we come.*
>
> *This afternoon I witnessed the vitality of several of our youngest shoots, which I confess I can countenance only so much of, dear little things though they are. In May I attended a large family*

fête at their parents' house, north of the city by way of a tedious hour's drive along the Coast Road. It is situated on the water's edge with a wilderness of woods all around it; I daresay it is picturesque, but I prefer the city. I fail to understand why today's young people are so enamored of nature. In any event the fête was enjoyable, and I may relate to you that the family are all thriving, as I am pleased to know from your last letter is true in Aarhus as well.

In June, of course, came the news of Waterloo. Although we agree on very little, I know you were as gratified as I to hear of it. What a mercy and a justice that this is finally the end of Bonaparte, although what he has wrought remains all too much with us. We must ever regret having let ourselves be forced into an alliance with him; thanks to our fighting on the wrong side we have lost everything. Our position among the nations of Europe has sunk so low that we can scarcely be counted as a country any longer, our great fleet gone, our maritime trade crushed, Norway ripped from us. We may recover from national bankruptcy, but as a power our sun has set forever.

It is not my nature, however, to bow to gloom. Indeed, one of your many criticisms of me is that I bow to nothing, while my chief criticism of you is your endless bowing to God. Now I am greatly annoyed with myself, for I had truly intended no disputatious thought to mar this letter. I might of course cross out the above lines so that they could not be read, but that would be dishonest. Let them stand. They are always between us anyway, and have been for eighty years.

I trust you are enjoying pleasant weather in Aarhus. Our summer here has been a very perfection of sun and breeze, in which I take my drive almost every day. This unfortunately reminds me that I saw Thorkild today on Købermagade. It is the worst thing I know to glimpse him heaving along the street for the sole purpose of frightening and disgusting people. As you well know, it is not his physical appearance which I deplore, but the perverse use he puts it to with his envy and fury and pity for himself. And I believe he has grown worse since his son's death, for there is greater intensity in that onrush of his, there is greater heedlessness and self-absorption. I noted this already when he paid me a surprise call early last year, a good several months after the son had died, yet he was weeping and frantic and completely demented with his self-pity. I wonder, if he continues this way, if he might not put an end to himself. Certainly nothing else will, for he is robust, he is even more robust than we. I would he had died long ago and you feel the same, but I state the fact because I am forthright and you do not state it because you are a hypocrite. Nevertheless, we are agreed that he has been the sorest of trials these many years. What matter if we never visit him or he us?—we cannot escape his existence, he has cast his stain on us every day of his life. Would at least that he went outdoors only after dark, but that is apparently asking too much of him. We can only be grateful that apart from his peregrinations he is a thorough recluse. I remember that when I was young and just married, I would sit in fear of his appearance in one of the neighboring boxes at the Royal Theater, but fortunately, that was an entirely unrealistic fear. Of course, it was not a fear which you would ever have entertained, since you do not set foot inside theaters and indeed are at pains to impose your restrictions on everyone else. I therefore close by telling you that I shall be attending Holberg's Maskeraden *tomorrow night, and now with sisterly regards I remain*

Bodil

· 11 ·

"I am tempted, my love," Grethe says, looking up with a smile from her translation work, "but I think I must stay put until I have these lines as they should be."

Holger touches his lips to her brow. "Then come when you can. We will be there all afternoon."

At the beach Holger sets up his umbrella, his easel and paint box and folding chair. The sand is hot, the breeze sultry. His two little sons have raced, jumping over amber seaweed, into the silken, shining water, and are splashing up a storm. He begins to paint.

Holger is of no school. Today he uses a palette knife to build up a vibrant impasto of bizarre colors. Other days he is inclined to classical detail in finely tempered hues, and often he works in the realistic mode. He accuses himself of eclecticism, but he is so appreciative of life's variousness, of its wonderful plethora of differences and contrasts, that he doubts he will ever adhere to a single style.

"And what might that be?" a voice enquired over his shoulder.

He added a slash of vermilion to the greens and ochers of the sky.

"Whatever you think it is," he said shortly, and eyed the stroller, who went on with a shrug in the direction of the bathing machines and paddling figures farther down the beach. Times were when you hardly saw another soul. But the old Coast Road had been widened to accommodate heavier carriage and coach traffic, and now bath hotels had sprung up, and weekend cottages, and new houses were being built throughout the region. He turned back to his canvas with a scowl for these newcomers who were turning the wild landscape into a suburb.

But though he longed for the unspoiled coastline of his boyhood, Holger believed in growth, for growth was a chief component of progress. He had no truck with the Right Party. As far back as 'sixty-four, more than twenty years ago, after the crippling war with Prussia, he had seen as a mere boy that the government in power was wrong. With the country in despair over the devastating loss of Slesvig-Holstein, one third of its territory, the government could only think of increasing its defense forces. As if there were anything left to defend, the boy had thought wretchedly, as if there were anything further to be ripped away. Denmark was now an amputee, reduced to one of the tiniest nations of Europe. Surely there was only one hope: to turn inward and cultivate their small field intensively.

And that was what had happened in the teeth of a conservative government. And was still happening in the teeth of a conservative government: the reclamation of the Jylland heaths, the growth of cooperative farms and Folk High Schools, the Labor movement.

Denmark's sun had not set in 'sixty-four; indeed, it was rising higher than ever, though in a manner his forebears would not have recognized, they who had had to be beaten out of Sweden and pulled off Norway, and before that, as Vikings, had massacred, plundered and burned their way into some of the blackest pages of history.

There was an irony in this which Holger appreciated. He had no doubt that given different circumstances, Denmark would be fully as grasping and greedy today as she had been in the past, as imperialistic this very moment as modern Germany or Britain. "But we were chopped away," he murmured, squeezing Thio Violet onto his palette, "and with so little left, we have no choice but to be peaceful and conscientious." That was survival. It was also the dream of mankind.

The sun burned down. The waves lapped. From time to time he turned around in his folding chair to see if his wife was coming.

He put away his palette knife and stood up from his canvas, which looked like nothing on earth. That pleased him. Why should the recognizable always take precedence? Ready for a swim, he got out of his shirt and trousers. Underneath he wore the bathing costume that had become *de rigueur* since his grandfather's day, when the few people who swam ran into the waves naked and unobserved. Of dark wool, short-sleeved, with trousers reaching to the knees, it could not conceal his smoothly muscular build as he kicked off his sandals and ran across the stinging sand. He stood in the water with hands on hips, his thick wavy hair burning like bronze in the sun.

"Shall I come after you?" he shouted.

With screams of delight, the boys splashed away as he gave chase, caught them, tussled with them in the waves—"What have I here, two fish?"—and hugged their wet, slippery little bodies. And then they swam, and floated on their backs, the three of them, looking up into the hot blue sky, Holger turning his head in the water now and then to see if his wife was coming.

⋘⋙

Grethe and Olaf lay asleep on a carpet of moss. From a rocky little spring there issued a limpid murmur. Overhead the beeches rustled with the passage of birds, whose calls filtered down through the greenness.

Earlier, Olaf had been startled from his slumber; in the space of a second he was on all fours poised to flee or attack. But it was his creature who had come; it approached toweringly, the biggest moving, breathing thing he had ever let near him.

Breathless from her walk, Grethe sank down by the cat, her face shining.

"Oh, I've missed you so much, Olaf. You've been gone for days."

And taking his head gently between her hands, she smiled into the pale green eyes and laid her cheek against the scarred muzzle and the little brick-colored triangle of the nose and the yellow tips of the two incisors. Olaf felt himself engulfed; he would have been terrified and enraged had this creature been any other; as it was, he merely squirmed, and immediately sank into the bliss of being stroked. Grethe ran her hand along the cat's knobby spine, and scratched the side of his head as the striped head bent, bent, pushing with joy against her fingers. He drooled in ecstasy. Drops fell from his furred chin to her pale blue-veined wrist. She laughed, and rubbing him between his ears, sat back.

"How cool it is here. How nice it always is."

Undoing the two glass buttons on either shoe, she flung the shoes aside, followed them with her stockings, and stretched her bare feet out on the moss. Rooks and thrushes called down. There had been birdsong since two o'clock this morning, so many hours she had had to wait before she could get away from the house. She listened to the trills and warblings. Only those sounds could reach the two of them. Nothing from the outside world could penetrate this green bower, this world lifted out of time, safe and changeless, where all was simplicity.

"I don't want ever to leave," she told him, smiling, and watched as he went after a thread of moss. "Wait, wait, this is better," she laughed, and scrambling to her feet untied the sash of her summer frock. She trailed it along the ground, ran in circles with it as Olaf pounced, rushed, went mad with joy. Her hair came loose as she ran, and out of breath, dizzy and laughing, she collapsed on the moss. Seeing his creature flat, Olaf hurried over and, after turning many times in a circle, curled up at its side. Grethe lay stroking his head, as he closed his eyes contentedly.

So many things vanished from life, but Olaf was the opposite: he had come all at once into hers, as if blown to her feet by the wind. She had been coming from the greenhouse one bitterly cold and already darkening afternoon. It had rained the night before and the snow had frozen. The woods were an ice woods, the roof of the house was an ice sheet. She went by way of the gardens, where the gardener and stable boy had covered the flowerbeds with straw and ashes, which in turn had been covered by snow that had become ice, and there at her feet lay a cat, all scars and wastedness, with white-frosted fur, shivering convulsively. She had extended her hand, at which it drew back in fear and lashed out. Thus began a long coaxing: scraps of meat from the kitchen, consumed in an instant, and gentle beckonings as the afternoon became evening, she herself half-frozen in the wind. Little by little it came, weakly and in fear, stopping for endless moments. But then they were inside. How emaciated it was, nothing but ribs. And Onkel, who was visiting, had exclaimed, "*Du godeste*, it's Olaf Hunger!" Olaf Hunger being a medieval Danish king who had ruled in a time of terrible famine. "But," Grethe had said, "no doubt he himself ate very well, for kings always do." Nevertheless, that was how the cat was named Olaf Hunger. How frantically the starved thing had eaten, and just as frantically had cowered and hissed and fled to the door, madly scratching the wood as if to scratch his way through it. And she had had to let him go. But the next day he was huddled on the frozen snow by the doorstep. And that was the beginning of their great friendship.

She lay back and looked up into the high green trees, lit in a thousand places by small sunbursts. The leaves stirred in a breeze, then were still. She put her head on her arm, in a state of perfect happiness, and closed her eyes.

When she woke she had no idea how much time had passed. Olaf was still asleep. She tried not to wake him as she stirred, but he jumped away and sat watching as she worked on her stockings and shoes. She felt uneasy to think how late it might have grown.

"I must leave now. I would like to stay, dearest friend, but I cannot. I cannot."

She retrieved her sash and retied it. She brushed off the skirt of her dress and smoothed her hair back into place. Kneeling on the moss, she tenderly stroked Olaf and kissed him. And then he watched his creature disappear through the trees.

Coming from the woods into the garden, Grethe heard the voice of the world.

"Since the first Labor representatives were elected to the Folketing last year it has. It has grown clear that the bitter constitutional struggle. Hearteningly clear. Will soon result. Will eventually result. May result."

Onkel paused and walked on. The old journalist often visited his nephew and niece-in-law for several days. He was deeply fond of them both. He enjoyed their company, and he enjoyed their lively social gatherings when wine and keen talk flowed into the small hours. In fine weather he sat in the garden and wrote his articles, often rising to stroll up and down the path while testing his sentences aloud.

"May result in—" He put his arm through Grethe's. "Hot. Hot. Been in the cool woods?"

". . . No. Yes. Just for a little walk." And she gave her hair another, covert, smoothing. "I'm going to the shore now. Come too, Onkel," she said, giving his arm an affectionate squeeze. "Finish your piece tomorrow."

"I cannot." Pausing, he removed his pince-nez, wiped the lenses with his cambric handkerchief, and replaced them on the keen bridge of his old nose. "But waste no tears on me. I sit in a surround of beauty, both floral and cultural."

"Do I detect a judgmental note?" she asked with a smile as they walked on. "Too many flowers? Too many artifacts of various periods and styles?"

"Indeed not. Eclectic. That is their charm."

"That is true," she said, "yet I can imagine a visitor from another planet looking at the Greek pavilion here, and the Viking dolmen over there, and the griffin further on, and being greatly confused as to which one spoke the truth."

"Interesting thought," Onkel replied. "Yes, he might well see them all in flailing contest." And he pointed. "You there with the talons, watch out for that Doric column!"

She laughed and went on.

But there were times when that very clash filled her ears. They were the same times when the tremendous glut of color made her head ache, and she would close her eyes on the mass of blooms. But today nothing drove itself in on her. The garden filled her with delight and gratitude—loops and chains and lakes of flowers, and their eager, trusting gift of fragrance. And the griffin in its reared stance was motionless, its great wings and talons stone still, as befitted a statue. Once it had dragged her up to the source of all life, the sun, and she was burned to a cinder . . . but what a terrible thought to pass through one's mind, and absurd, for she was smooth-skinned and whole, and serene as she walked along, entirely happy, except that lately, lately it seemed that in bed with Holger she sometimes wanted to turn away— no seed, no fetus, no furtherance—yes, to turn away. She stood still on the path with her brows knitted, and gave a confused shake of her head. Turn away? She had never wanted to turn away, she could not even imagine such a feeling, it was alien to her whole being. It was yet another of those dreadful things that sometimes went through her head, but it was gone now.

She walked on, breathing in the fragrant air and listening to the sparrows in the hedge of wild roses. Truly, it was the kind of day when one was filled with joy to be alive, although it was only by the grace of a millimeter that she was. If her grandfather had fallen a hairsbreadth differently, he would have perished on the fence spike, a child of tender age, without issue, a child with a child's seed dead before its journey. But for that millimeter her father would not have been born, she in turn would not have been born. Nothing. An eternal void. But the child had survived the pierce of the spike, and had given life before he was pierced again, by the fragments of a bursting bombshell. She sometimes heard his cry at that moment. The terrible cry he made as he reentered the void. A black paper cry. But there had never been such a cry. She had never heard such a cry. She did not hear it now. There was no sound but the busy chirpings from the sun-drenched hedge.

℃℈℥

At the beach she hugs the boys, who are building an extensive sand castle, and waves happily to Holger as she runs through the hot sand toward him.

"I thought you were never coming!" he calls, sitting up under the umbrella and beaming, yet troubled in some growingly familiar, but indefinable way.

· 12 ·

Paula hikes up the sun-flooded road with the resounding column of cows. In the village she stops to regain her breath from the climb, dusty and exultant. Everyone is out on the street to see the garlanded procession. Children run alongside the hoof clops and the lowing and the prodigious jangle of bells, which sway and catch the sun. And suddenly, astonishingly, she is embraced by her daughter.

In the kitchen her daughter sets down her overnight bag—she has driven up from Geneva, she says, where her husband is attending an international computer science convention—and looks painfully, almost shrinkingly around her.

Paula smiles.

"At least you're not like your uncle Philip. He wouldn't say anything. Your entire face speaks."

"I should hope so . . . God, I'm standing here trying to adjust to a major shock."

"Then sit down, my love."

"He said, Uncle Phil—we stopped over in Chicago—he said to expect something different, but *this*—"

"How is Philip?" Paula asked. She put water on for instant coffee.

"I don't know. As usual. Rushing off somewhere. His Tokyo office. He and some girl who works for him, I guess."

"The Alp Maiden, I suspect. What's she like?"

"I don't know. About thirty years younger than him. But the point is, Mom, we're not talking about him. The point is that I didn't even *recognize* you. Do you realize that? When I saw you with all those *cows* and looking like . . . and this *kitchen*—"

Paula turned around from the stove.

"Let me explain, so we can get it over with and have a nice visit. It's that I'm looking for something. In my work. And other things have lost their importance. It's simple, really."

"But Mom, your work, it's hardly—I mean . . ."

"I know. I know that."

"Then why put so much into it?"

Paula said nothing.

Her daughter finally sat down at the table, gingerly, as if the old chair might collapse beneath her. She wore a silk navy blue blouse, whose sleeves she neatly turned up to the elbows in the room's afternoon heat. She was thinking.

"Do you know what it sounds like to me? Depression. This is what happens. It's a divorce commonplace. You come up here to punish yourself for your failed marriage. You want to hide. To forget. You try to lose yourself in your hobby. You let yourself go to pot." She paused. "You must wonder why I didn't write that I was coming."

"I don't wonder at all," Paula said. "You wanted to surprise me in my unnatural habitat."

Her daughter did not smile. She lacked humor.

"No, but it's bothered me your staying and staying. You were going to regroup and get a condo somewhere. In Lausanne maybe, or Geneva, or back home."

"Was I? Did I say that?" She brought two mugs of coffee over to the table.

"No, but I *assumed*. Instead you just stay and stay. No phone or anything, no way to get in touch. Some back-of-beyond village nobody's ever heard of. At least I thought you were renting a decent place . . . Look, Mom, come back to the States. Get a nice place. And for heaven's sake, get some *counseling*. Do you know you're not even listening?"

"No, I'm drinking my coffee."

Her daughter cast her eyes heavenward, but then she sipped her coffee, for she was a practical woman. Paula knew her daughter would wait to press her argument until a more intimate atmosphere had been established. Just now they would have a pleasant chat, as if the surroundings didn't exist. Her daughter's eyes took in the ulcerated windowsill, the frayed oilcloth, the cheap thick coffee mugs, but expressed no dismay. It was all to be held back until later.

As they talked, her daughter frequently flung her hair from her forehead. Her hair was cut fashionably short as a boy's except for a wedge hanging to one eye. It was bright gold hair, returned by way of the bottle to the fairness of her first years. There was no other hint of her childhood. She was an eminently efficient woman. She endured the impracticality of flinging a wedge of hair from her eye only because fashion decreed it. Flesh of my flesh, Paula thought with self-reproach. I must have made her that way. Didn't I myself tend to fashions? Except that there was always more than that. I have to say that for myself. How, really, did she ever get like this? And Paula envisioned sperm meeting egg, an explosion and expansion of cells, then comes the baby in a chaos of blood and sudden light, who becomes the child of fantasy and impulse, who becomes—somehow— this downright, competent woman sitting there with the requisite wedge in her eye.

Paula asked suddenly, "Are you happy?"

"I would be if you'd move out of here."

"I mean apart from that."

"Let me think. No, there's not much I can complain about. Maybe blaring rock music. Speaking of which, I brought pictures."

From her bag she took out a thick sheaf of glossy Kodachrome shots. Almost all were of her teenage son and daughter. Paula looked and commented appreciatively. She had not seen the children for some time. Taller, fluorescently clad, sitting, standing, smiling, mugging, with and without dogs, in the recreation room, at the barbecue pit, on the ski slope, in the pool, on the beach, one picture after another in what appeared to be an hourly chronicle.

"They look very busy."

"And in every way. Always some project or other."

Paula learned that her granddaughter's latest project was genealogy.

"Everybody's into it, finding their roots. And Mom, I have a commission. She doesn't want your stepdad's roots."

"Well, fine," Paula said, "except I don't know anything about the other one."

"Why, may I ask, has it always been such a closed book?"

"I wouldn't call it that; it's more like no book at all. You know they weren't married even a year. Philip and I are ten months apart; the man died before Philip was even born. And Mother was definitely not one to live in the past. And we had our stepdad from the very start. He adopted us. He gave us his surname and he gave us his love. We just never thought about the other one."

"Well, you're certainly not one of those types you see on TV, sending out bloodhounds to track down their biological parents." She paused. "Was there something wrong with him?"

"Not that I know of. Well, boring, Mother said. But she said that about everybody."

"And that's all you know?"

"No, of course not. I know his name. It's on my birth certificate, but I can't think of it offhand. He was a Swede, or something along those lines. Worked as a structural engineer in Uruguay. And there was a trunk in our basement which I think now was probably his. Probably sent up from Uruguay to Mother when he died. Some old things in it. Mother gave it to the Salvation Army. Mother was not sentimental. Let's face it, your grandmother was usually in an alcoholic haze. Charming but . . . I'm trying to remember if she said anything else. I recall her mentioning that he was tall. And sometimes he'd say, 'Even the finest little pony brings no one back.' "

"Some Old World proverb?"

"No, presumably a joke. I don't know. Mother used it as an example of his boringness: a man who told pointless jokes. But that's all. The rest, as they say, is silence."

She herself was beginning to long for silence. Though she was fond of her daughter, her thoughts were straying disloyally to her work. And the assault was being renewed.

"Mom, do you really know how you look? I mean—and what were you doing with all those *cows*? And living like this—honestly, are you sure you're all right?"

"I'm perfectly fine. At least I was before you came. My dear child, desist."

And now it burst forth.

"But it's all *wrong*, this—this windowsill, this oilcloth, just everything, your hair, your clothes, how can anyone in their right mind *live* like this? You've got to get hold of yourself, Mom, you've got to move *out* of here—"

"Do you know what we're going to do? You're going to help me set up the cot. Then we're going to gather some fresh flowers from the garden. Then we're going to the *épicerie* to get something to make for dinner. The one thing we're not going to do is to sit here and talk at cross-purposes."

Her daughter flings her wedge from her eye. She knows when it's useless to argue. And, in fact, the visit evolves into a pleasant one for both. When her daughter leaves the next morning, Paula is genuinely sorry to see her go, although she is hungry to return to her solitude and her work, and although she knows her daughter has not said her last word on the subject of moving.

In the spring when their hibernation ends, the bats swarm out from the cave entrance in their thousands and fill the night sky with the sound of flapping. In the morning they swarm back in. Each night and dawn for millennia, the immense exodus and return take place as the entrance grows gradually choked with eroded earth, with rocks, trees, bushes, and the bats seek another domicile. The cave returns to silence.

· 13 ·

Autumn has come with heavy rains. Water streams down the leaded diamond-paned windows of the bedchamber, a spacious room whose floor is graced by the pastel garlands of a Savonnerie carpet, and whose furnishings are of handsome tulipwood inlaid with ebony, ivory and ormolu. Everything is dingy, including the blue damask hangings of the canopy bed in which the Counselor lies with eyes partly open, the lids delicately aflutter in strained alertness. Behind this safeguard the old man sleeps profoundly. Sleep has always been his greatest talent and boon: a sweet pasture of nothingness, empty and undisturbed, although in one way he would gladly have had it otherwise.

Only once had the Counselor known a bedmate. In 1790, at the age of fifty-nine, he had one day been apprised by his tailor that a young lady of great charm and excellent family, indeed, the daughter of one of his most fashionable customers, had seen the Counselor on the street and expressed a romantic interest in meeting him. "What! Why should that be!" the Counselor had responded in a savage voice, envisioning a female pervert. "Why not?" the tailor had answered, biting off a thread, and bidding him raise his arm for the fitting of a sleeve. Thorkild, standing in his bedchamber in the vast circumference of his underclothes, hated fitting sessions even more powerfully than he did the incursions of his barber. But he was a man who put much stock in sartorial and tonsorial dignity. Raising his arm, he had snapped, "Go on, you idiot, what are you trying to say?" The tailor began a running baste of the sleeve. In the thirty or more years that he had been measuring and sewing for the Counselor, creating ingenious if hopeless versions of gentlemanly attire to conform to the truncated body with its unique proportions, he had never dropped the remote mien clearly required of him in the execution of this intimate task; yet his conversation was informal, and he replied, "I am saying, Hr. Counselor, that you might look into it. Are you averse to marriage?" "Marriage?—hah, I see! A family in financial straits." "Possibly," conceded the tailor. "Possibly there have been severe business setbacks owing to shipping calamities in the West Indies." Thorkild gave a snort: "Your bills are going unpaid? Sorry, I am not in the market for daughters of bankrupts."

Yet he was, and had always been—daughters of any kind, destitute or otherwise. But none had ever been offered him. When he was alone he bit his knuckles, intrigued, terrified. From the bedchamber door he called the tailor back. Next day, in a state of rigorously controlled agitation, he presented himself at the family home of the young lady.

The young lady was clearly in her mid-fifties, bony, long-jawed, a meek and colorless spinster-daughter. She trembled at the sight of him, the look in her eyes was one of horror. But he had steeled himself against such a response, and from someone much younger and prettier, with greater claim to dismay. He felt vast relief that the gap between them was not as awesome as he had feared, while at the same time he was stung by the woman's lack of allure; but above all was he dazed by the thought of marriage within his grasp, and in a matter of minutes, though retaining his dignified manner, he was madly in love with his unprepossessing bride-to-be.

On subsequent visits he saw that she was a kindly soul who, unlike the rest of her family, abstained from sneaking him revolted glances as he hoisted himself up into a chair; that she valiantly battled her apprehensions, trying with timid smiles to make him feel at ease; and that the hand that tremblingly smoothed her mouse-colored hair was quite nice, lovely in fact. His heart pounded.

The wedding night found him almost ill with confusion. Did one wear one's nightcap on such an occasion? Did one climb into bed first, or did one's wife, or should it be done together?—these anxieties crashed through his mind as they entered his bedchamber, where his wife's sealskin portmanteaus were being unpacked by the servants, of whom he begged silently, "Stay! Stay!" even as they discreetly took their leave.

And then somehow he was in his dressing room, leaning with his back against the door. It was not a matter of nightcaps or the order of procession into bed that harried him so, but that in his entire life his only erotic experience had been the solitary solace of onanism. Never had he even approached a prostitute, always fearing to be met with murderous laughter. And now in the next room, as with shaking hands he began to disrobe, waited a wife. He had been swept away, crazed, inflamed, had flung aside all sense of reality, which was this body that was emerging, this great nightshirt in which he hid it while wishing desperately for darkness in place of the pale summer night. And half-swooning with dread, desire and pity, for he pitied her, he somehow got the door open, his face burning to the hairline, and tried vainly to conceal his massive waddle as he crossed the carpet.

The eiderdown was drawn to her chin. She wore a frilled nightcap, beneath which her long plain face was drained of color. There was about her a sense of mortal dread, of imploringness, yet she smiled, courteously if faintly, so that of a sudden he felt irradiated with welcome and climbed shaking and wheezing beside her angular body, which shook, too, through the fine weave of her nightgown.

This was the only time the Counselor and his wife lay together. Meek though she was, the next night, with lowered, apologetic eyes, she retired to her own room. He knew with churning regret that she had suffered. There had been cries of pain and there had been blood. But he knew that her far greater pain had been the sensation of a toad lying upon her, a panting, wheezing mate half her height and twice her poundage, a gruesome miscreation whom she had been forced to endure, this luckless pawn of a woman whose family had received from his hand, upon the betrothal, an enormous no-interest loan.

That night he climbed by himself into his canopy bed. He longed to have her beside him, but he knew this could never again be. And he groaned aloud to remember the anguish he had subjected her to, and the sordidness of having purchased her. And yet it had been the most profoundly beautiful moment of his life when, like a single breaking wave, semen, soul and cry had made him one with her.

His sister Bodil paid them a dutiful visit. He saw from her face that she had pictured just such an ill-favored and moss-grown bride; her congratulatory words seemed directed to two well-suited oddities who, it was to be hoped, would as a couple maintain the groom's long-standing habit of not calling on her. The groom's face flooded with fierce loyalty to his mate; like an enraged bull he charged the visitor, pounded down the hall after her fleeing form and, the footman leaping aside for safety, half-flung her through the door. His wife stood shaken by the sight of his violence, but seemed understanding of the gallantry involved.

Yet there was never to be a fond embrace. One day he brought her hand tenderly down to his cheek, and her chagrin, her meek and pained forbearingness resolved him never again to seek even that little. And truly, her wifely presence was enough in itself, a dream of many decades fulfilled. They took their walks—though not arm-in-arm, for she would have had to stoop uncomfortably—around the courtyard with its lilac-thick walls. They dined together at the long polished table, beautifully laid, crystal and porcelain sparkling. At night they sat in one of the smaller drawing rooms, she quietly plying her needle, he reading the pages of Virgil or Saxo Grammaticus. And often, turning to her, he would give expression to deep thoughts that had gathered within him for years. This was the most intimate part of their marriage, and though his wife was shy, and not given to conversation, he cherished each small nod of her head in the cozy candlelight they shared.

About a month after they were married, the Counselor's wife took to her bed with nausea and vomiting. The physician deemed it the grippe. Leeches were applied. She grew no better. On his second visit, the physician came from her room with raised brows and informed the Counselor that she was with child. The Counselor's jowls dropped to his neckcloth. At fifty-four? Unusual, he was told, but fecundation occasionally takes place even when the climacteric would seem to have terminated. The Counselor hadn't a notion of what the man was talking about—only that she was with child. He rushed to her bedside, astounded. She too was astounded. They looked at each other astounded.

In his own room he paced. Doctors, that scruffy breed risen from horse physikers and bloodletting barbers—what did they know? Cretins and mountebanks! It was indigestion. For the other was too fearful to think of. She was of no age to endure the harsh rigors of pregnancy and childbirth, and a frail, scrawny sort of woman to begin with. What if it all went terribly wrong? His big knuckles pressed against his teeth.

The Counselor's wife expressed no apprehension at all. Miserable and uncomfortable though she was, her eyes held an unanticipated quality of wonder, of enthrallment. And when she finally left her bed, the *mal de mer* and retching behind her, she asked in her timid way if she might order fine wool and lace for the infant's gowns. Of course, of course, but the Counselor was half-mad with anxiety, for she had been left even scrawnier and more pallid than ever. Then, as the days and weeks went by, before his eyes she changed miraculously: her sharp bones put on flesh, her cheeks grew rosy, her small pebble-colored eyes were lit in a pearliness; even her hair, flat and plainly dressed, of a dullish brown mixed with gray, took on a rich luster. She bloomed with health. Her appetite was a thing to behold, her quiet step held an eagerness. In the evenings, as she grew increasingly round-bellied, she would frequently remove her spectacles and hold up before her, with savoring scrutiny, whatever miniature garment she was sewing; and the Counselor would smile broadly over his book, for her zeal was contagious, and he realized that he had never been in the presence of total happiness: it flowed from her in a radiance, he felt it as an actual physical warmth, as bright and streaming as that of the sun.

The Counselor's wife went into labor very early and suddenly, the midwife arriving in all haste. For three days and nights the room rang with screams. When they ceased, it was the wife's family who grudgingly oversaw the arrangements, the Counselor unable to attend to anything. On the morning of burial in Assistens Kirkegaard, he climbed blind, rumpled and unshaven into his carriage. The coachman cracked his whip in the snowy air.

Afterward he shut himself in his room again, to pace and weep, unaware of his swollen face and bristled jowls, or that his wrinkled clothes were rank with stale sweat. The thought of the infant never touched upon his tortured soul. Stillborn or living he neither knew nor cared. Only on the third morning after the burial did he utter a question as to its fate when the servant came in to lay the fire in the tile stove.

It had not died, and so, with a feeble flicker of interest, he took himself along to the nursery, his huge waddle askew with grief and exhaustion.

Paper was his lifelong confidant: open-armed, embracing, understanding. From the nursery he blundered downstairs to his library, where he fumbled a sheet toward him on the desk, his hand shaking so badly that ink spattered as he dipped his quill.

22 Feb. 1791, on this fifth day since the death of my beloved wife, I write that the child she bore at such dreadful cost . . . oh, if a shred of mercy existed in her so merciless death, it was that

she was spared the knowledge of . . . though she was spared nothing else, nothing! cruelest, unceasing agony . . . I cannot believe that she is gone, my Darling One, my Treasure, my Sweet, always I yearned to call her by those dear names that filled my heart . . . but it was not a marriage of that sort, I think she felt but pity and meekness and tolerance, Oh God I think in her soul she abhorred me—why do I write these things! Why do I break the pieces of a heart already broken? I have no strength or sanity left . . . I cannot bear that my beloved one is gone, nor can I bear this new blow, cannot, cannot—

And the Counselor, weeping, rocked back and forth in his chair as he beheld again a thing more rodent than child: horribly small and wizened, its body covered with a scruffy black pelt, tangled black fuzz darkening the shriveled face, a sordid, ratlike thing, the miscreation of a miscreation.

The servants saw the Counselor depart each day for Assistens Kirkegaard. He did not go on foot, lunatic walker though he had always been, but was driven like an invalid in his carriage, his face still swollen with weeping and eyes festered like cankers. Except for these visits to the cemetery, he remained shut up in his bedchamber or the library.

2 March 1791. In this week since I beheld the creature I have not gone back. May it die. And may I die. It is all I want. I speak to her grave each day, I hear no answer. I am like the cold snow that blows outside the windows. Nothing matters.

4 March 1791. I have ordered the wet nurse and nursemaid to allow no servants to enter the nursery. Nor are these two to gossip when they eat downstairs. I did not speak to them more. I do not know them, I do not want them—but a *DIGNIFIED GENTLEMAN* must have them, as he must also have his tailor and barber, also exorbitantly paid for attending an aberration. I

can buy anyone, it sickens me, I hate their proximity, I hate their eyes—I do not want these nurses, above all I do not want this monstrosity. Though I kept face before the nurses, in my room I bit my hands in despair. Why does it not die! If it survives, it will live out its life eating and defecating and perhaps maneuvering around the floor in some scraping way, its cramped, tiny mind a perpetual darkness. Why does it not die! Why was it my beloved one who died, whose absence I cannot bear . . .

Later that day a carriage drew up before the house.

"Of course he will not receive us," Bodil said to her brother, "but that is why we have come, isn't it? Formalities are the glue of society. One practices them as a matter of course, but one is honest enough not to pretend that they mean anything."

The Bishop gave her a withering look and climbed out. Tall, as was the family characteristic, and imposing, dressed all in black and heavily wigged, he had recently sat for his portrait, which depicted him in his great white ruff and had captured in every brush stroke the power he wielded. The slight sensualness of the mouth, and a certain pliancy of skin beneath the severe, penetrating eyes, bespoke a man who liked his comforts and had been left on the palette.

He bent his head in the wind-driven snow, envisioning a glass of hot spiced wine, which he pushed from his mind as they entered the house of bereavement. Servants were lighting wall sconces in the darkening afternoon. A footman took the two calling cards upstairs on a silver tray.

"You did not mention the service," said the Bishop when the servants had gone. "In which church was it held?"

His sister shrugged. "I do not know. I was not invited. As I told you earlier, the single time I met his wife, Thorkild ejected me from the house for showing lack of esteem."

"And as I said, that was wrong of you. You are hard. You are hard and Godless, Bodil. If the miserable wretch was content with her, why insult him by showing what you felt? It was not for you to pass judgment."

"Well, since God was not there to pass His, it was left to me. But I was not so petty as to deplore her appearance, though she was long in the tooth and drearily appareled and homely enough to turn milk sour—what, after all, had one expected? Possibly something worse. No, it was her meekness, it was her unhappy acceptance of her lot with him. Intolerable. I could feel no sympathy for her, much less esteem."

"The vows of holy matrimony are to be esteemed," the Bishop said shortly.

"All marriages are financial contracts. But no contract should prevent a wife from asserting herself."

"It is unseemly that you exercise your sharp tongue on this woman. She is dead. Let us show respect."

"Why? You never met her. I met her once and disliked her. We both dislike Thorkild. We are here only that we may leave again. Is that footman never coming back?"

Upstairs the footman stood knocking on his master's door. One often had to knock for a long while.

The Bishop chewed the inside of his cheek. He was not used to be kept waiting. His sister tapped a gloved finger against her beaded reticule. "I am glad we will not have to witness his grief," she said. "Like everything else about him, it is sure to be excessive."

"So speaks one who grieved not at all for her husband."

"I preferred to get on with my life. It is life that is important, after all, not death."

"I see. The salvation of the soul is not important."

"Certainly it is important to the Church, as there would be no Church without it. As there would be no banks without money."

The Bishop's eyes flared, but he only said, coldly: "You should know that in some ways you are even more repugnant than Thorkild."

"And you should know that it is a treasure in my life that your bishopric is in Aarhus and that you visit Copenhagen but rarely."

Upstairs the door was finally opened. The Counselor took the two calling cards from the tray. He squinted at them. "Out! Tell them to get out!"

The visitors heard the angry bark, and despite their wrangling were united by a sense of relief. The footman returned to them with a bow.

"The Counselor sincerely regrets that he is indisposed. He begs you to accept his apologies."

"Of course." The Bishop bowed his head in return. "If you will kindly tell the Counselor that we extend our deepest sympathy to him in his great loss."

"Footmen will be a thing of the past if the situation in Paris worsens," Bodil remarked as the door closed behind them. She was tired of bickering. On the subject of the revolution in France the two of them were as one, even if she did not share her brother's outrage at acts against the clergy. "One hears that the National Guard now surrounds the Tuileries," she went on as the coachman helped them into her carriage, "and that the radicals may actually declare for a Republic." Her brother, settling himself into his seat, replied with a keen shake of his head, "We knew what to do with Struensee twenty years ago. But that was one man. This is so drastically different—who knows where it will all end?" He gave a look back through the flying snow as the carriage pulled away. "And what of the child? Do you say it lived or died?"

"I know nothing. I would not even have heard of the wife's death were it not that my cook happened to chat with a servant from over there on market day. What goes on in Thorkild's house does not concern me."

"Except for observing the formalities," the Bishop commented in a dry but conciliatory tone, and went on to suggest that the only hope was for the European rulers to unite in arms and restore full power to the French king, with which Bodil agreed; and then they were at her house, the drive from Thorkild's taking somewhat less than two minutes.

છ્જી

That evening Thorkild returned to the nursery. He had not been able to bring himself to look at the creature carefully. Perhaps, he thought, it was not truly as hideous as he believed. It was. He left the room at once, more than ever consumed by revulsion, loathing and shame for the thing he had fathered.

Each day he went back, as if he could not have enough pain. With a harsh glare at the nurses—Keep your eyes to yourself! Do not come near me! Do not speak!—he would stand mute and stony-faced by the crib. And then he came to realize that a seed of pity had grown in him for this helpless abomination. It had not asked to be born, yet blindly it wanted to live. It mewled and feebly waved its tiny, dreadful hirsute arms in the lace and satin of its crib. It was horrible in its finery. He felt a need to bring it solace, to touch its shaggy repellent head. He did this once, when the nurses were elsewhere in the room. Another time he put his great hand around a fluttering minuteness of fingers, and felt them weakly grasp his thumb; and at that moment he understood, with astonishment, that he loved this creature, this poor terrible mutation, with a deep and almost desperate love; and that the creature was gazing up at him with its small eyes, in their surround of tangled black fuzz, and that in some ineffable animal way, those eyes returned his love.

After this he suffered even more. The creature was doomed either to death or to a hopeless existence; and stroking its pitiful rodent face as the little eyes looked up into his, he could not bear the thought of either inevitability. His agony over the creature and his grief for his wife kept him in seclusion. As the weeks passed, he took on an unhealthy indoor pallor. His great rocking step had a brokenness. In his library he tried with futility to write or to read. In his room he wept.

He began to notice something puzzling. The tiny creature's

beribboned, too-large gowns no longer seemed as large. And the fingers he gently took up appeared less withered. And the scurf of fur along the limbs—was it becoming patchy? His heart gave a great hopeful lurch, which he checked: perhaps it was only his imagination. But it was not. The creature was growing, filling out, losing its black pelt. The Counselor was in a daze. Each day at the crib he hardly dared breathe lest the miracle cease. The feeble mewlings were taking on the sound of an infant's cries, the hands were becoming smooth and soft; scarcely any fur clung to the rounded arms, the tangled facial fuzz was wearing away, and from the skull the shaggy hair fell in strands, revealing a fine pale down. The Counselor was transported by joy, he could no longer contain himself.

"Are you not astounded?" he cried at the nurses. And received a cold answer: "What is there to be astounded about?" "But a miracle is happening! It is a monstrosity no longer!" And was contemptuously refuted: "It never was a monstrosity." "What? What do you mean! Speak up, damn you!" And was told in curt tones: "They're always runty and shriveled, and sometimes all covered with hair like a monkey, when they're so extremely early born, that's all. And if they don't perish right at once, they generally come round in time like him."

Speechless, the Counselor stared up at the two women. Why had they not told him this at the start, and spared him his so terrible suffering? Yet how could they have, and why should they have, treated as they were with such ferocious aloofness? He turned back to the crib with an inner groan—all that unnecessary pain . . . and yet he could not regret the depth of that pain, for without it, the extraordinary bond of love and understanding between him and the creature might never have been forged. And that bond was forever, he knew that in his soul.

One day he ordered the nurses to leave the room. He lifted the begowned infant from its crib. It felt warm in his so careful but clumsy arms. Tears glistened down the heavy folds of his face, and he felt that his wife was also touching the warm small body, and that she smiled.

It became his daily habit to order the nurses out for half an hour. His joy and eagerness and untrammeled sentimentality were not to be observed by eyes that would find them grotesque. Alone, he would with a wheeze hoist his massive bulk up into a chair, the infant in his arms. If it had been squalling in its crib, it was soon soothed by his rocking and patting. He would ask how it felt. Was it comfortable? Would it like to hear a song? And he would sing something from his childhood, in a low, quiet voice, so as not to jar its ears; sometimes there was a gurgle of pleasure, which so clutched the Counselor's heart that he could scarcely continue singing for joy. And if the infant eventually fell asleep, he would sit on in perfect contentment, lightly stroking the round, downy head.

The infant's eyes were turning from darkest blue to the blue of the sea. Its little legs grew plump and sturdy. In time it began to crawl. As soon as the Counselor opened the door—the nurses marching out at his command—it would come scuttling across the floor with crows of delight. The Counselor would with difficulty bend his misshapenness and lift the infant into the air, covering it with kisses. He would carry it to a window and point out the housetops, or a flock of birds, or perhaps a cloud floating by. "What do you think that resembles? A cow? A bonnet? Ah, you say a teapot!" The infant, round-eyed, would laugh, and he with it as he nuzzled the small cheek with his own, and then he would sit down with it in a chair, where they would gaze at each other in complete accord.

When the child began to walk, it would totter across the room to him in all haste, arms outspread in welcome. When it began to chatter and to listen, it would nestle at his side—for the Counselor had no lap—to hear stories told in a spellbinding voice, with every sort of fascinating gesture, and with a bear hug at the end. The Counselor's absence of a lap, the enormously broad, bulging overhang in its stead, and the two pegs dangling below, seemed not to trouble the child even as he grew older; nor did the waddling and wheezing, nor the fact that at four he was taller than his father. It was as if he had an absolute understanding and acceptance of these things. This was because of their extreme closeness, their indissoluble bond of love, the Counselor told himself; but at the back of his mind was fear that the bond might give as the child grew into boyhood and began looking at him with more sophisticated eyes. Already the child left their nursery sanctuary to run about the house and the courtyard. This, a normal life, the Counselor most ardently desired for him, but he knew what it might engender.

Still, there was no change in the lad as he grew older. His eager, affectionate ways did not diminish, nor the pleasure he took in his father's company. He liked to settle himself across from the Counselor at his desk, to draw or to read, and to ask endless questions, which became long conversations between them. He was very bright, and according to his governess very naughty as well. He was allowed to race around the courtyard, but not to climb the spiked iron fence. When he did this one day, and was carried inside having fallen from a tree limb onto a spike, the Counselor's terror knew no bounds. He rubbed the boy's hands, kissed them, begged him over and over to live. And only because of a few millimeters between the piercing point and the little heart, and the quick thinking of a scullery maid, was the child left among the living with no more than a raised red welt of a scar.

It was a miracle that the child had been conceived at all, and a miracle that he had not died at birth, and now this was yet another miracle. The Counselor felt that the lad had been destined in the face of every obstacle to live, and that he had a special gratitude for life, and a gift for living, and that life would be good to him.

Just how good the Counselor could not have prophesied. In addition to his bright mind and open, winning disposition, the lad was now growing tall for his age and striking, with thick, lustrous wheaten hair, a smile that dazzled, and a face possessing all the well-chiseled symmetry and clarity that the Counselor and his wife had so signally lacked. How had the two of them produced such beauty? the Counselor wondered almost with awe. How had this paragon come to be? And again he began to fear that his child would turn away from him.

When one day the boy, a strapping twelve, asked to come along with his father on his walk through the city—for the Counselor had years ago resumed his peregrinations, as he had his dignified grooming, hair powdered, jowls close-shaven and fragrant with scent, coat and breeches just so, boot buckles agleam—the Counselor felt a heavy sinking of his heart. "Now it will happen," he told himself. But with a sense of fatalism he assented. They walked down Bredgade together, through Kongens Nytorv, and along Vesterbrogade. The lad showed no trace of self-consciousness as people gawped at his companion, some even shading their eyes for a better look. It was as if they did not exist. He was as natural and attentive as when they strolled alone together in the courtyard. The Counselor, emotional as always, was obliged to blow his nose many times on this walk. His fear never returned.

The lad grew into an immensely tall youth, strong-willed but with a sweetness of nature, high-spirited and sunny. He was radiance itself, and the jewel of his father's life.

ᑲᑭ

The old man woke from his profound sleep beneath the dingy blue hangings. He lay listening to the rain pour down the windows. After a while he climbed from bed, washed and dressed himself, as always with difficulty, having to stretch and gasp in order to reach around his freakish proportions. The task took almost two hours, but even when he had employed servants he had never used a valet. He worked his quilted satin dressing gown over his clothes, and at nine o'clock his barber came in. The barber was the son of his old barber, as his present tailor was the son of his old tailor. He had outlived everyone in his generation except his sister and brother. He felt aged, a ghostly relic. The barber draped the powdering gown around him, combed and powdered his gray bristly hair, carefully shaved the sags and pouches of the face, patted in scent with his fingertips, removed the sheet, collected his things, bowed, and left, not having ventured a word, for it was obviously one of those days when the wretched gnome did not wish to speak.

Downstairs, the Counselor has his breakfast of hot chocolate and buttered rolls. He does not give his slatternly housekeeper his usual hostile look. He is distracted, inward. In his library, putting on his brown velvet skullcap, he sits down at his desk to write. He looks at the desktop before him. It has been the same for fifty years: the malachite inkpot and box of fine blotting sand, the two very old candlesticks, the yellowed globe of the world standing on ebony legs inlaid with mother-of-pearl.

16 October 1815. Today is the second anniversary of his death at Leipzig. He would be four and twenty had he lived. It is all finished now. The wars are over. Napoleon has been defeated once and for all and banished. It is all finished. But I cannot endure my lad's absence any longer. In the spring I shall go to Leipzig and find him.

· 14 ·

ℰ Going over faxes and business letters at his desk, Philip looks with curiosity at the sheet of fluorescent-pink stationery. It is graced with a Disney chipmunk holding the string of a purple balloon emblazoned with HI! The lines are written in vibrant yellow Magic Marker. They are from his niece's young daughter in Malibu, whom he has never met. Her message is that she's into doing her family tree and needs the name of his real father. Her grandmother in Switsorland can't find her birth sertificat, so maybe he'd take a look at his, any other info would be wellcome.

On a memo, he jotted, "Rosted, probably Swedish. Sorry, don't know more—best luck." He tore the sheet off, stuck it in an envelope, addressed it, and added it to the out pile, and glancing at his watch continued with the clearing of his desk preparatory to one of his trips. A few minutes later, getting into his heavy Burberry raincoat as he went, he strode from his private office through the outer office, and leaving behind its soft, rapid clicking of computer keyboards, its bulletin board thick with Kodachrome postcards from every inch of the globe, thumped on downstairs.

Recessions do not touch the sales of cameras or photographic equipment. The need to reproduce ceaselessly is too strong. It is built into the century. It is a need that will not be denied. This was his reasoning when he established his business, through whose sales-rooms he now passes. His aversion to photography had not stood in his way, nor has it since. His acute business instincts are such that no amount of aversion can militate against their effectiveness: the store flourishes, fructifies. Outside he heads with relief for the parking garage.

The drizzly afternoon had turned to dusk when, a traffic-thick hour later, he arrived at his house in Kenilworth. This he had bought after his last divorce, impatiently taking the first thing the agent showed him. Executive style, semicustom; talcum-white walls, plantation shutters, gourmet-tiled kitchen, recreation room with built-in widescreen TV, wall-to-wall tangerine carpeting throughout. On moving in he had hired workmen to revamp the whole thing, but had rapidly grown tired of the mess and dismissed them. Except for the master bedroom partially wainscoted and an oak beam in the living room ceiling, the house remained unchanged.

His assistant was propped on an elbow at the kitchen counter, talking on the cardinal-red phone to Montreal or Mexico City or Greece or England. She knew people everywhere. She ran up staggering bills. "No, hey, I'm a survivor. Hey, look, you've got to preserve your inner space . . ." He took a piece of cold chicken from the refrigerator and walked into the recreation room where, in his coat, he stood gnawing. This would be the extent of his evening meal; he never had an appetite when he was going to fly. By rights, he thought, I should be a very thin man. He looked over at his assistant's cameras lying in a tangle of straps on the sofa. She saved all her phone calls until she came over to his place. It was a minor thing, it didn't matter. Except think of that drivel being served by millions of feet of intricate, painstakingly created wires and underground cables. He threw the chicken bones in the fireplace, which was of whitewashed brick flecked with sparkling mica, and went upstairs.

In his partially paneled bedroom he tossed his old pigskin bags on the unmade bed and acknowledged a stomach flutter. O'Hare coming right up, then Dallas, Los Angeles, Hawaii, Tahiti, and finally a prop plane to Bora Bora. An excruciating chain of takeoffs and landings for the sake of checking into one more resort hotel. He drew in and expelled a long breath. It was something he lived with, as others lived with migraines or rheumatism. His assistant advised acupuncture. Paula had once said, sensibly enough, at least don't fly if it's not necessary. He shrugged off all suggestions. If it was your fate to feel this way, it was your fate. His palms were already damp.

Downstairs, having set his bags by the door and phoned for a cab, he picked up the mail from the floor—she could have done that—and brought it into the recreation room, where she was sitting on the sofa with her Walkman on, its inner crashings causing her kinks and cork-screws to jolt in rhythm. He sat down beside her with the mail, all junk except for a blue airmail envelope from Paula. He opened it and withdrew a drawing, if it could be called that—a mess of blotches and sharp angular lines. Evidently his sister was now attempting the graphic arts. He sat trying to appreciate the scribble when a jolt of fear went through him.

"Look," he said to his assistant. "Look at this." There was no response. He waved the drawing at her.

"Huh?" She moved the earphones forward.

"Look." His lips felt dry. "Is this an air crash or isn't it?"

She ran her eyes over the picture.

"I don't know. Could be. Where'd you get it?"

"My sister. She sent it."

"Is she a sadist?"

"A sadist? Of course not."

"Then I don't suppose it's an air crash."

She replaced her earphones.

He looked again at the black scribble. It could be anything, an effort at a landscape maybe, or a street scene, God knew what, but certainly it wasn't meant to be a plane crash. Yet the thought was now stuck in his mind like a burr, an omen. He felt shaken. He got up and went over to the bar, poured a shot of Scotch, downed it, and walked around the room with his hands thrust deep in his coat pockets. Outside it had begun to rain. Also bad.

After a while, his assistant took off her earphones. She frowned at the sight of him dolefully pacing.

"I don't think this trip's going to be exactly *Saturday Night Live.* You know?"

"It's incredible." He shook his head. "She draws even worse than she sculpts."

"Who?"

"*Her.* My sister."

"Oh, we're back to her. Your sister that goes wandering around the Alps."

"The Jura."

"The nut."

"Just who the hell do you think you are?" he demanded angrily.

"A nut case." She yawned. "That's what she is, isn't she?"

"I never said that. I said eccentric!"

She shrugged and looked at her watch.

He scowled at his.

"Bora Bora," he said. "You know what it makes me think of? Some Grade-B movie from the thirties."

"I wasn't around then."

"Only updated. Sanitized. Worse."

She stretched her arms, and got up from the sofa. She was in a gold-knit tunic, black tights and combat boots. She pulled on her prefaded, prefrazzled denim jacket. He watched her sling her several cameras over one shoulder. She never stowed them in her tote bag. They had to be displayed because, like everything else she had or said or did, they expressed a compelling facet of her uniqueness, this self-intoxicated, walking cliché. And he winced at the sound of the door-bell, a melody of nauseating fake chimes which he kept meaning to remove, and which suddenly filled him with a ferocious urge to rip the mechanism from the wall.

❦

The ride to the airport was long but, as always, Philip found himself too soon inside the terminal, too soon passing through the metal detector and beginning the long, irrevocable walk to the waiting area. His assistant was involved in a monologue that he would ordinarily have lent half an ear to, as a distraction from his flying nerves, but tonight his dread was so intensified by the scribbled air crash that he heard nothing, and thought of nothing except the unavoidable moment when he would feel the jet begin to move down the runway in the rain. With a sense of tightly controlled panic, he was certain beyond the smallest doubt that this time he would not escape God's wrath.

An hour later he sat looking out at the night sky. The rain had been left behind, stars sparkled. Usually after the takeoff Philip felt spent, wonderfully relaxed, thankful to have been spared and gratified to be on his way somewhere. This sense of well-being, mixed with tedium, would endure for hours, disappearing only with the approach of landing.

But this time he felt none of his usual repose. His tension persisted, thanks to that mess of a drawing, which he tried to forget by thinking of Australia. They might go there after Bora Bora, or India, maybe Turkey, maybe Europe. That was the way they traveled. Extemporaneously. That was the way they liked it. That much at least they had in common.

He looked at her sitting next to him. Soon she would get up and roam. Her combat boots would take her from business class into off-limits first—rules didn't apply to her—or up and down the clogged aisles of tourist, where she would press around backsides and food carts with a casual unconcern that amounted to elbowing, and where she might flop down in an unoccupied seat to converse with some promising intellectual whose sweatshirt announced "Harvard" or "A Dirty Mind Is a Terrible Thing to Lose." Or she might not get up at all. She might decide to sleep. She could turn herself off at will, click, like a machine.

He looked irritably away. Why bother with her when she roused such contempt in him? It wasn't as if she were necessary to him. She wasn't even essential when their trips were of a business nature; he needed no assistant. She was a convenience, as he was to her. She accompanied him, interrupting whatever other liaisons she was involved in to reap the benefits of free travel. There was also his store, where she got her cameras and photographic equipment reduced in price to nearly nothing. And he? He reaped the benefit of her embraces, which were able, athletic and brief, and conveniently so, since he was not of an age to excel in all-night marathons. Also, he didn't like traveling alone. They were the same. He had no right to feel contempt for her, especially as the much older partner who should provide patience, wisdom and understanding. But instead he felt more and more irritation with everything she did.

He shut his eyes and tried to find sleep. No plane seat was big enough for someone his height, but it wasn't lack of leg space that denied him rest as the minutes passed, it was his mind: glaringly awake, it refused to be shut off; his thoughts were like billiard balls clacking in all directions. He cursed the scribbled air crash for this high level of adrenaline. If only the thing hadn't arrived just as he was leaving, but it was his big day for personal mail—and his mind jumped to the gaudy schoolgirl note, and from there to the interior of his garage. The BMW took up less space than the clutter. Sprung tennis rackets, defective lamps, toppled piles of books he'd never got around to shelving, and some battered old cardboard boxes full of papers, among which, in his mind's eye, was an official form entitled *Certified Copy of Birth Record.*

He hadn't thought of that piece of paper for years. Decades. He'd got it to apply for his first passport, 1945, a lifetime ago, the summer between his high school graduation and first year of college. Tourists weren't allowed into Europe so soon after the war, but his family had connections, and off he went on a stormy Atlantic passage that thrilled his soul. Snatched back from the plunging rail by a deckhand, he survived to race down the gangplank onto French soil, rucksack thudding against his knobby spine—one of those adolescents with long gangling limbs, feet that got entangled with each other, and a raging inflammation of Romantic Sensibilities. Could anyone else at seventeen have been so green, so gauche, so credulous? Got himself a beret first thing, and swept it off in the hush of great art museums covered from floor to ceiling with beauty, glory, magnificence, eyes bedazzled . . . well, watch where you're going, idiot. A country road, a Peugeot barreling by, skidding to a stop, backing up—"Hop in." Jumped inside with his rucksack and sped off through the poplars. Fellow American as it turned out, son of a brigadier general posted in Berlin. Terrifically nice young guy, terrifically friendly, kept smiling at him from the steering wheel. How would the poor moron like to see Berlin? "Where I'm headed back, could easy wangle you a pass at the border"—a finger-snap, the general's son. Why not? Nobody got into occupied Germany. A supreme adventure. On they sped, he and his benefactor, who began sending him little nostril-flaring looks, which Philip supposed were a tic of some sort. By the time they reached Berlin—and it was an endless day-and-night drive, punctuated by drawn-out waits at military sector checkpoints—his companion's indefatigable pawings had him squashed against the car door ready to leap out. Which he did. Bolted off into the morning like a terrified rabbit. And then, with a hammer blow of disbelief, he stopped. He stood in an infinity of destruction. After some moments, open-mouthed, he walked on. Ruins wherever he stepped, wherever he looked. Walked a long time, nothing ever changed. Ruins, and only ruins. Began seeing American Jeeps and Army personnel, hardly registered them. Walked past pockmarked Brandenburg Gate, saw red-starred soldiers, scarcely noticed them. Eyes glued to the ruins. All day, astounded, walking through the gray skeletal wastes of the immense city, shoes coated with dust from the rubble. Astounded. Of course he knew. He knew the whole war—magazines, newspapers, newsreels—but that wasn't to know. To *know*. At nightfall, after hours of red tape in the American sector, he boarded a dilapidated train that would take him back to France. Exhausted, he fell asleep like a stone. Woke a while later, when they jolted to a stop in Leipzig. And when the train chugged away from what was left of the station, he saw, with indrawn breath, spreading from either side of the tracks, a city burned almost level. A few lit windows here and there. Then they dwindled to nothing in the clattering expanse of the night.

And that was his supreme adventure. What did you expect, moron? Now you return to France with a broken heart. All misery and Weltschmerz. You go back to your great museums of art and cloud-piercing cathedrals, and try to fit them into what you now know. No luck! And in your poor little beret you struggle to figure it all out. Oh, the turmoil, the torment! And then the earnest, ridiculous, gangling-limbed suffering creature fades into the mist of time. Never saw him again after a couple of years. The turbulent poems and midnight-oil debates tapering off as the feet grew less clumsy, the limbs more solid, the mind taken up with each passing day. Which was only natural, for who could have lived forever with all that juvenile intensity . . . ?

He tightened his eyes. He was determined to slam a lid on his overactive brain. But his thoughts continued to leap everywhere, landing now on one thing, now on another, now landing again on the birth certificate, where he saw "Rosted" typed beneath "Father's Full Name." This he had always remembered, but he couldn't bring to mind the first name. Nor after all these years could he visualize what stood beneath "Father's Place of Birth." Sweden, it seemed, or maybe Denmark or Norway. None of it had meant anything to him then, and none of it meant anything to him now. The past was dust, the man was dust. As kids he and Paula had heard bits and pieces from their mother . . . brief shipboard romance, knot tied in Uruguay, life in the back of the back of beyond with an elderly structural engineer who was dullness itself, his boring sense of humor, his one tiresome joke about a pony . . . big, old and boring was all he knew about the man, and that after their mother had left with Paula just born, and pregnant again, he'd died of a ruptured appendix, "peritonitis in the pampas," as their mother had put it, but she had seldom made reference to him, their swilling, wisecracking mother . . .

He felt the sharp prod of his assistant's elbow. The seat-belt sign was on: they were approaching Dallas. The thought of the black scribble clamped itself around his innards. He gave a sharp headshake to be rid of it, but only saw more vividly than ever its crude delineation of crumpled fuselage and shattered wings. Somehow, with shaking hands, he got the belt fastened with what he knew was the hard, cold click of absolute finality.

❦❧

There was stone dust in her hair, and even on the fine dark brows above her surprised eyes. Rain dripped from his coat to the worn linoleum as they hugged each other. The window streamed, misted on the inside with heat from the old stove's open oven door. Her face beamed as they stood away. The surprise!—where in the world had he come from? And she took his coat, hanging it on a peg by a plastic rain cape with taped rents.

"Zurich," he said, drawing a chair out from the table and flopping down. His entire body, from the top of his bald head down to each of his ten toenails, pulsed with fatigue. "Zurich by way of Istanbul and other points east." The most excruciating, exhausting trip he had ever endured. He felt in a way that he had become unhinged.

"And you can stay a while?"

She was already putting water on for coffee. She was in a shapeless sweater and a pair of flannel pajama bottoms whose cuffs, none too clean, were coiled around run-down carpet slippers. Her gray-streaked, stone-dusted hair hung loose.

"Till around five," he told her, stretching his sore spine. "We're driving on to Geneva to catch a plane home tonight."

"We? Who, your assistant?" she asked. "Where is she then?"

He shrugged. "Who knows? Waiting out in the car. Driving around maybe. I told her to get lost while I visit."

"But Philip, really. You can't treat someone that way—and in this pouring rain? You should have asked her in with you."

"She'd have stared you up and down. She'd have been amused. She'd have walked around picking things up. She's stupid and arrogant."

Paula was startled by his candor. Wonderfully startled. He would never have talked like that last time.

"Well," she said, rummaging through the cupboards and ancient refrigerator, "if she stays out there long enough, maybe through some process of osmosis she'll realize it's not the Alps but the Jura." She brought things over to the table. She said there were dark bags under his eyes. He rubbed the thick, grizzled hair at his temples, and commented on her own face. Thin, he said, was she okay? Very okay, she assured him, and sat down with a hospitable gesture that reminded him of the very polished hostess she had once been.

Lunch consisted of a couple of tomatoes and hard-boiled eggs, of rolls a little stale, butter in its wrapper and a jar of marmalade, sliced fruit from a can, instant coffee. It was what she had on hand, and it was more or less what she had served her daughter when she had appeared unexpectedly, for the second time, a couple of weeks earlier. She described the visit with an exasperated laugh.

"Just like the first time. 'Think about it, Mom, a nice condo back in the States, an upswing wardrobe, good nutritious food' . . . I can't possibly want to stay here with these stale rolls. Next time she'll probably bring a psychiatrist to back her up."

"Naturally she'd think you're cracked."

Again Paula was startled and pleased by his openness.

"It's what you think too," she said.

"I may have."

"Good. I like this. But you don't have a leg to stand on. What with your terror of flying, and the huge unnecessary amount of it you keep putting yourself through? If that isn't cracked." And she cracked a hard-boiled egg on her plate. "You're like one of those medieval self-flagellants."

Surprisingly, he agreed.

"And I'll tell you something else," he said, "that drawing you sent—I thought it was a plane crash. I know, I know," he responded to her incredulous look, "but that's what I thought. What is it anyway? What the hell is it supposed to be?"

"But I thought you'd know. I was sure you'd know. Don't you remember that when you were here last we talked about the ones in Evanston? When we were children?"

"No, I don't. I don't know what you're talking about."

"Look again then. Behind you."

Turning in his chair, Philip saw the black scribble thumbtacked to the wall. He untacked it and sat back. It had been cut from a newspaper.

"I thought you drew it yourself."

No, she said, she'd seen it on one of her walks, in the arts section of a discarded newspaper. The paper had blown across the road and she'd picked it up, and the drawing had spoken to her so deeply that she'd hiked to the next village, which had a Xerox machine, and made him a copy. Couldn't he see what it was?

"An *ant*," she said finally.

And before his tired, searching eyes, the massed black with its sharp angular lines came into focus, and he saw not his persecuting air crash, but a single, solitary little ant rendered a thousand times larger than life. The insect was sleeping, or maybe it lay in deep concentration, or maybe it had sunk to its final rest. The drawing's crudeness was now resolved into something powerful and fragile both, odd, unreal, yet more real than real somehow, with a feeling of deep, of infinite poignance. He nodded.

"Yes, I see it now. An ant."

And didn't he remember the ones in Evanston, she wanted to know, when they were children? How they had used to watch them in the backyard, crouched side by side? The fascination? The sense of discovery? Before the world had come crowding in? That's what the drawing had made her think of: those days. That's why she had sent it.

He thanked her, and put the picture down. It didn't seem strange that they, two grown people, should be talking about the ants in their old backyard. Nothing seemed particularly strange. He felt drunk, lightheaded with fatigue.

"But how you could have got a plane wreck out of it. God, I'm sorry, Philip. It must have made the trip even worse than usual."

"Worse?" He almost laughed with exhaustion. Incredibly, indescribably worse. Unrelenting tension, sleep deprivation, hardly a moment's respite from his clattering, overactive brain. And yet . . . "In a way I'm not sorry I went," he said. "Like this guy I'd lost track of years ago. I saw him again. I kept meeting him all through the trip. He was in a beret and had dust on his shoes."

"Who was that?"

He shrugged. He felt embarrassed by what he had just said, theatrical and melodramatic. "Just somebody I used to know." He sipped at his coffee from the thick mug. The rain was still falling hard, but the room was pleasantly warm. "That oven actually does a fair job," he told her.

Oh, it worked wonderfully, she said, although her daughter had made a big fuss. "One of the things she threw her hands up over. Heating a place with the kitchen oven, like a slum dweller! Everything upsets her so—why doesn't she stay home with her children? Which reminds me, my granddaughter's doing her family tree. She wrote asking about our real father, and if I'd get out my birth certificate. Which is God knows where, maybe stored with my things in Neuchâtel, in one of a billion boxes. I told her to write you instead. The child seems earnest, if given to atrocious notepaper and worse spelling."

"I know, she wrote me. I wrote her back his name and—"

"What is the name, anyway? I've been trying to remember."

"Rosted."

"That's right, Rosted."

"And the birthplace. Sweden, I think."

"Or maybe Denmark? I think Mother mentioned it."

"She mentioned damn little," he said, chewing. "Of course there was peritonitis in the—"

"—pampas. Alliterative and amusing. And when she said we were lucky he'd still been able to produce viable sperm?"

"Jesus," Philip sighed.

"She always had to be funny."

"I don't think Uruguay even has pampas grass."

"It does," she said. "I read it somewhere." The rain swerved rattlingly against the window. She broke off and buttered a piece of roll, and gave a slow shake of her head. "The whole thing was that she was bored down there in the middle of nowhere. She said he was boring, but anyone would have bored her down there."

"Bored her anywhere," Philip said.

"Everyone bored her. We bored her."

"We bored her."

"A boring, doddering old man, she called him, but could he have been so old if he was an active engineer? She always had to exaggerate. Like that one joke he was supposed to have told over and over. He probably told it once."

" 'Even the finest little pony brings no one back.' "

"I have to admit it's completely pointless."

"Maybe it was just the punch line," Philip said.

"Maybe it wasn't even a joke."

"Maybe he never said it. Probably she made it up. Half-swacked anyway."

"Half-swacked." And again Paula shook her head. "You realize that's all there is? Just a few facetious bits and pieces? He was about as real to us as thin air. But you know, I did see his clothes once."

"You did?"

"I think. Clothes and books and things. When I was small. In that old steamer trunk down in the basement. It must have been sent up from Uruguay after his death. I'm pretty sure it was his, although I didn't know it then."

"What were his things like?"

"Just some anonymous belongings as far as I was concerned, un-interesting. Except for a little rolled-up rug, and I snitched it because it was nice. You remember, I had it in my room. Then later, of course, she gave the trunk to the Salvation Army. Just gave it away, imagine. Everything still in it. Except the rug; I still have it. I think now it must have been done by someone in his family."

"Did you ever wonder," Philip asked, "about the estate? It must have been family money. He couldn't have made all that as an engi-neer."

"No, I never thought about it," she said. "You reach your majority, you come into shares. It was an abstract."

"That's how it was for me too. I knew it was his estate, but it didn't mean anything. I never thought about him."

"Not a letter, not a photo. Nothing. But I've been thinking about him lately. So have you."

"I have," he said, and slowly swirled the coffee in his mug, the engineer being another one he had kept meeting over and over on his trip. "I've thought of him dying down there in the back of the back of beyond. Peritonitis in the pampas . . . a few fatuous words for who-ever he was. It's a lonely ending."

"It was immoral of her," Paula said. "It was immoral of her to leave us with nothing of him but her joking remarks. Nobody has a right to do that."

"Still, what does it matter? He's dust. He is now, and he was then. Seriously, why do people do family trees? What's the point?"

"Not much in this case, I'm afraid. The child will come to a dead end with him."

When they finished their canned fruit, Paula brought out peppermints from an opened cellophane package that lay on the oilcloth. Philip remembered the gold-foiled after-dinner chocolates in her small crystal dishes. He looked at the windowsill with its jar of late wildflowers, where rain had seeped in along the ulcerated wood. He looked at the old linoleum, at the big sloping stone sink in the corner, at the stove and refrigerator standing at their slight tilt, and at Paula sitting there with the stone dust of her secret labors in her ungroomed hair. Last time he couldn't wait to leave, had been unnerved, depressed. This time he wasn't bothered. He had come over the edge himself.

"Does it worry you," he asked, "her wanting you to leave?"

"Worry me? I don't know. It's just that she comes and makes such a scene. I know she means well, but I really think her horror has less to do with my well-being than her idea of correct living. She can't get past that. She's like a battering ram."

"You should have my children," he said with a laugh. Each had been born of a different mother and grown up in places distant from Chicago, with one or more stepfathers, and half-and-step-siblings. Their lives had little connection with his. "They'd never question my lifestyle any more than they would that of some stranger on a street corner."

"I guess that's worse," Paula said, "although there's something to be said for it."

"Not much."

"Would you like to have done things differently?" she asked. "I don't mean just in regard to your marriages, I mean everything. I know I'd like to have. Because it's hard to know what you're doing while you're doing it. I mean it's hard to understand how you're living your life while you're in the middle of living it. And then suddenly you realize decades have rushed by—thirty, forty years—and somehow they've been wrong."

Philip nodded. He supposed he knew only too well, racketing

around the world like a—what had she called him? A medieval self-flagellant.

"There's a quotation," he said, again feeling self-conscious and embarrassed, overly dramatic, "do you know it? 'Die and become what you are.'"

"I don't know it."

"It says everything."

"It does," Paula agreed, nodding. "From the first minute of our lives, it's what we should remember."

After this, they sat without talking. They ate their peppermints and looked out through the condensed moisture on the windowpane. The mountainside above was blurred, and the slope below, and the great distances below that. The rain fell heavy and straight, now and then swerving in a wind. Philip, looking down at the drawing on the table, at the insect lying in its solitary sleep, or in its final dissolution, felt tears prick his eyes. For himself, for the engineer, or for everyone on earth, he didn't know.

"I was thinking," Paula said after a while, turning her gaze from the window, "there must still be papers from when the estate was litigated."

"What, from sixty years ago?"

"Banks keep records. Law firms keep records."

"Not for that long."

A steady blast of a car horn carried up through the rain. Paula put her fingers in her ears.

"It's nowhere near five," she complained. "What's she honking about!"

Philip looked at his watch. "It is though. Unbelievable."

After a series of shorter, jabbing blasts, the noise finally stopped. Paula took her fingers from her ears. "Well, you suppose she's sat there long enough by now to know it's the Jura?"

"Don't bet on it," Philip says with a shake of his head. "But she knows by now that she and I are through. Kaput."

"Well, that's wonderful! I'm delighted to hear it," Paula tells him in congratulatory tones. "Only haven't you gone about it in a somewhat crappy way?"

"There's a heater in the car. She hasn't suffered."

Philip unfolds himself from his chair and stretches his sore bones, still feeling exhaustedly over the edge, unhinged, yet weirdly happy. He takes his sister's hands in his.

"It was a good visit, Paula."

"It was. The best of visits."

They embrace and wish each other well.

· 15 ·

One of the Rosteds' informal social evenings is in progress. Guests serve themselves from a buffet table set up between the two tall palms, some people are sitting on the rug where others step casually around them, the air is filled with flowing talk and with the zestfully plucked resonance of a mandolin. Through a fragrance of flowers and cigar smoke, Grethe has gone over to check the table. The open-face pâté and pickled-beet sandwiches need replenishment. So does the apple cake, and the coffee is almost gone. The maid should be seeing to these things, but the maid is busy listening to the mandolin. Grethe beckons her.

"I think you've forgotten the table, haven't you? Will you see to it please?" And she adds with a smile, "No, the mandolin won't go away."

Then she joins a young poet who wants to talk about Zola, telling him with friendly humor, "I believe you are a contradiction in terms."

Returning to the kitchen, the maid put water on to boil, and then leaned her arms on a chair back as the cook prepared more sandwiches. Nearby, Olaf crouched over his plate of scraps, tail tucked in to avoid having it squashed by a careless foot. The maid moistened a fingertip with her tongue, smoothed a scant eyebrow.

"They'll want more apple cake too."

"It's right there in front of you," snapped the cook. "Put it on the tray."

The useless thing, she thought crossly, and so above herself to boot. And it wasn't even her role to bring in the buffet tray. It was that of the kitchen maid, but this brazen lump here had begged the mistress and got her way.

"Rinse out that coffeepot and rinse it good! And don't hang about when you go back in there."

The girl carried the tray back in, her broad doughy face flushed by the talk and laughter and mandolin music. This is where she wanted to be, but she didn't approve of people sitting on the floor. That was queer and uncouth, you wouldn't find ladies and gentlemen doing that. And hardly a woman in the room dressed up proper for a party. Or the men either, and some with beards what looked like they'd never been cut. An odd crew. Anarchists maybe? You heard about them, fearsome types. But no, because the words she caught in passing were downright silly. Here they were talking about Peter Ox—Peter Ox, a tale from the land fit for children. And here somebody was saying you couldn't step into the same stream twice. "Why not?" she said boldly as she passed. "I have." No, they were a pretty poor lot, but it was a party anyway, and the mandolin raced up and down inside your veins.

She passed the master, standing in conversation with one of the beards. He looked sociable but he didn't look good. And she knew why, because the other day in the woods, where she sometimes sneaked off from her boresome tasks for a boresome walk, she'd heard twigs crackling and like any truant ducked behind a hawthorn. The mistress it was, walking fast and setting her mussed hair to rights and brushing off her skirts and looking around in a secret sort of way. The girl had gaped after her—who would have thought it! And she was shaken from head to toe with admiration. To have everything in the world—the tremendous wealth, the golden beauty, the big handsome husband—and now a lover too. All the two-øre novelettes the girl had

ever read sent up fireworks in her bosom: she could almost hear the
passionate gasps that had rent the quiet green air only moments ago.
And him?—a baron probably, from some estate nearby; no stenchy
oaf for *her*, like the stable boy with his grunts and sweaty groping, no,
of course not; and as she turned and walked on in her mistress's wake,
heading back to the beating of the rugs, the girl's flat lips went sullen
with the injustice of life. At least she herself wasn't a cheating whore,
an adulteress. But to be an adulteress was daring. Fru Rosted was
daring, a heroine. And always so kind to her too, but it wasn't hard
to be kind when you had everything; and anyway it wasn't kindness,
it was weakness, and sometimes you felt contempt for it. And what
she did under the trees was low and disgusting, except that it wasn't,
no, it was secret, grand, thrilling . . . and as she came through the
garden onto the carriage drive, she saw the mistress in pleasant conversation with the nursemaid, as cool and unruffled as if she hadn't
just torn herself from the hot arms of her lover. That was breeding,
that was the power of having everything.

See her sitting over there with a little fellow in thick spectacles, just
nodding and talking in her quiet way, outshining every other female
in the room and didn't even have to try. And again the girl was torn
between veneration and ire, sorry she had told the other servants what
she had seen in the woods, and at the same time not sorry. After all,
it would soon come to a head anyway. You only had to look at Hr.
Rosted with those dark circles under his eyes, like he couldn't sleep
for worry. He was still talking to the sprawling beard, but his eyes, as
he sipped his wine, were on his wife across the room. Did he suspect
that shrimp? With his thick spectacles and nothing chin? And she felt
a surge of insult on the mistress's behalf.

At the table she set out the savory sandwiches, the apple cake covered with whipped cream and glistening dots of jam, the shapely silver
coffeepot. Now she should go back to the kitchen and return later to
check. Instead, she plumped herself down in a chair, the mandolin
gorgeous in her ears. It was played by a squat, dark fellow in knick-

erbockers, with a sash around his middle like a gypsy. Afterward he'd want food on top of his pay, all gypsies begged, it was their nature. Cook would give him a hare in the kitchen, or a sack of apples, and would have to keep a sharp eye on the silverware. But he played wonderful, he played like anything, and her fingers jumped in rhythm on her broad aproned thigh.

At the other end of the room Onkel's flinty face creased in a smile. "A parable of the Resurrection? No, no, I don't say you're wrong, but let us recapitulate. Here we have a little red calf named Peter whose owners, a rich old peasant couple, love him as their own son. Indeed"—and kindling with his considerable powers as a raconteur, he pushed his pince-nez up the keen bridge of his nose—"indeed, they take him to the sexton and ask if he will teach Peter how to talk. The sexton assures the simpleminded old pair that he will do this, pockets a hundred kroner for the costly books he says will be needed, and afterward slaughters Peter and sells the meat. And every time the old pair come to his house he regales them with dazzling reports on Peter's progress in his studies, and pockets another hundred kroner for more advanced books. And when at last they beg to see Peter, for it has been so long, he tells them alas, the calf has bolted off that very day. Galloped into the horizon. Lost. Gone forever. The old couple are devastated, they weep, they lament, they are inconsolable. They return home shattered. Sad dark months go by. Then it happens that a new merchant settles in a nearby village. A man with the surname of Ox. Peter Ox. He hangs his sign out. When the old peasant comes to the village on an errand one day and sees this sign, he rushes inside. There before him stands Peter! Full grown now and amazingly changed, but still with the same thick neck and broad forehead and red hair. 'Oh Peter!' he cries, throwing his arms around the astonished merchant. 'Oh how we have missed you! And how you have changed! Why, if I wasn't absolutely sure, I'd never dream you were our little red calf all grown up. Now I'll retire and you can take over the farm. But if you prefer to stay in business, my love, that's fine too. Your mother and I will move in with you and you shall have all our riches, you being our only son and heir.' And the shrewd merchant, having gathered his startled wits together, replies, 'Why, what an excellent idea, Papa.' And so the old couple, after presenting the sexton with two hundred kroner for having educated Peter so well, move in with the merchant and live in happiness with him for the remainder of their days."

Onkel brought up his hands, palms out.

"No, no, I don't mock. The Resurrection, as experienced through purity of heart and shining faith, is as valid an interpretation as any. But so is that which sees the story as a triumph of avarice, deception and exploitation. And so is that which accepts both versions, since everyone in the tale triumphs. Except poor little Peter himself, of course, who has been slaughtered, eaten and digested at the very start, who does not exist except as excrement that has rejoined the earth. Which is yet another interpretation one could uphold. Where is one single, unassailable truth, even in a humorous old folktale? But I have perorated long enough. No, no, do not demur. One always over-indulges one's native tongue after a trip abroad, but I give you rest now—"

And the old journalist moved on through the room. He had just returned to Copenhagen from a trip to Italy, had driven out to say hello to Holger and Grethe, and had found himself in the middle of one of their gatherings. These he always enjoyed, but mingled with his pleasure tonight was an uneasiness. In his warm welcome from Holger and Grethe he had paid no heed to the touch of haggardness in Holger's face, for his nephew sometimes worked too long on his paintings. But later, glancing over at him, Onkel had sensed there was pain in that haggardness. Preoccupied with this thought, he strolled on now and half-listened to the mandolin, which was played by a fellow journalist with whom he habitually enjoyed exuberant political clashes. With a lift of his goatee, seeing his colleague set aside the instrument and take out a cigar, he went over to lose his uneasiness in a rattling good dispute.

The music had stopped. But she would stay where she was. None of the guests seemed to care that she sat among them in her apron and cap. Some even nodded pleasantly as they passed, and said good evening, a peculiar, underbred lot. She looked over at the table. Why shouldn't she have some of the apple cake? But that was going too far, even for her. Yet why not? Fru Rosted sat talking with the shrimp, she wouldn't notice. And if she did, what matter? Because what if Fru Rosted had glimpsed her peering through the hawthorn, and knew that she knew? And that was why she'd let her serve tonight, for fear of crossing her? The more the maid sat thinking about this, the more certain she became. She felt almost awed by her power, she felt a shimmering. She stood. She went to the table. She slid a big spoonful of the crumbly, creamy cake onto one of the pretty blue and white plates, clattered a fork onto it, and reseated herself in a vigor of satisfaction.

"No, it's not so much Cezanne's colors as his broken light," Holger said, but he was not thinking about Cezanne; he was remembering when he and Grethe came home from their wedding, and above every door, in the old custom, flowers had been hung. Now every door was shut and locked. "I know," he went on, urging his thoughts back to the conversation, "prints are no good. One must see the originals. One must go to Paris. Yes, we went two years ago." Ago. Ago. The word was beautiful. He was at sea in the present, lost. "Yes, how true," he responded to something being said, and even laughed, for it was evidently humorous. And with a departing smile, he moved on.

Onkel, bowing from the debate with his confrere, took Holger's arm.

"What is wrong?" he asked, dropping his voice.

"What, am I not the soul of conviviality? No one else sees anything wrong with me."

"Perhaps not, but I do." They had strolled over to a corner of the room where things were quieter. "Are you ill?"

"No. Not I."

"What does that mean?"

Holger sighed. He shook his head.

"It's not the time or place," he said.

"But later then. Please promise me."

"It is Grethe," he said abruptly. "She is ill. Ill in her mind."

"What, Grethe?" The old man stared at him. "Why, that's preposterous. Why, just look—"

"What do you expect?" Holger bit at him in a whisper. "Wild eyes and gibberish?"

They were silent.

"I'm sorry, Onkel."

"Don't be. But I wish I understood."

"It has come on gradually . . . a strangeness. As if suddenly she disappears, though in body she remains. It's not simple distraction, Onkel. It's something else, something terrible. I can't explain it. I ask her what is wrong, I want to help her, but she says she doesn't know what I mean. I cannot reach her . . . there is a chasm."

And of late that chasm had crept into their bed. He could not put it into words, but he knew in some inexplicable way as they made love that she was no longer with him, no longer part of him. And when with tears in his eyes, which he could not prevent, he begged to know what was wrong—to this too, lying in his arms, she would tell him: I don't know what you mean. Lately he had not even tried to touch her.

"Terrible. Terrible," he said aloud, and ran his palm over his face. "Of course, I know that, to look at, Grethe seems perfectly herself . . . believe me, Onkel, I sometimes think I'm the victim of my imagination, and that everything is just the same as always. But it's not so. There has come in Grethe a strangeness very deep . . ."

Onkel turned away from the darkly circled eyes. He pinched his goatee. He turned back.

"I take your word, Holger." But he did not. It was his nephew in whom there had come a strangeness very deep. He gave the boy's arm a pat. "Come, let's have a drop of Madeira." That being the only thing he could think of to say for the moment.

"Bjørnstjerne Bjørnson's wife has a dress that she has cut down the back and hangs on a peg, and when someone comes to the door she simply steps into it . . ."

Vulgar. Shameless. The maid stared up from her plate at the two young women as they passed. And idiotic—what kind of a fool did they take her for? Bjørnstjerne Bjørnson was a famous Norwegian writer, did they think she didn't know that? In school hadn't she had to listen to his boresome long poems till she was half-dead? And this great man should have a wife what went about the house naked? And him too? Did he have a suit cut down the back that he jumped into when callers knocked? It was unbelievable what these people here talked about. Weren't they going to say more? But the two young women, both smoking cigarettes of course, and the hair of one escaping from a careless and unfashionable bun, had passed out of earshot. Good riddance to shameless twaddle. So stupid, why, you'd get chilled to the bone if you sat about the house without a stitch on. But naked in the woods . . . she scraped up the last of the whipped cream from her plate—naked in the woods, that was something else, for passion turned the flesh to fire, to fire . . .

Now the mandolin music resumed, bringing her to her feet. She returned her plate to the table with a keen and knowing look at the back of Hr. Rosted, who was getting some wine with his old uncle, and took herself boldly through the flux of figures to those gathered around the gypsy.

"So you see," the young poet said, "I'm drawn more and more to the realistic form. I tell you, I burn to write like Zola—execrated everywhere by the middle class."

"Is that your objective?" Grethe asked with a smile.

"No, but you know what I mean. Grand-scale exploder of society's ills." And his thick spectacles flashed. "There's no one like him!"

"It's true," she agreed. "You will love *Germinal*, I promise you."

"And are you soon done?" he asked as they got up from the sofa.

"Quite soon, yes," she replied, but she felt a shadow of confusion. Wasn't the stack of translated pages actually meager, and filmed with dust? Yet how could that be, when she took up her pen every morning, and had done so for months? What would she have been doing all this time if not working? Staring out the window? At the desktop? But where did this idiotic thought come from? The stack of completed pages was quite high, quite high. Wasn't it? And she said again, "Yes, quite soon. And you will love it, for he is at his most explosive yet."

"Who is explosive, Bjørnson?" asked the young poet's wife, joining them as they strolled on. "We visited him this summer, did you know? And *she* is delightful. When visitors come, she steps into a presentable dress which she has cut down the back and keeps on a peg, so as not to bother changing from her gardening clothes. How practical, yes? I now do the same when I've been painting. And you could too, Grethe, when you are black with ink."

Grethe saw for an instant the blackness of the Pierced One's silhouette. "Yes indeed," she laughed, touching her brow.

"*He* was fulminating against Brandes, naturally," said the little poet, and again his spectacles flashed. "*Gud hjalpe os*, who could have foreseen such a puritanical streak in the great Bjørnson!"

"But at least," said another guest, drawing them into a circle of conversation, "Bjørnson has opened up discussion everywhere. What he thinks. What Brandes thinks. All Scandinavia is thrashing out the question of bourgeois morality, which is more than you can say for the Continent."

"But only morality's sexual side," protested the poet's wife.

"Exactly," the poet agreed. "Bjørnson sees modern society as strangled by sexual hypocrisy. He blames men and demands that they practice the same purity as women. Brandes demands that women be free to practice the same impurities as men."

"What a dreadful little nutshell you put it into," a woman objected.

"I do not. It is an issue of the greatest importance. But I would that *all* inequities were the issue."

"You want the ultimate explosion," Grethe said quietly. "Of everything that is wrong and bad and cruel. Yes, that is understandable."

"Understandable, but unfeasible," someone else put in. "There will never be an Eden blasted out on our planet. Still, we must be thankful for our iconoclasts—thank God for Brandes. Whom, by the way, we had hoped to see here tonight, but Holger says he is abroad?"

"Yes," Grethe said, "visiting a Swiss writer. Or I think he's German, but a Swiss citizen. Not well known, but Brandes says he should be. Do you know the name Nietzsche, or something like that? You must ask Holger."

"And what of Holger's work? He looks as if he's been at it very hard."

"Oh, he's worn himself out, but he is very pleased with what he's done. You must ask him to show you the canvases."

And excusing herself with a smile, she passed on from the group. But again she felt confused. For Holger had not been painting at all lately. He was too worried. His eye sockets were dark, there was a look of suffering on his face. She could not bear that he suffered. What could worry him so badly that he did not paint?

Scharwenka's "Polish Dance" was ringing out from the mandolin, the gayest of all melodies. Her cheeks were pink. She wanted to be happy.

"Every time I come, Grethe, I mean to ask you. Who is the young man in the silhouette?" A woman friend drew her over to the wall of pictures. "The line of his features is yours exactly."

"He is my grandfather," Grethe replied with a pleasant nod.

"Ah, it shows. And have I met him? Is he here tonight?"

"But my dear, he would be almost a hundred. No, he is dead. I never knew him. Nor did my father, even, for he died before my father's birth."

"Ah, the pity. An accident."

"No, he was an officer with the Grande Armée, a volunteer. He was killed at Leipzig."

She sat deep within the petals of a flower that swung gently in the wind. Everything was quiet and beautiful. At some great distance, far beyond the flower's rim, she talked easily about the Pierced One while looking at his framed silhouette on the wall. Though always she kept her distance from it she was not disturbed as she stood there, for she was not there at all, but in a wind-swung velvet bell, in a silent, cradled world where nothing happened and nothing mattered. And presently, as they walked on talking of other things, the flower dissolved in the surround of music and voices.

As they neared one of the voices, that of a bearded sculptor, her friend gave an amused headshake.

"Is he still going on about his rubbings? His entire atelier is hung with them. It looks more like the interior of a church than the studio of an atheist."

"But don't forget," Grethe reminded her, with quiet humor, "he takes rubbings only from the most ancient churches, only those bearing the pagan influence. Does that not restore him to our enlightened ranks?"

"One may use either chalk or charcoal," he was telling a captive audience of two or three. "The finest I have ever done was at Ribe Cathedral, of the lion head and dragons on the great bronze cat portal. Which portal is so named because tradition has it that the church was built in honor of a cat, and that this cat is commemorated by the lion head."

Grethe turned.

"But how charming," she interjected, although it was much more than charming: she was certain that Olaf was the cat honored in the great bronze door of Ribe Cathedral. "And which do you prefer, chalk or charcoal?" she enquired in her friendly manner, while busily consigning the portal to a bright corner of her mind. When she told Olaf about it, he would meow back with pride: yes, I founded Ribe Cathedral . . . but a sudden small frown came cutting between her eyes, for somehow this thought was terribly wrong, was frightening . . .

"Each has its merits," replied the sculptor. "But I didn't know you were so keen on the subject, Fru Rosted, you look positively riveted. You see," he said to the others, "I am not such a bore as you think."

There was laughter and Grethe laughed too, the preceding moment vanishing from her mind.

"He plays good," the maid said. She stood with her arms crossed, one big broad foot tapping in rhythm on the floor. She felt perfectly at ease to address the nearest of her neighbors, who answered agreeably.

"Yes, he does. He would rather play than write."

"Well, naturally," she replied with some impatience. "They can't write."

Her neighbor gave a puzzled nod and sipped his wine. His hair fell to his shoulders. He had on a worn corduroy jacket no gentleman would be seen in. What did the Rosteds want with people like this? Then her attention was caught by the opening of the double doors and the appearance of Cook's angry red face. She stared around, but the girl was unperturbed: Cook would never dare to step inside. The door closed. But now the music had stopped again. He was relighting a cigar—a cigar, what nerve, a hired gypsy—but her thoughts were on other things as she went back to the table. Why shouldn't she take up one of the delicate, long-stemmed crystal glasses, pour into it the lovely ruby wine—the plain white did not appeal—and walk around where she pleased?

Sipping, she moved among the figures in the rosy glow of the lamps. She had no fear of the mistress's glance, for the mistress knew that she knew, and would not dare cross her. Indeed, the girl wished for the great moment of confrontation. But when it came, when she found herself passing right by Fru Rosted's shoulder, she felt suddenly uneasy, the glass in her hand felt enormous.

"Really, aren't you overdoing it a bit?" Grethe remarked.

And that was to be all, the girl realized. For the mistress was already turning back to her conversation. She walked on. It had been a dramatic, a splendid moment. If only she had music too—and at that instant it broke forth again. Everything, it seemed was in her power.

Latecomers were arriving, cheeks red from the cold autumn night outside. Grethe went to welcome them, detained for a moment by a guest who sent a beaming nod in the direction of the strolling, sipping maid.

"How very democratic. How original."

"How perhaps too original," she answered with a smiling headshake as she went on. And she did not even care for the girl, with her false, whee- dling ways. But she was sorry for her, so matronly looking, so dreadfully, cruelly plain, as if God had singled her out for punishment. It was little enough that the girl should also take pleasure in this evening.

"I am so glad you could come," she said happily to the late arrivals, shaking hands, kissing cheeks, indicating the table of refreshments, and to the tingling brilliance of the mandolin she joined Holger and Onkel, putting her arm through her husband's.

"Do you know," she said to Onkel, "I've not heard a word about your trip."

"Don't worry," he told her in his drily affectionate way, "you will hear more than you wish to."

"You will stay over? You must. Mustn't Onkel?"

"Of course you must," Holger agreed, as if he and his uncle had not already decided on that, for in the morning they must talk about Grethe. And yet, with her arm so warm in his, her face smiling up at him with animation and love, he wondered how he could have thought such a discussion necessary.

Onkel fitted an Italian cigarette into his ivory holder. He lit it and blew the smoke away.

"I will stay over with pleasure."

But he felt guilty toward his nephew, for he intended not to discuss Grethe with him, but to discuss him with Grethe. He was glad that she bore up so well under her husband's unsound imaginings, that she possessed the inner strength to maintain her charm and naturalness in what must be a crushing situation. He was sorry for them both, these two young people whom he dearly loved, and he said with de- termined cheer, "And how have the boys been? Getting along all right without their old uncle?"

"Oh, they've grown so much over the summer," Grethe told him.

"But they're still the same, one all crayons and colors, the other all mathematics."

"And still wants to be an engineer?"

"Oh, wants to build a bridge to China," Holger said with a laugh. "Not impossible at seven."

And it was all so pleasant and usual, Onkel thought, that he could almost believe nothing was amiss. Holger bright-faced and easy, and Grethe the same. He wondered if it was his imagination that had so darkly colored Holger's words. He would be more than relieved to think so; he would give great thanks.

"You have returned to an early autumn," Grethe was telling him.

"Early and severe, but invigorating. Ah, it's fine to go away, but much finer to come home."

She heard the Pierced One's cry. Anguished, anguished. Then only music, voices all around, Holger saying, "Then you'll enjoy a dip in the sea tomorrow," and Onkel replying, "No, I'll enjoy *you* enjoying it," and to Grethe their faces were as remote and unhuman as diagrams, as were all the faces in the room, but now she sat deep within the bell of a flower that swung quietly, quietly, in the sunny air, and now she stood again with her arm in her husband's, and listened to Onkel describe the sea at Rimini. She gazed around the room filled with music and friends. Love and friendship were the true things. And kindness, courage, honor. The true things, the real things. She cherished them. And beauty. And faith. And the happiness of Holger's warm arm in hers.

All three people were happy, Grethe smiling up at Holger, he smiling down at her with all his anxiety banished, and Onkel thankful to admit to himself his alarmism. And the maid was happy too, pouring herself another glass of the lovely ruby wine.

☙❧

When the last carriage had driven away, when the maid in several trips had returned the plates and platters and bottles and glasses to the kitchen, she sat down with the remainder of the apple cake.

"You should be dismissed," Cook snorted. "Staying in there the whole time. What's the mistress thinking of?"

"She likes me."

"Nobody likes you."

The girl shrugged. She and the other servants ate very well, but a cake like this, smothered in whipped cream, was a delicacy not often on their menu. There were a few good mouthfuls left. "What about the gypsy?" she asked when she had swallowed them. "Did he come by for a hare?"

"What gypsy?"

"The one what played the music."

"Wasn't any gypsy came in here."

"He played good. But the rest, I wouldn't give you an øre for the lot. Not dressed proper, and half of them sitting on the floor."

"Because they're bohemians. That's what they're called. What would you know?"

"I know a lot more than *you* do."

And filled with the shimmering power that had been hers all evening, she got up to leave.

"No, you don't, Miss. This here's for you to clean up. Her who takes in the tray, she does the dishes. And do them good!"

Conceited lump, she said to herself as she went upstairs to bed.

The maid grimaced at her task, but got through it with great dispatch, splashing water everywhere. Barely washed and not dried, things were clattered into cabinets and drawers. "That's that!" Then she checked to see if the window was partly open on its hasp for the wretched cat, who, as she extinguished the gas lamps and took up a candle, was roaming through the woods, fur stirring in the cold wind, nostrils filled with the smell of damp, pungent soil.

Before retiring, Grethe, in her nightgown and robe, took a candle into the boys' room. Both were deeply asleep. Asleep they could be twins; awake they were very different, though united in rambunctiousness. She should be sterner, but it was not her nature. Leaning over, she kissed one on his cheek, and turning to the other, kissed him on his. On the floor by their bed lay the little rug of yellow roses she had done last year. It sees good use, she thought with a smile. Sometimes it was a ship they sailed away on, sometimes a flying carpet and they swooped around the world, always squashed close together so that their toes didn't touch the floorboards. And when they came back they had been to Arabia, they said, or to where the wild Indians were, and once to the moon. The rug was also a place to wrestle on, or to lie across as one colored his pictures and the other wrote out his figures. Both of them quiet now, eyelashes like miniature fans, hair tousled in the candlelight.

Softly closing the door behind her, Grethe blew out the friendly glow of the candle and stood still. In the darkness, that was when she went down to the Pierced One, when others slept. Because he called to her. He was calling now. "Grethe! Grethe!" came the terrible cry, and she must go to him, she must or else he would devour the world with his pain and horror and anguish—devour Holger, the boys, herself, all the world—

Coming along the hall downstairs, the maid blew out her candle. It was Cook, the old bitch, descending the stairs to see if she was still scrubbing and polishing, doing everything right. But it wasn't Cook's heavy tread, and whoever it was had neither lamp nor candle. It was the mistress whom she made out. She stood flat against the wall as the figure walked past her, hurriedly, intent.

Grethe opened the double doors to the drawing room. His cries had stopped, now that she had come. She went inside, recalling that there had been a party earlier. A lovely party, but now the room was dark, silent. "Why have I come here?" she asked herself. She could not remember. Perhaps to find Olaf? "Olaf, where are you?" she called softly, and heard his meow from a corner: "I founded Ribe Cathedral." "Oh, I know, Olaf, and that is so splendid," she whispered, looking in the dark for him, feeling around furniture and softly calling his name. Suddenly she was jolted by the Pierced One's cry—of course, that was why she had come, and she went in terror toward his silhouette on the wall. She could not see it in the darkness, but she knew where it hung among the other pictures. Never in daylight did she look at it, would not, could not, but when he called her at night, then she was forced to; and he knew if she trained her eyes somewhere else. She must needs stare through the darkness, straight into his darkness, and that brought him peace, that quelled his terrible cries . . .

The maid had followed her mistress into the room. How grand and reckless of Fru Rosted to have her lover here—right into the house the baron had crept, and they were playing a love game in the dark, him hiding, her calling and searching, and now standing very still in her robe, hair all down, waiting breathlessly for him to leap forth and pulsing, panting, drag her in his arms to the floor.

Prickles of excitement ran down the girl's spine. It wasn't proper to watch, she knew that, but how could she help herself? And in her eagerness not to be seen, she darted, bent low, to crouch behind a table, tripping heavily and sending the table over with a crash of itself and everything on it.

Fru Rosted screamed. She screamed and screamed. She kept screaming. The girl, lying frozen with fear on the floor, finally scrabbled to her feet and blundered through the room to the open double doors, where she ran into what seemed to be the entire household, which had come thundering down the stairs.

Grethe's screams had become sobs when Holger reached her side. He sat down with her, holding her comfortingly until she grew quiet.

She looked around the room with no understanding of why she was there. Her heart pounded in her chest, her hands in her lap shook.

"What is it, Grethe? What has happened?" he asked her.

"I don't know . . ."

"I thought you had gone to the children's room."

"I did . . ."

"But why are you down here? Why were you screaming?"

"I don't know . . ."

And she broke into sobs again.

The maid stood looking on in a tremble. The old uncle was asking everyone to go back upstairs. Only she was requested to stay, and the nursemaid, who sat down by the mistress as Hr. Rosted, with a worried, lingering caress of his wife's arm, got up. The girl's shimmering power had collapsed. She wanted only to crawl into bed and forget the whole night.

"You were here too," Hr. Rosted said to her. He and the old uncle stood before her in their bare feet and nightshirts, horribly embarrassing.

"I was, Herre," she answered nervously. "I come from the kitchen and seen the mistress go in here . . . like sleepwalking, you know? So not to scare her I blew out my candle . . . and I come in and I bumped over the table there. That set her to screaming. I'm sorry as anything, Herre."

"But Fru Rosted doesn't sleepwalk. She never has."

"Only it's what I thought, Herre."

"We'll send for the doctor," Onkel said to his nephew, for Grethe's sobbing, as the nurse tried to soothe her, was clearly hysterical. He rubbed his brow, knowing that what Holger had told him earlier was true, and stood listening to the poor fellow interrogate the frightened maid, as if she could somehow put everything right.

"Mightn't Fru Rosted just have come down to retrieve something she forgot at the party?" Holger asked. "Isn't that more likely?"

"That's it, Herre, she was searching all over . . ." But now her story was getting mixed up. Rattled, she bit her lip. "I mean I didn't see anybody. She was talking, but they didn't answer."

"But who should be here?"

"Nobody!"

"Why do you shout?"

"Leave her alone," Onkel whispered.

"Why do you shout?" Holger insisted.

Then anger surged up in her—always to be polite and bobbing her head with Fru and Herre, and being grateful to drink a glass of wine with those seedy bohemians, and putting up with Cook's insults and having to do all the dishes, and only wanting to fall into bed and forget everything, but having to stand here before the magnificent Hr. Rosted in his nightshirt which he didn't even notice, so anxious was he to pound her into the ground with his questions.

"She's got a lover!" she said in a furious rush.

Then she felt better. More trembly and nervous, but strong, seeing the look on his face.

"Rubbish!" Onkel spat out. "How dare you!"

She needn't say she'd sneaked around in the dark hoping to see the baron leap out and crush Fru Rosted in his arms to the floor; even now she feels hot-faced and guilty for wanting to watch—and she feels stupid too, because the baron isn't here at all. But she's put a wrench in the spokes of these two high-and-mighties before her. She can say what she wants.

"No, he wasn't here, but that's the thought what struck me—that she'd brought him into the house. I was shocked. It's why I turned in a hurry and bumped the table."

"What *are* you talking about! Liar!" shouts Hr. Rosted.

"You can call me a liar, but it's the truth," she shouts back, feeling the power inside her grow and shimmer. "I didn't want to tell, but you forced me to. She's got a lover! And I'm not the only one who knows, everyone knows!"

❦❦❦

Over the ages erosion has broadened the fissure in the cavern roof. Through foliage and gnarled roots a mottled wash of daylight falls, subsumed by darkness almost at once, illuminating nothing of the chamber below. Down there, and in the labyrinth of smaller chambers, water trickles unseen, unheard. Down there nothing changes, although on the earth's surface human creatures have covered their nakedness with animal skins, have gone on to make tools and weapons of stone, and lately to gather and grind the seeds of wild grasses.

· 16 ·

On a raw April morning the Counselor boards a sailing ship in Copenhagen harbor, the wet stone quay a madhouse of wagons and neighs and shouts and bales swinging up in a racket of screaming gulls. Never before has the old man set foot aboard a ship. Never has he sailed anywhere, nor even traveled anywhere by coach—except for his short and futile trip to Helsingør—for the thought of enforced proximity to strangers, of inescapable, scouring eyes, is anathema to him. Even when, in a state of exaltation over his impending marriage, he had entertained visions of a wedding trip to the ancient splendors of Rome, his fear and loathing of travel had prevented anything more than visions. Only because he can no longer exist without his son, because he must go to the battlefield where he fell, because he is driven to it inexorably, is he laboring up a ship's gangplank behind a navvy who bears his portmanteau. The early morning sky is heavily gray, with a slicing wind that plasters wet snow against his cloak. Spring has not yet come, but he can wait no longer.

His exceedingly old face, all sags and brown liver spots and gnarled potato nose, is dominated by fiercely glaring eyes as he gains the deck. Passengers and crew alike, even in the turbulence of thudding bales and swinging hooks, cannot help but turn and stare as something like an immensely broad black bug, heaving from side to side, makes its way rapidly past them, eyes shooting sparks in every direction. Then it is gone.

Down in his cabin the Counselor thrust a handful of coins at the navvy and stood wheezingly alone in a sharp, clean smell of varnished wood. The cabin rocked slightly, with a regular creaking of wood that sounded through the muted loading noises from outside. A single porthole, too high for him to see through, admitted a dim gray light. Setting aside his stick and tapestry-worked satchel, he shook the wetness from his cloak but he did not remove it, for the cabin was not only dim but cold. He did not care, he was already busy. He took out a packet of bread, cheese and dried eel from his satchel and set it on the small table. Laboriously bending, he opened his portmanteau and withdrew his nightclothes and quilted satin dressing gown, and laid them out on the narrow inset bed. He searched for a chamber pot—surely there must be one—and found it in a low cupboard. This he set by the bed. Finally he hung his hat on the knob of the cupboard, the clothes pegs being too high for him to reach. There was nothing more to do. He began to pace.

Every article of clothing the Counselor paced in, as well as those in his portmanteau, was newly made. His tailor had been kept busy for weeks. (The tailor, like his father before him, received enormous payment for his labors, but was sometimes inclined to say to his stubborn client, who insisted on breeches and tailcoats thirty years out of style, "For heaven's sake, Hr. Counselor, trousers are now being worn, and short jackets with flaring lapels, and the Polish greatcoat is much in fashion," but he said nothing, for of course it made no difference what was worn by those less than three feet of squashed proportions, it would always look dreadful no matter the excellence of material and craftsmanship, in fact, to be perfectly honest, an old horse blanket would serve just as well.) Even his cloak was new, although the other was in excellent condition and precisely the same as this, of finest-quality black wool and lined throughout in red-silk rep. But this one was fresh, immaculate. He would have everything fresh and immaculate for his journey.

Thudding back and forth, the Counselor went over in his mind all his preparations. He had his passport, pouch of exchanged money, letter of credit. He was thoroughly familiar with the coach route to be taken when the ship docked at Stralsund tomorrow, for he had traced it many times on the map with his forefinger: from Stralsund to Berlin to Leipzig, a simple and almost straight line south. And there would be no language difficulty, for he spoke German fluently—not to mention French and Latin, in addition to a reading command of Old Icelandic.

"But will we never start?" he asked impatiently.

It seemed a very long time before the loading noises ceased, to be followed by a flurry of shouts and commands. After a while there came a sensation of something huge bearing itself free. There was a swaying, an ardent creaking of wood. He stretched himself on his toes in a vain effort to see out the porthole. Standing back, he could only envision the city as it receded, its flags and green copper spires growing ever fainter through the wind-driven snow and sea spray. He relished the strong roll under his feet. The great sails must be billowing.

The Counselor never did sit down to his bread and cheese and dried eel. He never sat down at all. Reeling from one side of the cabin to the other, smashing forward into the varnished wood and flung back with another smash, he finally managed to toil up on the bed where, with his powerful grip, he clung to a wooden handle mercifully attached to the wall. All day and all night he rose high with the ship and plunged low with it in a shuddering jolt, and rose high again as the crazed creaking of wood vied with the chamber pot's skidding clatter. Groaning with nausea, jarred and battered, he begged that his torture might end, but he never begged to be elsewhere. Nor did he ask himself if it was wise for someone of eighty-six years, hale though he was for his great age, to have set off alone on an immense journey perhaps fraught with unforeseen rigors all the way. He did not ask because he did not care. He cared only that he was going to his son, whether to find his bones, his ghost, or his real, fleshed lad as his lad had always been, he did not know.

The sea began to calm in the morning. The heaving and pitching and the great crashing noises all grew gradually less. The Counselor lay dazed as if he had been pounded with mallets. But he was in one piece, he had survived. He floated along. And eventually, through the high, dim porthole, came a welcome cry of gulls. They were nearing land.

When they docked at Stralsund there came again a tremendous muted flurry of shouts and bustling activity. The Counselor stood waiting impatiently by his portmanteau. His clothes were stale and wrinkled under his cloak, his eyes burned from want of sleep, every bone in his body ached. He did not care. He would rest on the coach to Berlin. Hat clamped on his head, stick and satchel in hand, he spoke to himself with deep seriousness.

"Now you will be stepping on foreign soil. Keep in mind that the Germans will stare just as the Danes always have. You know your shortcomings—your irascibility and rage—but you must not let them interfere with your journey. You want no scenes, no impediments. Remember that people cannot help themselves. You too would gawk if you saw someone who looked like you. This you know very well, and in your journals you have even endeavored to be just and fair. Well, then, endeavor to be just and fair in your actions. Otherwise, your journey might be a very difficult one."

When a porter came into the cabin, stopping dead in his tracks with bulging eyes, the Counselor fought down his usual surge of fury.

"If you will avail yourself of my portmanteau," he said, nostrils distended, "I should like to be conducted to the town's principal coach stop."

But to his amazement this simple request, spoken in perfect, formal German, was not understood. Nor when the man opened his mouth could the Counselor make head or tail of the thick Pomeranian dialect that issued from it. Long minutes were required, the eyes still bulging down at him, before results evolved from mutual linguistic struggle. Then, at last, he was laboring up on deck. There he stood stunned. For he saw no sea or sky, no quay, no town. Only dense dripping fog in which the thighs and hips of passengers bumped and crowded past him after laden porters. Clenching his stick and satchel, he thudded hurriedly after his own.

୦୫ ୫୭

Following the porter along wet cobblestones, the Counselor had almost arrived at a befogged bustlement of horses and coaches when at his heels he heard the gleeful cry of guttersnipes. They came running abreast, crouching low and lurching from side to side with whoops and hoots as the Counselor's pulse banged through his veins. He clenched his teeth. The Copenhagen guttersnipes, whole generations of them, had felt the crack of his stick against their skulls if they dared come near, but these—and it was only a few steps to the coach stop—these he would endure. No clash, no discord, no impediment to his journey. It was no use. Shaking with rage, he lashed out with his stick and sent two of the wretches sprawling, at which moment everything became chaos. The guttersnipes fled, but were replaced by travelers crowding around, jostling, jabbering, gaping down at him. He tried to calm his enraged shaking as he stood inside this ring of trousers and skirts and consuming eyes, but so violently discomposed was he that he jumped when the porter swung down his portmanteau, and in the crowd's resounding babble he grappled, thick-fingered, with the string of his pouch, dropped his stick, spilled coins all over, and in a rage of confusion swung his tapestry-worked satchel in a wild arc at the nether parts surrounding him. The swing missed, and took him in a complete circle from which he staggeringly emerged to a sound of pealing laughter.

"Murderers! Murderers!" he cried.

And he began to spit at them, but his mouth was so dry that despite convulsive efforts he produced hardly any saliva, and still puckering and spluttering, he swung at them again with his satchel, swung at the porter too, swung blindly at everything and everyone, and grabbing up his stick in the babbling and laughing, he brandished it ferociously and plowed through the parting figures to the nearest loading coach.

"The transportation charge!" he cried at the gawking driver. "What is it! What is it!"

He saw that the words met with no understanding.

"I go to Leipzig via Berlin!" he cried again, wheezing like a bellows. "What is the transportation charge to Berlin!—*Berlin! Berlin!*"

And in the noise of the crowd, which had followed on his heels, he cupped his madly shaking hand to his ear. The driver's thick dialect told him nothing, but the headshake did: this was not the coach to Berlin.

"I will go anyway!" he almost screamed—anywhere, anywhere to be gone from this nightmare town. "Do you go south at least?—*South! South!* Do you go *south?*"

Another headshake, joined by a thumb pointing west.

"I care not! I care not!"

Thus in less than the half of an hour since he had emerged from the depths of the ship, the Counselor, with his portmanteau strapped to the roof of the coach, sat headed in the wrong direction. He sat dazed, wheezing, still shaking in every limb. He fumbled straight his hat, which had got badly awry, and shot the stares around him a trembling look of hatred. The coach creaked. Moisture trickled down the outside of the windows. Streets passed in the thick fog. All at once he was deathly tired. Everything had collapsed in those few horrible minutes—his dignity, his fortitude, his well-laid plans. And he had brought it all on himself. Had he remained calm, as he had determined to do, he would not be sitting here in a blundering detour. Yet he had survived, even as he had survived the battering of the ship. Fogged streets gave way to fogged countryside. The wheels began to rumble. The wet panes rattled.

⊂℞℈⊃

The Counselor had got himself badly off the beaten path. When the coach reached the distant village which was its destination, he commenced his journey south, but his map had pitched from under his cloak during the wild swings of his satchel, and he could not divine his whereabouts. Moreover, language difficulties prevented light from being shed on this predicament. Days passed. The dense fog never lifted. What little he could see of the land was flat, desolate. He felt himself borne deeper and deeper into uncharted territory.

"Berlin" and "south" were the two words he relied upon, anything more complex proving hopeless in these hinterlands whose dialect was even more impenetrable than the obscure slurpings of Stralsund. Who knew if he was comprehended by the drivers of the small, shabby coaches that carried him from one isolated gray village to the next? The hooves clopped. The rustics he sat with drilled holes through him with steady, beady eyes. In one coach he had been prodded experimentally with the ferrule of an umbrella. At this he had almost screamed aloud, but he knew from that terrible day in Stralsund, if he had not been sure before, that he must never grow frenzied.

He put up at village inns that were not much more than hovels, and here too he kept tight control of his combustible nature. Though confronted by bug-eyed innkeepers, by patrons hurrying over to see what this was that had entered, by domestics gaping from the kitchen, he expressed no more than his fierce glare. And having requested a night's lodging and his meal brought up to him—this done in sign language, words being useless, and written words too, since no one could read—he eventually found himself wheezing up dark stairs behind a servant lugging his portmanteau.

The rooms were all similar. Very small with grayish whitewashed walls. A basin and jug, an iron bed with straw-stuffed mattress, a table and chair, a window looking out on fog. Damp and chilly rooms, but at least private. Alone, he removed his hat and worked off his cloak.

He was always tired, he never had sufficient sleep. At home it was no matter that he needed some two hours to make his morning wash and struggle into his garments, but here he must rise in the dead of night if he was to accomplish his task in time to catch the early coach. He had grown sorely tempted to retire in his clothes, but this was repulsive to him as a fastidious gentleman.

"Fastidious!" he spat.

His unpowdered hair felt barbaric on his head. Bristles covered his jowls. In all his planning, he had forgotten that he would need the services of a barber. But to have a strange barber lean over him, bulging eyes only centimeters away—no, the thought was too much. Yet it was the least of his troubles. The coach journey from Stralsund to Leipzig would have taken perhaps five or six days, whereas he had been on the road a week already and had not even reached Berlin.

"Will I never get where I am going!" he would ask himself, each evening coming closer to panic. "Will I never come free of this godforsaken back country!" And then, "Enough, enough. It will come out all right."

He worked his quilted satin dressing gown on over his clothes. For further warmth he wrapped one of his huge pairs of drawers around his head. Then, turning to what was important, he maneuvered himself up into the chair and with his tinderbox lit a stump of tallow on the table before him. Putting on his spectacles, he withdrew from his inner pocket two letters. One was written in French, dated 20 November 1813.

. . . knowing of course that you will receive official notification of your son's death, but knowing too that that cannot assuage your need as a father to know the circumstances surrounding it. As a fellow officer of your son, I can tell you at once that his death was swift. He did not suffer. On that morning of 16 October we were deployed some two leagues from Leipzig near the village of Möckern, where at about nine o'clock the shelling commenced.

Hours later the ferocity of the battle had not diminished. To our left Möckern was burning, and the setting sun shone through its flames, while around us there was scarcely a space in the air or on the ground where shells were not bursting. In this chaos I saw your son, who was riding a short distance from me, sit back suddenly in his saddle and fall. I pursued him, his foot was caught in his stirrup, and halting his horse I dismounted from mine and knelt beside him. I saw that he had been pierced through the heart by a shell fragment. His face was untouched and was calm. I was then forced to remount and leave behind this young foreign volunteer who was the best of comrades and bravest of soldiers. Where he is buried, or indeed were all the men who fell that day, and the next and the next, I cannot tell you . . . what was left of the Grande Armée was three long and indescribable weeks in its retreat to the Rhine, which is why I write only now . . .

The other letter, dated 13 October 1813, and written in Danish, was the last word the Counselor had had from his son. The letter was far more frayed than the other, for it had been reread endlessly, although when it had arrived fully four months after its writer's death, the old man had been thrown into such anguish that for many hours he had been unable to bring himself to read it.

My Dearest Father,
*We have been on the march for a week, much rain but now sun. We are not far from Leipzig and are readying to move on, thus these lines must be extremely brief, but they will at least let you know that I am well. And you, Father, you must keep very well, for you are as dear to me as I am to you. And you must not worry about me. Can you feel the sun on the page as I write? It is a fine morning, warm and fresh and clear—*de bonne augure *as they say. I must leave you now. I embrace you.*

Your devoted son

The Counselor smoothed the page with his broad, gnarled fingers, and it seemed to him, as it so often did, that he could feel the sun's warmth in the fibers of the paper. Was his lad not warm and alive this very moment, waiting for him . . . ? The thought was entirely irrational. His quest was to find the boy's grave. There he would put flowers, lilac, as grew in the courtyard at home where they had always walked together. He would find nothing more than the grave, for there could be nothing more than that.

Pierced through the heart. But the French officer had dismounted for only a moment. How could he have been certain of what he saw? And in such chaos? Perhaps the lad was only wounded, only unconscious. And then, his foot caught in the stirrup as it was, he had been dragged away by his horse. Yes, dragged away from the field of battle. Yes, and had somehow survived, lived on, and at this moment stood waiting near Möckern . . .

It was a senseless, senseless thought. Yet in the course of these two and a half years, this thought had come to seem the only possible truth. Had not the boy always been attended by miracles? His very conception had been a miracle. And when the fence spike had pierced so near his heart but not through it—surely that miracle was also true of the shell fragment, and had the French officer remained a moment longer he would have realized this . . .

It was all feverish imagining. The fever of sorrow that had never calmed. He understood this. The grave was all that he would find, if indeed he would find that much. He knew only that it must be near the village of Möckern, where he would take himself directly from Leipzig. Möckern, of course, had burned down, the setting sun had shone through its flames, had shone in a streaming, radiant light . . . truly, could his lad have been annihilated, any more than the sun itself could be, which rose ever and ever again . . . ?

He started at the sound of a knock on the door. He unwrapped the drawers from around his head. A maidservant entered, eyes on stalks, hastily set the tray down and hastily departed. Cold cuts of mutton, gherkins, barley soup. He rewrapped the drawers around his head. His spoon clinked in the silence.

☙ ❧

The hugely broad beetlelike dwarf was gaining fame throughout the countryside, word spreading from one remote village to the next. A small crowd would now stand waiting in the fog as he labored down from a coach, all eyes consuming this amazing apparition in its black enveloping cloak. It was said to be mute, ancient. The superstitious among them believed it was a creature that had crawled up from the netherworld through a crack in the earth, perhaps centuries ago. Others, equally mesmerized, believed it to be an aged circus grotesque. All moved with it as it plunged to the inn door, several hands managing to tweak its cloak or bump fleetingly down its back before it banged inside, where more people than ever converged around it. They watched its fingers tumultuously request a room. They followed its plunging course to the staircase up which, thunderingly, blunderingly, it disappeared into the darkness.

In his room, the Counselor no longer tried to fight down his panic.

"I am lost! Lost among deaf, brutish, benighted clods! Lost in fog that never lifts!"

The days went on. The Counselor no longer knew how long he had been traveling. His goal of Berlin, not even to speak of Leipzig, had come to seem a hopeless fantasy. He felt that he would never come free of these fogged wastelands, of hands that snatched at his cloak, of legs that pressed around him in every dingy inn, of eyes whose devouringness seemed to rise from the depths of the Dark Ages.

As the days went on, the Counselor began to feel himself coming apart. It was like a cracking and breaking inside of him, inside his mind, his body, a crumbling, and he knew he had not survived his journey, although his heart still seemed to beat and his legs to move.

He now went to bed in his clothes and cloak and boots. He had no energy for his morning ablutions, nor to bend down and work open his portmanteau, nor often even to eat. In the darkness, lying haggard in his unchanged and fetid garments, he would sometimes feel his mind give a jerk: had he latched the door? What if they all came bursting in? Had he latched it? Had he forgotten? What was to keep them from bursting inside and perpetrating some depraved medieval cruelty upon him, some unspeakable horror? But even in his pounding fear he seldom labored down from bed to feel for the latch, for he was too weary, too broken, and perhaps, after all, it would be a mercy to be finished off.

One night his door was flung open with a bang. The Counselor clutched his face. His fingernails dug into his whiskered flesh. The door slammed to. Someone walked across the room bumping into things, scraped back the chair and flopped into it. The Counselor heard a groan, the deep, comfortable groan of someone stretching his arms. He heard feet put up on the table. And hiccoughs, a series of hiccoughs. More confused now than terrified, though still trembling, and with a heart that pounded, he settled slightly. The straw mattress crackled.

"Who is that? Is someone there?" asked a voice.

The shock of these words was almost as great as had been the Counselor's initial shock, for they were spoken in a fine and coherent German.

"Who is there?" the voice came again. "Why are you in my room?"

The Counselor tried to collect his flustered thoughts.

"But this is . . ." he began, his voice thick with disuse, as if caked with rust. He cleared his throat. "But this is my room . . ."

"Ah. Apologies. Apologies. I've had too much ale."

And indeed, there was a slight slur to the words. It was a warm, pleasant, good-natured voice.

"I'll leave, if I can get my feet down."

"But stay—" The Counselor lifted a trembling hand in the darkness. "Stay, if you are comfortable. I do not mind. I was not asleep."

"Small wonder. Who can sleep on these straw pallets?"

"Indeed," said the Counselor, clearing his throat once again, and feeling little pricklings all through him, like those in a numb limb coming back to life. "Indeed, our hosts do not err on the side of lavishness."

There came the sound of a laugh, followed by two ringing hiccoughs.

"Forgive me. Most rude. And forgive my familiarity, but do I remark a northern accent?"

"You do indeed, sir. I am from Denmark. From Copenhagen."

"Ah, I have been there. A most beautiful city."

"How true, how true. I never tire of its beauty. *Pulcritudo animam alet.*"

"*Et anima est aeterna.*"

The Counselor felt as if riches were being spilled upon him. Could he be imagining this marvelous conversation? His weariness had vanished; his odorous clothes, the chill of the small drab room, the heavy fog that hung outside—none of it mattered. He was suffused by a glow of well-being. He felt as light, as easy, as if wine flowed through his veins. He smiled broadly into the darkness.

"I had not thought to be speaking Latin tonight."

"Nor I," said the voice. "A most agreeable surprise. But shall we not see each other as we talk? Let us light a candle."

"A candle?" The Counselor bit his knuckle. His mind rushed in circles. "No, no, we cannot," he said in an inspired lie, "for they have neglected to provide one."

"There you are. What can one expect of these cowsheds that pass for inns? I would not be staying here but that my carriage cracked a wheel, and I must wait until it is mended on the morrow. I'm on my way to Wismar. And you, sir, where do you go?"

"I—? Why, I go to Leipzig."

"Leipzig? But my good sir, you are exceedingly distant from any high road. How come you to be in so remote a region?"

The Counselor pinched his lips in the darkness. Then he came out with a sociable little laugh.

"Well, you see, I chose to go by way of the lesser traveled roads so that I might view more than is the lot of the usual tourist. But what an irony, for I have viewed nothing but fog, fog and more fog. And the poor accommodations are scarcely to be borne, not to speak of these poky little country coaches, which," he added for the sheer delight of it, "cramp the legs dreadfully when one is as tall as I. Yes, in fact," he went on with a dawning thought, "you might advise me, for I should like to avail myself of a better traveled route."

And he waited with indrawn breath.

"Leipzig, you say? Then you must go by way of Berlin. Let me think a moment . . . Yes, take the coach to Karnitz. From there take another to Krause. And from there take another to Neustrelitz, which is on the Stralsund–Berlin high road, and there board the Berlin coach."

The Counselor's heart banged in his chest. He repeated aloud: "Karnitz. Krause. Neustrelitz."

"And in Berlin, I recommend the Bayrischer Hof. If you plan to stay a day or two, it is near everything you might wish to enjoy—the Tiergarten, the German National Theater, the Royal Opera House."

"Excellent! Excellent! I thank you heartily." And in his bedazzled state, the Counselor actually envisioned himself entering these places and partaking of their various pleasures.

"Here in these Mecklenburg backwaters, I think not a soul has ever traveled farther than to the next village, that in itself being an event. They are starved for events. Were you downstairs this afternoon when the grotesque came in?"

The Counselor's face clenched as if from a blow. He swallowed. He ran his tongue over his lips.

"No, I was not," he said.

"Why, it was a festivity. They almost trampled the poor wretch in their excitement. I caught but a glimpse of him in the melée, a homunculus most dreadfully deformed. And mute, as I learned later. An imbecile, I suspect. And think, this poor miscreation is being exhibited throughout the region."

The Counselor fought to keep his voice steady.

"Exhibited?"

"From what I understand. I have been sitting for hours in the ale room downstairs, there being nothing else to do here. And the abysmal things I listened to—you cannot imagine. Yes, drivers take this hapless freak aboard and set him off wherever a crowd awaits. The entire countryside wants to see him. He has already been transported nearly everywhere."

The Counselor began breathing hard. He felt cold all over.

"And the superstition is—I do not lie—that this aberration has crawled up from the netherworld, worked himself out from a crack in the earth like an overlarge bug."

The Counselor suddenly feared he would sob.

"They snatch and poke at him. And do you know why? Because this brings them great good luck. Oh yes, it is far more efficacious than poking a humpback's crook, for our fellow here is a true creature of nightmare come from another world. Another world, my foot—he has clearly wandered from an asylum, poor wretch."

"And you!" The Counselor burst out in a sob. "Why did you not help him! You call yourself a Christian!"

"I—I do not recall that we discussed religion . . ."

"You have no mercy! You are all the same!"

And shoving himself violently off the bed, he kicked with all his strength at the chair and its occupant.

"All the same! All the same!"

No longer sobbing but snorting and raging, he felt tumultuously around the tabletop for the candle stump, struck fire from his tinderbox and lit the wick. He flung only a brief glance at the figure who stood flattened against the wall as if carved from stone—a white-faced, youngish, plumpish man fashionably dressed. He was of no interest. The only thing that boiled and crashed in the Counselor's mind was to be on his way, to gather his things and be off. He barged around in a fury, clamping his hat on his head, grabbing up his stick, his satchel.

"Carry my portmanteau!" he cried at the figure.

And he banged out the door. He pounded down the dark stairs and through the deserted ground floor.

"All the same! Vermin! Vermin!"

Outside on the dirt street he stood wheezing and catching his breath. Then he began to pace back and forth in the black night fog. The door opened. His portmanteau was quickly set down. The door closed. Moisture fell in drops from the brim of his hat as he thudded furiously to and fro. Thudded, thudded until the black fog turned slowly to gray and he heard the sound of hooves. When the coach came to a stop and the driver climbed down, the Counselor shouted up into his face:

"Karnitz! Karnitz! That is where I want to go! Do you understand, you piece of filth! Karnitz!"

Inside he heaved himself up onto a seat and shook an enraged fist at the other occupants, an elderly peasant couple.

"Bring you luck! I'll bring you luck, you vermin!"

Then, attending to what was important, he wheezed hoardingly to himself, "Karnitz, Krause, Neustrelitz. Karnitz, Krause, Neustrelitz."

That afternoon in Karnitz he transferred to the coach to Krause.

"Krause!" he cried at the driver. "Do you understand, you swine! Krause!"

And laboring inside, he heaved himself up by a window. He sat jouncing and rocking as the day wore on, exhausted to his very marrow, bewhiskered, smelly under his cloak, but exultant, for the fog was growing less dense. It was thinning, thinning all the time.

Suddenly he felt the kiss of the sun through the glass. Green meadows went by, grazing cows. So great was his joy to have come free of the cruel gray labyrinth that laughter shook him. His fellow passengers stirred in their seats and exclaimed to each other. He threw them a contemptuous, dismissive swipe of his hand and kept laughing. The sky that stretched to the horizon was blue, the clear young blue of his lad's eyes.

"I am coming! I am coming!" he cried joyously, and he saw the lad wave from the sunny field near Möckern.

In the evening the coach rumbled alongside a lake. The moon was full. It sent down spangles of silver along the water's surface.

"The beauty, the beauty!" he breathed, and his whole soul ached with joy, so that again he began to laugh aloud, in the overflow of his happiness.

In Krause he took a night coach to Neustrelitz. The moon followed, raining down its silver.

Neustrelitz was a large town. He met with no impenetrable dialect at the coach-stop inn where they arrived in the morning. He requested a room, snarled "Out of my way!" to gawkers, and in his chamber at once began to undress. An hour's struggle had him out of his sour garments. Another hour and he had scrubbed himself almost raw at the basin, splashing out every drop of water from the jug. Wrapped in his quilted satin dressing gown, he climbed onto a chair by the sunny window and rubbed his thick bristly hair with a towel.

"I consider that only now have I begun my journey," he said to himself as he worked. "Yes, now it goes swiftly and well. And all around me is beauty . . . the moon at night, and in the day the sun . . ."

And leaning back, he let the warmth fall across his face. "Yes, beauty is everywhere. Except in man. To think of the tormented pages I have written over these many years, struggling to uphold a just view of humankind. Love of my fellows I could not aspire to, but to fairness, yes. I tried. I tried. Thousands of pages—trash, trash that should be burned! For the honest ravening animal pack is preferable to human beings—butchers, murderers all, vermin, garbage! Thousands of worthless pages . . . but I suffer no pain to know this . . . if I weep, I weep with joy, for soon I shall be hastening across the fields to my lad, ah God! ah God!"

And climbing down, he waddled across the room to the bell cord. He gave his hat, cloak and boots to the servant who came. He ignored the great fish eyes.

"Brush the hat, polish the boots! Clean the spots on the cloak! And send me a barber!"

When the barber arrived, also fish-eyed, the Counselor underwent a moment of irresolution at the thought of being touched by his hands. Then he said, "Shave me!" and got himself into a chair. He clamped shut his eyes at the feel of the cringing fingers on his skin, the knowledge of those bulging eyes centimeters away. He pushed his thoughts to other things. His mind was sharp, crackling.

"And when I wrote to Goethe, I was right! All things are woven into the whole, said Goethe. No they are not, I wrote him, and I was right! Who desires, in any case, to be part of the rot that is humanity!"

"I cannot work, sir, if you talk."

"I? I have not said a word. I have sat here thinking."

The barber shrugged.

"As you wish."

"And I wish my hair powdered."

"I do not have powder. No one uses powder."

"I do! Find some and return tomorrow morning. You will be paid well for your trouble."

In the afternoon the Counselor dug into his meal like a starved man. In the evening he stood by his window and gazed up at the silver moon, enraptured, laughing aloud from time to time. He retired early and slept powerfully.

Fresh, immaculate—boots shined, hat brushed, cloak spotless, wearing clean clothes from his portmanteau, hair powdered, cheeks shaven and fragrant—the Counselor stumped out into the morning. There it stood: the long-sought coach to Berlin. He was flooded with rage as he labored up to an outside seat.

"What is the date!" he demanded of the passenger whom he heaved himself beside. The man, bug-eyed and cringing, pressed himself away.

"What is the date! The date! Are you deaf!"

The man stared before him and murmured coldly, "The tenth of May."

The Counselor flung his head back. He had left Copenhagen the fourteenth of April. More than three weeks he had been led around in circles. "The infamy of it! The infamy!" he cried, but the coach had started, the hooves thundered. He laughed with joy until tears ran down his cheeks. "I am coming! I am coming!" he cried. "My God, how the horses go!"

12 May 1816
Copenhagen

My Dear Brother,

I come immediately to the point of this letter. For some weeks I had not experienced my usual carriage glimpse of Thorkild, thus today I went to his house to ascertain if he was deceased. But his housekeeper—so she referred to herself though it appears an egregious misnomer—told me he had gone on a trip. Yes a trip, you may imagine my astonishment! And when I asked where, she did not know, for he "would not open his trap" as she put it. He has been gone since mid-April. There has been no word from him. In short he has disappeared.

I cannot believe he is alive. Either he has met with foul play, or indeed he went somewhere to put an end to himself. For as I wrote you some time ago, I sensed that this extreme act was building up in him.

The housekeeper believes he will return, for she is without insight or analysis and believes what suits her, and it would suit her ill that he lies dead somewhere though she clearly dislikes him as who does not. In any case I took advantage of my presence there to see for myself the grandchild.

The house is appalling, everything is dusty and dingy and tarnished. Upstairs I conversed with the nursemaid who was hungry for company and said but for prodigal pay she would have left long ago, so uncongenial was the disorder of the house and its hanging silence. The Counselor never came to the nursery, she said, though he had used to visit the babe but frightened it so horribly that it would howl and flee and she confessed she felt the same but practiced control.

He is a child of some three years and is as normally proportioned as his own father was. This confirms what I have often said: that Thorkild's affliction is unique to him and not something carried in the family, about which we must ever worry ourselves lest it suddenly crop up in one of our own. I confess that I had not known what to expect of the child's physiognomy and was greatly relieved, as you will also be to know it.

But to proceed: the babe has no one on his mother's side. This the nursemaid told me, and this is the crux of the matter. For it means all responsibility will fall upon us as nearest of kin. Indeed, all matters of the estate will devolve upon us. Should the house be sold? The child cannot stay there alone with a nursemaid and housekeeper. He must be placed somewhere under a guardianship, and I do consider putting it all in the hands of my lawyers and Thorkild's. They can see to the will, they can see to everything. Yet still we must be involved, simply by virtue of blood. It does not end even with his death! I will write you again soon. You must think about all this.

Bodil

The Counselor on his rumbling perch watched Berlin unfold before him, a large city at whose heart they passed through the columns of a great monument sparkling in the sun.

"Brandenburg Gate," a passenger informed another in loud tones above the noise, and described the Prussian Army's glorious return through this gate after Napoleon's defeat at Leipzig.

The Counselor's head swung violently around.

"I damn him!" he cried. "I damn him who abducted and mis-led the idealistic young! I damn him a thousand times over! I damn him!"

He was still muttering with fury when the coach came to a stop and he began to labor down. The other passengers kept their distance; he did not care, he did not even notice. The baggage was unloaded in a welter of voices, and the Counselor gave a loud laugh, for the

Berlin accent was a collection of clucks and quacks and explosive hissings. Fortunately, he would not have to fathom the splutters of Berlin, for he would be gone again in no time. He gazed with impatience at the massive baroque buildings, at the wide street before him lined with linden trees. Holding his stick and satchel, he stood with his head thrown back, entirely lost in the flickering greengold beauty of the leaves above him. Only the thud of his portmanteau returned him to his surroundings. An hour later, from his rumbling perch atop the Leipzig coach, he watched Berlin fold back, fold back, until open country again spread before him.

❧ ❧

Three days later, on a clear sunny morning, in a jangle of horse bells and clatter of hooves, the Counselor entered Leipzig. His excitement had mounted to such heights that his whole body trembled. Labyrinthian streets, high-pitched roofs, Gothic edifices—these impressions flooded in on him but took no hold. Nor did he remember that this old cultural center had known the likes of Luther and Leibnitz, or that he had ordered many of his books from this city famous for its publishing. Leipzig was but a place he must pass through to his goal of Möckern. He must hire a hackney coach. A hackney coach. This was the thought that filled his entire mind and trembled throughout his body. In perhaps an hour he would be in Möckern.

It was fortunate that the day before, at the stopover at Dessau, the Counselor had replenished his funds at a banking establishment, and had had a barber shave off his newgrown stubble, and a bootblack polish his boots, for in his present state of excitement he could not have attended to these things. Nothing mattered but to find a hackney coach. No sooner had they disembarked, in a large market square, than he rushed thuddingly to the nearest such conveyance.

The driver, florid-faced, with thick gray side-whiskers, dressed in a worn, olive-brown skirted coat, looked down with mouth agape. As with everyone else he encountered, the Counselor did not care about the bugging eyes, scarcely noticed them. Other people were not of his world, they counted for nothing.

"Are you for hire!" he shouted up, and the fellow not answering, still gaping, the Counselor dragged his money pouch out from under his cloak and shook it loudly. "You will be paid double! Triple!"

"Ah no. Ah no," the driver protested, finding his tongue. "I've a deal of respect for circus people."

"Idiot! I am not from a circus. Can you take me to Möckern? Möckern!"

"Möckern? Aye," the fellow answered in his extremely slow, sing-song dialect.

"My portmanteau is by the coach. And make haste!"

While the fellow went for it, with no haste at all, the Counselor climbed, wheezing hard, up onto the driver's seat. He would not be boxed in. He wanted the view.

"I want the view," he told the surprised face when it appeared beside him. The driver shrugged, and slowly stretched his arms.

"We had a circus troupe here five years ago. No, 'twas six . . ."

"I do not care about circuses! Let us start!"

The horses moved off across the square. They passed flower stalls riotous with color, stalls of vegetables and fruit, pens full of cackling fowl, bargaining voices, the Counselor taking no notice of faces that squinted up at his squashed form and stared after him as the hackney passed. Then through winding streets they clopped. His heart pumped harder and harder.

"When shall we be in Möckern?"

"Under the half of an hour. 'Tis not far. And 'tis not much to look at. But Leipzig had its bombardments too. That we did. You must have noticed when you come in."

The Counselor hungered to be alone with his anticipation. He did not want someone talking at his side.

" 'Twas even worse when the fighting was over. We had them all here, French, Prussian, Russian—all the wounded dragged in from the battlefields. I never saw anything like it. Thousands lying in the streets. You'd see some eat on a dead horse and then start in on a dead comrade. And the stench? Shit everywhere. Rotted in their own filth, poor sods. The ones killed in battle, they were the lucky ones. We could smell them too, when a wind come up. Thousands and thousands and thousands—so many that the peasants were put to work burying them. They did a great lot of corpse looting, I've heard. You can't blame them. They were hit harder than we was."

The Counselor tried to block out the voice, but a shaft of clarity penetrated his mind like a knifeblade: he would find nothing but a field with bones beneath it. Nothing else. Then the clarity, even before anguish had fully seized him, crumbled, vanished, had never been. He wondered why he sat twisting his hands. He smoothed the folds of his cloak. Sunlight fell hot on his face. They had emerged from the streets and were clopping across a bridge into open country.

"Can you not speed up the horses?"

"What for? They go as suits them."

"Very well. Very well."

He did not want to argue. He did not want even to speak. His eyes consumed the landscape. How beautiful it was! Wooded hills, green fields, blossoming trees. He felt that his pounding heart would burst with joy.

"I am coming! I am coming!" he cried.

"Why, what is it? Why do you shout?"

The Counselor glanced at the face beside him and, laughing, turned back to his panorama. Odorous hot grass filled his nostrils, and the sweet scent of blossoming trees. He leaned forward, as if to urge on the horses. And then, as the minutes passed, his wildness of joy became an utter stillness of joy, a holding of his soul's breath.

They arrived. There stood the ruined village, and here—"Here! Stop here!" he cried, in a release of his soul's breath. Here stretched the green, sunlit field. The horses drew to a halt. His blood pounded so crashingly in his veins that he very nearly fell from the side of the vehicle as he climbed down to the dirt road. The driver, face wrinkled with puzzlement, watched the creature plunge off through the grass. Heaving from side to side, sometimes stumbling and righting itself with its stick, it made its rushing way to the middle of the field. There it stopped and stood absolutely still, as if waiting. Suddenly it came plunging back.

"Go away!" it cried. "Go away!"

Shrugging, the driver twitched his reins and drew up a little distance to the edge of the village. It consisted mainly of blackened stone ruins with vines growing over, but some cottages had survived and were still lived in. A few peasant folk had come out on the road, where they stood looking out across the field. What was that out there? they wanted to know as he climbed down to stretch his legs.

" 'Tis a circus freak," he told them, "and a very fine one. But odd. No doubt they all are."

Suddenly he yanked back by their collars a pair of children pushing past their elders' legs in a burst of excitement.

"Stay here, you little pisspots. Leave him be."

"What is it he's doing?" one of the peasants asked.

He shook his head.

"I've not the faintest."

They stood looking on. The squashed black form in its tall hat— almost as tall as itself—was plowing all over the field, going in one direction only to veer off and pursue another, rocking from side to side like a ship in a storm.

"He's of a great age," the driver said. "He'll soon wear himself out."

Presently the little group saw that the figure was headed toward them. The peasants watched with enormous eyes. The children hopped up and down, hands pressed with excitement to their cheeks. The driver sighed, for there was nothing worn-out about his onrushing passenger.

"Did you see a horse!" the creature cried up at the peasants, so frenzied his voice, his whole shaking appearance, that the driver put a soothing hand down to his shoulder, which jerked it away.

"In the battle, this horse—the rider's foot caught in the stirrup—this horse, did you see it go by? Did you see it!"

The peasants, still with enormous eyes, looked around at each other at the senselessness of the question.

"A horse?" said one. "There was hundreds."

"But *this* one, did you not see it! Where did it go!" he cried, his face a sweating knot of panic. And given no answer, the creature swung around, cloak whirling, and plunged off again across the field.

Where would a horse go? To flee the chaos, where would it go! And his eyes flared wide as he saw the answer. "I am coming! I am coming!" he cried, pounding and floundering toward a copse of willow trees at the field's far end. There it would have galloped, there the lad waited. Why did I not realize it at once? My God, my God, to waste so much time when all the while—"I am coming! I am coming!" he kept crying in his wild rush, and he stumbled badly, fell hard, and with pain, and raised his head gasping, and in his pain came a rapture so great that he could only press the lad's hand to his breast, sobbing uncontrollably. Then they clung together, rocking back and forth on the grass; and still sobbing, the Counselor lifted his hand to the beloved face, stroking it over and over in trembling tenderness. The boy smiled.

"Why do you weep, Father?"

"He's fell down," one of the peasants said. "Looks like. Hard telling from here."

"I hope he's not hurt himself. No, best you stay," the driver said. "I'll go alone."

"I've missed you so dreadfully, so dreadfully," the Counselor said, still weeping.

"And I you, Father, so dreadfully. But I always knew you would come."

After a time, his sobs diminishing, the Counselor sat back.

"Oh, let me look at you."

His young blue eyes, and his dear lips, and the little mole by one brow. His thick wheaten hair, ruffled by the breeze. His uniform bright in the sun. The grass was bright too, and where they sat was splashed with white wildflowers. Smiling, the lad leaned over and picked one.

The Counselor took it with a radiant smile.

"Do you remember our walks on the Commons?" he asked.

"How fine it will be to go there again." The lad smiled. "Let us go there our first day home."

The driver squinted as he trudged across the field. His wild dwarf was sitting quietly on the grass, a flower in his hand. He appeared to be talking to himself. Hearing someone approach, the creature got to his feet, or rather—fascinating in an awful sort of way—he rolled and heaved and worked his misshapen bulk to a standing position with the help of his stick. He beamed.

"We will be leaving now. Kindly drive us back to Leipzig."

The driver worried all the way back. The dwarf sat inside this time. "We have a great deal to talk about," he had said as he climbed in, making room for another on the seat. From time to time the driver heard a loud, delighted laugh from the interior. What was he to do with this poor creature? You couldn't just leave him and his portmanteau on the market square, like you would an ordinary person with all his mental parts. No, you couldn't, for whatever would become of him?

But in the square he was faced with such briskness, such certitude, such shattering dignity that he fingered his worn olive-brown coat in confusion, and wondered if earlier he had been given to imaginings. He was paid quite enormously, then stood alone.

In the market-square inn, the Counselor orders a double room. The next day he hires a private carriage and coachman, and the journey home begins. They travel a different route from the one he had come on, "for I do not need another sea voyage," he laughs, and the lad laughs too. They go by way of Braunschweig and Hamburg and up through Holstein and Slesvig. They cross on the carriage ferry to Fyn, and on another to Sjaelland, and arrive in Copenhagen on the twenty-seventh of May, a fresh, gusty day with scudding white clouds overhead.

· 17 ·

ᴄ❧ A commotion has dragged the two small boys from the depths of sleep. After some moments, they climb down from their bed and go hesitatingly to the door. The crack they open it to admits a storm of sobs. In the light of a candle held by their great-uncle, their father is helping their mother along the corridor, her sobs as they pass so shrilly tearing that the two watchers are stupefied, hardly even aware that their nurse, who follows with wringing hands, sees the door ajar and is leading them back to their bed with hushed, distracted sounds.

ᴄ❧ ❧ᴆ

Downstairs in the drawing room, the maid had been left standing alone. The master had told her—shouted at her—to stay there. The room was very quiet after all the screaming and sobbing and shouting. And it was cold. The great seagreen ceramic stove, with its painted flowers and winged animals, no longer gave off any heat. During the party, with its mandolin music and ruby wine, and how long ago it now seemed, the room had been filled with cheerful warmth. Now it was filled with coldness and silence, and was nearly as dark as when she'd crashed the table over, for only a single lamp had been hurriedly lit. She could barely make out the table lying on its side over there, but she didn't have to see it, or to dwell on all that had followed, to know that she'd now be sacked.

"So what? It was worth it," she said aloud.

She sat down next to the lamp to wait. The clock across the dark room chimed twice. In her entire life she had never been up so late, but she felt neither sleepy nor tired. She felt only power and impatience. She brought her cold fingers to her mouth, and blew on them with her hot moist breath.

The clock chimed the quarter hour, the half hour. She waited on. Outside the wind was blowing. Sometimes it fell, and was still, and then you could hear sigh after sigh of the surf, like the deep sighs of a lover.

The clock had chimed three times when she heard a carriage draw up outside. The doctor probably. Voices at the door, feet hurrying upstairs. She was the one who had caused all that. She was at the center of it all. And she looked at a vase of big yellow flowers next to her, bright in the lamplight, and at the graceful velvet contours of the sofa she sat on, and at the illumined patch of carpet below, with its so rich and beautiful designs. A lot of good all this finery would do them now. She had said the truth, and their lives had come crashing down in pieces.

She waited on. When the carriage finally departed, she heard Hr. Rosted come into the room. With a deep, sure breath she stood up as he came striding into the lamplight. The dark circles under his eyes were darker yet for his paleness. He had thrown on a robe over his night shirt, but his big angrily striding feet were still naked. They planted themselves before her.

"I want to know what took place here," he demanded.

"I already told you," she answered him boldly.

"What you told were lies. How dare you have said such things!"

"It's the truth!" she shot back, and her power swelled and shimmered within her. "The mistress has got herself a lover, he's a baron!

They meet in the woods, that's where they got their love nest—you go to the woods any day, you only need eyes in your head!"

Holger's brow, as he listened, had slowly wrinkled.

"What kind of asininity is this?" he asked.

"Don't know that word," she muttered, going suddenly sullen, for all the anger had drained from his eyes; the night's great crashing drama, whose very center she was, seemed in danger of fizzling out to nothing.

"It's the truth!" she flung at him again, but he didn't catch fire.

"How old are you?" he asked after some moments.

She shrugged. "Seventeen."

A square, bulky, dough-faced seventeen, more matron to look at than young maiden, but seventeen nevertheless. "Asinine means silly," he said. "It means you've read too many two-øre novelettes."

Insult shot through her, but at the same time she realized that she might not be sacked after all. And that was not the most unwelcome thought in the world, when you came down to it. In fact, it was worth making sure of.

"Well . . . could be I did talk foolishness . . . maybe so, but I didn't mean no wrong, Herre. Believe me, Herre, I never meant no wrong. . . ."

And she stood looking at him with eyes of tragic innocence.

"I'm tired," he murmured, as if to himself, as if he had forgotten all about her. And he left her standing there.

Hr. Rosted was more than tired as he climbed back up the stairs, he was exhausted to his core, and deeply, wretchedly ashamed of himself. Of course the allegations she had shouted earlier had turned out to be rubbish, a witless schoolgirl fancy. Had he really given them credence, even for a second? He felt he could not forgive himself. He well knew that Grethe's estrangement in bed, that chasm between them so agonizing to his heart, had nothing to do with a lover, but was only another and more unbearable expression of the smaller, daily chasms he had come to know—those frightening, indefinable moments when she was there and yet not there. It was an illness of her mind. Nor could he forgive himself his mishandling of this illness, certain of it one moment and certain the next that he had imagined it, doubting his own sanity because she was so often, so entirely, so unquestionably herself. He had fluctuated endlessly, seesawing from low to high, and even tonight, at the party's end, he had felt—God help him—a strong, glowing sureness that all was well.

Onkel looked up from where he sat by the bed.

"You must put some slippers on, my boy. You'll catch pneumonia."

The calm, practical voice was welcome. He nudged his cold feet into his carpet slippers. His uncle, rising from the chair, pressed his arm and left him alone. He sat down and put his hand around Grethe's. The doctor had given her an injection. She slept deeply, with slow, even breaths, her closed eyelids swollen and red from her catastrophic weeping.

♧♥

Holger sat by her bed the remainder of the night. Gradually the room paled to gray, then filled with the lemon-colored tones of a clear, cold, windswept morning. It was late when he saw that Grethe was waking. With a great stretching of arms, her cheeks rosy, she pushed back her tumbled hair.

"Why, whatever are you sitting there for?" she asked with surprise, and yawned cavernously, spreading her fingers over her mouth. "I don't know when I've ever slept so well," she murmured, rubbing the yawn tears from her eyes. "But my dearest, why are you sitting there?"

"Do you not remember?" he said gently. "The doctor gave you an injection."

"An injection?" she asked, puzzled. "The doctor?"

"We called him because . . . do you not remember last night?"

"Yes, of course," she said. "The party."

"No, but after the party. Later."

Sitting back against her pillows with another yawn, Grethe tried to remember. It did seem that something had happened, and then, slowly, it came back to her.

"I do remember . . . yes, I remember that I went down to the drawing room . . . yes, for I thought I heard Olaf meowing, and that perhaps he had been shut in there by mistake. And then—and then while I was looking for him, there came such a sudden loud crashing noise—"

"That wretched maid! The one who served at the party, you know the one. The idiot followed you in there and knocked over a table and everything on it in the dark. Of course it was a shock—we found you in a state of hysteria."

"Hysteria?" Grethe repeated, and shook her head ruefully, with wonder. "But how completely ridiculous of me. Oh, how stupid. What a commotion I've caused, upsetting everyone."

"It wasn't your fault. It was hers alone, and I mean to discharge her."

"Oh, but Holger, surely that is harsh. Surely it was inadvertent."

"Of course it was, but do you know why she followed you in there? She entertained the cretinous notion that you were meeting a lover. Oh yes, in the drawing room, why not? And with forest trysts as well. A baron, I should add."

"A baron?" Grethe was laughing. "Why not a count?"

Holger too was laughing. "But really, it's too much. She's impossible, she does and says whatever she pleases, and she's bone lazy to boot. And it's your own fault, Grethe, you don't put your foot down."

"I know," she sighed. "And I shall. I certainly shall. It's just that she is so ill-favored, Holger, she has been so meanly cheated by nature. And to be so young, it must be dreadfully hard."

He sighed too, with a smiling headshake. "You will never change."

And only then did he realize that he had been conversing as if everything were perfectly normal. He had seesawed right back into the unrealistic frame of mind for which he had condemned himself only hours earlier. Yet he could not question his sense of cheerful ordinariness as they sat there talking, could not restrain his certainty that all was well and good. And when Grethe began to get up, and he suggested she stay in bed until the doctor returned at noon, he could find no argument at all to her reply: "There is no need for him to return. He is overly conscientious."

A rap sounded at the door. Holger went out into the corridor.

"Grethe has rested wonderfully well," he told Onkel, with perhaps too much light in his eyes, for his uncle replied sharply:

"Well, you haven't. You look a wreck."

"I'll bathe. I'll shave."

"That won't help. Don't get your hopes up—I can see it in your eyes."

"But with reason."

Onkel left him with an exasperated shake of his head.

Breakfast was served late. In an apricot morning dress with pleated bodice, her honey-colored hair done up in its shining coil, with rosy cheeks and clear eyes, Grethe looked fresher by far than her husband or uncle-in-law or her two children. The usually lively boys were quiet. Earlier their mother had sat down with them in their room and explained the night's upheaval with a soothing cheer that had at once restored their merriness, but now, above the table talk, her frantic sobs had worked back into their ears; and after a while, finishing their portions, they asked to be excused and went quietly outside to their play.

Grethe told herself that she must talk to the disruptive maid, and sternly, although she had no wish to involve herself further with the events of last night; for it seemed to her, as she took a *rundstykke* on her plate, that more had contributed to the hysteria about which she had been told than a piece of furniture knocked over, at which a black scrap of recollection flew into her mind and out. Buttering the *rundstykke*, she listened with a smile to Holger's rendition of a party guest who had had to be poured into his carriage.

"I hope he wasn't poured out the other side," she remarked with a laugh, and was subjected again to the sweeping black fragment of memory. With a smoothing gesture to her temple, she asked Onkel if he would pass the citron marmalade. "And we must hear more about your trip," she said, noting for an instant that Olaf sat on his shoulder.

As breakfast wore on, as Grethe talked, listened, ate, sipped, she was sometimes in the blue depths of a flower, rocked quietly by the wind; sometimes, with a surge of joy, she saw Olaf hurrying among the plates and dishes toward her; but more often she was struggling against the Pierced One's black silhouette and his horrifying cries, which came sweeping and cutting into her mind with more insistance than ever before.

Onkel marveled at the ease and lightness with which Grethe sipped her coffee and conversed about the party, about Italy, not in the slightest way reminiscent of the wildly weeping figure of the night before. She showed not even a trace of wanness or fatigue, rosy and clear-eyed, imparting the same fresh, quiet, natural radiance as that which always characterized her, and as lucid as the clear blue sky outside. In spite of his best efforts, he felt himself gladly recant his earlier certitude; and as for his nephew, although his bathe and shave had done nothing for the dark circles under his eyes, he looked positively buoyant. But Onkel himself, up in age and thoroughly worn out from the long night, looked forward to a good nap after breakfast. What a pleasure it would be to feel the soft, beginning snore in the back of his throat, he was thinking, when Grethe suddenly rose from her chair in a flurry, capsizing her coffee cup, and ran headlong from the room.

He sat stunned—had he dreamed it? But her chair was empty. So was Holger's. A moment passed before he got stiffly to his feet and hurried into the hall, where he followed a running servant into the drawing room. Other servants stood looking on in frightened bewilderment as Holger struggled with his wife, who was attacking the wall as in a blind fury. Under the pounding and scratching and flailing of her hands paintings madly swayed, and some had struck the floor.

When Onkel had hastened across the room she was straining from Holger's arms.

"I can't bear the cries!" she panted. "I can't bear the cries! I can't bear them!"

Her panting was like an animal's, spittle was on her lips. Holger threw him a trembling, hopeless look, and between the two of them they helped her up to the bedroom once more. She was very quiet now, as if drained, and she lay down on the bed with closed eyes. Holger sat down beside her and took her hand, feeling her fingers tight around his.

"When the doctor returns," she whispered, opening her eyes, "whatever he suggests, I will agree to."

Admitted 14 September 1888. Margrethe Kristine Rosted, age twenty-eight.

Height somewhat above average, weight normal. Fresh complexion, healthy muscle tone. Patient has two children age seven and six, deliveries and recuperation normal. Vision and hearing normal; motor responses normal. No physical disease or malfunction.

Patient was oriented and reasonable, and expressed her desire to cooperate and to be helped. Asked if she could describe her nervous affliction, she did so but could speak only in unspecified terms such as memory difficulties and sporadic feelings of distress. Our clinical picture is thus based on separate interview with her husband, Hr. H. Rosted.

Patient was raised by maternal relatives, having lost mother at birth and father at age seven. No family history of mental disorder, as far as is known. Hr. Rosted describes his wife as lucid and responsible, of a quiet, warm and open nature. Behavioral changes commenced some three months ago, perhaps earlier: gradual withdrawal from sexual intimacy; periods of clarity alternating with increasingly frequent lapses of awareness, patient unable to remember or acknowledge said lapses; within the last twenty-four hours two episodes of extreme and abnormal excitation, the first involving protracted hysterical weeping, the second violence and auditory hallucination.

Provisional diagnosis: dementia praecox.

Treatment: rest; electric massage; camphor baths; chloral hydrate to be administered in the event of mental agitation or insomnia. To ensure her quietude, patient is to have no visitors or letters during the first two months of treatment.

It was a private sanatorium situated in the country some forty kilometers west of Copenhagen. Untouched by the gloom associated with lunatic asylums, its rooms were spacious and tastefully furnished, like those of a fine hotel, and its grounds an attractive, well-tended park, which Hr. Rosted saw blurred as he and his uncle climbed back into the carriage and were driven back down the drive. Through the film of his eyes, the drive gave way to the gates, the gates to the country road.

The old journalist too was grieved to leave Grethe behind, grieved by all that had so calamitously taken place since the small hours of the morning, and spent, hardly able to credit the fact that it was still the same day, if dusk.

From time to time the sound of trotting hooves was overlaid by a boom of wind against the carriage side. Chaff blew by, and dry leaves, and dust from the fine white dirt of the road. He looked out at bending trees, and at the stubble of harvested wheatfields stretching into the distance. From the flatness of the land the sky rose immense, a vast reach of deepening gray through which winged a V of migrating geese.

"They promised nothing," his nephew said huskily, and broke off. From his frock coat he brought out a handkerchief and with it wiped his eyes. He blew his nose. "But they said Grethe has much in her favor . . . her strong desire to be well, and her good physical health. These things are much in her favor . . ."

"They are sure to stand her in good stead," Onkel told him, reaching over and pressing his hand.

They fell silent again. They might have tried to sleep, even in the jounce and sway of the vehicle, but they had entered that stage of fatigue in which sleep is not possible: the bones are leaden but the stomach feels sour and fluttery, the eyes gritty, lidless, incapable of closing.

From time to time, the steep thatched roofs and low half-timbered walls of a farm came dimly into view and passed. The road was a pale ribbon in the gathering darkness. Presently the coachman drew the horses to a halt and lit the lanterns. They started on again in the boom and rattle of wind.

"One has to have faith in them," Holger said at length.

"One can, I think. They're presumably the best."

"They're thorough and conscientious, at any rate."

"Yes, they kept you a long while."

"Their questions were many."

And some he had had no answers to. Was there a history of mental disorder in Grethe's family? He had no idea. "Most of what they asked me I could answer, but not everything," he said. "Grethe's family, for instance. On that subject I could tell them but little."

"Well," said Onkel with a tired hint of his old humor, "you could certainly tell them about her maternal side."

"I did." And even in his sorrow and exhaustion Holger gave a snort of dislike. "A stodgy hidebound lot, I said, and no kindness on their part that they provided a home for Grethe when she was orphaned, for she was lonely there. Stuffy, self-centered prigs, it's a wonder Grethe's mother escaped being like them."

"Yes, she impressed me very favorably the few times I met her."

"I know. You've told us. Nothing like her dreary kin—but at least kin *exist* on that side and one knows their history. On Grethe's father's side there is no one at all. Even about him I could tell them but little. Say again what he was like."

"A fashionable man. A man about town. I quite liked him."

"And you traveled with him that time."

In spite of his own weariness and heavy heart, Onkel laughed a little.

"What a trip . . . Back in 'forty-three, yes. I was twenty." And removing his pince-nez, rubbing his gritty eyes, he felt his raconteur's soul begin to percolate a bit. "Well, you know we were slightly acquainted as distant cousins, but only slightly. He was some ten years older, and a very active figure in the social world. To be honest, and I've told you this before, our family wasn't keen on him. They thought he overdid everything. They've always prided themselves on quiet money, and he was noisy money. Anyway, I scarcely knew him, but then on my first trip to Italy I bumped into him in Trento on my way home, and since he was also returning to Copenhagen we decided to travel back together. Instead of which—"

"You found yourself in Poland."

"Poland," Onkel said with another laugh. "Because suddenly he decided we must change coaches and go to Krakow, for I must see its curious architecture. It's how he was. Impulsive. And possessed of prodigious energy. Hundreds and hundreds of kilometers off our route, but I didn't care, it was an adventure. He was a passionate traveler, had been everywhere. And bright? Witty? You couldn't ask for a better companion. But I'll spare you my usual prolix rendition of our extensive sidetrip. Suffice it to say that fully five weeks after our departure from Trento, we arrived vigorously back in Copenhagen. After which I didn't set eyes on him for perhaps a year."

"Because of his activities."

"Never still. Attending receptions, balls, opera, theater, hosting lavish parties, and an ardent sportsman as well—hunted, rode, sailed, and took up archery, and took up tennis, and took up the piano too, after meeting Liszt on one of his travels, and always traveling, always off somewhere. Among so many activities, one's friendship with him was necessarily of a sporadic nature. I cannot say I ever came to know him well, although I knew him long. He did settle down a good bit when he married, late in life as you know, mid-forties. And extremely happy in that brief year before she was taken in childbirth. And a devoted father to Grethe, as Grethe still remembers from the few years they had together. Yes, I quite liked him. A highly personable man, bright, vital. Too many directions, of course."

"And to go farther back?" Holger probed, rearranging his tired legs in the cramped and rattling darkness.

"His parents?" asked Onkel. "I tell you, I think more young women have died in childbirth than young men have died in war. Truly, the world over, all through history. Well, he got both barrels, as you know. The mother at his birth, the father even before, he who was killed so young at Leipzig."

"Grethe's grandfather, yes. One can see from his silhouette how young he was."

"Twenty-one or two, I think. Whereas his own father was enormously old."

"And what do we know of him, Grethe's great-grandfather?" Holger asked. "Apart from his having been related to our antecedents?"

"That is all, I think. But give me a moment..." And Onkel searched back through his memory, but came up with not a thing. "No, I don't recall anyone in our family ever mentioning him. Apparently no one remembered the man. Possibly someone who lived abroad for long periods? I've no idea. He wasn't in my lifetime."

"Did not Grethe's father remember him?"

"Yes, of course. It was he who once said how enormously old his grandfather was when he died. But he said no more than that. Well, he would scarcely have remembered more, being but a small child then, still called the babe. In any case, he was not at all interested in the past. Only the present."

"It's good you're not like that, Onkel, or else we would be without our family historian."

"Sheer flattery. Like all old people I am merely verbose."

"Not so. Nor do I consider that you've entered the realms of old age."

"You would, if you considered that as a small boy I laid eyes on your great-great-great-grandmother."

"True," Holger agreed. "She who was a hundred."

"Very nearly. I remember she sat in a large gilt and white drawing room and she was very wizened, and her eyes were almost nonexistent, so faded they were, the lids so droopingly wrinkled. And her hands shook in her lap. And her voice shook too, but even so it was a ghostly cackle of command. We children must be introduced to her, bows, curtsies, and then our parents must chat with extreme loudness into her ear. What was said I have no recollection of, for my entire interest in this aged ancestress lay in the knowledge that our papa as a child, and his papa before him, had been given—"

"—bonbons."

"I waited with supreme faith. Any moment those shaking hands would drag out the little treasures from wherever she kept them, perhaps in the folds of her shawl? My faith did not waver even when the brief visit ended. We all departed with a great clatter of feet across the room, but I stared back over my shoulder all the way to the door, for I believed—yes, fully and absolutely believed—that she would raise her arm, whirl it around and around, and send a bonbon flying through the air. How unaccountable that she just sat there gazing after us with those old, old eyes . . ." Onkel gave a smiling headshake in the darkness. "Such is one's singleness of mind at the age of four. A droll little memory. But told all too often, I'm afraid."

"No, it always has charm. Indeed, send a bonbon flying through the air."

A boom shook the carriage side.

The wind was growing stronger yet as they neared the coast, the booms louder. In the increasing noise the two men fell silent again, Onkel with the hope that he had taken his nephew's mind from his pain for at least a little. He stretched the sore muscles of his back and resettled himself stiffly as Holger moved his cramped legs once more.

His legs were heavy as lead, his heart felt heavier yet, as if it filled his whole chest with a sorrowful, dragging density. Even as they had talked, he had kept asking himself underneath, is she lonely? is she frightened? If only, he thought, he could tell the coachman to turn the horses back.

The Sound was turbulent, with whitecaps rushing through the blackness, and a pounding of surf that mixed with the beech woods' churning roar. They climbed down from the carriage holding fast their top hats in the battering wind, and came into an emptiness of warmth and light.

Their things were taken. They declined supper, too tired to think of eating. Holger went upstairs to the boys' room. When he came down he found Onkel warming himself before the great tile stove in the drawing room. The old man looked worn as he stood there, bent, sallow.

"I've put you through so much, Onkel . . ."

"Nonsense! Come get warm. How were they?"

"They cannot understand. They're too young," he sighed. They had asked if she was going to die. Poor small souls, all day fearing, and their nurse unable to set their minds at rest. And when he had reassured and soothed them, they had begged to know when she would come home. Tomorrow? The next day? "No, they cannot understand," he said, "nor can I."

And he walked across the room to the opposite wall. The servants had tidied things. Pictures that had been swept wildly crooked now hung straight; those that had been torn to the floor, some showing damaged frames, had been leaned in a neat row along the baseboard. He could still feel inside him the shock of those few minutes, the violence, the crazed anguish of those tearing hands.

"So many," said Onkel, who had come over beside him. He shook his head. "Everything in front of her came down."

"I want to understand," Holger murmured, his dark-ringed eyes moving slowly along the row of pictures against the baseboard. A seascape he had done last spring. The black cut-out silhouette of Grethe's grandfather. Two small pastoral etchings. A still life with red fuchsias. An old genre painting of a springer spaniel. "It must be possible to understand. There must be some sense one can make of it."

"It was a wild sweep, a frenzy. How can one make sense of it?"

"Could it have been the dog?" Holger pulled pensively at his lower lip. "Only the dog that she was actually assaulting? And in her frenzy everything else came down with it?"

"I don't follow."

"She couldn't bear the cries, she said. When she was panting so afterward. That was what she said. She couldn't bear the cries."

"But a dog doesn't cry. It barks."

"True . . ." And his eyes returned broodingly to the other pictures. "Ah, but of course!" he uttered after a moment. "Of course, it was the seascape. It has gulls. Don't you see?—two small ones up in the corner? Gulls cry."

"Holger, you torment yourself," the old man said wearily. "You cannot make sense of a crazed act. It was crazed, can you not accept it? Come, let us have some sleep."

Holger undressed in the noise of the night, the howl of the woods mixed with the flapping flurry of ivy and racket of wind against the panes—none of it, as he lay down in exhaustion, with eyes over-brimming, as loud as the silence beside him.

❧

"Did the wind disturb you last night?" the doctor asked.

"No, I rested very well," Grethe told him from her pillow.

"Indeed, you look fresh as the morning," he said genially, a stout frock-coated man with a kindly, ruddy face and a trim ginger beard that shot to his waistcoat and spread rushingly off to either side filling the air with its rampant growth, then was abruptly as before. "And how do you find your room? Is it to your liking?"

Grethe touched her hand to her temple, smoothed a strand of hair. "Thank you, yes. It is very comfortable."

"This morning, as you know, the nurses will begin the daily regimen, this being a therapeutic treatment consisting of baths and massage."

"I shall put faith in their salutary effect."

"Rest is also important. Rest is in fact of the greatest importance."

"As I am confined to bed," she said with a smile, "I surmise that."

The doctor smiled too. He liked a sense of humor, which he did not frequently come upon; nor was he entirely indifferent to the fact that the patient was a very lovely young woman.

"Well, now that we've got the question of rest settled, there must be other things you would like to ask."

"I think not, at the moment."

"If you do have any questions or complaints, please don't fail to tell me."

"Thank you, but I doubt that I will have complaints."

"I hope that will be the case."

"I would be doing myself a disservice if I weren't to accept and comply with all that is offered here. I wished to come, after all. I was in full agreement with our family physician. I knew it was necessary."

"To know that," he said, "is as important as the treatment itself."

But he sighed as he went out the door, for he had no idea, nor did the other staff doctors, if the treatment was remotely useful. He sometimes felt that the sanatorium was no different from the public lunatic asylums—only more humane and more attractively furnished—for if nothing was understood or achieved in those bleak and often brutal places, neither was anything understood or achieved here. And not for want of medical terms—what an impressive nomenclature of madness he and his colleagues possessed. But the causes, origins and reasons, these remained as mysterious as the darkest night. Give them camphor baths and electric massage, feed them large nourishing meals, quiet them with chlorides or other drugs if they grew agitated, and hope for the best. A few patients did recover and return home for good, but most who were released as cured suffered recurrent breakdowns

and were brought back again and again. Some, he didn't have to remind himself as he continued his rounds, had been here twenty years.

When the doctor had gone, Grethe lay looking at the room she
would occupy for how long she did not know, two months or so she
inferred. Fine rugs and handsome heavy carved furniture. Vases of
fresh flowers. Large windows with drapes drawn back. It was still
windy, she could see the tops of trees blowing. She tried not to think
of the woods at home, or the garden or the beach, for she and Holger
might be taking their walk now, even in this wind. She missed him
with a deep and ragged pain that brought tears to her eyes. Most of
the night, muffling the noise in her pillow, she had wept. But she had
not disclosed this to the doctor. It was not for him to know that she
had slept badly, or to know of the confusion inside her. Tell nothing.
Show nothing. Reveal nothing that might stand in the way of recovery.
She would be the worthiest of patients. She would follow every rule
with calmness, faith and fortitude. And wiping her eyes with the sleeve
of her nightgown, she lay waiting for the nurses.

After breakfast Holger and his uncle went for a walk with the boys.
The wind was still strong, if not as fierce as the night before. The
garden paths were littered with leaves and petals. The boys would run
on ahead, but not as roisterously as was their wont, and then would
stop quietly and wait; they had in a way grown up overnight, Holger
thought. He tried to be cheerful, and ruffled their hair when he and
Onkel came abreast of them. Then they would run on again for a
little.

"You must get back to Copenhagen today," he said to Onkel as
they walked.

"Why?"

"Why? You've hardly unpacked from your Italian trip. You have
things to do."

"Nonsense!"

"It's good of you, Onkel."

"Nonsense!"

From the little tea pavilion, where he lay under a chair out of the wind, Olaf watched the two great murmuring creatures pass by. He did not see his own creature with them or hear its sounds. They were gone now and gone from his mind. He contemplated some things in the air—these being leaves and petals—that came whirling by. When they reached the ground they fluttered along and then lay still. Not grasshoppers, not butterflies, not birds. The cat's thoughts were on food. The night before he had been unable to get into the kitchen. He had jumped up against the window many times but it was shut. Somewhere deep within him Olaf had been puzzled by this, being a creature of habit, like all cats. He still felt puzzlement, but nothing more troublesome. Coming out from under the chair, he stretched, pulling himself high on his legs and arching his knobby back as great quiverings and flexings rode all through his musculature. Then he set off to stalk a meal.

The two men had walked on from the garden. The Sound was dark gray-green, still rough. The sky was clouding over, and in the ripping wind came a smell of rain. They walked along the damp sand where black sodden branches had been washed up, and ropes of shiny kelp. Holger was glad to see the boys run along the surf, splashing and soaking their shoes, as if perking up a bit. But his own thoughts stayed with Grethe. Listening to the cries of gulls overhead, he felt with an almost physical pain how alone she was inside her mind. And could they really help her? Had he done right to take her there?

"I don't know what to think!" he said aloud, pushing his fingers through his hair in the wind.

"Better if you stopped thinking," Onkel told him. "Come, let us go back. I could do with a second cup of coffee. And the boys' shoes are soaked."

Rain had begun to spot their shoulders as they came through the door. A maid was coming along the hall with a stack of linen; Holger registered the square shape, and the indolent step which picked up under observation. An ingratiating smile creased the girl's big flat matronly face. Holger looked at her coldly.

"Will you keep her on?" Onkel asked over coffee.

"I told Grethe I would. But by God I dislike her. All that smutty rubbish. And crashing tables over— I tell you, if not for the shock of that, Grethe would never have had this breakdown."

"You know that isn't true, Holger. Grethe broke down because it was going to happen. Because her mind is ill, not because a table fell over. If it hadn't been that, it would have been something else."

"I know," Holger sighed. "I do know."

⊂ℬℬ∽

Grethe found the camphor bath pleasant. One sat immersed in water that stung the skin slightly, refreshingly. Afterward one was rubbed with soft thick towels, put into one's robe, and taken to a room in which stood the electrical massage machine. She was frightened to step into its metal intricacies, but she expressed no reluctance; and she discovered that the massage, too, was a mildly invigorating and pleasant experience.

When she was returned to bed it was still morning. It had begun to rain in long swerving spatters against the windows. The nurse smoothed the covers as Grethe lay back.

"Are you comfortable then?" she asked with a friendly smile.

"Yes, thank you."

"You need only ring if you need anything."

"May one read? Or do needlework?"

"I'm afraid not, dear. Complete rest, that's what's called for."

"Of course. I understand."

The nurse went to the door in a crackling of starch. The nurses wore stiffly starched aprons over cotton gowns with narrow pale brown stripes. The stripes detached themselves, whirled rapidly around the room and dissolved. The door closed and was locked. Grethe already knew the sound, a small metallic clunk, very discreet. They needn't be so discreet, she said to herself. After all, we're all crazy here, it wouldn't do to have us running about. And in spite of herself she smiled at the picture this evoked, and thought that perhaps nothing could be too bad if one maintained one's sense of humor.

And in the stillness of the room, tightly intertwining her fingers, she lay listening to the sound of wind and rain.

❧

Holger was incapable of settling down to anything that afternoon. He wandered around the rooms, picking something up, putting it down. In Grethe's study he stood gazing at her empty chair and at the books and papers on her escritoire.

"It's odd," he said to Onkel, who was reading *Politiken* in the library, "I was looking at Grethe's *Germinal* translation, and there are not even seventy pages of it." "How can that be?" Onkel asked, looking over from his newspaper. "Even before I left for Italy, she told me she was nearly finished." "Yes, of course, that's what I thought too." "The rest is somewhere in her study, Holger, surely." "That must be," he agreed, "I'll look again later."

And he wandered out into the hall. How quiet the house was. The boys, as if reverting to babyhood after their vital splashing along the surf, had accepted their nurse's injunction to nap. And the servants, who had seen all that happened . . . there was a deep hush about them, part sympathy and part embarrassment. He put on his frieze coat and went out in the rain to his studio, a whitewashed cottage at the foot of the garden, consisting of a single skylit room. He stood fingering his palette, its encrustment of pigments as hard as rock and coated with dust. He brought a crumpled paint rag to his nostrils and breathed in its aroma of turpentine and linseed oil. It still left him unimpassioned. Nothing here engaged him. He wandered back through the garden.

"Poor Hr. Rosted," murmured one of the maids, looking from an upstairs window, "and poor, poor Fru Rosted. To think of it."

"Well, what's so awful?" asked the square-shaped one. "She's not in any plain old crazy house, after all. You can be sure it's some fancy expensive one."

"So?" flashed the other. "Wouldn't you want that too if you could afford it?"

The girl shrugged. "Maybe. Never thought about it."

"You never think about anything, only how to shirk your tasks. And gossiping your stupid gossip."

"Wasn't gossip," the girl said equably. "I saw what I saw in the woods."

"Bah!"

"Bah yourself!" she said, extending her tongue as the other walked off. Then she retracted it and looked down again through the wind-driven rain. The master had gone in. The master had looked at her coldly this morning, but he hadn't sacked her. In fact, no one in this house had ever been sacked. They were kind, the master and mistress, no question about it, especially the mistress, and her heart was truly sorry for what had befallen her. But it wasn't wrong that it had happened, that their lives had come crashing down in pieces. Why should they be happy? Other people weren't happy. Other people didn't have their money and their manner and their looks. Maybe that was how the world was ordered, but it wasn't ordered right. What had happened was right: there was justice in it. And she was the one who had done it. She was the cause of it all. Maybe she was sorry, in a way, but mostly she wasn't. What she'd be sorry about would be if she was sacked; and she took herself downstairs to do some diligent and observable dusting, for to be on the safe side she was on her best behavior.

How quiet the house was, like a shell. Hardly a footstep, no sounds of laughter or echoing talk. A lot of good these fine things of theirs would do them now; and her power shimmering inside her, she took her dust cloth to tawny wood carved rich with leaves and clustered fruit.

"The bath and massage weren't at all disagreeable," Grethe told the doctor on his evening round. "In fact, I'll look forward to them."

"Good. And the rest of this rainy day?"

"The time passed well enough."

"The hours can be long."

"Of course it would be nice to read, but if one is undergoing a rest cure, one shouldn't be disturbed by the outside world which is to be found in books."

"Alas, yes, that is the nature of a rest cure."

She did not ask why needlework was also forbidden. One was not to have sharp objects. That was also understandable.

They talked a little about books.

"Ewald. And Goldschmidt and Jacobsen," she told him, "they are some of my favorites."

"Ah, and mine. And Drachmann and Oehlenschläger."

"And—" And Bødtcher, she was going to say, but whenever those lines of Bødtcher came to mind, " '. . . my ears may capture, a nightingale's rapture . . . ,' " whenever she thought of that joyous poem of love, she felt a tearing sadness. "And Holberg," she said. "And Grundtvig. There are so many fine writers."

"You will get back to them again," he told her, and after a few more words he departed, his figure breaking momentarily into five men.

The kitchen window again being shut against his leaps, Olaf slept out of the wind and rain behind some heavy boards that leaned against the stable. The stable itself would have been warmer, but Olaf feared the massive creatures therein, with their stomping and blowing. He was content to lay himself down in his sheltered recess, which was fairly snug and dry, but puzzlement accompanied him into sleep.

In the house too sleep had come. One by one the lights had gone out, and after a while the chimneys no longer sent smoke into the wet black racing wind.

All the days were the same, merging one into the other almost indivisibly: early morning therapy; then the long solitary hours; meals brought in on a tray; lamps extinguished at half-past eight; then morning again and the same. The tops of the trees were dim, blowing shapes beyond the blur of the windows. Except for the sound of wind and rain, the room was silent.

Sometimes she saw the quick flashing things. An antimacassar convulsing on the back of a chair. Wallpaper shredding. Sometimes she found herself inside a flower in one of the vases, curled up within the petals' pale blue velvety light. Then she was lying in bed again, and the silence throbbed. She wished she had her needlework to concentrate on, she longed for it in her hands, her own clearly drawn pattern, her own steady route through all confusion. And she would try to think of nothing, to be nothing.

When Olaf first came, she was not sure. She heard him. Heard his sudden, familiar meow. And then she saw him leaping from one piece of furniture to the next, almost flying, like a bird. She was not surprised, but her heart pounded with joy.

"Oh, Olaf, Olaf!" she cried as he landed on the foot of her bed.

"I would have come sooner, but I was detained by the rain," he meowed.

"Oh, how are you? How are you? Have you kept well?"

"Very well." He settled in by her feet, tucking his paws under his chest. "And you, dear friend, are you well?"

"I shall be. It's why I am here."

"Are they kind to you?"

"Yes, very. The nurses and the doctor too. He is a stout gentleman with a ginger beard, and we have conversations, but they are brief and of a slight nature." And she added with a gentle laugh, "And that is good."

Olaf laughed too, his little cat face lighting up with conspiratorial humor.

"Yes, that is good. Show nothing. Tell nothing."

"Fortunately he believes only in rest, baths and massage. And I believe in them too, Olaf. Very much. I have great faith. I am improving every day."

"But are you not lonely here?"

"Indeed I am, 'yet I could be bounded in a nutshell—' "

" '—and think myself a king of infinite space, did I not have bad dreams.' "

"Are they only bad dreams that I suffer from, Olaf? You must know, for you speak Hamlet's lines so well."

"Perhaps, but what Hamlet knew he never told. Was he the best or worst of men? Was he mad or not? We will never know. And we may go to Kronborg but we will never find him there. I have been to Kronborg. I have walked in the Great Hall. I have chased the royal mice—"

The attendant with her dinner tray opened the door and Olaf vanished. But he had returned many times since.

◌ ❧ ◌

"I am often terrified, Olaf. I cannot tell anyone else of this, but I tell you because you understand."

"I understand because I have suffered."

"You have suffered as the workers suffer down in the mines. And the ponies, dear God, the ponies never come up at all, they live and die down there—I could not go on with it. I could not—"

"You should have, dear friend. You should have finished your translation, for you well know that in the end the mine workers rebel. Just think how their grievances explode in righteous blood and violence."

"But don't you know that a thousand explosions are not enough, Olaf? Nothing is enough."

"I do know. How well I know that nothing changes. In my kittenhood everyone I held dear was slaughtered. All my sisters and brothers. Three were pushed into a sack struggling and screaming and flung into a pond. Another, playing innocently in a field, was killed by boys with slingshots. Another was seized by her tender neck and dropped down a well, another eaten alive by rats. These things never end. Under the sunlight and bright foliage lie darkness, slaughter and anguish."

"You understand."

☙ ❧

"My father played the piano. He was inspired by Liszt, his touch was *molto vivace*. He was full of life and brightness, and when it rained we would have hot chocolate and *lagkage*."

"Did it rain like this? It has been raining so long that we will soon float into the sea."

"I took a sea voyage once with my father, and there was a cat aboard."

"The cat was later. The cat was in the house of your mother's kin where you were lonely."

"The kitchen mouser. Oh, how we played, what splendid times we had, not a blemish existed in the world when we were together. But they said we got underfoot, and I was banished from the kitchen. I never saw him again. And he was such a friend, such a friend. Although not as great a friend as you, Olaf, for we have known each other a very long time now."

"God be praised."

"God be praised for all good things. On my seventh birthday my father had a party for me. Onkel was there, I remember, and other friends. And someone played the piano, although not as wonderfully as my father, and my father and I danced together."

"Was it raining?"

"No, it was a lovely summer evening. But in the autumn my father died. He went out one day and fell over on the street. I never saw him again."

"But we will take a sea voyage, you and I."

"Oh, let us, let us when I am well. They are very pleased with me. Each morning I step with good will into the camphor bath, and into the cold arms of the massage machine, and whether I am hungry or not I eat every morsel of the robust meals set down before me, and I never complain when the lamps are extinguished so early. I follow every rule. I practice calmness, faith and fortitude."

∽ 𝄢 ✇

"One must eschew the amorous embrace."

"I know nothing about amorous embraces. I have no amorous life, nor have I ever had."

"But that is a pity, Olaf. Why is that?"

"Why is that? How could it be otherwise? There are no other cats living in the woods. There was never a wife I might have taken."

"That is sad, Olaf. For there is no joy like the joy of two loving beings united in their marital bed. But take comfort in knowing that you have not added to the endless cycle of generations."

"Still, I would have liked to have a wife."

"A wife brings sorrow. Think of the sorrow I have brought Holger."

"That is true but it was necessary. The garden grows and gluts and dies, and grows and gluts again, and is a chaos of growth and black decay, and there must be no more seeds sown."

"For if one cannot bring God's Kingdom to earth, if one cannot end all suffering, then one must at least end one's own begetting. Otherwise the griffin drags one up to the sun, and one is cast into its flames and is burned and burned and burned as punishment . . . yet there could have been no greater pain than when I did finally turn from the lips I loved, although it was necessary. It was necessary. But I cannot bear to remember how my coldness brought tears to his eyes, I cannot bear to remember it . . ."

"Hush. What are tears compared to such necessity?"

"You ease my heart, Olaf. You are my savior."

"I wouldn't go so far as to say that. Although I do have my religious side. You know I founded Ribe Cathedral."

"Oh, I know, Olaf, and that is so splendid. One may use chalk or charcoal, and the mandolin plays so brightly, or perhaps it is my father at the piano, *molto vivace*, he was of great good cheer—"

"Not always."

"I saw it happen. He would press his temples, and in his eyes was horror. He was so stricken that he was not even aware that I was there. And I was frightened, and I would watch as he went to his room to stay there all day. But always otherwise he was so lively and good-natured."

"But these other times. His eyes saw darkness and slaughter and anguish—"

"His eyes were filled with horror, and I was frightened . . . no, no, I don't remember. I don't remember anything, how can I? I was so small. I remember only that every day was bright . . . and how we talked, Olaf, all my childish questions were met with happiest patience."

"And you asked him about the Pierced One, whose name makes me think of Christ on the Cross, who was given vinegar mixed with gall and pierced in the side by a spear."

"No, he was not Christ, Olaf, he was only my grandfather. Yes, and so young and fetching in his silhouette, which hung on our wall. I was quite taken with him. And then to learn that he had perished in battle, that was so sad. My father called him a brave soldier who had died for his ideals. And what are ideals? I asked, for I was so young I did not know what the word meant. And my father said that ideals are good things, but that people sometimes die for them uselessly. And how did he die? I asked. Pierced through the heart by shell fragments, my father said. And he was also pierced when he fell onto a fence spike as a child, but survived. And my father described the house-keeper who never stopped talking of this. Oh, I believe she was indeed a character whose tongue never ceased its flapping. My father was only a small child himself then, and he laughed heartily to remember that he had once told her she talked too much. He told me these things because I asked, but otherwise he never spoke of the past. I thought it did not interest him greatly. It was only when I was older, and living in such loneliness with my mother's kin, that it came to me that my father had not dared to think of the past. No, for then he beheld in his mind the Pierced One's death. That was the horror in his eyes that I had seen."

"The darkness and slaughter and anguish."

"To be so young and to die for nothing. Torn by metal through the heart for nothing. Nothing. Darkness, slaughter and anguish yes, and I felt great pity for my father and greater pity yet for the Pierced One, of whom nothing remained but a piece of cut-out black paper to show the charm of his features, already so long dust and for nothing . . . and then I began to hear him calling out to me in his loneliness . . . that was long ago, I don't remember when his calls became cries, oh they are loud, they are terrible, his cries. He cries out as his heart is pierced, he cries Grethe! Grethe! he cries Grethe! Grethe! and I must go to him and assuage his anguish. But it will not be assuaged, Olaf. It is profound. It is unanswerable. I cannot assuage his suffering or the world's—for it is not only his but all the world's suffering that I must end. He wants me to bring God's Kingdom to earth, Olaf, I try, I try, but I cannot do it—how to end pain and cruelty and evil which go on forever, the garden rampant with growth and black decay and horror and I cannot end it! And he calls Grethe! Grethe! and if I cannot end his anguish and the world's he will devour us all with his pain and horror—I cannot bear his cries, Olaf! I am terrified, terrified that I will hear them again—"

"Hush, calm yourself, dear friend. You have not heard them in all the time you have been here. You will not hear them again, for you are getting well."

⚮

"The nurses tell me you are their best patient," the doctor said to her.

"That is very nice to know," she replied. "However, I *do* have one complaint."

"No, I don't believe it. And what is that?"

She smiled.

"I don't hold you responsible," she said. "The rain."

"Ah, I agree. Three days of it has been enough."

Grethe gave no indication of her astonishment and dismay at how little time had passed.

She said, "It is probably good for the soil, at any rate. But I don't mean to bore you with talk of the weather. It is not you who needs to be bored, after all; only me, in the interests of the cure."

"Well, and do you think you are sufficiently bored?"

"Oh, I fear not. With vases of lovely flowers to look at? And one's fingernails to contemplate? And immense meals that use up at least three hours each in the eating?"

The doctor laughed.

"And you continue to sleep well?"

"Very well."

"All to the good."

⊛

"I could not believe it. I had thought so much more time than that had passed, two weeks, three. It was such a surprise, Olaf. Such a terrible disappointment."

"But you must accept it. You must go on as you have, with calmness, faith and fortitude."

⊛

Holding a wind-snapping umbrella over their heads, Holger accompanied his uncle down the steps to the carriage. He saw Olaf dart across the splashing drive, looking more bedraggled than ever, and squeeze under a hedge. He had forgotten all about the cat.

"Take good care of yourself, my boy."

"And you, Onkel. A thousand thanks for your company. I could not have done without you."

"Nonsense!" The old man climbed inside. "Now see that you eat well."

Holger waved after the departing vehicle, then went inside to the kitchen.

"Is the window kept ajar as usual at night?" he asked the cook. "Fru Rosted wouldn't want the cat out in this weather. And it needs its food."

"I know how fond the mistress is of that animal," Cook sighed, "but I tell you, a lot else besides itself comes in. The rain for one thing. It gets on the floor."

"It cannot be very much."

"Maybe not but rain's rain. And a dormouse once and once even an owl."

"They did no harm, did they?"

"They did no good."

"Please keep the window as usual at night."

Cook nodded, but she intended to forget, her dislike of the ratty thing being pronounced. And Hr. Rosted looked too preoccupied not to forget the matter too. He went out the kitchen door with a nod, and indeed he had other things on his mind.

He must go into Copenhagen next week to interview a tutor for the boys; it was something he should have done during the summer, but along with much else it had been let slide. And this morning he must search again for the rest of Grethe's translation, and check the carriage-house roof to see if it was leaking, as it tended to do, and go into Hørsholm to order glass for the replacement of several green-house panes smashed by the wind, and he must spend the afternoon with his account books. And he is glad to have these homely duties to perform, for they will help to keep the rawness from spreading through his chest.

. . . Why do I have to write a letter that will take days to get there, why can't you get a phone? *Last night the news showed whole villages over there snowed in, and you don't even have a phone to let us know if you're okay or if you're sitting there with that decrepit oven going day and night and have burned down the whole building and yourself included.* Please *call when you get this,* somebody *in that godforsaken village must have a phone. It's the most catastrophic snowfall in years over there in case the fact has escaped you . . .*

℃ Tossing the letter aside, Paula gets into her padded jacket and woolen cap and goes downstairs out into the icy air. The sky is magnificently blue, everything else white and sparkling—the slope and the mountain rising above and even the snow that has been plowed to either side of the street along which she crunches in great annoyance. In the hole-in-the-wall post office she puts through a call.

"Is that you, Mom?—are you *okay?*"

"Of course I am."

"We saw on the news how awful the—"

"You watch too much news, it's all exaggeration and aggravation. Our sky here is probably bluer than yours in Malibu."

"Well of course it is, it's eleven at night here. The fact remains that—"

"That the snowfall's been very heavy for early December. But we're not snowed in, and what harm if we were?"

"Because as I said in my letter—"

"Your letter was offensive. I am not an imbecile. I am not negligent. I don't burn down buildings."

"That old stove is *unsafe*."

"It may be unattractive to your eye, but it is not unsafe. As for this godforsaken village, the people here do have telephones. Yes, they're actually that advanced. You do sound incredibly ignorant sometimes."

"The fact remains that *you* don't have one."

"I have the public phone here at the post office if I need it."

"It's not the *same*. We should be able to reach you at any time, especially at a time of crisis like this. Listen to me, Mom, your situation over there just continues to be totally off the charts. Can't you understand that? How can we *keep* from worrying?"

"I won't have this, will you stop your carping once and for all!"

"If I carp it's because *somebody's* got to. You go wandering around with a bunch of cows, you sit there banging on those crazy stones with that decrepit old oven going—"

"Didn't I just tell you—"

"All right, all right. So what do we talk about, the weather?"

"We already have." And she hung up.

Crunching back down the street she grew gradually less angry. Her daughter was insulting, nagging, officious and persistent, but inside that obdurate mind of hers she was acting with concern and helpfulness. And to be hung up on, cut off, smacked into muteness across the miles . . . she felt twinges of regret. She wondered what the child was doing now, getting ready for bed probably, flinging that wedge out of her eye as she briskly pats aloe vera into her face and the ocean five minutes away and has she ever noticed it except to be reminded that the pool needs cleaning?

"That is a small, mean thought. Mean and undeserved." And turning around, she went back to the post office.

"I'm sorry I hung up. I shouldn't have."

"And I'm sorry I went on and on, but you've got to realize how—"

"I'm calling back so we can have a nice conversation. Let's start all over. Unless it's too late, were you on your way to bed?"

"No, no, it's fine, I'm just sitting here looking at toilets."

"At toilets?"

"Pictures. We're having the master bathroom done over. God, it looks like a disaster area."

"When will they be finished?"

"I don't know. A couple of weeks, God *willing*."

"Well, I'm sure it will be very nice when it's done. Have you found the toilet you want?"

"No. It's not easy when you've got so many styles to choose from."

"Well, don't worry, I'm sure you'll come to a decision. But how are you? How is everyone?"

"Fine. We're all fine. And you're all right?"

"As I said earlier, yes."

"I know you said that, but the fact remains—"

"And how is our young genealogist coming along?"

"Who? Oh, she got bored, she's into something else. Clothes. But totally."

"She's only thirteen though, isn't she?"

"Only? It's pretty *late*, if you ask me."

"Well, you must be relieved. But tell me what else has been happening, what other news is there?"

"Just the usual, always busy. And that's the thing, Mom, you've got too much time hanging on your hands. No wonder you're—"

"Are you starting in again?"

"Oh, everything's just fine you say. But look at yourself. Please.

Look at your appearance and the way you live and the things you do. Everything's *not* fine, can't you see you're totally in *denial*? Can't you see that the bottom line is that you can't go on like this, you've got to let yourself be *helped*?"

Paula hung up again, hard.

When she got home she squashed her daughter's letter into a ball and threw it in the garbage bucket. She took off her cap and jacket, face stinging from the cold, and looked around at the off-kilter floor, the ancient stone sink, the shabby refrigerator and stove. "So? *I* like it," she said. She lit a match and turned on the oven. "And for your information I don't leave it going day and night, I turn it off when I go out, I turn it off when I go to bed . . . damn, why should I have to justify myself to her!"

In her bedroom she changed from her wet shoes into slippers. The furniture was scuffed, the wallpaper discolored and the mattress sagged. But the sag was very comfortable. And the bed was brightened by throw pillows, the wall by a shelf of books, and on the floor was her small rug. What more was required?

The rug, especially, brought resonance to the room. In the clear winter light from the window she looked down at its yellow roses, its greengold leaves and russet background. Old it was, and frayed in places, but its beauty was irreducible. What fingers, she sometimes wondered, had worked the rich, quiet colors, the fine gradations of tone, the wondrous harmony? What fingers had understood so much? It was something she would never know, but it didn't matter, the rug was there. And not one of her possessions in the commodious Neuchâtel storeroom—not all of them together, plus her stored Mercedes—came near the worth of this frayed old rectangle of needlework by her bed.

That was something her daughter would never understand.

In the kitchen she put a pan of water on the stove for coffee. If her daughter had her way, she would find herself in a Geneva high-rise. All her things out of storage and in pleasant surround, the Mercedes in the vast underground parking garage below. Except that the Mercedes might be dead by now. Didn't cars die if they weren't taken out and driven now and then? Never mind, a spotless new condo with all the conveniences plus a live-in maid and a cleaning woman once a week. Little luncheons with other loaded expatriates, fun trips to the hairdresser and boutiques, maybe membership in a state-of-the-art gym where she could find exercise on any number of marvelous machines. And don't forget those well-balanced meals: there were many books in which you could read up on the subject of nutrition, and that would also occupy your time nicely.

But no, her daughter's true wish for her would be a condo back in the States. Same kind of life but on home soil, Europe being lovely to visit of course, but if you didn't *have* to live among foreigners why would you? Not Chicago, too cold. Some sunny enclave in Florida or Arizona or California. Why not Malibu?—I should write and suggest that I move into her guest room where she could keep a really sharp eye on me. Maybe that would stop her carping. Except nothing seems to.

Does she really worry about me? Burning the place down?—good Lord. Or could it be something as simple as money? Really, as simple as that? Being of unsound mind, why, I might suddenly convert all my assets and sign everything away to some charity or con artist. Or cash it all and turn it into a huge bonfire here on the kitchen floor, which would seem more in keeping with her incendiary picture of me. Naturally I should be prevented from doing such things. For my own sake. And possibly for hers?

But be fair. Her daughter was not avaricious, she was not grasping. Nor should she be, considering her own extremely affluent circumstances. No, she was motivated only by concern for her poor demented mother. Well, I wonder what she's got in mind. Will she come swooping down with a battery of shrinks and a court order flapping in her hand?

She sat down at the table with her mug of instant coffee, and looked out at the intense blue and sparkling white, against them the green of a potted fern standing on the windowsill. The jar of wildflowers would reappear in the spring, when the earth put out blooms again. Her daughter would have it that she never saw another spring from this window. But there wasn't a thing her daughter could do, there was not one legal step she could take. So she had an eccentric mother. So?

The stillness of the sky and snow was profound. In other seasons you heard birds chattering, the distant clunk of cowbells, the barks of a dog, voices filtering up from the street. She was never lonely. Even in this great winter silence she was not lonely. She thought of life in a high-rise somewhere, and gave a shudder.

An ant moved along the oilcloth, skirting the huge tower of a milk carton, now tracking the immense metal length of a spoon. She watched it circle and zigzag its way along the vast, obstacle-cluttered plateau until, long minutes later, it finally gained the ulcerated windowsill where it traversed the deep craters—down, up—down, up—and disappeared through the crack between window and sill.

"Bravo! Onward, Ulysses—" she called after it, and lifted her mug in a toast.

She sipped her coffee.

"I suppose that's what she means. Is it normal to sit here lost in the peregrinations of an ant? Is it normal to read a Homeric journey into those hurrying little insect feet? And to toast and cheer it on? I can see her roll her eyes . . . well, roll on, roll on . . . I don't care. I wonder what she's doing now. Probably gone to bed, tired after studying so many toilets."

She looked down at her hand lying on the oilcoth, her fingers calloused and crosshatched with small black cuts, and at her sweater sleeve which, if she gave it a shake, would send up a small gritty cloud of stone dust. She would go back to her work now, she had been diverted too long by this stupid business. She would return to the demands and rigors of her quest, and as always she felt excitement building up inside her, a heightening, a gripping, as if she were going into battle.

☙ ❧

In the evening she came back into the kitchen for dinner. She had worked long and hard. Her fingers still throbbed. She felt tired and she felt good. She ate a fried egg with mayonnaise, a can of pears and a candy bar. And as she ate she looked around the room again.

Actually, why shouldn't she give her money to charity? Keep enough to live on, but she didn't need all the rest. It wasn't right to live like this when you had ample means to do otherwise. She could move out in a minute if she wanted, the poor couldn't do that. It was an insult to the poor. Not that money did them much good, a drop in the world's bottomless bucket of misery. A person should go out and help them, like Mother Teresa. But she herself wasn't a saint, she was just someone with a lot of money she didn't need. If others could make better use of it, why shouldn't they have it?

After dinner she turned off the oven and the light and stood for a while by the window. Some nights you saw the moon clothed and unclothed by tattered clouds, sometimes the clouds were gray, stupendous mountains, barely moving, and sometimes, like tonight, the atmosphere was of such clarity that every star in the galaxy seemed visible, an incredible multitude, incredibly bright.

They filled the window of the bedroom, too, when she went in to undress. Standing barefoot on the small rug, she shivered enjoyably in the room's already growing hint of the biting, bracing cold she would wake up to in the morning. She wondered if the ant had completed its great journey down the side of the building. She wondered how Philip was, and if he would suddenly pop up again as he had in October. She wondered if she should brush her teeth but decided against it, climbing into her pajamas and sinking heavy-lidded into the deep sag. She fell asleep almost at once.

☙ ❧

In October, when the jet from Geneva had landed at O'Hare International Airport, Philip had disembarked exhaustedly from his round-the-world trip. Gritty-eyed, in sheets of rain, he had stuffed his irate assistant into a cab, slapped some bills for the fare into her hand and, relieved that with a splash of wheels she was gone forever from his life, climbed into another cab and sank back in the seat. He reflected that it had also been raining when he left for Bora Bora, and that it seemed a long time in the past, but was actually only a few days ago. He closed his eyes, opening them when his shoulder was shaken by the driver in front of his house. Inside, he lugged his wet bags up the tangerine-carpeted stairs and threw himself on his bed without unpacking. For two days he stayed home resting and sleeping, then he returned to work.

In retrospect the trip was embarrassing to Philip. What was supposed to have been an ordinary two- or three-week jaunt had been compressed to almost nothing because of a persecuting little blotch of a drawing. He had become an adrenaline-pumping, brain-jangled, sleep-starved wreck, had put oceans and continents behind him for the sole purpose of exorcizing that scribbled little mess. He could hardly stand the thought that he had traversed three quarters of the globe, fifteen thousand miles, haggard and driven, for such a humiliating reason. Or maybe he had just felt like dropping in on Paula for a cup of coffee?

He wrote her saying he had enjoyed their brief visit, but he mentioned none of the things they had talked about, for the high seriousness of their conversation, its lugubriousness, was also an embarrassment to remember. Had he really brought up that gangling wanderer in his beret and dusty shoes? And delivered himself of heavy quotations over his coffee mug? And actually shed tears at some point, or at any rate felt them prickling? Prickling for all humanity, as he recalled, for everyone on earth. The presumptuousness of it, the drunken puerility of fatigue.

And the scribble itself, his persecuting air crash, of course it was no air crash—that was his own overwrought imagination. No, all it had turned out to be was a little solitary dead ant, which, he had discovered on boarding the plane home from Geneva, was no improvement on what he had misconstrued it to be, and which was not only humiliating but idiotic.

The whole trip chagrined him. The only good thing about it was that he'd broken off with his assistant. Yet the way he had gone about it—so crude, so conscienceless, letting her sit in the rented car in the rain, like a pariah, while he and Paula visited—was also embarrassing to remember. And when he'd climbed in behind the wheel after her furious, protracted horn blasts—"Three fucking hours I've fucking sat here in this fucking rain!" he hadn't even bothered to answer. And then at O'Hare, stuffing her into the cab like a piece of rubbish.

He was deeply relieved to be rid of her, but he knew he should have ended their alliance in a less shabby way. Yet he couldn't have, for he had been too exhausted. His every thought and action on that trip had been set askew by fatigue. He had been in a way unhinged.

⊗

Philip had gone back to work restored to his usual energy and acuity of mind; and like most people who have had an uncharacteristic and unsettling experience, he gladly welcomed the resumption of his ordinary life. It was a pleasure to drive as always in heavy morning traffic into the steel and glass ravines of downtown Chicago; to emerge from the underground garage and walk the brisk block to his store; to pass through the outer office with its soft rapid click of computer keys, its bulletin board thick with Kodachrome views from every corner of the globe; to take the rumbling freight elevator down to the basement— he owned two warehouses as well and was in the process of buying a third—and go checking through room after room of stock; to tour the salesrooms, bounteous and glittering, always taking time to chat with customers in regard to their needs and preferences; to sit working in his private office with memos and faxes, dictating tapes, making phone calls, holding discussions with department heads. After work he usually met with friends for dinner, and three nights a week played indoor tennis at his club; he arrived home late and got up at seven.

Not only did Philip welcome all this back, but he felt a strong new dedication to his work. He set his clock-radio an hour earlier, to six. He took work home at night. He came in on Saturdays. No detail was too small for him to set his mind to, no effort was too great. When he rose in the mornings, it was with a gratifying sense of duty and direction.

The trip, like a bizarre and mortifying bump on the graph of his life, faded behind him to nothing: overwrought brain, scribbled air crash, ants, everything. He felt virtuous, content, fulfilled by the clarity and order he was bringing to his life. One Sunday he even got out the vacuum and plowed it back and forth over miles of tangerine carpet. He thoroughly swept his gourmet-tiled kitchen. He went through the entire house with a dust rag, snapping it vigorously at banisters and furniture. He plumped up sofa pillows, threw out old newspapers, straightened magazines, and with a feeling of accomplishment thought how surprised the cleaning woman would be when she walked into such tidiness.

After a few weeks, all this lost its novelty and grew increasingly unsatisfying. He set his clock-radio to seven again. He stopped going into the store on Saturdays, and no longer brought work home at night. He left the state of the house to the cleaning woman. At work he found it hard to concentrate. He felt restless, full of disquietude.

One night he picked up the phone and punched out his assistant's number. He had been in the wrong but he had never apologized, and he thought maybe this was what was bothering him.

He got her in the middle of a party. He raised his voice against the noise.

"Look, this isn't the best timing, but I won't keep you. All I want to say is that I owe you an apology."

"Hey, you're funny. You ought to get up an act," his assistant yelled through the tumult, and resumed a yelled discussion about getting more ice. He waited patiently. "So what d'you want? I don't take shit like that from anybody."

"I apologize. I'm not sorry we're finished, but I am for the way I went about it. My behavior was shabby and uncivilized, and I fully—"

"Oh, fuck off," she yelled, turning away in a screamed exchange of greetings with new arrivals.

He hung up satisfied that he had done the right thing, but feeling no less restless and discontent than before.

A couple of days later there was a message from her on his answering machine: she wanted to pick up the clothes she'd left at his place, let her know if he'd be home the next night.

He left a message on her machine saying he would be.

She wasn't coming to pick up any clothes, because she hadn't left any; only some burned-out flashbulbs and a tube of lip gel. Their two messages were an unstated agreement that their breach was behind them. And he wondered how that had happened, because it wasn't what he wanted; it wasn't why he'd called and apologized. Yet somehow he was now slipping and sliding back into the old habit.

Driving home the next night in blusters of snow that did nothing for the traffic, he thought: maybe she'll decide the drive isn't worth it. But it would be. He wondered what had tipped the scales for her, the gratis trips or the cameras and photographic equipment reduced in price to nearly nothing. He parked in the garage, made his way through its clutter into the house, and walked around in the dark turning on lamps. He picked up the mail from the floor, all junk. What he didn't understand was his having forgotten how relieved he had been to be rid of her.

By the time the door chimes sounded their vomitous melody, he knew he would have to tell her that her drive had been for nothing. He would have to sit down with her and explain that their getting back together was pointless. After all, she had other lovers, other benefactors, it wasn't as if he were an essential part of her life. Granted, no one else owned a cornucopia of photographic supplies, but she could continue getting her stuff for practically nothing, he didn't care, he wished her well. He would say those things, and he would bring up their ages too. She was what, twenty-seven, twenty-eight, and he was a mountain of years. Truly, a mountain of years, people looked at them twice. He was tired of that, if she wasn't. Also, he would remind her that they had nothing in common. Except that didn't hold much water, since the one thing they had in common was making good use of each other. He was tired of that too, sick to his marrow of it, and he could go on to tell her more: that she irritated and depressed him, that she was empty, stock, banal—that their whole relationship was repulsive to him, that he felt contempt for her and greater contempt for himself, and that he couldn't stand the thought of going back to all that.

But as he went to open the door, he knew he couldn't say any of these things; they were harsh, cruel, and he was determined to be civilized this time. He must think of something tactful to tell her. And there was always the hope that she really had left some clothes in the corner of a closet, and that was all she was coming for, with coldness and brevity in her face.

But the familiar round young face, eyes strikingly accented, expressed neither of these things. She was already unbuttoning her coat as she came in, shaking out her massed corkscrews.

"Hey, you're looking better," she greeted him. "Better than on that fucking trip. What'd you do, take a course in stress management?"

The immediate intestinal clenching, the insufferable barrenness of jokeland. He helped her out of her coat, trying to think of something sociable to say.

"So how was your party?"

She shrugged. "So-so. The usual freaks."

He had truly meant to sit down and explain things, to behave in a civilized manner, but he was suddenly getting her back into her coat. She pulled away.

"Hey, what is this?"

"Look," he said impatiently, "all the time we didn't see each other, did it matter? Was it any great blight of the soul?"

"Great blight of the soul?" she repeated, staring him up and down. "Where the fuck are you coming from?"

"I'm just saying there's no point our getting back together. And no point dragging things out."

He went over to the door and opened it. Snow was flying by.

"Hey, you, I just got here! I just drove fifteen miles!"

"Can't be helped," he said. "Vamoose."

"What is this?—the same crazy shit you were pulling on that trip? Are you nuts? What's with you anyway, male menopause?"

"Could be." He pulled the door more widely open.

"Only that's in *early* middle age!"

"Then it's probably senility."

"What are you, funny?" She gave him a hard push with both hands. "I don't call it funny when my time's totally wasted! Fifteen fucking miles! My time's not shit, you fucking waste of time!"

And her voice, with its wondrous gift of repetition, was gone through the door. He pressed it shut and breathed a sigh of relief. In the kitchen he had some leftover ham and pesto pasta salad from the deli, with a glass of Chassagne-Montrachet, and read the *Tribune*.

Philip had no regrets about his assistant. He didn't miss her and he didn't miss their flying jaunts. But he continued to feel restless and desultory. When he had dinner with his friends, they said he looked distracted. At the tennis club he was told the same, and it was true that his game wasn't up to par. At work he would get up from his desk and wander around the room. It was as if something heavy hung over his head, or as if he deeply missed and needed something, but he didn't know what it was.

What it was, the thought came to him one night as he brushed his teeth, was precisely those flying jaunts he told himself he didn't care about. It wasn't the trips themselves that he missed—only the constant takeoffs and landings, when, with his terror and agony, over and over again, he paid his dues to the wrath of God.

This thought was embarrassing. How self-dramatizing it was to attach the wrath of God to simple aerophobia. And it was also senseless, since he didn't believe in God. His Episcopalian upbringing consisted of a single Sunday School class that he and Paula, as seven-year-olds, had sat through, blowing bubble gum behind their lesson books while plotting their earliest escape. When the maid came to collect them, they were playing leapfrog down the street. He had never felt the slightest religious inclination. So why should he think he owed dues to a nonexistent entity? And what dues?

He studied himself in the mirror above the turquoise sink. An ordinary sort of face. Good features, he supposed you could say. Showed the years, of course, thickenings and creases. Virile baldness set off by springy pepper-and-salt hair, well barbered. Complexion healthy, eyes clear blue, looking at him with an intelligent, alert expression. A decent, ordinary sort of face, what terrible dues could such a face owe?

He was imperfect. He had faults, made mistakes. Three failed marriages were a mistake. His business was a mistake. But it wasn't as if he were a criminal, a menace to others, a dark blot on their lives: a molester of children, for instance, or a heroin pusher or slum landlord. On the other hand, although he made frequent sizable contributions to charity, he claimed no great benevolence; never spent what free time he had going from door to door with worthy petitions, or giving volunteer English lessons as a second language. He was like most people, not particularly good and not particularly bad. But all things considered, he came off all right. Honest in his business dealings; a responsible and generous employer; a dependable friend; worked hard, played hard; wished no harm on anyone and brought no harm to anyone. It was difficult to see why he, as apart from everyone else, should deserve the wrath of God.

He rinsed his mouth, spat and went to bed.

He woke, the luminous digits of the clock-radio slipping to 2:28, and couldn't get back to sleep.

The clicking of cameras wherever you went, as if people thought that by recording every moment of their lives they verified their existence, when in fact they'd been handed a substitute for looking inward and remembering. A frenzy of mechanical duplication. An endless production and consuming of images. A crime against authenticity. A mindless, flooding fraudulence of bits and pieces.

And was it honest, was it even palatable, to abet something you hated? He had been over this ground often enough. The dialogue was always the same:

I have a flair for commerce. More than a flair, a talent, like a talent for the piano or higher mathematics. What was I supposed to do, throw it out? A gift?

No, but you could have chosen a different species of merchandise to apply your talent to.

Nothing seemed to me as viable. Cameras. Image-making. The ever-expanding heart of the age.

Okay then. Put up or shut up.

"Why not sell?" he asked himself suddenly. But the idea was too big. He couldn't get his hands around it. He punched his pillow and tried to sleep.

What he would really like would be to leave everything in the hands of his staff. After all, they were able, they carried on with no difficulty when he was gone on his trips. In fact, the damn place could practically run itself, growing and swelling like an irrepressible toadstool. He *should* sell—and the house too, why had he ever moved in? Impatience, indifference, and in the dark he envisioned the bedroom's blank, talcum-white walls with their unfinished wainscoting, the ubiquitous tangerine carpet, the king-size bed where he lay, its great width stretching off from his side like a desert.

He slept badly the rest of the night. In the morning, tired out, he called the store to say he wouldn't be in. He dressed and had breakfast, but there was nothing to do. Even if he had felt up to jogging, he would have been prevented by the foul sleety weather that rattled and obscured all his plantation-louvered windows. He thumped halfheartedly around the recreation room for a while. He put a compressed-wood log in his mica-glittering fireplace and lit its wrapping. He sat down with a crossword puzzle, but his boredom and restlessness were hard to bear.

In the afternoon the junk mail came, but also a blue airmail envelope. He and Paula kept in touch every few months, a few lines, neither of them being great letter writers. Today even a few lines from his sister were an event. She thanked him for his note in October when he'd got back, hoped he was busy and well. They'd had a big early snowfall, apart from that not much news. Heard from her daughter, more importunate than ever—getting to be *très agaçant*, though she meant well. Did he ever look for his birth certificate by the way? Her granddaughter had abandoned her project, no further interest in the engineer, but it would be nice for their own sake to find at least that little bit of something about him. She was fine, busy as always. No hikes in the deep snow, but some good walks along the cleared road. Enjoying the keen bite of winter, also enjoying the warmth inside. He should drop by for a cup of coffee. All for now, love from Paula.

How simple her life was, he thought almost with longing. Yes, well, simplicity could be yours too, if you wanted to stick yourself in some tiny rooms in some remote village and pound on a bunch of rocks with a mallet. No, thanks very much. And no, he hadn't looked for his birth certificate. Maybe Paula lived in the past, although he wasn't really sure where in her mind she lived, but he himself had no interest in digging through a lot of moldy papers.

But having given up on the crossword puzzle and walked around trying to think of something else to do, he put on his jacket and went out into the garage. Turning on the harsh overhead light, he made his way through stacks of old newspapers, toppled piles of books he'd never got around to shelving, broken kitchen appliances and defective lamps, and knelt by a couple of old cardboard boxes. In one he found a slew of tarnished Christmas ornaments; the other he lifted onto the dusty workbench, where he dumped out its contents.

They were mostly drawings in crayon, mixed with grammar school and high school report cards, letters, frayed pocket notebooks. He spread everything out and began to look for the certificate, taking his time in order to use up as much of the afternoon as possible. The drawings were of everything: space ships, elephants, gangsters with tommy guns, streets, trees, kings on their thrones, grasshoppers, birds, furniture, storm-lashed desert islands, roller skates, a child's perpetual attempt to embrace the world; he must have used up tons of crayons; he remembered the small cardboard boxes they came in, orange-yellow, with dark green lettering. Here was a certificate. It declared him a "Fish of the First Class, 1939," signed by the Director of the Crystal Plunge Summer Swimming Program. More drawings, of waterfalls, cannon, cowboys, cats. Another certificate, his high school graduation diploma, 1945. A lot of letters, maybe a couple dozen. He took up one of the envelopes, adhered to by a decayed rubber band; apparently they'd been in a bundle like love letters. He gathered them together, all bearing the return address of one Bucky McNie, 212 Grand Avenue, Albany, N.Y. Who in hell was Bucky McNie? Withdrawing a sheet of notepaper, he read, with deep puzzlement: c5Xd4. That was all. From another envelope he read: Nf6. Then it came to him: they were chess moves. And he remembered that at fifteen or so he'd carried on a fervent chess correspondence with a pen pal, evidently the forgotten Bucky McNie; had rushed out to mail his long-pondered move as soon as he'd made it, and waited with tremendous impatience for the postman to deliver the countermove. It was hard to believe he had ever taken chess so seriously. And hard to believe he'd had a pen pal, that quaint term. Did boys still have pen pals? Did they still use terms like pals, chums? Buddies maybe. A different connotation, less corny, less naïve.

And in the meantime he'd gone through every piece of paper in front of him and hadn't come up with his birth certificate. Now that he'd actually tried to find it, he was disappointed. Probably it had been in some box that had got thrown out during one of his moves, compressed to nothing in the jaws of the garbage truck and flung into the smolder and smell of the city dumps. Anyway he'd used up a good portion of the afternoon looking, and to use up more time he took up one of the small dog-eared notebooks. *Pocket Memo 5¢* on its cover, the unbelievable prices back then. He turned its pages, written crowdedly in pencil but legible in the harsh light.

—last night went over to Sally's, we necked on her back steps, we discussed Schopenhauer—get passport next week, am I really going? Crossing the ocean & stepping on foreign soil? Can't believe it!—Scraped fender of Dad's Lincoln & he wasn't too thrilled, said to daydream less & concentrate more on what I'm doing, what I think is streets should be wider—Subjects of paintings shall be grand, as are battles, heroic actions, and divine things! Nicolas Poussin 1594–1665—Phrases to memorize:

> Quel est le train pour Paris?
> Où est le Louvre?
> Le Palais des Beaux Arts?
> Notre Dame Cathedral?
> Je vous remercie bien.

—we necked again, is kissing necking? ("Good God," Philip sighed.) Since knowing Sally I know what love is! How it fills your soul! We talked about the meaning of life & if the soul is immortal—Give all thou canst; high Heaven rejects the lore of nicely calculated less or more! Wm. Wordsworth 1770–1850— Do animals have souls? If so where would you draw the line, with amoebas? But I think animals do & maybe even amoebas.

When Paula was home from Bennington we discussed this & she agrees. She won't kill an ant—Sally came over last night, we necked out back while one of the bashes was going on inside. We talked about the universe & what was there before it began, we looked up at the stars. Mysterium Tremendum!—What is life? What is eternity? What is God?—Got passport today, it's big and green. ("Like you," muttered Philip.) Tomorrow buy rucksack, three pairs [illegible], pick up shoes. One week to go!— The tree of man was never quiet, then 'twas the Roman, now 'tis I! A. E. Housman 1859–1936—Tomorrow: dental appt, haircut, return overdue lib. books. Three days to go!—I'm writing down what I believe in: to seek the truth, to feel deeply and passionately, to strive for the highest in this mighty tumult of life!—

Philip left off reading, tossed the memo book and the rest of the papers back into the box and dumped it down where it had stood. He snapped off the light and went inside. It didn't seem possible that he could have been even more ludicrous at seventeen than he remembered. Life! Love! God! You felt a cringing embarrassment for all that pulsating half-bakedness . . . but entertaining, you had to admit. Is kissing necking? This six-and-a-half-foot virgin with his exclamation points flying in all directions . . . and the divine Sally, who was that? Gone the way of Bucky McNie . . . but no, he dimly recalled a girl about as gawky a beanpole as himself and how neither of them knew how to kiss, heads like two melons stuck hard together, immobile, as if sheer pressure were the answer. Knew how to talk though, apparently—all that lofty adolescent quacking. And yet, and yet . . . the profound questions were always adolescent. Eternity. God. The human soul. They were the things you asked when you were young. Age wore them away.

"I'm in danger of growing maudlin," he said to himself with a slightly forced humorous smile, coming into the recreation room and sitting down in his jacket. The afternoon was growing dark. He thought of driving into the city and having dinner at the tennis club, but the weather wasn't for it. He sat on.

Quel est le train pour Paris? The gangling wayfarer in his ridiculous beret. He thought how he had kept meeting him on his October plane trip, in his adrenaline-clattering, sleep-starved mind, after not having thought of him for years. "There was this guy I kept meeting, he was in a beret and had dust on his shoes," he had said to Paula, sitting there in her kitchen, an exhausted wreck. He had said a lot of things he wouldn't ordinarily have said, or even have thought of. Their conversation had been very serious. He had pushed it behind him and forgotten it along with the whole bizarre trip, but now the scene came back to him intact and vivid. The rain had pelted down outside, and it was as if he could hear its sound again, and could hear his voice saying over his coffee mug, "Do you know that quotation: 'Die and become what you are'? It says everything."

Everything. What you will have been when your life is consummated, when you can make no further alterations on it. He turned on the lamp at his side, feeling a ghastly, lonely melancholy spread through him.

He deserved the wrath of God not because of what he'd done to others, that wasn't his crime. His crime was what he had done to the writer of the memo book, to the wanderer in his beret, whom he had so long ago turned his back on, abandoned, forgotten. His crime was to himself. And for that most terrible of transgressions, God's wrath was just. Only it wasn't God's wrath, it was his own.

"This is overdoing it," he muttered, and stood up with a blink of stinging eyes. "It's maudlin. Lugubrious. It's having too much time on your hands and thinking depressing thoughts."

He took his ghastly melancholy into the kitchen and opened a can of vichyssoise for dinner. He went up to bed very early, and because he was exhausted from his sleepless night before, he slept heavily. He dreamed heavily.

He was sitting on the cold cement floor out in the black clutter of the garage. People were walking around talking and drinking from paper cups, it was a convention of some sort. The people began to leave; they got into a big Lincoln, and he was driving. They kept talking with each other as he drove. The wanderer in his beret was there, and Sally, Bucky McNie, and Wordsworth and A. E. Housman, and the engineer was there too, with the birth certificate folded like a sad handkerchief in his breast pocket. When they all disembarked from the car, Philip didn't want them to; he turned around and tried to grasp their hands, but they couldn't see him because it was dark.

He woke at seven, the dream not yet faded from his mind. "I guess I don't have to take it to Freud for analysis," he murmured as he got up. Yet he felt better this morning. The ghastly black melancholy was gone. He felt purged in a way, drained, museful and quietly objective.

At work, in the bustle and bright decorations of approaching Christmas, he thought: I might in fact sell the business, and the house too. It's something to think about. And what then? . . . What would you do? Put a beret on your head? Look up Bucky McNie? Reread the classics? Make friends with your far-flung grown children? He hardly knew them. They had other fathers.

As the days went on, his thoughts began to center on one thing.

⊂⟨⟩⊃

Paula received an attractive Christmas card from her daughter. The enclosed letter was less attractive, but at least it was restrained, no doubt by the Yuletide spirit.

> . . . *Please consider what we've been discussing these past months. And if it's your hobby you're worried about, remember that if you move into a condo there's no reason why you shouldn't have a studio, because you could rent a really nice spacious one. You might even want to take some lessons. You might find that you meet a lot of interesting people. So many retired people are into art now.*

I'm not pushing you, I'm just giving you a few little things to turn over in your mind as the New Year approaches . . .

Paula tossed the letter into the garbage bucket, the dimpled, patronizing words actually more offensive than the usual double-underlined exhortations. But she wondered if the phrase "as the New Year approaches" was in fact a veiled ultimatum.

"Such as what? All she can do is show up unexpectedly again, if that's what she's got in mind. But there's not a single legal step she can take."

Even so, the thought of another argumentative visit was vexatious, distracting. She bundled up and went outdoors. The great snowfall of two weeks ago had melted in a sudden thaw, followed by an even more sudden frost that had glazed every surface, as if with crushed diamonds. Then it had begun to snow again. It was snowing now, from a dark overcast sky, in hard wind-driven flakes that stung her face invigoratingly as she hiked along the slope. The slope was spotted by big hard snowdrifts, white whales they looked like, in a slanted, gray-green sea. And after a while, under the icy battering of flakes, she felt scoured of her worry and climbed back home.

Soup, a roll; she sat watching the flakes fly by. Down on the street someone was carrying a small fir tree over his shoulder. They cut their own Christmas trees here, they didn't do much else, Christmas in the village was very quiet. Not like Chicago, good God the crowds, the stores, the carols and cash registers. And her thoughts turned to money, yes, she would definitely give hers to the poor of some blighted land. Not that she had a better opinion of the poor than of anyone else, human nature being what it was. Most paupers, given the chance, would leap into the saddle of galloping swank and never once look back at the rest of them stuck in the mire, who would do the same if they could. Human nature also accounted for the ultimate failure of revolutions. What happened after the great ideals had been secured?—a settling back into the same old greed and inequities that had been fought against. It was as if God, if one believed in God, had forgotten to finish His task when He created human beings, had left out some essential, some terribly needed ingredient.

She looked down the slope at the white whales in their slanting gray-green sea. She missed a sea, a river, a lake. But she had her bathtub on its grimed old lion claws, and submerged to her chin beneath the miniature waves she was down among flickering fish and sunken Greek statues, or in the middle of a raging Atlantic, or in some silent stream, in some silent land unknown to time.

She finished her soup, but kept sitting. There in the distance the young farmer had climbed crazily to his house. Yesterday, at the *épicerie*, where she overheard most of the village news, she had learned that his young widow had remarried and was expecting a child. She was very glad to know this, and the thought of daisies came into her mind: the freshest and whitest of all flowers, the very embodiment of beginnings, each with its yellow, seed-bearing disk like a shining little sun. The name was from the Middle English, "Day's Eye," she remembered that from school. The fresh, innocent eye of dawning day. Perhaps that eye was in the stone's tiniest, innermost grain. And yet, for all the gladness one felt for the young woman, for all one's thoughts about the regenerative force of life, nothing could change those few minutes of the past, the chopping red blades and razor-slashed throat. And perhaps it was that which was in the stone's tiniest, innermost grain.

Whenever Paula's thoughts fell too hard on the side of unanswerable agony, or when she focused too long on the usual fate of revolutions, or even when she was unable to push aside a sweeping fear of her daughter's possible plans, she would go in and sit down on the side of the bed, her eyes resting on the small rug. Whoever had made it had understood very deeply what design and balance and grace were. Those things existed, and she was comforted to remember this, and was brought back to a frame of mind in which the dark things did not weigh the scales to the ground.

On Christmas Eve Paula attended Midnight Mass at the village church. She went for the singing. She supposed there would be singing. She had scrubbed the stone dust from her hands, combed her hair, and tied a kerchief around her head. She supposed a kerchief would be more seemly than a snow cap.

The service had begun when she sat down at the back. Villagers were kneeling in pews while the priest was intoning something at length. She had never been inside the church. It was small, stony, ancient, and almost as cold as the night outside. Numerous candles illumined the altar. Smaller candles, in small red glasses, made blossoms of light throughout the dimness, casting glints from paintings and statues. The priest's incantation came to an end and was taken up by the villagers. Then that came to an end and the priest began again.

Her thoughts wandered. She looked at a painting of the Annunciation on the wall beside her, dimly lit by one of the small candles. It was not very good, a humble little country cousin of Van Eyck's masterpiece. She tried to see beauty in it, even though she did not believe in the Annunciation, and even though she herself would have been furious if, as an unsuspecting young girl going about her daily tasks, she had suddenly had a divine pregnancy thrust upon her. The nerve. The gall. It should be called the Presumption. These thoughts, she knew, were disrespectful, and she respected the faith of others; she would even have liked to have some of it herself. And again she tried to see beauty in the stiff, stilted figures, because they had been painted with humble faith. But a bad painting was a bad painting.

Her breath was white in the stony air. Her buttocks were growing sore from sitting. But the back-and-forth incantations went on and on until she began to wonder if maybe this was what a Mass consisted of entirely. She gazed at the backs of the kneeling villagers as they chanted whatever they were chanting. What stoicism, what single-mindedness—no squirms, no stretching, no thought of hard floor and bitter cold. She doubted that they would ever stop. She herself was like that when she worked on her rocks.

And her thoughts wandered again, to the things she had in storage. She would give them away, she had no need of them, clothes, linens, furniture, porcelain, crystal, Venetian glass and odds and ends of every kind, so many crates and boxes that she wouldn't know where to begin looking even if she thought her birth certificate might be in one of them. Since her granddaughter had written, on her fluorescent Disney notepaper with her amazingly deplorable spelling—did American children learn anything, even in the best of schools?—her thoughts had rested more and more often on the engineer. She wanted to know his full name at least, and where he had come from. Everyone deserved that much authenticity at least: a name and a place. She wanted to acknowledge him. She wanted to honor the fact, however belatedly, that he had existed.

The incantations came to a conclusive end. Then the choirboys lifted their voices in a sound of ravishing purity. The damp cold and the hardness of the bench vanished, she felt a joyousness swell within her, as if riches were spilling down upon her, as if she and the singing and the candles and the villagers all existed in one eternally sublime moment.

When the singing ended, Paula rose and took her leave before anything else could begin. She doubted that anyone had noticed her sitting there; and if they had, surely they wouldn't begrudge the village idiot's presence among them. She smiled, feeling in very fine spirits as she crunched back to her apartment in the darkness. It had been a perfect Christmas Eve, and before going to bed she poured herself a glass of cider and stood with it by the kitchen window in the silence, looking out at the night sky.

The next day she resumed her pounding and chipping and chiseling, her battle, her quest for the true thing. It was fiercely cold when she went out on her tramps. She saw not a soul as she made her way along the snow-crusted slope. In the spring and summer she occasionally caught sight of and avoided a hiker, but in winter there was no one. She saw no ants either. In winter they lived underground, in small chambers where they had stored food from their forages. Usually she brought a roll and dropped pieces along the hard snow, in case they ran out of what they had. When she came in from the outdoors, face red and tingling, she would turn on the oven to heat up the cold rooms, put water on to boil, and get out of her heavy outer clothing, leaving them on the floor where they were as she made a cup of instant coffee and returned to her rocks, to sit pounding and chipping and chiseling in the profound winter silence.

⳾

She had a letter from Philip in the New Year. They usually wrote a few brief lines; she was surprised to withdraw three pages from the envelope.

Dear Paula,

I've got his full name & homeland & a lot more—didn't find my birth certif. so asked in the trust dept. of the bank how long they kept their records—only as long as the funds are in trust, after which they're discarded, but I asked them to look anyway. Gave them the year of the original transaction, 1928, & whatever other info I could think of & paid a search fee, & they called a week later to say the microfilm had been located in their warehouse files.

Damn it I wish you had a phone like other people, there's too much to write—will try to boil it down—Info from the microfilm included the name of the lawyer who handled the transaction, an A. J. Taylor—knew he'd be long dead but the law firm is still around so I called. Taylor's son is with the firm, he's preserved his father's legal papers & today he had the relevant ones for me to read.

Taylor was retained by Mother to go to Denmark & settle the estate, he kept a detailed record—pges & pges of negotiations with a Copenhagen bank, savings, investments, etc.—real estate too, house and land north of Copenhagen, he describes the house Paula, he even gives the location—he & appraisers spent a couple weeks going through every room, his instructions from Mother (no surprise) were that everything was to be auctioned—there's a detailed list in Danish. When Taylor left he gave the Cop. bank power of atty. to carry out the auction & sell the house & land. These funds with all the rest were later transferred here, end of story.

Or beginning. I want to know how he looked, what he was like & I know you do too. I want to go to Copenhagen—I think of the times I've been there & never given the place a thought as having anything to do with me. I want to go again & you ought to come too—with the leads we've got it shouldn't be too hard to find out who our engineer really was. Is resurrection the word? Redemption?

Try to decide to come, we ought to do it together. And it might be a good thing, in any case, for you to get away from those clamorous communications from Malibu. Only you'll have to comb your hair & put on some decent clothes—that'll be your sacrifice, mine will be facing a plane again. Write—or if you can bring yourself to use a phone, get down to that P.O. of yours & call.

Philip

Two torches sweep through the vast darkness of dripping stone. Illumined are incredible formations—a shadowed and flickering labyrinth of jags and chasms and shapes unimaginable.

On the earth's surface, where human creatures have considerably evolved, a plumed nobleman out on a hunting excursion, hearing of a strange natural shaft said to lead to an underground palace filled with magnificent statues and precious gems, has had a miner and a goldsmith lowered by ropes through the mysterious hole.

But the torches disclose no sculptures or precious gems. In the deep, dank chill the two explorers fill a basket with sandy debris from the floor. With hammers they knock off the tips of numerous stalactites and fill another basket with these. Then they are hoisted back up into daylight.

An anticipatory week passes, but the sand from the cavern floor fails to turn into gold. Attempts are then made to produce gunpowder by grinding up the stalactite fragments. This also fails. The absolute darkness and silence are not intruded upon again.

· 19 ·

& Sitting in the kitchen, its outside door open to the fresh sunny air of the courtyard, the housekeeper and nanny are suddenly aware of noises from the front entrance of the house. Getting herself up with a yawn, the housekeeper shuffles slappingly across the unswept red-tile floor out to the entrance hall. There the Counselor is clumping along to the staircase in his cloak and tall hat, his stick and tapestry-worked satchel in hand, a coachman following with the dwarf's portmanteau on his shoulder.

"He's back," she says, sitting down again in the kitchen.

"He is back?" asks the nanny, her face amazed under its great white beribboned headdress. "Why, I can't believe it. Why, I was sure we would hear he had been found dead somewhere."

"Him? Too ugly and nasty to die."

"But where can he have been all this time?"

"No idea. Visiting other freaks maybe."

"Well," said the nanny, taking up one of the housekeeper's sugar-tops and putting it in her mouth, "I am very glad indeed that he has come to no harm."

"Very glad your pay won't end."

"And so? What of you? You have given me to believe that your pay is yet more than mine."

"And with good reason it is, what with all the work I do around here—I'm at it from dawn till dusk. And on top of that, let me tell you there's not enough money in this world to pay for having to look at that foul old thing. You've got it easy, you sit tucked away up there in the nursery, but me—"

The nanny could not abide the flapping tongue once it got started; excusing herself, she went back out to the babe in the courtyard, where he sat playing quietly with some sticks. She wished she could tell herself that it was not her munificent wages that kept her from leaving, but her love of the child. But though he was pretty he was not winning—pale, somber, nervous. And no wonder, living in that house with its dust and hanging silence, and with that ancient grotesque always about, for whom the child—and for that matter she herself—felt a horror. The babe's brooding, fidgety ways were understandable but off-putting, as was his precocity, his keen judgmental baby's eyes, and his impudent tongue. Only this morning he had told the house-keeper in his tiny, piping, nervous voice, "You talk too much!" But at this, the nanny had had to smile.

In the kitchen the housekeeper heard the coachman stride back down the hall and shut the door behind him. She put a sugartop in her mouth, displeased that the nanny had taken one and, settling back in her chair, closed her eyes for a snooze.

⊂⊃

"Is it good to be back?" the Counselor asked as he worked himself out of his cloak, and he laughed aloud at the bright smile he received from the lad, who was walking around the room in his uniform, stretching his back and arms after the long carriage trip. Flinging the cloak aside, the Counselor waddled over to one of the windows, ex-claiming, "See what a fine day has welcomed us!" The roofs and green copper spires of the city sparkled in sunlight. The sky was wonderfully blue, with small clouds white and scudding. "And what do you think that one looks like?" he asked, beaming and pointing. "A teapot," said the lad, and they both laughed.

"Now sit, my darling, be comfortable," the old man urged, bustling over to the chaise longue and patting it, upon which a puff of dust rose. He gave a look around at the musty Savonnerie rug, at the great bed with its dingy blue hangings. "Things have gone to pot, as you see, but what does it matter? Sit, sit, lie down, be comfortable! Let us rest before eating. Are you hungry?"

"A little," the lad replied as he stretched out on the chaise longue, his booted, very long legs extending beyond its foot.

"Of course she is an abysmal cook," wheezed the Counselor, hoisting himself into a chair, "and an abysmal everything else."

"Lazy, mean and stupid," said the lad.

"Yes, in that lump you see the collective stupidity of mankind—its narrowness and small-spiritedness, its heartlessness where thought and sensibility should be. And you see its greed too, for she is the most miserly of misers, never spends an øre of what she is paid but hoards it away, she's a Croesus by now. Moreover she inherited a property up in Helsingør which she subsequently sold, and you may be sure she drove a mean bargain. Ah, it was a nice cottage let me tell you, extremely small and plain, yet so deeply appealing in its way ... but did she appreciate it? Of course not. She has a soul of mud. The soul is eternal—*anima est aeterna*—but I hope to God hers will not be."

"But Father, why do you not give her notice? You have always desisted because of what she did for me when I was small, you have been loyal to that act for my sake, but I tell you there is no reason for you to put up with her any longer."

"Why, those are exactly my own thoughts," the Counselor responded buoyantly. "Come then, let us go down—and I will not mince my words!"

The housekeeper, awakened from her nap, looked over at the old beetle stumping across the room.

"So you're back." She yawned.

"I give you three days' notice! Three days, then out!"

Getting up from her chair, and planting her hands on the hips of her shabby skirt with its several lengths of soiled petticoats hanging below, she squinted down at him.

"And what kind of nonsense is this? What idiotic thing has got into that thick old head of yours now?"

"It's no use flapping your tongue! I should have done it long ago!"

And the lad said, "Yes, long ago, Father. She has a soul of mud."

"Three days, then out! Meanwhile, I want you to prepare a decent dinner tonight." And turning, he looked up at the lad. "What shall we have? What would suit you?"

"Why not roast goose, Father? I have not had that for a long while. Yes, with red cabbage and browned potatoes."

"Perfection!" agreed the Counselor.

"And apple cake after, with plenty of whipped cream."

"Ah, what an appetite. What an appetite!"

The housekeeper, staring with wide and frightened eyes first at the Counselor and then at the empty space beside him, gave a start as he turned back to her.

"So you have heard what dinner is to be!"

"Heard? Heard what . . . ?" she faltered.

"And now—!" he exclaimed, turning away with so loud a laugh that she jumped and knocked over her chair, "let us go into the courtyard! Smell the lilacs! Smell them!"

Seeing the Counselor come into the courtyard, the nanny gave a brief, polite nod in his direction and suppressed a shudder. The babe, scrambling up from where he sat, raced over to hide behind her. She took him by the hand and went inside.

"Why, what is wrong?" she asked the housekeeper, whose face was white, and she told the child to run up to the nursery. "He's mad," the housekeeper hissed when they were alone. "He's mad. He talks to the air! See him!" She pointed out the door. He was waddling along talking, gesturing, now listening and nodding with animation, now laughing.

"*Gud hjalpe os,*" murmured the nanny, her hand going to her cheek, "what are we to do?"

"Best we stay calm." The housekeeper breathed deeply and set right the toppled chair. "Could be the trip was a strain. Could be it will pass off."

"Oughtn't we to inform his sister? She who came by that day? She told me her house number, she lives but down the street."

"What for? Not yet. We'll wait and see if the old horror comes out of it."

◌୫ ଚ◌

In order not to stir up the old horror more than he already was, the housekeeper slapped off to Gammel Strand and bought a fresh codfish. She scrounged up an old dusty bottle of wine from the mess in the pantry. She attempted to make a decent meal. When at dinnertime she brought the platter into the dining room, he was seated at the table barking a complaint at her.

"You have set the table with only one plate! Are we to eat off one plate?"

"You mean," she asked in confusion, astonished, and also appalled at the thought, "I'm to eat with you?"

"You? You, the collective spiritual mud of mankind? No of course not, it is for him! We sit here waiting! Set that platter down and bring another plate! How she tries one's patience," he sighed when she was gone. "But not for long," he added with a laugh, and the lad laughed too.

The housekeeper returned with another plate, wineglass, knife, fork and serviette. She set them out with nervous, trembling fingers and slapped hastily back to the doorway, where she hovered with craned neck, watching.

"Don't stand there like a big gawk!" cried the Counselor. "Get on with you, close that door!"

The door closed. The Counselor merrily shook out his serviette and began to eat. He had forgotten all about the roast goose.

⋐⋑

Having closed the door to a crack, the housekeeper glued her eye to it. After a time the nanny tiptoed up to her. "What is he doing?" And she peered as the housekeeper stood aside. At the long dusty table, in a little pool of candlelight, the Counselor sat eating and addressing in festive tones the empty place setting across from him; sat lifting his wineglass in toasts, talking, and listening raptly, nodding, laughing.

"At least he is happy," she said with a helpless headshake. "But what are we to do?"

"Don't keep asking! I don't know."

They closed the crack.

⋐⋑

"And how many *Kro*s did you go to?" the Counselor laughed, shaking a finger in mock admonishment. "And trying to climb the pillars of the Raadhus!—*Gudbevares*."

"It wasn't every day one graduated."

"And with such marks!"

"They weren't bad," the lad agreed, his eyes very blue in the candlelight.

The Counselor's own blue eyes, little deep-set chinks beneath his shaggy brows, were shining. "Oh, how good it is to have you back! How good everything is! How happy we are! Come. Come—" And forgetting his food, grabbing up a candlestick, he maneuvered his bulk down from the chair and thudded from the room. Bustling into the library, he stood on his toes and lit the two candles on his desk. Papers lay strewn across it just as he had left them. "I shall burn these papers, trash to be burned!" he muttered, getting into his chair and pushing them aside. "But here, here is what I want to show you." From one of the desk drawers he took out a morocco-bound portfolio and opened it before him. Inside were letters and a few official papers.

"How often while you were away," he said, "did I sit here rereading your letters. See, they're quite worn. But not as worn as these." And he brought out from his inner pocket the two frayed letters he had carried with him throughout his trip, and put them back with the others. From another pocket he withdrew his square, metal-rimmed spectacles, and put them on, beaming. "But here, here is what I want to show you—that which caused you to celebrate so exuberantly!"

He laid the paper down as the lad leaned over and smoothed it with his hand.

The Royal Danish Academy for Military Cadets Cadet Class of 1809			
Marks Received at the Examination	Good	Fair	Bad
General conduct, and when on duty	8		
Higher Mathematics	8		
Applied Mathematics	8		
Chemistry	7	1	
Fortification	8		
Strategy	8		
Military Geography and Statistics	7	1	
French	8		
German	8		
Philosophy	8		
Military freehand drawing	8		
Total	86	2	

Passed with the best of character as first.

The lad smiled. "No, I didn't do too badly."

"Too badly!" scoffed the Counselor, laughing, and going through other papers. "As you see, I kept everything for your return." He unfolded a heavy sheet struck with royal seals. Adjusting his spectacles, he began to read aloud.

" 'We, Frederik the Sixth, by God's grace King of Denmark and Norway, of the Goths and Wends, Duke of Slesvig, Holstein, Stormarn, Dithmarschen, Lauenburg, etc., on this day the first of June 1813, make known the following . . .' " He slapped the paper. "No, by God, I never understood it. Why you had to get this thing."

"Royal dispensation is necessary to obtain a military discharge in time of war."

"Of course, of course, I know that. But to obtain a discharge only in order to join another army? *His* army?"

"Father, surely we discussed Napoleon often enough before I left."

"A monster of carnage," the Counselor said with sudden tears in his eyes. "His glory rests on a million corpses . . ."

"No, Father, he was the torchbearer of the Revolution. His were the forces of freedom and progress, he was the leader of humanity into the light of reason—"

"Oh, how often I heard you say those things, and those same words are in your letters . . . oh, your credulousness, your blind faith! oh why, why did you have to go? . . . and yet, yet what does it matter? For you are home now safe and sound. Safe and sound!" The Counselor laughed, closing the portfolio and sticking it back in the drawer. The lad was walking around the room, smiling and looking. "Here is the bookcase ladder. How often I used to sit at its top reading."

"And when you were very small," added the Counselor zestfully, "how you loved to roll it back and forth on its casters!"

"How well I remember. And here is the bust of Holberg. And the etching of Kongens Nytorv. No, nothing has changed. And here is my silhouette." The silhouette was hung very low on the wall, at the Counselor's own eye level, so that he would not have to see it from a distance, looking up, but could gaze upon its beloved features closely. "It is the only likeness of you I have," he said to the lad, "but now that you are back, why, we must have your portrait painted."

"Why not? Although I am not much good at sitting still. I am like you, Father, full of energy."

"Ah, but we could have the finest painter in Copenhagen! Eckersberg!"

"Or Senn!"

And they both laughed with pleasure.

Outside the closed door, the housekeeper and nanny had stood listening for some time. Now and then they could hear a sound of laughter. "It does not seem to be passing off," the nanny observed unhappily, at which moment the Counselor came through the door with his candle, causing the two women to jump back with theirs, their faces lit and anxious. "Who are you!" he barked. "Who are you!" For the Counselor had briefly forgotten where he was and what he was doing and where he was going. He sometimes underwent these moments of confusion—he might be disembarking from the ship in Stralsund, or singing by the harpsichord as a child—which moments when they passed left him no less sanguine than before. "Idiots! Away with you!" he laughed, and clomped on down the hall with the lad.

"It will be good when they're gone," he wheezed cheerfully, climbing the stairs. "I always used to keep a large house staff, but the fact is, I never enjoyed having them around. Eyes, eyes everywhere, that wasn't something I was too keen on . . . paid them exorbitantly too. That goes without saying: one learns early on what is required when one is—not to put too fine a point on it—of unusual appearance." At the top of the stairs he gave a laugh. "And so one day I dismissed the lot!"

"I know, Father. It was when I left for the Academy."

"That is so," he said after a pause. "I have to be honest. With you gone from the house, all at once there seemed no reason to keep them on."

"You were lonely when I left."

"I was," he said, walking on down the corridor. "But I wanted you to lead a life like other people. I never wanted to stand in your way."

"You never did, Father. But I know you were lonely when I entered the Academy. And I know that one can be loneliest of all with many people about."

"It was why I wanted them to be gone. And it was the eyes too. There had been too many years of it."

"I understood that."

"We have always understood each other so deeply. Whenever you came home to visit, and you came often, you were devotion itself, there was never a cloud between us."

In his bedchamber the old man set his candlestick down and began to bustle around. "Oh," he said, drawing up, "but will you want to sleep in your old room?"

"Of course not, Father. Why should we be parted even for a night?"

"Then you take the bed, for it has been a long journey and I want you to rest well. Be comfortable, my darling, be comfortable!"

"Nonsense, the chaise longue is fine."

"No, no, it is too short, Your legs hang over."

"I'll sleep like a top," the lad assured him, and sat down to remove his boots. And as the Counselor stood looking on, he beheld the lad in a great radiance; for this too was something that happened to the old man at times: it was as if for some moments his eyes and soul were filled with golden, streaming light. Then he began to bustle around again, and came waddling over with a lap robe, wheezing and beaming.

"You mustn't fuss so, Father," the lad laughed as he lay down. "It is a mild night, I am not cold at all."

"No, you are home, my darling. You will never be cold again."

And tenderly smoothing his hair back, kissing him good night on his brow, the Counselor too went to bed.

CROSS

Despite his robust constitution, the Counselor was tired after his long journey from Leipzig and he slept extremely late. The housekeeper and nanny heard him thud down the stairs at about two in the afternoon, at which the housekeeper got up from her chair and slapped out to the hall. She came slapping back in. "Gone off on his walk. And talking away to the air just like yesterday: 'Ah, the fine weather holds! Ah, how fortunate we are!' " She sat down broodingly, and shook her head. "No, doesn't seem to be passing off."

"And last night he did not even know who we were. Oh, it is frightening!—we should go to his sister."

"And have him carted away? Then where are we?"

To this the nanny had no answer.

Having left home late, the Counselor returned late. The sky had gone from blue to flaming tints of pink to deepest violet when he came stumping back in, full of delight with their walk on the Commons. "Ah, the beauty! The beauty! Was it not just as you remembered?" Then, catching sight of the housekeeper peering from the end of the hall, he suddenly advanced upon her in a rush, crying out, "You! Why are you not gone! Where is a basket!"

Horrible images flew through the housekeeper's mind—she had heard of the revolution in France when chopped heads fell into baskets, why did he want a basket?—and turning, she fled to the kitchen with the thuds of the crazed miscreation behind her. There she stood speechless in a corner as he stared around, suddenly dumped out some withered turnips from a large wicker basket and rushed off with it.

In his study the Counselor began sweeping his papers from the desk into the basket.

"How could I forget that I meant to do this? Yes, I am going to burn all my papers!"

"What a good idea, Father," said the lad.

"Trash. Trash to be burned!" he said exuberantly. "Discourses, disquisitions, dissertations—all an egregious waste of time!" When the desk was cleared, he began yanking open the drawers of his cabinet and pulling out more papers. When the basket was overflowing, he started back to the kitchen with it.

The housekeeper stood in tense conversation with the nanny, who had come downstairs at the sound of the Counselor's return. They both jumped back as he came thudding in, headed for the great blackened hearth. There the Counselor threw his writings into the flames. Grabbing a poker, he jabbed and stirred as sparks shot high and scraps of burning paper floated to the floor. "Trash, trash," he laughed, "I shall burn it all, everything!" And forgetting the basket, he rushed back out.

"Where has he gone?" cried the nanny, stomping around on the tiles to extinguish the bits of flame, as if in a sudden wild dance. "He will set the house afire! I care not what you say, I go for his sister!" "Go then, yes go!" agreed the housekeeper, and the nanny hurried from the house, holding her great headdress in place as she ran.

"Where is the basket?" the Counselor asked, looking around as he grabbed up more papers from the cabinet. "Ah well, I will finish up tomorrow then. It has been a very pleasing activity. Altogether it has been a splendid day! Shall we go up now and rest a little before dinner?"

In his bedchamber he lit a candle, and sat down with a reflective expression.

"I must ask you something. Do you want to see the babe?"

"Oh, not very much, Father. I have done this long without him."

"I want to be fair, you see. I don't care about being fair to others, no, no longer, but I could not face myself if I were not fair to you. He is your son, after all, and you have never seen him."

"What is he like?" asked the lad.

The Counselor sighed. "I don't really know. I have seen him but seldom. He took against me from the start."

"That is a shame, Father."

"It is understandable." The Counselor sighed again, and smiled. "But it is you I am thinking of. Do not worry about my feelings. I want to do what is right, what is fair. And if it would make you happy, what makes you happy makes me the same."

"Perhaps a small visit then. We need not stay."

"No, we must shortly go down to dinner."

In the nursery, walking as noiselessly as he could, the old man carried his candle over to the babe's small low bed. The amber glow fell soft on the sleeping face. "He looks a good bit like me," whispered the lad, and the Counselor nodded and smiled as the child stirred, drowzily opening his eyes, the lashes fluttering.

"He has come to see you. Welcome him," the Counselor said warmly, but the child scrambled maniacally away on his back, banging up against the headboard and screaming in terror.

"No, no, you mustn't scream," soothed the Counselor, leaning toward him and extending his hand, at which the screams grew wilder yet. "He is here, greet him!" he urged, having to lift his voice in a loud cry over the ear-shattering noise. "Please greet him!"

"Perhaps he will grow calm if we wait," suggested the lad.

"Do you hear? We are waiting for you!" cried the Counselor.

Then of a sudden the babe stopped screaming. His small body jerked and writhed most horribly. He had gone into convulsions.

"What is wrong? Oh, this is bad!" gasped the Counselor, and stomped hurriedly from the room. "Oh!" he cried to several figures running along the corridor. "Help the babe, he is not well!" Then noting that Bodil was one of the figures, huffing and puffing, her face a curious purple hue and her eyes popping out of her head at him, he slammed back into his room and locked the door.

He listened to the commotion outside.

"There are far too many people in this house," he said to the lad.

"Come out, Thorkild! Come out!"

"That is Bodil. The ultimate soul of mud."

"Why must we put up with her, Father?"

"Get out!" he yelled.

On the other side of the door Bodil, fanning herself with her hand and catching her breath, nodded at the two manservants she had brought with her. They began pounding.

"She is much stronger than I thought," the Counselor remarked, and waddled over to a chair where he sat down to think about things.

"There is too much mud in this house," he said as the pounding went on.

"Why should we put up with so much mud, Father?"

The Counselor got down from his chair and began working himself into his cloak. "Come. Come," he said with great good cheer, and bustled over to his bed. Bending with a laborious grunt, he pulled out from under it a wooden coffer. "People think I am impractical, but I am not. I always keen extra funds on hand." He bustled around for his satchel, and into it stuffed all the coins and paper currency that the coffer held. Then he clamped his hat on his head and grabbed his stick. "Come. Come," he said happily, and clomping to the door, he unlocked it.

The housekeeper, who had been madly slapping back and forth from the Counselor's door to the nursery, where the nanny sat in a hysterical state with the babe—a third manservant had already been sent to fetch a doctor—was astonished to see the Counselor emerge quiet and beaming.

"What is your wish?" he pleasantly enquired of the little group.

"We will take him to my house," whispered Bodil, her face still empurpled and eyes popping, and nodded at the two manservants, who accompanied the complacent dwarf down the stairs. At the front entrance, as the door was opened, the Counselor dealt two powerful blows of his stick against the men's two shinbones and rushed thuddingly off into the night.

"They will not run after us," he wheezed, laughing, as he made his escape. "For one thing their legs are smarting, and for another they are too dignified."

❧

In the morning everything is serene. He sits in a hackney coach gazing out at the passing Sound, blue and sparkling in the sunlight. "Now you will see," he says to the lad as they enter Helsingør, and a little while later they are disembarking before the cottage.

· 20 ·

A few small showers have followed the heavy rain and wind, but by and large the sky outside Grethe's windows has been intensely blue, and against its brilliance she has watched the trees turn, day by day, from tints of yellow to flaming orange and gold. Now a month has passed since her arrival and she is allowed to take walks outside with a nurse, both wearing warm coats, scarves and hats.

"Nice to be out again?" asks the nurse in a breath of white.

"Oh, it is wonderful. I have missed it."

"I tell you, if it was up to me, there would be walks right from the start."

"Would that *you* were head of the hospital," Grethe said with a rueful little laugh, gazing all around her, for the pleasure of being outside again was indescribable—the trees no longer separated from her by glass, but alive and goldly rustling in her ears, and on her face the cold autumn air as clear and pure as brook water. Yet for all the loneliness of her isolation, the regimen had worked, for she was no longer tormented by those fragments of terror and confusion manufactured by her own mind. She had known her mind was ill; that was why she had elected to come to a mental institution, after all. To get well. And now those terrible, fragmented moments were no more—

251

she did not even remember what they had consisted of, they were so totally extinct. Her mind was whole and clear. She had followed every rule, and with patience, faith and fortitude she had come through. And with the help of Olaf, who had visited her so often. She had unburdened her soul to him, and he had unburdened his to her. Their talks had at first been very intense; she remembered that, although she no longer remembered what they had talked about, only that she had felt eased as the days passed; for Olaf was so encouraging, so faithful and good, and gradually their conversations had become calm and sunny. Olaf still came to visit. He was with her now, scampering through the fallen leaves, as happy as she that an entire month had passed and she was allowed walks, that the worst was behind her and she could see the light at the end of the tunnel, where her beloved Holger and the boys stood waiting.

The square-shaped young maid had gone back to her usual ways, managing to be elsewhere when the linens were distributed or the brass stair rails polished. Yes, she said to herself, everything was back to how it had been. The dark circles under the master's eyes were gone, and each day he was down in his studio-cottage painting like always, and her fellow servants no longer went around all long-faced and hushed, and the two spoiled brats could be heard making their usual rumpus. That feeling she'd had that the Rosteds' lives had come crashing down in pieces, that the house was an empty, broken shell, that was a thing of the past. The great drama was gone. True, the mistress was locked up in a crazy house, but things here were just as ordinary and pleasant as before. The new young tutor didn't help. He was a perfect nothing of a fellow, little and plump and pink-nosed, and looked like he had chalk in the creases of his coat, but the master liked him, and in the dining room there was no longer that great tragic, empty silence, with only the clink of the master's fork on his plate— no, they talked and talked, and they laughed, laughed a lot.

It was hard to believe that in only a month's time the tremendous night of screams and sobs and yells had been forgotten, her shocking words cast to the winds. What good had the truth done? Where was the ruination, the justice? Things were so jolly it fairly made you puke. And as she swept the carpet with damp tea leaves—for it was impossible to escape every chore—she felt that the power within her had no place to go, that it was banked down and suffocated like an ash-covered heap of glowing coals.

◌

Today is clear and cold, Holger wrote, *wind not too high, the Sound all dark blues and greens. I took my walk and, as always, pretended you were with me. I miss you so terribly, our absence of communication is so hard to accept. But accept it we must, and though I cannot send you these letters it gives me comfort to write them, and to know you are writing me too, in your thoughts.*

I have painted all morning, and I must report that the still-life I told you about is coming along well. I think it will be quite fine, if I may say so. Yet even as he wrote this, Holger shook his head. He was painting again because one had to resume a normal way of life, but he was not swept up in what he did; every stroke of the brush had a mundane, tasklike quality to it. *And I continue pleased with the tutor. The boys like him very much, and he keeps them without difficulty at their lessons (which is not to say they aren't their usual unquiet selves afterwards!). I too like him greatly, and we have good discussions at the table.* And what a welcome change it was not to sit there night after night in lonely silence. It did him good to talk, to laugh, to get outside himself, and he wished deeply that Grethe too had someone to talk with. He could hardly bear to think of her loneliness, yet isolation being the nature of a rest cure, one could do nothing but hold faith in what the doctors deemed right.

And now I must tell you that I met Onkel for lunch in Copenhagen yesterday. We decided on the Hotel d'Angleterre, although he said the food there is not what it used to be. We have always found it excellent, haven't we? but he

was in one of his militantly nostalgic moods. Yes, the d'Angleterre lobster may-
onnaise has definitely gone down in quality, and steamships have all but sup-
planted schooners, did I realize that in ten or fifteen years schooners will have
disappeared from the seas? And typewriters, he wonders if in time he will be re-
quired to use one of these contraptions instead of his perfectly good pen. His
friend and antagonist, the mandolin player, is already considering the purchase
of a contraption, of course it is fine for him, Onkel says, he is clever with his fin-
gers (not so clever with his head, he adds with satisfaction), but then we must
needs go back to his childhood, and when did he last see a sugartop, that succu-
lent candy made of coarse brown sugar from the West Indies? Why, you can
still buy them, I say. But they cannot be as good, no, for nothing is as good in
this day and age, and he remembered as a boy listening to an old servant talk
about a grotesque creature who many years before had used to go pounding
along the streets, an ancient dwarf no higher than your thigh and monstrously
broad and misshapen, shrouded in a black cloak and lurching most horribly
from side to side and with ferocious tiny eyes, not something you'd care to meet
at night had said the old servant with a shuddering grimace, and do we have
anything like that nowadays? asks Onkel. No, there is no room for the unusual,
everything is homogeneous, produced in mass, even people. But the wonderful
thing about Onkel, as we know, is that he can laugh at himself, of course I am
all for progress, he states—somewhat needlessly, as a political radical—but at
my age I reserve the right to indulge in nostalgia from time to time, and I
stand by what I said about the mayonnaise. (I think he stands by what he said
about our era itself, and indeed, for all the steamships and typewriters loosed
upon the world, one wonders if there is such a thing as the progress of human
wisdom.) In any case, I thought you would be entertained to hear our conver-
sation. How I wished you were there with us—how I long for the day you come
home. And when would that be? Another month? Two, three? Six? A
year? He missed her so achingly that he put his pen down and sat for
some moments with his head in his hands.

Yes, we are all fine here, he resumed, *and Olaf too, whom I must not*
forget to mention. Of course he will come to no one but you, so we never see
him in the house. But Cook leaves the kitchen window open for him at night

as always. At least he supposed Cook did, for he had asked her to. But the cat was not around outside as it had used to be. Only once had he caught a glimpse of it, streaking off into the woods, and he wondered if it had reverted to its feral beginnings. He must remember to question Cook again, for Grethe would be heartbroken if she came home to find it gone.

Now I will end this for today, my darling. It is yet another long, long month before I may visit you—would it not be the most wonderful thing if you could come home with me then? That is my every moment's dream and hope.

Holger

The tutor was in the habit of walking in the woods when the day's teaching was done. He waded ankle-deep through fallen leaves, his eyes on the birds and squirrels above, then he was stumbling into someone, grasping an arm to right himself, and stepping back from a kerchiefed matron in a heavy brown shawl.

"Oh, I beg your pardon a thousand times," he apologized, clumsily tipping his hat to the broad, doughy face, "I was in my own thoughts." She shrugged. "Well, so was I. No harm done." And as she was evidently going the same way as he, she strolled along with him. He saw that below her shawl she wore the long dark skirts and white apron of a housemaid.

"You too are from the house?" he asked.

She nodded.

"I like to get out for a walk sometimes. The woods is nice."

"Yes. Very," he agreed.

"The house is too." She looked over at the pink nose, which had gone red in the cold. "I never worked in a better place. You can't find better people than the Rosteds. The salt of the earth."

"Indeed, Hr. Rosted impresses me as such."

"Her too, only she's gone now."

"In a rest home, I believe."

"Rest home?—would that it was! No, she was put away. For she's given to screaming and shrieking and tearing pictures from walls and such as that, and when that happens why everybody's beside theirselves, so now she's finally locked up, poor crazy thing. And before that, oh the turmoil and troubles, for she had a lover. She had a lover and they met here in the woods."

"Really, I . . ."

"Better you hear it from me than the other servants, for they're nothing but meanness and malice. Don't you ever listen to a thing they say."

"I have no intention of . . ."

"Oh, the low things they call her. They're glad she's gone, they've got no pity. All they think about is how awful it will be when she comes home and the same craziness all over again, the whole house shaking. They can't take it no more, some have already quit. But what I say is you've got to be loyal even if the ceiling comes crashing down. Yes, even if the ceiling comes crashing down," she finished, her power shimmering within her, for the tutor would now pack his bags and flee such a frightful household, and the master's evenings would go back to their bleakness, their loneliness, the way they should be.

The tutor said nothing. He had no interest in the woman's gossip, although the mistress of the house might indeed be in an asylum; if her husband preferred to call it a rest home, that was understandable. As for adultery, he was very young but he was not easily shocked, for sex was in the air. Wherever you went people were passionately discussing Brandes and Bjørnson, pulling apart traditional morality, shaking loose the whys and wherefores of erotic behavior . . .

"Just around here," the housemaid said, pausing and pointing, "is where they had their love nest . . ."

"Well, it's in the air, you know, sex."

She gave a sniff of the cold wind. In the air? He talked as stupid as those bohemians at the party. And she didn't like him saying the word "sex"—it was crude, and she felt her face blush hot in spite of the bitter cold.

There was a sudden flash of fur through the fallen leaves.

"A fox," the tutor observed. "Or no, a cat, I think."

She gave a grunt. Olaf. It hadn't been around the house for weeks. Living in the woods now, good riddance. And good riddance if a fox or weasel got it.

They turned and started back as a wind brought down leaves in a golden drift. The tutor put out his hand as if to touch them, but as far as she was concerned, fallen leaves were a boresome bother to wade through, there should be a machine invented to suck them up. Wrapping her shawl more tightly around her in the cold, she wondered what it would be like married to somebody like him, didn't own enough salt for an egg. All you'd get would be a couple of cheap rented rooms and the chalk in his coat creases and that fat little body. She wanted a man like the baron. Or the master. She'd never settle for some pink threadbare tutor who talked vulgar. If he thought using words like "sex" made him more attractive to her, he was sadly mistaken. If he thought she could even take notice of a nothing like him, well, it was a laugh. She wanted butter on pork, and she wasn't afraid of admitting it.

The tutor bent down and picked up a leaf as they went. "I collect leaves, it is a pastime of mine," he explained. And for the sake of politeness, he added, "Have you a pastime?"

She shrugged. Then, "Singing," she declared, but with a scowl, for the other servants always shut her up as soon as she let out a note. "I sing good, even if some say it's screechy and loud."

"Well, that is no drawback in the Copenhagen revues. Perhaps that is your destiny," he remarked in jest as they came out from the trees, "especially as it is also no drawback to be"—and he almost said "homely," for the singers tended to a stout coarseness like hers, but caught himself—"to be, well, as charming as you. For love of music always expresses itself in charm," he finished inanely, and tipping his hat, he bade her good day and went on through the garden, there pausing to admire the griffin and thinking of her no more.

"Charming," she breathed aloud as she walked on. No one had

ever said she had charm. But if he thought she was going to waste it on him he was sadly mistaken. But it didn't hurt that he was smitten, because when he packed his bags and fled she'd flee with him to Copenhagen, because it was her destiny to be a famous revue singer, yes, in a gown with flounces and jewels . . . only he'd better not try to warm with her, that pink little tub. Or better yet she would stay on when he fled and get to her singing destiny later. She would watch the ruination creep back into the house like it should, hear again the lonely clink of the master's fork on his plate . . . but what if the tutor didn't flee, was too lovesick to part with her? These problems banged noisily through the girl's head but caused her no distress. Drama had been restored, and her broad feet stepped with new vigor along the path.

෬෯

October passed into November. The spell of crystalline weather dissolved back into rain, then fog, and the gardener covered the flowerbeds with straw. The first snow fell, those swarming, powdery flakes that children called white bees. The boys were playing in the flurry of white bees when they saw their father hurrying toward them not even in a coat, as if lit inside by the sun, and smiling with all his face.

"Your mother is coming home!"

They ran to him. "When? When?"

"Tomorrow!"

Tomorrow, he wrote to Onkel in the library, *I had thought to have my first visit with Grethe, but instead I shall be bringing her home! The sanatorium writes that she has responded extremely well to treatment during these two months, and that no further stay is required—I have just received the letter and am sending you the splendid news at once . . .*

Suddenly, without the sound of a rap, the door was flung open. The square-shaped maid entered with the tutor, who said in puzzled tones, "I am told you wish to see me?" as the maid stepped forward, a flush suffusing her broad features.

"He acted indecent to me," she stated. "In the woods. He forced himself on me!"

"I?" the tutor exclaimed, his mouth falling open, and Holger slammed his fist on the desk.

"I want you gone the end of the week," he told her furiously—like a succubus the girl was, an evil spirit, never done with her lewd troublemaking. "You've told too many filthy lies in this house, I'll have you here no longer!"

"You ask him yourself! You ask him!"

"I would answer anything if I understood—"

"Can you say we weren't in the woods together?" she demanded.

"Some time back, yes . . . I was on my walk and—"

"And so was I, and you talked indecent to me. Used the word 'sex'—'sex'!" she flung at him who hadn't packed and fled, leaving the master to his bitter, needful loneliness—and who in all this time hadn't cast her one melting, lovesick glance which she wouldn't want anyway but why hadn't he, what with all his mooning and lusting in the woods? The days had just dribbled on like usual, and her power inside her with no place to go, but now it beat strong all through her veins. She didn't care that she was sacked. She had her great destiny. "You said 'sex'! You tell me you didn't?"

"I think . . . I think I may have, but in the sense that Brandes and Bjørnson—"

"And told me I was charming!"

"Oh, but that was not meant as—"

"And pressed yourself against me, grabbed me!" She clutched her arm with her thick fingers. "Grabbed me! You say you didn't?"

"But surely you cannot mean . . . for that was inadvertent—"

She swung around to the master.

"You heard it out of his own mouth—there's not one thing I say that he can say different, because it's all true!"

And she turned and swept past the tutor, ruination raining down on his head like boulders, and pulled open the door, flushed and radiant, a heroine in a drama where justice has been done. She turned again.

"And what I said about your wife, Hr. Rosted, don't you ever doubt for a minute that that was true too."

The door shut.

Twenty minutes later Holger pushed her into the carriage, and climbed in with the nursemaid to serve as chaperone. In a heavy brown shawl, the maid clutched on her lap a hastily packed pasteboard suitcase and an envelope containing two weeks' wages. Through whitening trees they traveled the few kilometers to the village of Hørsholm. There he bought and thrust at her a coach ticket to her home village. In the swarm of white bees she watched the carriage drive off, all her courage gone, feeling only the flimsiness of her scant seventeen years, and the solidity of her so terrible plainness. Then, before she lost her nerve entirely, and giving a headtoss like they did in her novelettes, she exchanged her ticket for one to Copenhagen, where her great destiny awaited her.

Her eyes opened to dim, gray morning light. She lay naked under the eiderdown, her breasts and stomach and thighs warm against his sleeping flesh. It was not a dream. None of it was a dream. Yesterday, bags packed, she had sat waiting in the rosewood and velour of the visitors' room, and when he came in she had wanted to dash to him with the abandon of a child, elbows sawing back and forth for all speed, and in him was the same hungering urgency. Yet they crossed the room like two proper adults because others were present, and took each other's hands and with trembling restraint kissed each other on the cheek. In the carriage, their embrace a fusion, a soldering, they were kissing each other's mouths, cheeks, eyes, hair, and presently, her head resting against his shoulder, they had sat in a kind of blissful torpor as the carriage swayed and creaked and the snow swirled by outside. And then they had talked—talked all the way, it seemed, as if they had been parted not for two months but two years. The ride had seemed very short, although it was dusk when they reached the Sound and the boys were racing down the steps, her arms around them almost before she had alighted, and inside she was dragged off in their jubilant chatter to meet the tutor, a pleasant pinkish young man with whom she exchanged only a word before she was dragged off again, for she must see their notebooks and the globe of the world, and then came dinner, festive as Christmas, and then she and Holger were alone together in their room, it was not a dream, and now his warm body stirred against hers, and they lay smiling into each other's eyes.

In the dim, gray morning light Olaf crept along looking for prey, but there was snow under his feet and snow that came blowing through the trees against him, and he knew that when the cold whiteness came, the small forest beasts disappeared. He should leave, go elsewhere, but he had been here so long now that he could not conceive of anything beyond the woods, only more woods. The morning grew lighter, grew full, but the wet blowing snow became thicker. Sometimes he was blown over, flailing and blinded, and he would creep on hunched, flatter yet, with slitted, stinging eyes. Suddenly his good ear cocked. Distant, distant, it was a sound he knew—could not place, but knew.

Cook didn't wish to welcome the mistress back with a lie, but her clean kitchen had never been the place for a ratty thing like Olaf that made you think of mange, so she had to say what she'd said to the master, "Oh yes, been coming in each night for its scraps," though the window had been shut so long that by now the cat was probably some fox-chewed fur moldering away in the woods. She was truly sorry for the mistress's innocent smile and eager voice as she pressed open the window, leaned out and called, "Olaf . . . Olaf . . . ," as if it were just around somewhere like always, "Olaf . . . Olaf . . ." And then, Cook could not believe it, way at the garden's edge by the woods a tiny dot appeared, came streaking through the flying snow, and a few moments later—no, she couldn't believe it, here the thing was back in her kitchen again! She had to pretend she wasn't surprised, and even managed a grim smile as the mistress kissed and petted it in her arms while a sound like a sewing machine came from its wretched head.

In the storm of his purring, hugging him and nuzzling his damp fur, Grethe carried Olaf into the drawing room and sat down by the heat of the great tile stove. "Now you must get warm, dearest, dearest Olaf... oh, how happy I am to see you again!" And stroking his knobby back and his striped little head, over and over, she could smile at the absurdity of having thought he visited and conversed with her at the sanatorium; even on her first walks, when her mind had become quite clear about everything, she had thought he was with her, bounding through the fallen leaves; then gradually there had been no more bounding, no more Olaf, and she had realized that his visits too had existed only in her mind. But now Olaf, the real Olaf, lay here purring in her lap; they were reunited and joyous. But how thin he was, how thin, poor little Olaf Hunger. Cook's scraps must have been very much on the meager side.

⚮

Holger was delighted that the cat was back, for he had worried that by now it might not come even to Grethe. He had also felt a little uneasy about mentioning the square-shaped maid; he had no wish to upset Grethe by telling her he had fired the girl, and least of all did he want to explain the ugly scene that had precipitated her dismissal. It was too close to the other scene. But in the pleasure and excitement of her first day home, Grethe took no notice of the girl's absence. She wanted to do everything at once. They must have their walk, even though the wind was fierce and the snow flew thick. And when they returned, laughing and out of breath, and had labored out of their heavy outer garments, she said, "Now I want to go into every single room and simply stand and look, and then I want to go to the greenhouse and bring back armfuls of hyacinth and hibiscus, and I want to see everything you have been painting, and I want to read all the letters you wrote to me, oh, I want to do that now," and in the library, sitting together by the desk, she had read aloud all that he had thought and felt during her absence. Her eyes sometimes filmed with tears, and she would press her hand to his cheek, and sometimes she laughed at the entertaining things he had written, as when she came to the lobster mayonnaise and the sugartops and the typewriter contraptions ". . . oh, but here, this poor grotesque whom the old servant describes . . . so monstrous a creature. Oh, how cruel nature can be. How cruel. Do you think he had a home? Did anyone care about him, I wonder?"

"I wonder if the servant didn't invent him—or more likely Onkel himself, to prove his point about the homogeneity of our own times."

"I do long to see Onkel, we must have him over very soon. Perhaps he can stay for some days, and we can arrange to have one of our gatherings then."

"But is it not too soon, Grethe? Will it not be too much for you?"

"Too much? Why shouldn't we have a party? It is the way we have always lived."

"Well then, we shall," he said, with a slap to his thigh. "And we'll ask the mandolin player. We'll learn if he's bought a contraption."

⊗

The boys had shown him her framed photographs, and had pointed out their father's portraits of her on the wall. Thus the tutor knew she was beautiful, but he had not foreseen the loveliness of her voice and manner, the quiet wit, the captivating laugh. He became as devoted to her as he realized everyone else was—the elderly uncle who often visited, the friends who came for evening gatherings, and all the servants. He sometimes thought back to what the burly maid had said about her fellow servants, and what she had said about Fru Rosted. And what she had said about himself—he had not been sorry when she was shoved into the carriage forthwith, the vile-minded hysteric. Hr. Rosted had never referred to her again.

He saw that Hr. Rosted was very happy. In spite of his geniality, and beneath his laughter at the dinner table, there had been a distractedness, a sadness. Since his wife's return there was no trace of it.

❧❧

After Christmas Holger completed a large canvas: a field of wind-whipped snow with trees the color of blackened rust, and then a rocky shore with pack ice extending thirty feet into the dark gray waters, and the dark gray skies blowing above. Life had been loosed anew from his brush, the dull and dutiful strokes were no more.

And Grethe had gone back to her translation. "Don't push yourself," he had said, for he had realized early on, after searching everywhere for the remainder of the manuscript, that her illness had prevented her from concentrating and that there was no remainder of the manuscript. "Don't try to catch up all at once."

"No, but it is scandalous that I didn't finish it on schedule."

And it was coming very well now.

The winter months proceeded in their usual unpredictable fashion. A great snowstorm with thunder came blowing in, carriages and wagons along the Coast Road were stranded, mountainous waves halted ship traffic on the Baltic, after which there came a long chain of fine, clear frosty days, and then there were days of still and heavy fog, and then the snow began again. They went skating with the boys on the small lake in Hørsholm, they had their gatherings with friends, they drove into Copenhagen to attend the theater, took their walks, did their work, sat reading and talking in the evenings and, with the ardor that never ceased to glow between them, would early ascend the stairs to their bedroom.

❧❧

Grethe saw her face in the mirror, young and luminous with health, and she smiled with all the happiness within her, because her happiness was far stronger than the fleeting moments of anxiety. They had begun coming upon her a week or so ago, it seemed, when she realized she was no longer working well, the pages lagging . . . or perhaps they had begun earlier, when the familiar sight of the griffin, in his rearing stance, with snow caught upon his great wings, had one day suddenly seemed frightening to her. And until now she had been so well, so clear-minded—although she had never mentioned the absence of the squarish maid, for there was something in her memory of the girl that she did not care to think about; something so indistinct she could give it no name; nor had she cared to think about the pictures on the walls, for they too brought her a faint, unplaceable sense of disquiet—but so very faint, the merest touch of unease, dispersed without difficulty. Not until now had she known these anxious moments, this sense of being subjected to jagged mental intrusions . . . but they were fleeting, they were infrequent, they could not touch the dominion of her restored happiness.

❦

In the sanatorium she had longed to do her needlework; and now she sat with it each evening as she had always done, the thread following the needle, the design so beautiful, so clear. Design presupposes God, but design was failing, she could no longer deny it, and alone in her study one day, sitting with motionless pen over Zola's suffering world and prey to fragments of sounds and images, she put her face in her hands and cried like a child.

"I am becoming ill again . . ."

And she thought: if only she could tell someone, if she could run this very moment to Holger and throw her arms around him and share with him this terrible burden . . . but she knew that was the one thing she must not do. It would put him in the greatest danger, and herself, and everyone, the entire world. Say nothing. Show nothing.

No one noticed the growing chaos within her; not the children when she read aloud to them at night, from H. C. Andersen or Jules Verne, and tucked them into bed afterward with a kiss; not the pleasant, pink-nosed tutor, with whom she had enjoyable conversations about Jacobsen's lyric prose style; not dear, flinty Onkel when he came on his welcome visits; not the servants, not anyone, not even Holger, who was her, as she was him, the two of them one beating heart, one soul. Only Olaf noticed. In the evenings she sat with her needlework or book, and talked with Holger, talked about everything, and smiled and laughed while trying to push from her mind the Pierced One's silhouette on the wall and the remembrance of a horrifying crash behind her, trying to push away jagged images of a crumbling moon, a decaying garden. Talking and smiling, and Olaf tucked in the folds of her gown around her feet, she saw from the expression in his pale green eyes that he understood her suffering and loneliness.

"In the spring," she would murmur to him in her lap, stroking his raddled fur as they sat together of a snowy afternoon by the great tile stove, "we will go to the woods again, to our green bower." The ground would be carpeted with the small white stars of anemones, and they would lie down, and in their ears would be the sound of the birds and the small brook. "We will go back," she assured him, scratching the side of his beloved little head, and for a while she would feel soothed.

※

". . . in the woods . . . I want to be with him in the woods again . . ."

Holger was not sure that he was hearing these murmured words. A heavy sleeper, he was always muzzy when he awoke in the mornings, a few moments always passed before his perceptions came clear . . . "I want to be with him in the woods again . . ." He could not have heard that. If Grethe had murmured in her sleep, she was quiet now, breathing softly. He must have misconstrued the faint words, or else she had never uttered a sound, and it was only part of his morning muddledness, similar to his hair which always stuck out in every direction, and which he smoothed back, yawning; and then with a smile he touched her sleeping cheek, and lay with his arm around her as the morning lightened.

ॐ ॐ

Grethe gently rubbed eucalyptus oil into the younger child's chest, and rebuttoned his nightgown. She gave him a sip of water. That was all one could do, the doctor said; as children's throat infections went, it was not the worst, but it was painful, and the fever would rise yet higher. Keep him warm, and if he grew restless he could have a few drops of valerian to help him sleep; the tonsils would have to come out eventually.

She smoothed his hair back in the candlelight. It hurt her heart that he was so miserable, and miserable too that his brother had been moved into the nanny's room, for they were never parted. She put some drops of valerian in a spoon and gently eased it between his lips.

"Try to sleep now," she whispered to him, smoothing the eiderdown, and softly kissing his fevered cheek.

Outside the door, she blew out the friendly glow of the candle. In the darkness, that was when she went down to the Pierced One, when others slept. That was when the anguish of his cries grew unbearable. "Grethe! Grethe!" and she must bring him solace, she must give him peace.

A while later she came back up the stairs, softly, that no one should hear. She had stilled the terrible, the piteous cries, but they would begin again. They would never end.

Holger drew her into his arms when she got back into bed.

"You will wear yourself out, my love, sitting up like this each night."

"Yes, I am tired," she sighed, burying herself in his embrace. In the darkness she tenderly stroked the hair by his ear. "I am so tired, Holger."

"He will be his usual boisterous self in a few days. You mustn't worry so. Sleep now. You must have some rest."

But she lay awake as he slept beside her. She was going to hurt him badly and deeply, he whom she loved more than anyone else on earth.

She would turn from his lips, she would lie motionless in his arms, cold to his touch though desire burned all through her. She would see the tears in his eyes again, the depth of his pain, and she could not bear it. But there must be no more seeds, no furtherance. For the garden grows and gluts and dies, and grows and gluts again, and is a chaos of black decay, and there must be no more seeds sown, no more suffering generations. For the suffering never ends; under the sunlight and bright foliage lie darkness, slaughter and anguish, and I cannot end it . . . the Pierced One cries to me that I must end it, he cries Grethe! Grethe! but his anguish is profound, it is unanswerable. It will never end. And I am so weary, so weary, all I wish is to be with Olaf in the woods, together in our green bower, our own little world lifted out of time, safe and changeless . . . but there is too much snow. And snow on the griffin's wings, he dragged me to the furnace of the sun, oh I burned, I burned to cinders, for I had not brought God's King-dom to earth. Grethe! Grethe! But I cannot do it, I am too weary, I cannot go on, I should like to end it all, to sleep forever . . . and I should like to think that everyone I love might be released from suf-fering too, and sleep in the hand of God . . .

"Come," she whispers, waking him gently. She has slipped a coat over her nightgown. She holds his own heavy winter coat in her hands. He is feverish, and groggy from the valerian, his eyes half-closed. She helps him out of bed, and in the candlelight buttons him lovingly into his coat. He looks at her questioningly, but his sleepy, feverish eyes are full of trust.

"Where are we going?" he murmurs. He is so tottery that he leans against her.

"We are going to a lovely place."

"Oh," he says.

With her arm around him she goes to the door, and she is aware of his smallness, his child's love of fairy tales and flying carpets.

"It will be an adventure," she whispers to him.

· 21 ·

ℭ The landlady answers her door to find an elegant woman with a suitcase standing before her.

"Yes? What may I do for you?"

"I just want to let you know that I'll be away for a week or so. If a visitor should ask for me while I'm gone, will you tell them that please?"

And squinting, the landlady is astonished to recognize this sleek and stylish person as her daft, disheveled tenant from under the rafters. She nods, speechless, and watches the apparition depart down the stairs.

Paula climbs aboard the morning bus to Neuchâtel, where she has already gone the day before to take some clothes out of storage. She wears a tailored, ankle-length charcoal wool Versace coat, at her throat the gleam of an emerald scarf. Her hair is smoothly drawn back under a Russian black fur hat. Her face is enhanced by eye shadow, blush and lip gloss applied with artful understatement. She has not lost her touch. But all this formality and burnish is a tremendous change, it will require getting used to.

From Neuchâtel she takes the train to Zurich, and from Zurich the plane to Copenhagen, where, coming in over a body of iron-gray water, she arrives an hour and a half later.

⳼

Philip had no trouble recognizing his sister: she had always dressed well before her conversion to fieldstones. He had arrived from Chicago the day before, gotten hotel rooms, rented a car, and now watching the passengers come in through the gate, he raised his arm in a wave.

Paula spotted him at once—he was so tall you couldn't miss him—and waving too she made her way through the crowd, unaccustomed to the noise and milling of many people, but with spirits too high to be impinged on. They hugged in an exchange of greetings. He took her suitcase.

"You look very presentable."

"It's a sacrifice, I assure you. How was your sacrifice?"

"The flight? The flight was great. No problem. No panic."

"But that's amazing," she exclaimed as they moved on through the crowd.

"Not so amazing, actually. What about baggage? You've got more than this carry-on, haven't you?"

"No, that's all. I've put on these clothes in honor of the engineer, but even for him I draw the line at two suitcases."

He laughed and took her arm.

Darkness had already fallen when they drove from the huge complex of the airport. High winds splattered snow against the windshield. Philip said cheerfully, "I suppose anyone with common sense would have waited till spring."

"But how could we wait?"

"We couldn't. We're like the Vikings setting off in their longships, across the swells of unknown seas."

"What a poet you've turned into," Paula laughed, giving his arm a punch. "You know, I feel like a truant. I do hope my daughter comes while I'm gone."

"As long as she doesn't think you've fallen off a mountain. Gets up a search party."

"No, I left word with my landlady—and the surprise on her face! What about you? Do you feel like a truant?"

"The very word," he said.

⊶⊷

"I didn't even ask if you wanted to go to your room first," he said, turning on the lights in his. "Or if you wanted to eat. It's only going on four."

"No, I don't want to eat—don't keep me in suspense," she told him as he went for his briefcase. She took off her coat, and thought how odd it was to sit down in such spaciousness, to see around her these tasteful furnishings all standing at a level angle, every surface spotless. Drawing off her gloves, she was pleased to be restored to her calloused fingers with their small black cuts.

"The typed pages on top, the ones in Danish," Philip explained, pulling up a chair and handing her a sheaf of photocopied papers, "are the appraisers' inventory of the engineer's house. The lists are endless."

"Endless is right," she said, slowly leafing through the pages. "It's a tome."

"I bought a Danish-English dictionary yesterday. I've picked out a fair number of words with it. *Maleri*, for instance, means a painting. There were a lot of paintings. A lot. And porcelain. Royal Copenhagen, Rosenthal, Meissenware—I swear every separate piece of every setting is listed. And crystal. Silverware. Items of fine needlework, a lot of those."

"Didn't I say it was made by someone in his family—that little rug of mine?" Paula broke in. "What else?"

"What else? Tables, chairs. Bedsteads. Credenzas, armoires. Books and bookcases. Carpets, mirrors, chandeliers. Clocks. Lamps. I even figured out 'ivory shoehorn' and 'gold thimble.' They itemized every last thing."

"And all of it auctioned off to strangers. It's sad . . . I wonder what the engineer would have thought."

"A good thing he never knew."

"And these pages? The handwritten ones?"

"Taylor's notes, they're in English. Read that page there, it was his first drive out to the house."

Paula read aloud: " 'House is located twenty-five kilometers north of Copenhagen by way of coastal road, Strandvejen. Near turnoff to village called Hørsholm, on east side of Strandvejen, is private road leading to house. Building faces Sound, is set back some hundred and fifty yards on slight rise. Two stories, half-timbered brick, well maintained. Extensive gardens, woods. Surveyor to do map of property lines.' "

"There's no surveyor's map with the notes," Philip told her. "That would have been done after Taylor went back to the States. But I think his description is enough for us to find the house."

"You'd better get a road map though."

"Never use them. I go by road signs and instinct."

"Really, Philip? I wonder you ever found your way up to my place."

"Speaks well for my sense of direction, doesn't it?"

"Like the Vikings," she said with a laugh, getting up and taking her coat. "I'll go unpack. Whenever you want to have dinner is fine with me, I don't keep regular eating hours."

"What about seven? And tomorrow let's start early—not that you can, it doesn't get light here till after nine. But let's definitely start as soon as it's light."

"Definitely."

"They say it's a severe winter this year, so the weather isn't likely to change. But what do we care?"

"We don't care."

⬥

In the morning, which finally distinguished itself from night, the weather could be seen to have improved. The wind and snow had left off, the sky was dark, low, still. They drove from their hotel near

Raadhuspladsen, the town-hall square; and though they had both been to Copenhagen before, they knew only its clear summer light and holiday crowds. They felt they were seeing the true city now, emptied of frolicking tourists and concerned with its own sober, wintry affairs, yet still beautiful, with its snow-bordered dark canals, and its pale green spires against the heavy gray of the sky.

Philip drove through the old streets in a northerly direction, presently turning onto a boulevard, which became Strandvejen.

"See? Unerring instinct."

But they were surprised that Strandvejen was a six-lane highway, and that the attractive suburbs it took them through did not end. Sometimes they drove along the very edge of the Sound, a heavy gray in color, like the sky; sometimes the highway curved a little inland, and trees and houses intervened before the water reappeared. The suburbs were always with them. They deplored their stupidity.

"It'll be impossible to find," Philip said, gesturing at Taylor's note on the dashboard. "That was 1928, for God's sake. Naturally everything would be all built up now, totally changed. How could we think it wouldn't be?"

"Because we wanted to, I suppose," Paula said with disappointment. Then impatiently, "Well, find it anyway, damn it."

"What d'you think I'm trying to do?"

"You ought to slow down. You ought to let these cars pass."

"Don't give me any backseat driving, or you can get out and walk."

They drove in irritated silence. And the weather was reverting to its former state: the wind was blowing hard, it swiped the side of the car in booms. When the Hørsholm exit appeared ahead, they saw that it too was a modern highway.

"How do we know it's the same intersection Taylor meant?" Paula asked, studying the sign as it neared.

"That's the trouble. Roads get changed around when things get built up. The old intersection could be defunct. Probably has houses on it. Another thing, we've come more like thirty-five kilometers than twenty-five. He says twenty-five."

"But it could have been a slip of the pen, couldn't it? Maybe he meant thirty-five."

"Not likely. But within the realm of possibility, I guess."

"Anyway, we ought to look for the road on the right."

They drove another kilometer or two, and then their journey, which had begun so simply and had become so depressingly problematic, suddenly took light again as they saw a road and turned off on it.

⋆⋆⋆

"Of course it would be changed too, like the rest of the region," Philip said as he parked. "We expected it."

"I suppose we did."

But both had kept a stubborn, unrealistic vision of the house standing by itself, simple to recognize, simple to approach. It would have seen them coming. It would have welcomed them.

They had parked by the beach. The gray waves washed up on dark, sodden sand, which was mottled with snow. They climbed out into the wind.

"My God, it's cold!" Paula cried.

"It's the dampness. Cuts right through you." From his pocket Philip took a navy wool cap and tugged it down over his ears. He pulled up the collar of his overcoat and stood looking across the road. "How many yards from the shore?"

Taylor's note flapped wildly in Paula's gloved hand. She subdued it. "About a hundred and fifty."

"It's got to be behind those other houses."

"I don't see anything like two stories," she said, holding her fur hat down in the wind. "Or maybe. It's hard to tell with the trees."

Crossing the road, they crunched along a lane packed with snow. It led among tree-flanked houses, some of them cottages, others larger. They saw no one around. The sky seemed still lower and darker, and the wind thrashed at them bitterly as they became lost among lanes and drives. The place was like a maze, though it had a pleasant rustic quality they might have appreciated under other circumstances. Paula grimaced from time to time. Her fashionable boots, with their pointed toes, were pinching. She was used to big boots, hiking boots, and she wondered how she could walk in these things, though she had no inclination to give up.

"It's got to be here," she said loudly through the wind's battering.

"I know. Somewhere."

And then the wind began assaulting them with sleet, and at the same time Philip was struck by a disastrous thought. He hit his forehead.

"What if it's been torn down? No wonder we can't find it—but no, it can't be torn down." For it seemed to him that because he wanted so much to find it, it had to be there.

"No, it can't be torn down. It's got to be just past these houses. If we could see anything—"

"We should be on a slight rise," Philip complained at length. "We're not on a slight rise."

"Because we're going in circles—we're just going in circles."

"All I know is we're getting soaked in this goddamned, lousy sleet—the place is a refrigerator."

"There's no sleet in a refrigerator," she retorted sharply for the sake of argument, her boots pinching, and her arm aching from holding down her hat. They pounded on in the lashing sleet, shoulders hunched, eyes squinting. And then a two-story house was before them. But modern, all wood and glass. There were lights on inside. Philip marched up and gave the doorbell a vigorous punch.

"What if they don't speak English?" Paula asked as she joined him on the wet porch, lowering her hand with relief from her hat, and for good measure giving the bell another resounding punch.

"They all speak English," he said, swinging around to a small man in horn-rimmed glasses who was opening the door. "Excuse me, we're looking for a house. Two stories like this one, but half-timbered brick. Old. Can you tell us where it is?"

"Half-timbered brick?" The man gave a shake of his head. "I'm sorry, there is nothing like that around here."

"This is the only two-story house around?"

"No, there are a couple of others, but not as you describe."

"The Hørsholm turnoff on Strandvejen, has it always been there?"

"Always been there?"

"Were there woods here once?" Paula broke in.

"Possibly. I couldn't say."

"What about a slight rise, do you have a slight rise here?"

"A slight rise?"

"What about the Hørsholm turnoff?" Philip repeated. "Don't you know if it was ever somewhere else?"

"I have no idea. If you will excuse me, I am getting wet."

"Is there anyone else around here we could talk to?"

"Unlikely. These are mostly summer houses."

The door shut hard.

"I think we were rude," Paula said as they hunched back into the wind and sleet. "We've lost perspective. We're acting like fanatics."

And still searching, plodding through the snow of curved lanes and brown-hedged drives, past the dark, wet trunks of leafless trees, they felt like two driven, middle-aged adolescents, two truants, gray-haired, intense and futile.

⌘⌘

They emerged where they had begun. They climbed back into the car, slamming the doors against the sleet, which was turning to hail, and sank back in their seats. Small hard pellets clattered against the windows.

"Even if the house had been there," Paula said, shivering, "I wonder what we thought we would accomplish. It was sold sixty years ago, after all, and it's probably been sold since. What could we have learned from anyone living in it now? They wouldn't have any connection with the engineer."

Philip nodded, sighed. "That's true. I hadn't really thought about it."

"We had the strange idea that finding the house would somehow be the same as finding him, that everything would fall into place."

Dejectedly, he started the motor. "It all seemed so simple."

☙ ❧

"Still, it's only our first day," Paula said at dinner.

"And it isn't as if we didn't have other alternatives."

Their spirits had lifted since their barren travail that morning. They sat at a window table at Frascati's, where they looked out on the vast expanse of Raadhuspladsen, the lights of cars and trams moving across it and the weather now showing itself more agreeable. No sleet, no hail, and the icy wind had been strong but not fierce as they had walked the few blocks from their hotel. Old streets, elegant buildings, the trams' cheerful clangor, and then the enveloping warmth of the restaurant, the perfection of the artichoke soup, the roast pork.

"For one thing," Philip went on, "we can go to a title company. We give them the name and date of the house sale, and they send out a search for the surveyor's map. It might take a few days, but we've got time. And there's the bank that Taylor dealt with. If they keep records that long, and I was lucky in Chicago, they'll have a mine of information. In fact, I should have gone there yesterday when I got in—but I liked the idea of our just setting off for the house."

" 'Vikings on the swells of unknown seas,' " Paula quoted him, but not ironically, for she too had been fired by the idea. "Then we can go to those places tomorrow. And also I have to buy earplugs. I meant to today when we got back, but I forgot."

"Earplugs?"

"I didn't sleep well last night. Not that there was noise, it was very quiet. But it wasn't the absolute silence you have at night in the mountains."

"I take it you're not being tempted back into the great world?"

She held up her roughened fingers, as if they spoke for her.

"Guess not. No reason you should."

"A week in the great world will be enough for me. But I'm glad I came. I wanted to come. It's necessary that we do this."

"And we'll find him. There's no doubt in my mind."

The waiter, his brass buttons glinting in the lamplight, came with the dessert menu. Philip enquired as to what *lagkage* was. Layer cake, he was informed, and not just one or two layers but very many layers very close together. "It sounds irresistible," Paula exclaimed, and Philip laughed. "You may yet be converted back to the great world."

After dinner, crunching along the streets in the cutting wind, they found an *apothek* still open. Paula bought earplugs and also a box of Band-Aids, for her toes were still being pinched, if not so badly as during the morning's grim pilgrimage. Afterward, passing the brightly lit bookstore where Philip had bought his dictionary, they took themselves gratefully in from the wind and browsed.

"She looks like she could really belt it out," Philip remarked as they paused by an old art nouveau poster on the wall. Above the name *!Mandolina!* stood a hefty, broad-faced revue singer smothered in flounces and finery, arms boldly akimbo, head flung back with rouged lips opened wide for maximum volume. "Do you have a yen for entertainment of any sort?" he asked as they went on. "I don't want to hold you back."

"My entertainment," Paula replied with a laugh, "is going to consist of retiring early with my earplugs."

◌⳹◌

The following day they learned at the bank that no records of the sort they described would have been kept, the bank having acted merely as an intermediary.

Back at the hotel desk they ascertained the Danish term for "title company," and were further assisted by the making of a phone call and the writing down of an address. They climbed back into the car. The brief day had darkened by the time they found their way there and entered an office whose clerks were as pleasantly cooperative as those at the hotel desk, but from whom they learned that the surveyor's map, or plat, as it was called, would not meet their particular needs. A plat marked out property lines, yes, but nothing more than that; it did not show the larger picture, it was not a map of a region. A plat was confined, and what they seemed to want was an idea of the surrounding area, yes?

Yes. And with courteous if discouraged thanks they left.

It had begun to snow. Flakes flew forcefully, diagonally, through the beams of the headlights.

"So what do we do now?" Paula said.

"I don't know," Philip sighed. "Hire a detective."

"Well, a detective would at least do something sensible."

"Such as?"

The long dark stretch of Tivoli Gardens went by as she thought.

"Check birth records," she said finally. "Isn't that what a detective would do?"

"And what information would we give him? Do we know what year the engineer was born? We don't even know the decade."

"Mother, of course, said he was doddering. Do you know where we're going?"

They were driving alongside a black body of water, with a bridge dimly bejeweled through the flying snow.

"No, I don't. But the hotel's got to be around somewhere."

"Old and doddering. Which could mean he was forty. She always had to exaggerate."

"And play the child bride. Swizzling and cute."

"He couldn't have been so old if he was an active engineer. It stands to reason."

"Except it doesn't help us in judging his age."

He turned onto a street that took them past the bourse, whose magnificent spire of four dragons with tails entwined they had seen the day before, but which tonight vanished up into darkness and wind-driven snow.

"Even if we knew *when* he was born," he went on, "we don't know *where*. Who's to say his family wasn't living in some other house at the time of his birth, some other place entirely? Our detective would be checking through the birth records of every city and town in Denmark."

"I think you're being unduly pessimistic."

"A corrective to being unduly optimistic."

Neither of them would have hired a detective. They would not have given over their quest to someone else. Their way was their own, private, instinctive, spontaneous, everything left in the hands of divine providence, as it were; and though disheartened by the day's failure, they kept within them a hard little nugget of faith. After driving around a good deal, Philip finally found his way back to the hotel—"instinct not working too well tonight," he confessed—where they sat in the plush sofa chairs of the lobby, having nothing else to do. Though it was dark, it was too early to eat; and though it was early, there was nothing left of the day to make anything of. Paula had a glass of sherry as they sat, Philip a Scotch and soda. Neither had much inclination toward drink; wine with dinner, and Philip might down a shot if he was especially jangled before flying, but like many children of dedicated drinkers, they had no trouble eschewing excess. They sipped, they talked, they watched people coming in and going out, and after a while they turned to each other with a half-smile reminiscent of their childhood when they both had the same thought at the same moment, for it occurred to them that in a wishful sort of way they wouldn't be surprised if the engineer came walking in through the door.

"How much simpler it would be than searching for him," Paula said. "If we suddenly saw him coming over to us saying, 'Ah, there you are!' "

"Too bad it's the sort of thing reserved for the mad."

They sat on, and as Philip looked around him, he realized that this was probably the first time he hadn't sent a postcard to the office.

"I'm thinking," he said, "of selling the business."

Paula looked at him with surprise, yet not deep surprise.

"It has to do with your flying, hasn't it?" she asked. "With your not feeling the panic, what you said at the airport."

He nodded. "They're connected."

"It seemed amazing when you told me. But when I thought about it, it didn't, and this doesn't either. Because you've changed, you know. You'd changed even when we last saw each other."

"In your kitchen." He gave a half laugh, followed by a sigh. "Well, I'd gone through a lot. And I went through a lot more later. That must sound overly dramatic, but—"

"But it doesn't."

"Anyway, sounding overly dramatic doesn't embarrass me."

"I know. 'Vikings on the swells of unknown seas—' "

"Mysterium Tremendum—"

"Mysterium Tremendum," she said, raising her glass with mystery's scored and calloused fingers. They clinked their glasses and drank. "And you're really going to sell."

"I haven't decided for sure. I'm just thinking about it. The house too."

"And then what?"

"I don't know."

"Well," she joked, "you can always come and set up housekeeping in the village."

"Jesus, I may have changed, but not *that* much."

They both laughed, and Paula gave a testing touch to her chignon. "I keep having to check it. I keep thinking it's falling down."

"It's not."

"At home it doesn't matter how my hair looks. When I get back I'm going to give it a good shake and send the hairpins flying. And then," she said, "I'm going to give my money away."

Philip's eyes closed. "Don't tell that to your daughter when she comes around with the shrink."

"I have no intention of telling her anything. And I'm not a complete imbecile, Philip, you needn't close your eyes like that. I didn't say I was giving it *all* away. Certainly I'll keep enough to live on. But there's buckets. I don't need all that, I don't want it, so let those have it who need it. It's simple enough. I intend to discuss it all with my lawyer in Neuchâtel."

"You know what, Paula? You've turned into a saint."

"Not at all. I'm the farthest thing from a saint that a person can be. I live for my fieldstones. And I don't think you should speak so lightly of my daughter coming around with a shrink. It worries me considerably."

"Well, it shouldn't. There's not a damn thing she can do except keep on harping and carping."

"That's what I keep reminding myself. I'm eccentric. So? Eccentrics have as many rights as anyone."

"Exactly. In my case, since nobody's bugging me, I don't have to keep reminding myself."

At this they laughed again, and then they grew quiet as they returned to thoughts of their search and of the blank wall they seemed to have come up against.

⁂

In the morning when Philip drew the drapes back, he looked out at a cold white sun in a cold white sky. He felt heartened. When he joined his sister downstairs for breakfast, he saw that she too felt more optimistic.

She greeted him over her coffee.

"Do you know what the Danes call Danish pastry? Vienna bread."

"And in Vienna?" he asked, sitting down.

"There the mystery deepens."

"Supposing we followed through on the idea of birth records. Well, say he *was* born at the house. Which isn't where we thought it was, but wherever it is, and it's somewhere around there, his birth would have been registered in the nearest town or village."

"Which is where we should go. I've been thinking about that too. And that the nearest village would probably be Hørsholm, because it's the only place Taylor mentions."

Once more, but with sunlight sparkling off the windshield, they drove north through the city. The snow on the ground was blinding in its brilliance, the tall brick buildings were etched sharp in the clear icy air. Cars and pedestrians seemed imbued with vigor and purpose. Even the distant high speck of a bird had a quality of brisk and confident destination.

Retracing their route along Strandvejen, they took the much-discussed Hørsholm exit and drove through more suburbs, which soon merged with Hørsholm—a town, as it turned out, no longer a village, but whose center retained the old part. They had decided the place to go was the church, where parish records would be kept. Parking and climbing out into the wind, they saw it set back behind a small frozen lake. It was a handsome old church, white as the dazzling white snow around it, and with what seemed to them an eager and welcoming countenance, as if it smiled with happiness at their arrival.

A few minutes later they were climbing back into the car. The parish records were not in the church. They were in the process of being transferred onto microfilm.

☙ ❧

"Why are you going this way?" Paula wanted to know.

"What would you rather do?" he asked, turning off on the road to the right. "Go back to the hotel and sit around trying to come up with another futile idea?"

"The house isn't here. We looked. What's the point?"

"There is no point."

"Have it your way. I'm too depressed to argue."

Philip drove down alongside the deserted, snow-mottled beach, the car passing someone who was pushing an old man in a wheelchair along the road.

"It's providential," he exclaimed, slowing the car to a stop and looking back. "That's the kind of person we wanted to talk with when we were here before. Someone old."

"Someone old. Someone who's been here a long time."

They got out as the pair approached. The man pushing against the wind was burly, ruddy, middle-aged. Of the old man in the wheelchair not much could be seen. Blankets and robes engulfed him. His face, of which only part was exposed between heavy scarf and sheepskin hat, had the pale transparency of someone possibly past ninety.

Philip stepped up to the ruddy man and spoke to him. He described the house and asked if he knew it.

The man gave him a broad, sociable smile. "English?"

"No, American."

"How do you like our weather? It is not so good this year. You should have come last year. You are wishing to visit someone at this house you speak of? But there is no house like that here."

"Would you by any chance know the name Rosted?" Paula asked him.

"Rosted? No," he said cheerfully.

"I wonder," Philip suggested, "if it would be too much trouble to ask these questions of this gentleman here."

"This gentleman here *must* have his promenade in every weather," the ruddy man complained, but just as cheerfully as before, and leaned down to him with a few words in Danish. "Yes, he knows it. He knows the name Rosted," he said straightening up.

"He does? Would it be possible—"

"We wouldn't want to impose, but—"

"Do you think we could have a few words with him—?"

"Why not? Come along from the cold. We're on our way back."

They were informed, only half-listening as they went, that the two men were neighbors. The old man lived with his daughter, who was out today. Philip and Paula could help get the chair up the front step. It always gave trouble.

The old man's cottage, which faced the road and beach, with large windows looking out across the water, had light and cheerful furnishings that seemed to reflect the neighbor's disposition. He unburdened the old man of blankets, robes, coat, scarf, sheepskin hat, helped him into a sofa chair, handed him his glasses, arranged a robe across his lap and turned around with his sociable smile.

"He will be pleased to speak with you. We have liveliness in the summer, but in winter there are few visitors."

The old man looked at them in a composed and scholarly manner. His pale face, with its thin, almost transparent skin, showed two spots of wind-whipped color on the sharp cheekbones. His hair consisted of a strand or two. In one ear was a large tan hearing aid.

"Do you know—" Paula began, leaning forward in her chair.

"I must translate. You must tell me," said the neighbor. "We will be like the United Nations."

Paula gave him the full name, and asked if he would enquire if the old man had known him.

The neighbor put the question to the old man, and listened carefully to the reply of his thin voice.

"He said they worked together in Hørsholm. He says Rosted was a structural engineer . . . they knew each other in 1927 . . . wait, I will get it all together and tell you." When the old man had stopped talking, the neighbor turned back to them, "Rosted was retained as a structural consultant for a public building in Hørsholm, he says. He himself was a draftsman at that time, quite young. Rosted hired him to do the structural drawings. It was his first job."

Philip too was leaning forward from his chair.

"Would you ask him how old Rosted was?"

The neighbor replied after a moment. "He says in the middle of his forties."

"Could he tell us what he looked like?"

The question was put to the old man, who spoke again in his aged voice.

"He said he looked like you." This seemed to delight the neighbor. "Big, tall. King's Guard size. In the face too he looked like you, but with hair."

"What color was his hair?" Paula asked.

"I will ask him . . . He says hair-colored hair. I take that to mean brown."

"Could he tell us what Rosted was like as a person?"

The question was put to the old man, and again he replied.

"They got along well," the neighbor told them. "He liked Rosted. Wait, he speaks again . . . Yes, he says Rosted was a very interesting man. He had lived in China, Chile, his work took him many places."

"He wasn't a boring man, was he?" Philip asked. "It doesn't sound like it. Would you ask him that?"

"He says not boring. On the contrary. But he was a serious man. A very serious man."

"Did he know the family? Rosted's family?" Paula asked.

"He says no. He says they knew each other only through their work."

"Then he wouldn't have been acquainted with the house. But could you ask him anyway? It was a big two-story, half-timbered brick house."

Again the neighbor enquired, and listened to the frail and tiring voice.

"He knew such a house. It stood not far from here. He said much of it burned, there was a fire, it was perhaps twenty years ago. Then it was pulled down."

"That was Rosted's house," Philip told him.

The neighbor imparted this information to the old man.

"He says he didn't know that. He is always pleased to learn new things. Now he wants to sleep."

The old man gives a courteous nod and closes his eyes. "This has been a pleasure," says the neighbor, and accompanies them to the door. "If you ever come this way again and have more questions for him, he has a splendid memory. Remarkable for his age. One is very proud of him."

"It was providential," Philip says as they crunch back across the road in the wind. "That's the only word. Providential."

After the sweeping torches, the scraping up of sand and knocking off of stalactite fragments, the cavern returns to its silence and darkness, and for some three hundred years, while on the earth's surface alchemy and astrology give way to the Age of Enlightenment, the deep chamber of stone remains undisturbed. Then one day a hard-drinking midwife from a nearby village, having consumed more than usual and setting off for a tavern in another village, thinks to take a shortcut through the forest and finds herself falling into darkness between two trees.

The plunge, though far, has only a minor effect on her bones, thanks to her intoxicated state, but she is terrified, and screams and shouts without end. For three days her family gives search throughout the countryside, and finally, in the forest, hearing faint screams, they come upon a hole in the earth half-obscured by roots and shrubbery. Having hastened home for ropes they haul her up, freezing cold, stone sober, and scarcely able to speak for the horror of her experience.

After this the fissure becomes a local curiosity, but no one is the least tempted to go down. The cavern is not disturbed again.

· 22 ·

The door is opened by a shabbily dressed woman who, with a start, takes an involuntary step back. Beneath her wide and frightened eyes the Counselor, laughing loudly, presses past her skirts and in his great, lurching waddle begins at once to poke about the little room. The doorway is empty, the woman has fled, the Counselor takes no notice.

"Is it not as I described? And how pleasant with a fire in the hearth!"

"The house is perfection itself," exclaims the lad, looking all about him.

"Although it is not quite as clean as it was. No, it has not been kept as the old aunt kept it. That, however, will be easily remedied."

"Meanwhile, Father, shall we not refresh ourselves? There stands a coffeepot on the table, still steaming."

They were having their coffee when a man in a patched gray smock rushed in, the woman just behind him, pointing and crying, "There! There!" and smashing into him as he came to a dead stop, eyes popping and mouth issuing astounded splutters.

The Counselor sipped from his cup unperturbed.

When the man finally found his tongue, crying, "Get out of our

291

house! Get out!" and making wild sweeping gestures with his hands, as if expelling an oversized bug, the Counselor said to him with curt simplicity: "You live here no longer."

And the woman, peering in a tremble from around her husband's shoulder, whispered, "Oh, it is a mad thing . . . it is mad!"

"We will have the constabulary upon you in five minutes!" warned the husband, trembling too, and turned violently on his heel. Upon which the Counselor reached down for his tapestry-worked satchel, opened it on the table, and dumped out half its contents, notes fluttering, coins spilling and ringing.

"A moment. A moment . . ." the man said to his wife.

"This," murmured the Counselor to the lad with a cynical smile, while patting the scattered heap of paper and metal, "always speaks with the most eloquent tongue." And to the man: "Here is a substantial down payment on your house."

"But . . . but we do not own it," whispered the woman, staring with tragic eyes at the money. "We are but renters . . ."

"Quibble, quibble," sighed the lad from over his coffee. "Barren factologists."

"Listen to what my lad says"—their eyes darted about—"for it matters not if you own or rent. The money is yours. Now you may rent something twenty times finer. Or you may put it toward a dwelling of your own. But be out before nightfall. Oh yes, bring in a bed before you depart, for the alcove will be too small for him. And," he said, turning to the lad, "we cannot have your legs hanging over two chairs pushed together, can we?" He laughed, and the lad laughed too. "Here"—taking a note from the pile and giving it to the couple—"purchase a good solid bed."

Everything was accomplished by early afternoon. When the bed was installed, filling most of the floor space, the couple shoved their few belongings into boxes and sacks, loaded them onto a cart outside, swept the money off the table into a large felt bag and hastened out the door.

"How well it went, Father. As smooth as milk."

"Yes, excellent!" the Counselor laughed, and waddling over to the hearth removed the lid from a cooking pot. Finding a ladle, he dipped it in the pot and stood chewing, beaming.

"Meat in horseradish sauce. With currants. Very tasty! We shall have it for dinner."

☙ ❧

In the mornings the Counselor woke in the alcove bed, pulled himself up with the aid of the old aunt's dangling rope—how simple, how handy!—and climbed down to greet the new day.

The days were fresh, sunny, with skies of cloudless blue.

He and the lad would start off early on their walk. At a bakery the Counselor would buy fresh *rundstykker*, which they consumed as they went, conversing and from time to time laughing. The Counselor was sublimely indifferent to the stares of passersby, although he still swung a mean stick—not with rage, but as though swatting away pestiferous flies—if guttersnipes pressed close. When on one occasion a particularly nasty article jumped before him and made hideous faces, pulling his features grotesquely awry with his fingers, the Counselor rocked on past without a blink. Similarly, at the *Kro* where he went each evening, for he had no idea how to cook even a bean, the Counselor paid no heed to the exclamations and murmurs and bulging eyes that attended him as he sat eating and talking with the lad. Other people were not of his world; they counted for nothing.

He bought two volumes of Holberg at a bookseller's, and after the day was done—after their long satisfying walk, after they had performed the tasks of sweeping and bringing in water from the moss-covered well out back, after their filling dinner at the *Kro*—they would make a fire in the hearth, not for heat, the weather being mild, but for coziness, and sit reading together in its flickering glow.

"How happy we are! How good life is!" the Counselor would burst out every once in a while, and the lad would agree, smiling and sitting back in his chair, his eyes very blue in the light of the hearth. Then they would return to their reading, and very often it seemed it was not the volume of Holberg which the Counselor held on his lap but the old aunt's yolk-yellow glass bowl, whose warm luminosity he could feel through his cradling hands. He sometimes dozed for a little, and waking, he would see the old aunt nearby, nodding and smiling, and he would smile back to her, and sometimes she seemed also to be his wife, and his eyes swam with tears of joy, and he would doze again. Then he would hear the lad beckoning him. "Come to the window, Father." And the Counselor climbing onto a box, the two of them would gaze up for a long while at the moon, divinely bright.

6 June 1816
Copenhagen

My Dear Brother,
Your commiserations are of no use to me at all. You sit there unplagued in Aarhus while everything continues to fall squarely upon my shoulders although I am far from well, not yet having recovered from that horrendous night.

There has been no news since I wrote; and if and when it comes what will it consist of? One scarcely dares to think, for he is insane and he is dangerous. His terrorization of the babe was such that the child did not speak for two days and did not rise from his bed for three. God knows what Thorkild did to him. And this is not even to speak of my footmen who were so viciously attacked.

Who could have expected him to return from his first disappearance? Surely he should have been found dead on some distant road. Yet now he has come and gone again! He will not be stamped out!

So that you may have an idea of the obligations which I am forced to shoulder though I am far from well, I will tell you of everything I have had to attend to during these past ten days. The housekeeper and the nanny clamor to depart, for they greatly fear

Thorkild's return. Thus I must pay their wages from my own pocket and I must also go to the trouble of hiring a new nanny, and of finding a lodging house where she and the babe may stay for the time being, for I will not have the child under my roof nor will I put him with anyone in our family. On the subject of finances I have consulted several times with Thorkild's lawyer. I have no interest in Thorkild's money nor in anything that belongs to him; every penny will go to the babe, but I wish to be reimbursed for what I shall have to lay out. The lawyer advises me that this will occur when the Counselor is apprehended and declared non compos mentis, *or when he is reported deceased, or when his disappearance has continued for one year, at which time he may be declared legally deceased. Thus is one entangled in Thorkild's destiny while wishing only to be free of him!*

As if the above were not enough, I have also been kept exceedingly busy at his house, having hired two workmen and overseen their removal of all his clothing and small personal effects and the burning of these things with kerosene in the courtyard. In my investigation of the house I came upon a framed silhouette of Thorkild's son and a portfolio containing the son's letters and official papers. These I have taken for the babe, for they are rightfully his. As for the house itself, I intend to leave it as is and to have it closed up. The babe may do with it as he wishes when he comes of age. In the meantime I will not have him brought up in the family. These many years we have preserved our children and their children and theirs from the knowledge of Thorkild's existence. I will not jeopardize that now. The child must be raised outside the family by a worthy and responsible guardian.

This letter is written without my characteristic felicity of style, as I am much harried by my numerous duties. May Thorkild be found before he brings further disgrace upon us. Better yet may we receive news of his demise.

Bodil

8 June 1816
Copenhagen

My Dear Brother,

The very day I wrote you I entertained friends from Helsingør who in the course of conversation mentioned a new phenomenon in their city, this being a hideous freak of nature which goes rushing about the streets talking to itself and greatly laughing.

Have you the capacity to understand my mortification as I sipped my coffee and endeavored to pretend to myself that this creature was not my blood kin? No, you sit there far away in Aarhus and suffer nothing of what I have had to endure. And I have endured much! For the next day I climbed into my carriage and bumped along the Coast Road all the way to Helsingør and had my coachman drive up and down every street until I beheld that nauseous lump laughing and gesturing as he rushed poundingly along. I followed him in the carriage to where he dwells; it is a small sordid cottage in a poor part of the town. How he pays for this lodging I cannot guess, possibly someone as demented as himself has given him shelter. I was obliged to stay over the night at an inn. I returned today. First thing tomorrow I go to the lawyer and discuss with him Thorkild's commitment to a lunatic asylum.

Bodil

12 June 1816
Aarhus

My Dear Bodil,

Always and ever have I endeavored to serve God and to go the way of His path. I know I have often failed. I possess many faults, of which I am aware even without your constant reminders. Often have I fallen lamentably short of what He in His great wisdom and goodness has asked of me. In the eventide, nay, the night tide of my life, I see this with terrible clarity. And I tell you that we have sinned most dreadfully against Thorkild. Never have we reflected God's mercy in our dealings with him, our one wish being to erase him from the face of the earth. We thrust him from us, we disowned him, we kept his very existence from the family, now you burn his clothing too, and will have him disappear behind the locked doors of a lunatic asylum.

Be it upon your head if you do this, Bodil. For if in his madness he has found joy, then let him be. Ascertain facts about his living arrangements, contract with his lawyer to send funds to keep him. He has grasped happiness at the end of his life, we must not tear it from him! Let us act at last with mercy and kindness, as God would have us do, and hope greatly that He will forgive us for what has gone before.

Heed my words, Bodil. Do not destroy these last days of someone whose life has been naught but suffering. Heed me also in regard to his grandson, for I do not accept the plans you speak of: the babe is to be erased too, kept apart from the family, brought up by strangers. This is heartless. He should be raised within the family, sent to live with one of our own. What harm is in it? Do you fear he will speak of Thorkild? Then let him speak, rather than be raised as an outcast!

I tell you again to heed my words, both in regard to the child and to Thorkild, for in our lives we have not acted with mercy, and we have now to settle our accounts before God.

Your Brother

17 June 1816
Copenhagen

My Dear Brother,
I do not hold myself accountable to God. It will be done as I say.
Bodil

· 23 ·

The windows of the house stand open in the heat of summer. The curtains of reticella lace are drawn aside to views of the Sound and of the gardens and beech woods, all imbued with a quality of basking stillness. Occasionally a breeze from the water stirs the long edges of the curtains, which then fall motionless again.

Down in the garden a birthday celebration is taking place. Holger has given his son a Shetland pony, which the boy is riding along the garden paths as the grown-ups sit watching from the white wicker table of the tea pavilion. The traditional hot chocolate has been drunk, served from the traditional silver pitcher worked in garlands and rosettes, and the small preliminary gifts—a set of ebony dominoes, a miniature steam engine, a little telescope in its smart leather case—have been passed around and praised, and stand in festive disorder among the cups and crumb-strewn plates.

"You see, it has a mind of its own," the tutor pointed out, chuckling as the pony stopped to chew bluebells at the side of the path.

Onkel squinted over his pince-nez.

"In my misguided youth I once ate a bluebell. It was not tasty. He will soon move on."

"And so he has," Holger observed with a laugh. "There he goes at a trot."

298

From the pony's bridle streamed two red satin birthday ribbons. The boy, in his belted white sailor blouse and white knee breeches, rode his little mount to the end of the garden, and then rode back again, giving a wave to the pavilion as he passed.

"Take care you don't fall," the nursemaid called after him, though in truth he was going at no speed to speak of. There was a time, not many months past, when he would have galloped, when his white birthday clothes would have been dirty ten minutes after he had put them on, when he would have opened his gifts not with a quiet smile but with jubilation. She gave a blink of her eyes, which had moistened, and said in cheerful tones to the tutor, who was much taken by the miniature steam engine, "How might such a thing work?"

"You would do better to ask Onkel," Holger advised her, lighting a cigarette. "He is an authority on steam engines."

Onkel, his flinty face creasing with a smile, took a crumb from his plate and tossed it at him.

"I believe it is quite simple," murmured the tutor, studying the little engine. "I believe this copper drum is where the water boils . . . and then you have here a pipe connecting it with this steel cylinder, which must be the steam transmitter. And here you have a rod which attaches to this wheel, which will begin to rotate when the pressure of the steam . . ."

"No, it is too complicated," she told him, bringing out her knitting. "And if it is too complicated for me to understand, it is too complicated for a child."

"That does not necessarily follow."

"Am I being insulted?" she asked with humor.

"Oh, indeed not," he demurred, his pink face flushing pinker, for he always said the wrong thing. "It is merely a matter of where one's interests lie."

"My interests," said Onkel, "lie in that last macaroon. Cook has outdone herself, she has never made better."

"It is a matter of the proportion of egg whites to almond paste," the nursemaid told him, passing the platter.

"You see?" he addressed the tutor, taking a bite, "you know about engines, but what do you know about the proportions of egg whites and almond paste?"

"Absolutely nothing. I am in most respects an ignoramus."

"Now, now," Holger admonished him, "don't hide your light under a bushel."

"That expression has always puzzled me," Onkel confessed. "A bushel of what? Potatoes? Canary seed? Piano wire?"

They raised their hands in a wave as the pony and its rider came by again and turned onto the path to the drive.

There was a waning of the forced, trivial conversation.

How terribly aged he is, Onkel said to himself. Holger's hand, lying on the white wicker tabletop, was thin, the wrist bone like a knob. He had a stooped appearance, as if his chest had been crushed, hollowed out. His hair was flecked all through with gray. He sat gazing out at the garden.

Most of the flowers were still in bloom, a brilliance of white and purple and red in the hot August sun. The sky was flawlessly blue, the Sound a sparkling blue-green dotted with white sailboats. From time to time a breeze from the water stirred the flowers in a long soft ripple, then they were still again.

Holger's eyes had filmed.

I would reverse the earth's axis if I could go back . . . if I could go back, go back, and not sleep. If only I had not fallen asleep . . .

In the morning she was gone from the bed. He had not thought anything of it; no doubt she had slipped away to the sickroom again. But when he had dressed and gone to the room, she was not there, nor was the child. He had looked all through the house but they were nowhere. Frantically he had run outside, had searched everywhere, everywhere, and finally he had found them. They were washed up on the beach. They were lying not far apart in the snow and ice and water.

While he slept they had drowned. While he slept, Grethe had gone out into the freezing night with the boy, and taken him with her into the waves.

"Now he has ridden up the drive," the nursemaid said brightly from her knitting. "Now he has ridden behind the house. He is going everywhere with it."

"He will be wanting his lessons on horseback," said the tutor.

"That is so," Holger replied. More than he could ever have said, he appreciated their efforts to keep the table talk going, to make this birthday as cheerful as any other. "Of course that means you must also have a mount. Will one of the carriage horses do?"

"Oh, splendidly."

His remaining child was riding the pony back down the drive. Now he crossed the lawn in front of the house and disappeared from sight.

"A fine gift," Onkel said. "And just the right size for him."

"Yes. He is eight years, and it is eight hands."

The tutor was watching a small brownish shape, now and then obscured by flowers, which was moving along one of the sun-beaten garden paths. It always kept its distance. It would come to no one. It would come only to her. And he had taken it upon himself, during those chaotic, grief-racked days when the cat was the last thing on earth anyone had thought of, to set the kitchen window on the hasp each night and to put scraps in its bowl. That was his deep, his private homage to her. Now the scruffy little creature stepped in among the flowers and was lost from sight. And then it could suddenly be seen bolting off along the path as the pony reappeared.

The boy rode it up one path and down another, occasionally trotting, usually walking. The nursemaid pinched the bridge of her nose, unable to keep from her mind the picture of the boys' room, the two inseparables sitting on the small rose-figured rug pretending it was a flying carpet or a sailing ship, scrunched close together and usually making a racket—"Look out for that big wave!" or "There's Arabia down there!"

"The breeze," she said, "is very pleasant."

They all agreed that it was.

I will never see you again. I will never hear your voice. In the mornings when I first wake, there are always a few moments before I remember, and everything is the way it always was, and we lie in each other's arms. And then it all fades away . . .

Holger's grief never lessened; six months had made no difference to it, except that he was now able to carry on his daily life, to do the surface things. All was surface. Nothing and no one could reach inside him to his sorrow.

And yet his sorrow was not pure, and this made it the more terrible and unbearable. His grief for his dead child was unalloyed, but his grief for Grethe, whom he loved more than anyone on earth, was sometimes stained by a feeling of hatred. Why had she had to take the child with her? And when this bitterness was upon him, it carved a microscopic foothold for the thought: she was unfaithful too, she had a lover whom she met in the woods, she even spoke of him once in her sleep. And then he would lacerate himself as deeply for this ugly, disloyal thought as for his bitterness and hatred. How could he hate Grethe, his Grethe, whom he yearned for every moment, with all his soul? Yet why did she have to take the child? It was her derangement that had done it, that madness which he had not seen this second time, had not suspected, had not recognized. The madness had done it; it was not the act of the real Grethe, his Grethe. It was as if a huge and merciless fist had struck them all.

The boy came into view once more. He was still riding up one path and down another, desultorily, the pony at a walk, the two red birthday ribbons hanging down. It was a kind of wandering, Holger said to himself. The boy had gone everywhere, looked everywhere. He was searching, searching for what he had lost.

Onkel leaned over and gently pressed his nephew's arm.

"The pony is a fine gift, Holger."

Holger nodded his head.

"It looks as if it may be yet warmer tomorrow," commented the tutor. "I hope so. I like the hot weather."

"Who does not?" Onkel agreed. "You must go to Italy."

"They have the tarantella down there," put in the nursemaid from over the clicks of her knitting needles.

"Ah, now we learn more about you," Onkel said to her. "You danced the tarantella in your youth."

"Get away with you. I have read about it."

"Do you speak Italian?" the tutor asked him.

"Fluently."

"I've been to Switzerland, but only to the German-speaking part."

"Zurich. A fine city, but you must go to Italy."

"If you beg Onkel very hard," Holger said, forcing himself back to the conversation with a smile, "he may tell you how he once left Italy and arrived in Poland by mistake."

◈

Olaf has lain down on the carpet of moss. From the rocky little spring there issues a limpid murmur. Overhead the beech trees rustle with the passage of birds, whose calls filter down through the greenness. He stretches his knobby spine and tucks his paws under his chest, and for a while he sleeps. Then his pale green eyes open, and he lies there waiting. His good, his uncrumpled ear flicks from time to time. He waits for a sound, a scent, a touch.

· 24 ·

꙳ Paula takes the pins from her hair and shakes it free, gets out of her fine clothes and narrow-toed boots into a pair of old trousers and her work sweater, and goes from one small room into the other, and just stands looking. She has already turned on the oven for heat, and with a stretch of her arms she sits down at the kitchen-table window. Here is the green fern on the ulcerated sill; there outside is the white slope, the white mountainside rising above. She has come from snow back to snow. Everything is the same as when she left, and yet not the same.

They knew where he had lived, how he looked, what he was like. When they had come back to the car, they had walked on a little to the edge of the beach, and in the freezing wind they had stood for a while looking out at the gray waves, knowing that this was a view he must have been deeply familiar with. They were seeing it, in a sense, with his eyes, standing where he might have stood, standing there with him. They had honored the fact that their father had existed. That was something that could never be taken away from him or from them.

꙳꙳

Philip had the same thoughts when he returned home. His arrival was different from Paula's, although he also came from snow back to snow.

He did not go from one room into another and just stand looking; in fact, he ignored the rooms he passed through, as he always did, or always tried to do, tangerine vibrating from every square foot. He unpacked his bags, took a shower and went to bed early.

They had found him. They knew what he had looked like; he had looked liked himself, Philip, same height and build, same face, but with hair, brown. A face and a personality to give to the undefined figure in the backseat of the Lincoln with Bucky McNie and Sally, and Wordsworth and A. E. Housman—the engineer sitting there in darkness with the birth certificate folded like a sad handkerchief in his breast pocket. They could see each other now, and there was no sadness between them.

He could have gone about it differently, more efficiently, he knew that. No doubt there were scores of genealogical organizations you could connect with on the computer—a touch of your fingers and a huge network of potential springing before you. He hadn't wanted it. No electronic collectivity, no mediation, no processing. His and Paula's way had perhaps been amateurish, erratic, but it had been their own chosen way, relentlessly private, and they had found him.

∽

"Did anyone ask for me while I was gone?" Paula enquired of her landlady, who squinted again, seeing her daft, disheveled tenant back in the place of the sleek and stylish woman who had stood before her a few days earlier. Who was what? But she managed to reply, without actually scratching her head, "No, no one asked for you."

Paula would have liked very much if her daughter had come all the way from Malibu only to find her gone. Serve her right, turning up without warning. Now she would be turning up some other time, flinging the wedge from her eye, opening her mouth to fill the rooms with all that was alien, inconsequential, vexatious. No, nothing had changed in that respect: she still worried that her daughter might have some means of forcing her humanitarian plans upon her, giving her over to the succor of therapeutic counseling and eager support groups, installing her in a civilized condo with level floor and a phone in every room. Of course it was ridiculous to worry. Philip had said so. She herself knew it. Yet the fear still nagged at her. And why, at the very least, should she be intruded upon, lectured to, argued with, forced to waste time while her fieldstones called?

It had been wonderful to get back to the stones, center of her existence. And it had been wonderful too, in its own way, to go off. But she wouldn't have wanted more of the great world; those few days were enough. She and Philip had done what they had set out to do, two driven, middle-aged adolescents. She hoped they would never arrive at the estate of full adulthood.

∂℘

Nothing had really changed. He was still not certain that he would sell the business and house. And it would have to be that way: both. A clean break. Why did he hover, when inside himself he had already made the break?

One day shortly after his return, sitting at his desk in his office, he picked up a paper clip, musingly scratched his jaw with it and flicked the bit of utilitarian metal into the wastepaper basket.

I've started the ball rolling, he wrote Paula. *Store and house both. Where the ball will roll me, I don't know. A very nervous feeling at first, but now it gives me that good truant feeling—Vikings setting off on the swells of unknown seas.*

∂℘

Paula took her hikes in the snow, with her good big roomy boots on, no squashed toes.

She brought her rolls along and crumbled them for the ants, should they run out of supplies while still hibernating in their little underground chambers.

She lay submerged to her chin in her bathtub and thought of the Sound. The Sound had been a special bonus of the journey. She had been away from water so long, and had missed it so much, and then there it was each day before her, even if in fierce wind—that reach of gray rolling waves. She felt a particular closeness with those waves because of the engineer, because they had been a great part of his life, living as he did so very near them, and he must have felt a love for them.

She wrote her lawyer in Neuchâtel, asking for an appointment in the next week or two. Of course he would do all he could to discourage her from her plans, but she could be extremely sharp and firm when it suited her. In fact, it usually suited her. The only person impervious to her prickles was her daughter. Her daughter wore the armor of the crusader.

She wrote Philip. She told him how good it was to hear that he had started the ball rolling. Where indeed he himself was rolled who could know, but as he had said in his letter—those swells of unknown seas. They had clinked their glasses to that in Copenhagen. Mysterium Tremendum! She had written quite a long letter.

But mostly she worked. In the great winter silence she sat pounding and chipping and chiseling in her search for the one true thing in the tiniest, innermost atom of the stone—the fresh, innocent eye of the daisy? The overturned harrow with its mangled children?

She looked with new curiosity at the little rug, for she now knew for sure that it had been made by someone in the engineer's family: all those items of fine needlework on the inventory list, and the gold thimble. Who then, perhaps his mother? She wondered what she was called, what she had looked like. But it wasn't important. What she knew about her—had always known about the creator of this little rug, whoever she was—was that she had been someone deeply in tune with all that was balanced and beautiful. A gold thimble. That was nice. And it was as if she could see it on her grandmother's finger as she sewed, and she thought of it as a small and glowing sun.

Another letter came from Philip. *I'm going to be taking off in a few days, I'm not sure where. I've bought a beret—that must sound phony but I assure you it's not. I'll drop you a card from somewhere. And I may drop by for a cup of coffee, mapless as always, using my unerring instinct to get there.*

After the midwife's unceasing screams the cavern undergoes no further intrusion for more than a century and a half. Then something again comes falling down through the fissure. The disturbance is brief, only a thud in the silence, which then resumes.

On the earth's surface, in the green and quiet forest above, peasants had seen and followed a horse that was dragging its rider along the dusty pine needles. The horse had made its way a good distance from the battlefield, perhaps at first galloping in panic, now going at a leisurely walk. It was tired and calm; they had no difficulty taking its reins. The rider, in the blue tunic of the French, with blood soaked through the front of it, had his foot caught in the stirrup. He was very large, and very young, from what could be told from the abraded face, with dusty, wheaten hair. Like the face, the uniform was badly torn up from the long dragging, but its two slitlike pockets at the back were intact. They rapidly pulled out some coins, a watch. They worked off the boots, twisted a ring from a finger and then, with all their strength, hoisted his weight over the saddle and led the horse through the trees to the fissure in the earth. There they flung the corpse in and quickly went off with its mount.

The cavern's dark silence reigned for another half-century or so, while on the earth's surface the Age of Enterprise burgeoned, inspiring a sawmill owner and an innkeeper to brave the unknown, to descend by ropes and with miners' lamps to make an exploration of the deep chambers. Subsequently they discovered a place where the wall could be broken through, thus creating an entrance. A year later the cavern was opened to the public.

Visitors have now been coming to the cave for a hundred and thirty years. They are each given a brochure along with their ticket:

The cave is entered through an artificial opening that was created in 1863. Here visitors are provided with carbide lamps for illumination, for no electrical installments mar the natural environment to this day.

The walls and ceiling near the entrance are covered with a white coating that is called moonmilk and that consists of a microcrystalline deposit of calcium carbonate originally dissolved by water.

After the visitor descends a number of steps, a room called the Eagle's Grotto is entered. A portion of the flowstone that covers the wall resembles an eagle with enormous outstretched wings.

A passage now enters the Organ Hall, named after a flowstone formation that resembles a huge row of organ pipes. You will note a boulder to the right of your path. This exhibits not only vertical stalagmites but trunks at an oblique angle, which leads to the conclusion that the boulder was tilted at some time during the stalagmite's growing stage, perhaps by an earthquake.

A side chamber of the Organ Hall displays a massive stalagmite named the Iceberg. It is said to be one of Germany's largest.

After the visitor leaves the Organ Hall, the passage leads into a room where a great column formed by the joining of a stalagmite and stalactite guards the entrance. A recess on the left houses a group of stalagmites known, because of its size, as the Elephant. Above this is a drapery formation resembling a great sawblade. Each tooth holds a drop of water.

The following gallery presents a variety of beautiful stalactites. The path is cut into a thick layer of flowstone.

A further flight of steps leads down to the last and largest chamber, called the Dome. A faint glow of daylight may be seen where a twenty-four-meter (eighty-foot) above-the-ground natural fissure is located. On the floor of the Dome there can still be seen remains of talus (debris), which, during the construction of the tourist trail, yielded the bones of cave bears (*Ursus spelaeus*), and human bones whose remnants of clothing and insignia indicated a French cavalryman from the time of the Napoleonic Wars.

Fragments of the above bones are displayed to the right of the path. You are asked not to handle them.

When the echoing voices and ringing footsteps and the probing white of carbide lamps are gone until the next day's intrusion, the cavern returns to its absolute darkness and silence, which, in time—time as brief as a moment in the existence of stone chambers far older than man or beast—will know unbroken sovereignty again.